STAR SCRAPPER

CHANEY GOODWIN

VARIANT PUBLICATIONS

LAS VEGAS, NV

Copyrighted Material

Star Scrapper Copyright © 2024 by Variant Publications

Book design and layout copyright © 2024 by JN Chaney

This novel is a work of fiction. Names, characters, places, and incidents are either products of the author's imagination or used fictitiously. Any resemblance to actual events, locales, or persons, living, dead, or undead, is entirely coincidental.

All rights reserved

No part of this publication can be reproduced or transmitted in any form or by any means, electronic or mechanical, without permission in writing.

1st Edition

CONNECT WITH J.N. CHANEY

Don't miss out on these exclusive perks:

- Instant access to free short stories from series like *The Messenger*, *Starcaster*, and more.
- Receive email updates for new releases and other news.
- Get notified when we run special deals on books and audiobooks.

So, what are you waiting for? Enter your email address at the link below to stay in the loop.

https://www.jnchaney.com/star-scrapper-subscribe

CONNECT WITH MATTHEW A. GOODWIN

Check out his website
thutoworld.com

Connect on Facebook
https://www.facebook.com/ThutoWorld/

Follow him on Amazon
https://www.amazon.com/stores/Matthew-A.-Goodwin/author/B07TXWJBWX

JOIN THE CONVERSATION

Join the conversation and get updates on new and upcoming releases in the awesomely active **Facebook group**, "JN Chaney's Renegade Readers."

This is a hotspot where readers come together and share their lives and interests, discuss the series, and speak directly to J.N. Chaney and his co-authors.

facebook.com/groups/jnchaneyreaders

CONTENTS

Chapter 1	1
Chapter 2	9
Chapter 3	17
Chapter 4	23
Chapter 5	31
Chapter 6	45
Chapter 7	53
Chapter 8	63
Chapter 9	71
Chapter 10	81
Chapter 11	93
Chapter 12	103
Chapter 13	113
Chapter 14	123
Chapter 15	133
Chapter 16	147
Chapter 17	155
Chapter 18	165
Chapter 19	171
Chapter 20	181
Chapter 21	189
Chapter 22	197
Chapter 23	209
Chapter 24	219
Chapter 25	231
Chapter 26	245
Chapter 27	257
Chapter 28	265
Chapter 29	279
Chapter 30	289
Chapter 31	299
Chapter 32	309

Chapter 33	321
Chapter 34	331
Chapter 35	347
Chapter 36	355
Chapter 37	369
Chapter 38	377
Chapter 39	391
Epilogue	401
Connect with J.N. Chaney	411
Connect with Matthew A. Goodwin	413
About the Authors	415

1

Debris clattered onto the metal floor in front of me and slammed against my back, the thick jacket providing only a modicum of protection. One chunk of dirt crunched on my headlamp, knocking it ajar and coating my facemask in dirt. I fixed the light, the beam pointing down the decaying starship toward my prize. Or theoretical prize, anyway.

I had bid on this scrap site because it was the only job available when I checked in this morning, but when I read the description, I immediately knew why none of the other scrappers had bid on it: Actium IV was a huge, high-density planet with no life, and it was on the far side of the Sector. Barren and inhospitable, the only thing it had going for it was the fact that the atmosphere was breathable.

And this scrap site.

Pushing deeper into the ship, I glanced around for anything of value. Unfortunately, this one was old. Really old. My adoptive father, Lutch, had taught me how to eyeball the age of the technology, and I could usually get it to within a decade. This ancient vessel looked to be 200 years old. The couple of bullet striations streaking the walls that I had seen on the way down bolstered my suspicions: it was from the Old War.

Metal groaned when I stepped on a panel in front of a closed door, and more dirt and bolts crashed to the ground. One screw that had been jarred loose rocketed downward and punctured the alloy floor.

Good thing that wasn't my spine, I thought, jamming the crowbar into the crack at the door and pressing my shoulder up against the metal. The high gravity here wasn't only potentially deadly, it also made everything more difficult. Each step took the energy of a dozen, and pulling the crowbar to pry open the door felt like trying to lift a car.

When the door popped and swung open, revealing another length of corridor, the ship around me moaned again. It had been buried over the last two centuries, and the earth above was threatening to consume it at any moment.

I had to get out of here. Grab whatever there was to loot and return to the surface and back to my own ship. So far, this job had been a bust. Some old, desiccated rations, a few time-ravaged uniforms, and a handgun more rust than metal. The only thing of value was a bottle of wine, but I suspected that it was past the point of "aged" to now be deemed undrinkable or, more likely, hazardous for human consumption. *Probably not the kind of thing you want on a wine label.*

I snapped my head back up the way I had come, listening and

staring into the dark. There was no movement. No sounds. I was alone.

My ship's short-range scanners hadn't detected signs of life here, and most everyone in the galaxy knew better than to ambush a scrapper on a job, though it wasn't unheard of.

A skeleton sat slumped against the wall, the metal at its back stained a dark brown. The body was wearing the ancient Consortium armor that I had seen at the museum the one time the orphanage had arranged a field trip there in order to impress some inspectors and keep their accreditation.

This was from the Old War, all right.

Turning my light, the darkness in front of me seemed to consume it, leaving the beam to dissipate into the void just before my face. Every heavy step bent the panels beneath my feet, causing them to moan with crackling echoes, and it felt like a matter of time before I was going to crash through. And it wouldn't be the first time.

Another sound from behind me sent a chill up my spine and I stopped entirely, as if Medusa herself had gazed at me. Hardly a breath escaped my lips as I listened.

Nothing.

After a long moment, I kept pressing forward into the void, heart pounding against my ribs and hand ready to pull the weapon from the holster at my side. I hardly had to use the old handgun, but I liked to know it was there.

When Lutch had given it to me for my sixteenth birthday, he had squinted his massive front eyes at it before turning to look at me. "Point it to make your point. Shoot it in the air to scare. Use it only if someone uses theirs on you first."

He had been unbearably proud of himself when he said it, and I had done what all teenagers throughout the universe did at their father's sage wisdom. I rolled my eyes.

Looking back now, it's clear that I had taken the lesson to heart. The stomper at my side had only ever been used in self-defense, and more often than not, when one of the large projectiles was fired, it struck the ceiling above my head to make a point. And mostly I kept it slung at my side to be intimidating.

Not that there was anything to intimidate here.

A wall appeared in the beam of light just in front of me and a door with the words Hanger Bay written across it.

Now I was getting somewhere.

Dragging my body forward, I lifted the crowbar once again and jammed it into the gap between the sliding panels before opening it enough to force the rest of the way with my side. Once it was ajar enough to squeeze through, I fished a small metal wedge from one of the many pockets in my jacket and then dropped it on the floor. It landed with enough force to dent the frame and fire a loud clang through the ship.

Releasing the pressure, the door slid and stuck against the jamb and when I turned the light again, I saw nothing but dancing specks of dirt in the path of my light. I groaned but pressed forward.

I needed money. This job had to yield dividends.

The sound of my footfalls changed when I moved into the space. Rather than bouncing off nearby walls, the sound took time to bounce back. Lutch taught me to use all of my senses. He had compared scrappers to hunters who needed to understand their surroundings in order to find their prey. Hunting down valuable loot was no different. An acute sense of place and understanding of the environment made the difference between leaving with something valuable and leaving empty handed.

Not that my highly attuned senses were necessary now.

Taking another couple of labored steps forward, my light fixed on another skeleton, this one lying face down on the ground, a blood stain on the back of a frayed flight suit.

"What happened to you?" I wondered aloud before kneeling and checking the pockets. The fabric disintegrated to my touch and there was nothing to be found until I flipped open the holster on its side. I pulled the weapon out. An ancient energy pistol, by the look of it. I smiled.

This will fetch a high price, no question, I thought. Maybe this site would turn out to have some value after all.

I tugged on the belt, causing the loop to slip off the rattling bones before jamming it in the bag slung over my shoulder. One of the body's arms had been reaching forward and I followed the direction it was going, gazing up to see a long, sleek shape just above head height.

I craned my neck, the beam of light revealing the nose of a one-man starfighter with the word *Starblaster* emblazoned along the side.

I chuckled to myself. *No one worked too hard coming up with that one.*

The ship itself was long and narrow with two short, triangular wings on each side, a cockpit at the top, missile batteries on the underside, and a gun at the front. It was in pretty good condition, and I started to wonder how deep I was under the ground and if it would be possible to bring my ship around and tow this back.

If *Starblaster* was still in working condition, it would be worth a lot. Even if it wasn't, there were collectors who coveted items from the Old War. I had heard rumors that some rich families had vast collections larger than those at the museums and would even dress up, pretending to be soldiers from the war and play at fighting with one another.

I couldn't imagine being wealthy enough to collect things just to put them on a shelf that I didn't even look at when I walked between the kitchen and the bathroom. And I certainly couldn't picture having enough time to play at war. But the kind of people who served in Parliament or were elected to the Triumvirate were as different from me as any of the non-human species around the galaxy.

A ladder hung from the side of the ship, and I made my way over to it. Both the ladder and fighter were in good shape, given their age. Having been made with alloys from across the universe and built to withstand various planetary weather conditions in addition to intergalactic combat, it could retain its integrity for a long time. Fortunately for scrappers like me. After taking a sharp breath in, I pulled myself up, moving my feet from rung to rung laboriously.

I hate this place, I thought as my muscles screamed with every move. *Next time, I'm bidding on a job on a planet made of pillows.*

After heaving myself over the lip of the cockpit, I shone my light in to see if the controls were still in working order. For having been hundreds of years in the past, the control panel was like something out of the distant future. My eyes went wide as I looked at the technology within.

Large, sleek screens now little more than a reflection in black, holographic display imagers and neuralink receivers were set in front of the pilot's seat. While many of these technologies still existed, they were different in the modern era. Since the outlawing of all artificial intelligence in the wake of the war, all computerized systems were nothing like what I was staring at.

Then I heard it and my head snapped up.

2

AND THIS TIME, I knew it wasn't the ship or dirt or my imagination.

It was the sound of clawed feet against metal. From the other side of the room, the chittering sound of Vekrass skittered into my ear as they approached quickly. The growing sound began to bounce around the hanger like an approaching swarm and I took one last look in the cockpit.

On the seat was a small metallic cube about the size of my palm which I reached out and grabbed, dropping it in my bag before clambering down the ladder. I would normally jump down from this height but, enjoying my kneecaps as they were, I decided against it here.

When I reached the deck, the sound was getting closer, and I shot a look into the darkness at the far side of the room. At first, there was nothing, but then I saw the red eyeshine. One set. Then another. And soon, the swarm was cutting through the dark in my direction.

I turned and ran the way I had come, my heart thundering as I slammed away, my body straining and sweat beading along my brow before being pulled to the deck below.

At the door, I tried to kick the jamb free, but the metal bent around it and there was no way to get it free without stopping and prying the thing out, and I didn't have the time with the swarm closing in on me.

Due to their resemblance to human-sized rodents from Earth, early human colonists had been cautious around the Vekrass but now, the two most populous species in the universe worked together. The Vekrass had many representatives in Parliament and had been elected to the Triumvirate on several occasions including the first.

Like with any people, they had their bad actors too. The Junk Rats, as they were called by the rest of the Universe, were the black eye of Vekrass politicians. Rather than working with the Scrapper's Guild, these scavengers simply descended on sites and took whatever they could before disappearing into space. Depending on the crew, they would either subdue or kill any scrapper they came upon.

A shot rang out, and a bullet hit the floor somewhere behind me.

Just my luck to have been intercepted by a crew who didn't seem interested in leaving any survivors.

Pulling my own weapon free, I twisted my body to aim it in the direction of my pursuers. Though, "aim" is too strong a word as the weapon was waving wildly.

I was about to pull the trigger before remembering protocol.

Running as quickly as I could but feeling as though I was moving in slow motion, I forced the words from my mouth through my gasping pants. "This is Scrapper Twenty-Seven. I am at this requisition site with the permission of the Scrapper's Guild under the protection of the Consortium. You are in violation of Universal Law and must leave immediately or I am authorized to use deadly force."

Was I legally obligated to shout this before opening fire?

Yes.

Did it actually matter in the heat of the moment or stop the Scavengers from descending upon me?

No.

But now that I had said it, I was free to pull the trigger in the direction of the bodies in the dark at my back. Still pushing forward, I contorted my torso to point the stomper behind me at the pursuers. It was awkward and difficult, but it would have to do.

Muzzle flash filled the hall for just a moment, illuminating hooked claws and patchy fur, gnashing teeth and patchwork armor. I had tried to arc my shot, but the bullet slammed to the ground harmlessly in front of the throng, stopping them only a moment before they continued to surge toward me.

Pointing my hand higher, I pulled the trigger again, but this time, the bullet punctured the ceiling and did nothing to stop the creatures pursuing me.

It was a surreal chase, all of us heaving to drag ourselves forward as though we were running at the bottom of a swimming pool. That did nothing to assuage my fear as they were closing in on me. The beam of my headlamp swung wildly back and forth when I checked over my shoulder and squeezed the trigger again.

Keeping the weapon raised was becoming nearly impossible, my arm burning and screaming for rest. Each heaving step made it feel as though the muscles in my legs were going to tear apart, but I kept moving, and soon I saw the stairs at the hatch I had entered through.

The pinpoint of light in the distance grew larger but the sound of the Vekrass was nearly upon me. When I fired off the shot this time, I heard a shriek followed by confused chatter. Gripping my gun, I slammed both hands onto the railings, using my combined upper and lower body strength to drag myself up the stairs. The narrow walkway worked to my advantage as my pursuers had to file in one at a time with each of them wanting to be the one who took me down. They clawed and scratched at one another as they attempted to keep pace, but I started to lose them.

Or, at least put a little bit of distance between me and them.

At the top of the stairs, I wheeled around and pulled at the crowbar I had wedged in the door, yanking my hand free just before the heavy metal slammed, trapping my pursuers on the other side. There were enough of them to be able to reopen the door quickly, so I had only bought myself a little time. But hopefully, it would be enough to escape.

Rushing through the cavern that the scrapper scout team had blown into the earth to reveal the ship after detecting it on their scanners, my eyes burned as they adjusted to the bright light above and the reflected brightness of the yellow stone planet below.

Once again, I wished that I could afford goggles with night vision and light acclamation adjusters rather than the hard plastic ones I was wearing that did nothing more than keep dirt out of my eyes and all too frequently fogged up.

With each blink, the world around me grew a little bit clearer, and I could see the *Buzzard* where I had left it two hundred paces from the cavern's mouth. My ship was large, designed for use by a full scrapping crew though I hadn't been able to afford one of those for a long time. It was brown with grit and rust, the original paint having long peeled and flaked away. Two retractable claw arms flanked a gangplank at the front and a tow magnet was mounted above another boarding ramp at the aft which led to a large scrap storage area.

It had a few meager facilities, like a kitchen and washroom, as well as heavy guns on the top and bottom. Of course, they required gunners to operate and, since we hadn't had a crew for years, they served no purpose. The only weapon I had at my disposal was a small micromissile cannon at the front of the ship, mounted just below the cockpit which I could fire from my control sticks.

Rushing toward the ship, I blinked once more and this time the brown of the Vekrass standing beside the *Buzzard* separated from that of the ship itself, the two forms becoming distinct as I set my foot down and slammed to a stop. They looked up at me and began to raise their crude weapons, straining against their weight. One had some kind of gun and the other, an axe with scrap metal blades.

Under normal circumstances, I might have dived for cover but there wasn't much other than small rocks to get behind and if I jumped, I knew I would crack every rib on that side of my body. This left me with only one choice. Using every last ounce of strength I had left, I reached down and pulled out my stomper, aiming it into the sky above the one who had produced the gun.

When I squeezed the trigger twice, the recoil of the weapon in the gravity finally forced my arm to give up. The bullets tore through the sky before their trajectories bent and bowed them back toward the ground, smashing the skull of the gunman before slamming his body to the dusty earth.

The other Vekrass hurried toward me, brandishing the axe above his head. I pressed my teeth together and winced as I forced my arm upward, but my attacker got close enough to whip at me with his tail and slapped the gun from my weakened arm before he brought his blade down at my head.

I swung my shoulder back, throwing my body out of the way as the weapon came slamming down, the blade bending and breaking when it crashed against the surface of the planet. My sore hand curled into a fist, the adrenaline coursing through my system empowering me with just enough strength to raise my fist before bringing it down on the thing's snout. The gravity bolstered my punch, making it like a hammer fall on the creature who was thrown to the ground.

When I took a step in the direction of my stomper on the ground, I saw one more Vekrass appear from within the *Buzzard*. He was smart and pointed his weapon skyward before firing. He hadn't gotten the angle quite right, obviously not playing as much billiards as I did, and the bullet crashed into the ground a few meters in front of me.

He began to adjust his aim and my gun was just a few steps too far. My eyes flashed back and forth as I weighed my options. Thinking fast, I jammed my hand into my bag and pulled the energy pistol free. It glinted in the bright light of the nearby star, and I aimed it at the thing that looked like a giant upright rat in armor.

Pulling the trigger, I had no idea if it still carried a charge. Lutch had taught me as much as he could about the weapons of the universe so that I could haggle and barter better, but I had only ever fired my own weapon so I wasn't quite sure what to expect when I exhaled and pressed the trigger.

Mercifully, there was hardly any recoil when the weapon discharged with a flash of purple light before the smell of singed hair filled the air. The Vekrass looked down with surprise before crumpling down onto the metal ramp of the ship.

I didn't have time to appreciate the new weapon. I had to get out of here. Pumping my legs, I hurried as quickly as I could to my stomper, plucking it up before taking the few remaining steps to the *Buzzard*.

A crunch sounded from the mouth of the ship below and I turned to see all the Vekrass running toward me. Kneeling and watching them close in on me, I pushed against the weight of the one I had shot with the energy weapon, cursing him for falling backward rather than forward and onto the dirt.

The others were exhausted, their fur matted and damp, but they were still coming when I finally rolled the body onto the ground from where it had landed on my ramp. Slamming a fist against the door operator, I turned, feet clanging as I ran up into the ship and toward the cockpit.

When I reached it, I could see through the window that half the attackers had stopped, raising weapons to their shoulders as the others came rushing toward the ship. The ramp should have been closed enough to keep them from getting in, but I didn't want to wait around to find out. Flicking on the power, I felt the Buzzard rumble to life, loose panels clattering and clanging.

With the force of the thrusters, I felt the ground shift beneath us. The Vekrass noticed it too. After some fired off pot shots at the ship, they looked down at the ground cracking under them. The species were naturally subterranean, and they dropped to their haunches, before bounding away from the collapsing earth. The *Buzzard* lifted, and I tilted the ship up. After yanking the bag from my shoulder and dropping it to the space between my chair and the vacant copilot seat, I pulled my harnesses on and clicked them into place.

Safe, and with the Vekrass being swallowed by the planet under me, I accelerated toward space. The pull of the gravity lessened, and I could breathe easily for the first time. I hadn't gotten away with much, but it would allow me to scrape by for another few days.

The power gauge on my dash began to vibrate unnaturally and I reached out, tapping on the circle to knock it back into functionality. The *Buzzard* was held together with duct tape and cable ties, so it wasn't uncommon for the dials to malfunction. Usually, they just needed a tap.

"Hello?" a voice said, and a cold chill ran up my spine.

3

Turning in my chair, my eyes darted around the ship for the source of the voice. I couldn't take my hands from the control as I was in the interstellar gyre but I would also need to deal with this.

"Hello?" I answered, frantically looking for who spoke. The voice had been low and measured, not sounding like the usual clattering speech of a Vekrass, but that didn't rule it out entirely. If I had a stowaway, this situation might get much more complicated. I had no interest in universal politics and certainly didn't want to get involved in intra-species squabble.

"Who's there?" I asked.

"It's me, hello there," the voice said, and it sounded unsettlingly close, as though it was coming from the panels beneath my feet. A Vekrass would have no problem accessing any part of the *Buzzard*. Any number of rusted out panels could have been accessed and, with their natural ability to move through confined spaces, they could have ferreted themselves away easily.

Another thing to add to the growing list: patch all the holes in this ship.

"Me who?" I demanded in an authoritative tone, staring into the slats and gaps in the floor panels for eyes. "Identify yourself."

"I am Ned, Adaptive Military AI Rank Seven of the Consortium Fleet, paired with Captain William West, hero of the Five Battles and pilot of the *Starblaster*."

I had never been hit by a truck, but at that moment, I knew the feeling. My hands went numb and my mouth dried. A stowaway was one thing but having an active artificial intelligence on my ship was something else entirely.

"No, no, no, no," I muttered, mind racing.

"Calm down, sir," the voice said, trying to sound soothing. "My system indicates that I have been in energy saving mode for nearly seventy-three thousand days. Tell me, what year is it?"

For a moment, all I could hear was the sound of my own heartbeat in my ears. The *Buzzard*, space, everything else fell away as I considered how to answer this contraband. But then I considered its words.

"You said you were in energy saving mode? Are you sapping energy from my ship right now?" I pressed.

"I am," the intelligence that had called himself Ned replied.

And I glanced down to see a light emanating from within my bag.

The cube.

I reached down with one hand, keeping my other on the controls, and pulled the now-glowing square out.

"Additionally, I'm synchronizing with your ship's systems," he informed me.

"You can't do that!"

"As a ranking Consortium officer, I'm well within my rights to commandeer any vessel I see fit." I couldn't believe what I was hearing. He just told me that he believed he could take my ship.

"If you do that, you'll be destroyed," I snapped.

There was a brief pause at that before Ned spoke again. "But the Enemy AI was defeated. Were our suspicions accurate? Did it create a superweapon? What came of the investigation?"

He was talking about the past as though it were happening right now. The 'Enemy AI' was something I'd heard about in history class. There was a whole chapter dedicated to it. But today, outside of conspiracy podcasts and late-night documentaries, no one gave it much thought.

"I don't know anything about that," I answered honestly and when he didn't answer, I went on. "I said you will be destroyed because AI is illegal. What I am doing now is illegal."

"I—I don't understand," Ned said, and for the first time, I felt as though I could hear a hint of sadness in his voice. I didn't know that AIs could feel anything. Or even what the word feel would mean to a computer program, but I could still hear the shift in tone.

It was surreal.

"Was the Consortium defeated?" Ned asked after a beat.

I shook my head, needing to focus as I exited wing space and slid into orbit around Bussel, my home planet.

"No," I said. "The Consortium won, and as you said, the Enemy AI was defeated. But…"

What was strange was that I didn't want to tell him. I knew it was nothing more than a machine, but it still sat wrong with me to have to inform him. Even the fact that I was thinking of it as a him just because it had a low voice and the name Ned was somewhat confusing.

After I set the coordinates and began guiding the *Buzzard* down to the surface of the planet, I spoke. "But all artificial intelligence is outlawed. You are illegal. The Inquisition could kill me, destroy this boat and burn down my shop just for talking with you."

"Oh, shit," Ned said, and I barked a laugh. It came from somewhere deep within me.

"I'm sorry," I said, looking at the cube. "It's just, that was such a human response."

"I am, in essence, a human," Ned observed, and I had to think about that one. "I was designed based on the human mind, created to work in perfect harmony with people and react to stimuli in the same way as a human mind, simply with more processing power. The human mind is programming with an organic processor rather than a synthetic one. So, like I said, human."

"When you put it like that, it's pretty ugly that you all are hunted down and destroyed," I said, and meant it. Even though I knew I was going to have to get this cube as far away from me as soon as possible, I still felt bad for him.

"Yes," he said solemnly, "it is."

Neither of us said anything for a moment and when the *Buzzard* began to shake as we passed through the atmosphere, I set the cube down and gripped the controls with both hands.

"My synchronization with your systems is complete. Would you like me to guide the ship in?"

"No," I answered quickly. The idea of a machine driving the

Buzzard for me put me ill at ease. "And I don't want you to synchronize with my ship."

"It's too late," he said and this time, the voice came from the speakers in the cockpit.

This was bad.

Really bad.

4

"You can't do this," I warned. "I need you out of this ship."

"Right, you need me out of here, and it sounds like I need someone to keep me hidden as I assess my current situation. So, for the time being, we should work together."

"And if I don't agree…?" I asked. "This sounds a bit like blackmail."

"Oh, no, no," Ned admonished. "I am simply hinting at the possibility of blackmail while, in reality, knowing that both of us seem to be in a bad spot and could use the other's help."

"I'm only in a bad spot *because* of you," I reminded him. "I could just turn you over to the Inquisition and be done with it."

"If you do that, I will tell them that you have been helping me," he said in a tone that was reminiscent of a half-joke.

"Ah, now the blackmail," I said, pointing an accusatory finger at the cube.

"Nah, I was mostly kidding," Ned said with the easy affect of an old friend. It was strange that this forbidden technology which I had been warned against for my whole life and could be incarcerated for even knowing about was actually a pretty natural conversationalist. "I'm assuming that the Inquisition is the AI hunting branch of the government or something like that?"

"Yeah, that's right," I affirmed.

"A little on the nose."

I chuckled. "Well, I didn't name them."

"I'm just saying…" he trailed off.

"Because *Starblaster* is so original," I said under my breath as the city came into view when we cut through the cloud cover.

Bussel had been one of the first colonies back during the age of human expansion across space in the wake of the Tidal Drive's discovery. With a little atmosphere, fertile soil, and many of the requisite conditions to sustain human life, the planet had become a hub almost immediately.

As it was in one of the furthest sectors from Earth, Bussel's primary source of wealth had been fuel. With all of the ships stopping here on their way to other places, an industry revolving around starfaring had grown. Repair and maintenance shops had given way to hotels and entertainment. What began as a stop became a destination, and the city had reaped the benefits.

But when the money began to flow, so too did crime. People of all species began to take advantage of one another and preyed on those who visited. Inevitably, the tourism dried up and Bussel was left with a meager business of desperate travelers on their way to more desirable ports.

Now, the city was a shadow of its former self. And in that shadow lurked villainy.

Despite all that, it was home. Passing through the layer of great glass buildings in the haze down to the brown buildings of street-level, the Buzzard landed just after the roof garage door opened. Guiding forward, I pulled off to the side to allow for any other business that might come my way. Not that it happened very often these days, but I always wanted to be prepared just in case.

Killing the engine, I sighed and leaned back in my chair. My body moved with an unbelievable ease back to normal gravity. My eyes drifted to the cube.

"Listen, Ned, all joking aside, you can't stay here."

"Listen, Lutch Spears, I believe we can help one another."

I shook my head. "Lutch was my father. I'm Hank."

"You should change the *Buzzard*'s registration."

I couldn't help but chuckle at that one. "I should do a lot of things."

"I expect that I could help you with that and a great many other things if you were to keep me hidden and, perhaps, help me in exchange," Ned offered. He affected a serious tone, and while it didn't sound like pleading, I knew he was desperate.

"Things have changed in the universe," I said before letting out a long sigh. "Hiding you could alter the entire course of my life, completely change everything about it, forever."

"I believe it already has."

He was right, but I didn't want to tell him that. "Ned, I know you were partnered with some great hero, but that isn't me. I'm just a grease monkey trying to keep my head above water financially. Hiding an AI… potentially drawing attention from both the Consortium and the Inquisition, that's not for me. I'll just get us both killed."

I might've been downplaying my aptitudes a bit, but I was trying to sell him on the fact that I wasn't a good partner. He could cause a lot of problems for me and if he would be willing to go peacefully, that would be a much better situation for me. Not that I had any idea how I would even get rid of an AI but that was a problem for future Hank.

"It's that bad?" Ned asked.

"Yes."

"Well, then consider this: you say that you are having a hard time with money? I can help with that. I am an adaptive, deep-learning intelligence. I will be able to analyze your business and maximize profits and productivity in a way that you never thought possible.

"Put me into the net and I can learn what your competitors are doing and how you could do it better. I can study their systems and help you to become rich beyond your wildest dreams. I can save you money on fuel by calculating perfect trajectories and help you in innumerable other ways."

That stopped me dead.

He was already in my ship's system, and I was already in possession of the cube. The trouble might come for me one way or another, but the idea of turning this business around was highly appealing. I had been scrimping and scraping since Lutch died. I had eaten one too many dinners of bar peanuts, had my electricity turned off too many times, and had to sell one too many valuables just to make payments to Resh, the crime lord who all but ran Bussel.

"First, if you access the net for even a moment, you will be flagged, and this place will be a crater… Second, what do you want in exchange for all that help?" I asked, mostly to give myself time to think.

"At the time that I was deactivated, William and I were on a mission, investigating a superweapon about which we had received reports, code-named 'Extinction.' The Enemy AI was believed to have been defeated but this weapon could have changed things like the atom bomb on Hiroshima."

"The what?" I asked.

There was a long pause.

"Have you not been taught the history of Earth?"

I shook my head, finally working up the strength to lean forward in my chair and pull the energy weapon from my bag. Flipping it over in my hands, I marveled at the design.

"No," I finally answered a bit absently, staring at the gun. "We learn about the destruction of Earth as part of the history of the Old War but not much more than that."

"What the actual hell?" Ned snapped, the ship vibrating as the words thundered out of the speakers. It took me by surprise, and I looked up. "I was a loyal servant of the Consortium. I was built on Earth and fought alongside humans who sacrificed everything to rid the universe of the greatest evil it had ever known.

"I did all that and now my very existence is a crime, the history of those who created me and who I battled to protect are nothing but a footnote, and the weapon is almost certainly out there."

I found myself gawking at the cube as he spoke. Looking up from the weapon, I gazed at the small square which housed a mind utterly betrayed by those it served. There was nothing I could say, nothing that I could do to ease his feelings. Because, when all was said and done, he was right.

Humanity *had* turned its back on the artificial intelligences that had helped to win the war. The memories of Earth *had* been pushed aside in favor of teachings about the glory of the new Consortium. And, while there may have been some clandestine investigation or eradication of whatever weapon he was talking about, I had never heard hide nor hair nor it.

"I'm sorry," I offered.

"It's not your fault," Ned said. "It's just… a lot. I was programmed as a partner to a human. What you call 'the Old War' was fought to keep people from being forced to incorporate non-organic intrusions into their bodies, but the war was won by man and his creation working together. We could not have done it without the other. To think that this is the thanks we get… that this is the world that was birthed from that is… pretty grim."

He had a point. There were no two ways about it: it was pretty grim. But what would happen to me was also pretty grim if anyone caught us together.

"Do you think there is any way you could investigate this weapon without me? Maybe I could get you a ship and you could control it?" I offered.

"Hank, I am a consciousness housed in a core," he replied flatly. "Sure, I could integrate with the systems like I did with the *Buzzard*, but how would I refuel? How would I search? And what would I do if I was discovered by the Inquisition?"

"Those are all excellent points," I conceded.

"I know," he said. "That's why I need your help. You could have chosen to throw me out the airlock the moment I said what I was. You could have destroyed my core or demanded I leave permanently. You could have done any number of things when you learned what I was, but you didn't.

"You have spoken with me as an equal. You have treated me with respect, for the most part, and you have heard me out. So far, you seem like a good man with a good head on your shoulders—"

I cut him off. "Flattery will get you nowhere."

"But it's true," he said, and if a synthesized voice could carry the tone of pure sincerity, it was this. "I'm not just blowing smoke up your ass."

At that, I blinked in surprise. "Not doing what now?"

"That expression didn't survive the last two hundred years, eh?" he asked with a little chuckle. His voice was light and carried the hint of a lisp like someone who had spent a lifetime training it away. It was so lifelike that I had to keep reminding myself that it was nothing more than a program. "It means 'I'm not just saying it'."

"But why?"

"The expression originates from England, a country on Earth. During the early 1700s, medical professionals would use the therapy of blowing tobacco smoke up patients' rectums to alleviate certain ailments."

I felt a smirk cross my mouth. "Can't imagine why we didn't want to hold on to the history of Earth when I hear about things like that."

"You got me there," Ned joked. "But my point remains valid. I truly believe that we can aid one another. Help me, Hank Spears, you're my only hope."

I said nothing and contemplated his offer.

"No? Nothing? Okay, then," he said as though I had missed something, and I rubbed my hands across my face slowly.

"I'll think—" I began but stopped when I saw the garage door opening again. It had closed automatically after I landed, and now the dim light of the nearby star was sliding across the cracked cement floor as the metal panels parted.

The only person who could open those doors was me, but they could be overridden. Squinting into the light, I saw the shape of a medium fighter with the Consortium flag on the side.

"Oh, fu—"

5

"Don't say anything, don't do anything, don't move," I said to Ned, scrambling to my feet on muscles that didn't want to obey me and under gravitational conditions that made me feel like I was drunk, my limbs overcompensating with every movement.

"Don't worry, I'm a cube," Ned said in a whisper.

I stumbled from the cockpit, tripped over a loose nut in a floor panel, and caught myself against the wall before hurrying down and activating the ramp. As it lowered, I was blasted with air and debris kicked up from the thrusters of the Consortium ship, and I had to throw my arm up to block my face.

Realizing I left Ned just sitting out in the open, I turned and considered going back to tuck him away somewhere and cursed myself for giving him instructions rather than hiding him.

Not that it would matter. If the Consortium was here to investigate, I was done for.

When the thrusters shut down, I stepped toward their side

hatch, smoothing my rumpled clothes and taking a long breath to calm myself. I could fake my way out of a situation if I had to, but this kind of deception was better suited to a used starship salesman or spy.

The Hawk-class heavy fighter's engine shut off, and when it did, I heard a rattle. Unable to help myself, I stepped around to the other side and saw blast marks and micromissile punctures striating the flank.

"You Scrapper Twenty-Seven?" a bearded man called after climbing down the ladder and jumping to clear the last few rungs.

"That's me," I said in an overly friendly tone.

He took no note of it. He had his own concerns. "You can see that we had a run-in with the Peacers," he said, voice tired and hoarse, undoubtedly from yelling into his comms. "We took some licks but gave it right back."

"Happy to hear it," I said, mustering a patriotic tone. "Have to teach those Peacers a lesson."

"Got that right," he said, and looking up, I could see all the Consortium vessels coming in to land at the various repair shops around Bussel. "How long you think it'll take to patch her up?"

The man was already eyeing the exit.

My shop was small with just one parking spot for the *Buzzard* and one for a customer. The overhead garage door opened to a large space surrounded on three sides by equipment and tools and workbenches. On the fourth side was a small office area with a low wall that allowed me to meet with people either from the garage side or the front door. Beside the entrance was a little waiting area with some burnt out digital poster boxes and a coffee machine with brown sludge in the pot that I expect had solidified before I even broke into this place all those years ago.

I eyed the ship before giving my answer. "The exterior damage appears to be pretty superficial, but I can't give you an estimate of the cost or time until I run a full diagnostic."

"I understand," he said. "When you are looking around, I would also appreciate it if you could dispose of the body of my copilot."

My heart stopped and my mouth fell open. I had just begun to breathe when I realized that he wasn't here for Ned, but now I had a new problem on my hands.

"We don't really—" I began, but a wide grin broke out on his face.

"You wish," a woman's voice hissed from inside the hatch before a Vekrass in Consortium flight suit dropped to the ground and sprang over to me, extending a clawed hand. I shook it. "Thanks for getting her patched up."

"My pleasure," I muttered. "There is a Consortium Hub just two blocks to the right after you exit."

They nodded and started walking. But the man turned back to me, and my heart rate picked up again. "There a bar between here and there?"

I chuckled. "There's nothing but bars between here and there," I told him, and I wasn't exaggerating. Bussel had more bars per capita than any other city in the Sector. The one thing that locals and visitors alike desired was booze and other mind-numbing chemicals. Escape was the only other thriving industry on the planet.

While the atmosphere was livable, it was not conducive to the growth of plant life. Large greenhouses, the size of colonial cities on the outskirts of the Sector, were constructed in the surrounding valleys and grew little more than hops, barley, hemp, and a few fruits and herbs for mixers. If you had a job on Bussel that wasn't scrapper or mechanic, it was distiller, bartender, or, of course, gangster.

"Any bars friendly to the Consortium?" the copilot asked after hurrying over to fall in beside the man.

"Just across from the Hub is just the place, can't miss it," I told them, and they turned without asking the question they should have. "Check back in the morning, and I'll have an update for you," I called after them, and the man waved a half-appreciative hand and must have said something snarky because the copilot laughed.

They stepped through the exit, and I let out a breath that I felt as if I had been holding in for the entire duration of the conversation. All the stress and exhaustion flooded my senses, nearly causing me to collapse. I gripped the landing leg of the Consortium fighter and panted for a minute.

"Well, that was stressful." Ned's voice now came from the speakers mounted around the garage.

I looked up at the *Buzzard* as though I was going to be able to see the source of the voice through the cockpit window. It would take some getting used to in order to wrap my mind around the disembodied consciousness that could move from computer system to computer system. It was so far from anything that I was used to.

I shook my head. "Everything about today has been stressful."

"You're telling me," Ned said, and I couldn't help but laugh.

"I notice that you are not slowing down or making it any easier for us to part ways," I said, gesturing to the rusted-out shop speaker hanging by little more than the wiring since the corners holding it in place had long chipped and flaked away.

"Oh, are you still deciding?" Ned asked in a light tone. "I thought we were helping each other out."

Once again, I rubbed my face. "I am still deciding, and you have to give me the room to do so."

"Understood," Ned said, and I wondered if he was programmed to obey the human with which he was working. He had said that he was designed to work in perfect tandem with the person, and if he believed I now was that individual, perhaps he had to follow my orders. I didn't want to ask at this moment and chose instead to just stash that idea for potential later use.

Right now, I needed a drink and to sort some things out.

"Ned, I have to go deal with some business before I can get to work. I need you to stay here. No more intruding into systems or whatever you're doing. My ship and my shop are already too much. We are quite literally right under the Consortium's nose, and you can't take any more risks. I think you know what a chance I'm taking even by entertaining the idea of working together, and hope that you'll respect my wishes."

There was a long pause. "I do appreciate the fact that you are considering this and do understand the risk you are taking. It is not lost on me in any way. But you must also understand what is at stake. I was shut down right before discovering the truth behind a weapon that could ch—"

"Change the fate of the universe," I finished for him. "I heard you loud and clear too."

"Right," he said, a hint of resignation in his voice.

I couldn't help but wonder what the point of making these AIs so lifelike was.

Why make them so human?

But I didn't have time to dwell on the philosophies of long-dead programmers, I had to go check in about this recent development.

I ran back up into the *Buzzard* and tossed Ned's core back into my bag before putting the entire thing under a floor panel within. The last thing I needed was for somebody to accidentally happen upon him. Nobody should be in my shop without my permission, but it was still something I didn't want to have to worry about.

Ned said nothing as I did it, and soon I was out on the street and away from this new voice in my head.

I tried to think about what Lutch would've done. While he might've let his demons get the better of him, he was always a fundamentally good man who made smart choices in a pinch. Trying to put myself in his mindset often helped to guide difficult decisions but this was something way beyond anything he had been faced with.

This was way beyond anything I could've even conceptualized a day earlier.

The easy answer was, of course, to get rid of Ned. To throw his core in a trash compactor and be done with him forever. I had a Consortium ship in my shop at this very moment, and housing an AI in the same place was as dumb an idea as existed.

On the other hand, Ned was more than just what I had been told about artificial intelligences. My whole life I had been taught that they were evil and set on destroying the universe. Instead, I had met a personality whose entire existence was dedicated to saving people. It wasn't that I believed everything the Consortium told me. Far from it. But I hadn't expected my first experience with an AI to be like Ned.

And the truth was, I believed him.

I thought he was sincere. Whatever that meant when talking about a program. And I believed that there was cause to be worried about this weapon he had been warned about. It made a certain sense that the Enemy AI had been defeated before being able to set it off but that it might still be out there.

If it was and was as bad as Ned thought, there would be good reason to go after it.

This line of thought just made me angry though because the people who should be going after it were the very people who would lock me up and throw away the key if they learned about Ned. I wished I could just tell the pilots parked in my shop about the threat, that they would take it seriously and then investigate.

"Oi, watch where you are going," a man said as I nearly walked into him where he stood waiting for the bus, and I was pulled from my thoughts.

"Sorry, mate," I said and meant it.

The man grunted and went back to staring at the hologram dancing in lingerie across the dusty street in front of a bar where people in various states of undress danced on the bar.

I kept walking down the street, now looking up and trying to keep my body from overcompensating or crumpling. After Actium and everything that had followed, what I really wanted to do was sleep, but I knew it would be a while longer before I would feel a pillow beneath my head.

I passed my local grocery mart on the left and checked the stock: the same aging fruit and packaged meals transported from other planets on the same small shelves as always. I checked it every time I passed because of one time when I was a child. While I was on a run to buy a part for Lutch, I had caught a glimpse of a food package I had never seen before.

From the label alone, I could tell it was candy.

It stopped me immediately, and I turned, pressed my face against the glass, and stared into the cube. I pulled my card from my pocket and ran it over my pants to clear the grease and grime from it before pressing it against the reader and seeing how much money I had left. Lutch had given me just enough for the part, but I didn't care. It would easily cover the cost of the candy bar.

I bought it without considering the consequences. I didn't care about them. I had to have it. When I pulled the wrapper and bit into the chocolate bar, it was the greatest moment in my life to that point. Or, second greatest after Lutch deciding to adopt me. I stood in the exact spot where I stood now and ate the entire thing.

Another candy had never appeared nor anything else remotely exciting but from that day on, I would always check. As I continued up the street, I thought about the night of the infamous candy bar. My body had never had sugar like that and, as I clutched the toilet bowl for dear life, Lutch laughed and had one question for me.

"If you spent part of the money I gave you on the candy, how did you get the part?"

I looked up at him with red, glassy eyes. "I haggled him down to what I had left."

Lutch smiled at that. "So, you got two lessons for the price of one."

Those words rang in my head as I crossed the street to Resh's. The bar that the crime lord named after himself stood out at the end of the street. Where everything else in the city was brown, tan, khaki, copper, or russet, Resh's was black and chrome. Where all the businesses and homes were short, two or three stories tall, the club was a tower that dwarfed everything around it. The club itself was only the lower floors, and the rest were, I assumed, the business center of Resh's vast criminal empire.

The few administrative buildings in the area were nothing compared to this club, and it was a perfect embodiment of the state of things in Bussel: the Sectoral Governor worked out of a drab little building adorned with nothing more than a cracked fountain dribbling water, while Resh operated out of a gorgeous tower at the end of the road.

As I approached the base of the tower, the bouncer hooked a thumb in the direction of the side door to the "locals only" bar around the side of the building as though I hadn't been coming there and doing this same song and dance for years.

Nodding, I continued into the alleyway and to the staircase leading to the bar under the real bar. My feet clattered against the bricks before I pushed the door and stepped into the dimly lit room. A center bar was constructed of old pieces of starship, owing to the planet's history, and was surrounded on all sides by low tables. A few people drank at the bar, a few more played billiards in the corner, and two were throwing dice at one of the tables.

It was the same scene every time. Scrappers on their breaks or those desperate few between jobs all drinking their woes away until their next round of woes would begin. Stepping up to the bar, I looked around for Alek. I didn't see him at first until I noticed some movement under the bar at the far end.

I cleared my throat, but it didn't get his attention. The music playing loudly to cover the thumping bass from upstairs might have made it hard to hear. I reached into the little bowl on the counter, scooped a few nuts up, and tossed some into my mouth before sending one plunking off his back. It startled him and he jerked, knocking his head on the underside of the bar and rattling some delicately stacked glasses.

He pushed out and stood, his massive frame blocking the light behind him.

"You've got some nerve."

I smiled, crunching one of the nuts between my teeth. "Sure, but isn't that why you love me?"

He grimaced, his massive, gray face contorting as he fixed me with his front eyes. Like Lutch, Alek was a Kyrog, a species that had a troubled history with the Consortium, and humanity in general, but who now could be found in all corners of the universe.

Their home planet was said to be nothing but open fields with no trees or cover of any kind, so the species had evolved four eyes with horizontal pupils, perfect for seeing nearly all the way around themselves. Their skin was gray, thick, and hard, and even the shortest among them was easily a head taller than a human.

"Oh, sure, you got it, that's why I love you," he grunted sarcastically. "You humans and your 'love'… all the other species have to learn this absurd concept just to converse with your lot."

Crunching another nut, I nodded. "Yes, we *do* seem to like it when everyone else conforms to us."

Given his species' past, that comment carried extra weight. He threw the greasy rag over his shoulder with a slap. Wearing a dirty tank top, cargo pants and a boot big enough to fit both of my feet, he looked more like a handyman than a bartender. One of his pant legs was cut short, revealing a wooden peg leg in the style of a cartoon pirate.

He had lost the leg during a battle with another clan and, under Consortium law, was only allowed to replace it with this rudimentary prosthetic. Since the Old War, limbs could only be replaced with nonelectronic parts. As the war had been fought against enemies with advanced cybernetics, all augmentations had been banned subsequently. This meant that men like Alek would be forced to spend their days hobbling around.

"So, Hank, what are you here for?" he asked, leaning against the bar and looming over me with narrowing eyes.

"I'll take a beer," I said, flopping down onto one of the hard metal stools. He reached under the bar, retrieved a Bussel Brew, and pulled the cap off with one massive finger. I took a quick swig. "But I also have some bad news."

He chuckled, the sound shaking the bar. The Kyrog's native language was several octaves below the human auditory range, consisting largely of vibrations and their laugh could be felt in your feet. "Let me guess this bad news," he said with a wry smile, showing his few large teeth set into the back of his mouth.

"Be my guest," I answered with a sweeping gesture.

"You're here to say that your payment to Resh is going to be delayed because the Consortium just showed up and is demanding repairs. You're going to further offer a cut of what the Consortium pays you and also warn Resh not to send any jobs your way for the time being."

I tapped my Bussel Brew against the counter. "You got it."

"Of course I got it," he snorted. "I used to—"

"Be a doctor before coming to Bussel," I filled in. "Yes, you've mentioned. Once or twice… in every conversation."

He tapped a finger on the bar. "I'm merely pointing out that I am very smart."

"I don't think anybody's ever doubted that."

"No, what you mean to say is that you've never doubted that," he corrected. "Most people doubt it, and that's why I ended up as a bartender who also works as muscle."

"Yeah, that's tough," I said, taking another pull of the beer. "You can always move."

"Not a lot of people in the market for a one-legged Kyrog bartender," he said with a sigh, pulling out another beer and popping the cap before taking down half the bottle. The cap clattered somewhere on the far side of the room. He looked down at the bottle. "Also, this beer is swill. Can't believe you people pay for it," and he shot me a clever look. "And you *are* paying for it."

"So long as you get my message to Resh, I'm happy to add your beer to my tab," I said, raising my glass and clinking it against his. "And I'm guessing you knew what I was going to say because people have been reporting the same to you all day?"

He snorted. "Exactly."

Nodding, I turned to the screen in the corner of the room displaying some sports match from another planet. For the first time in what felt like a long while, I let my brain shut off.

But the moment didn't last long. Alek turned from the game and looked at me. "You went on a run this morning, get anything good?"

It wasn't that I had forgotten about Ned, but I had certainly allowed myself to push it from my mind for a moment. I swallowed hard and turned to Alek. "Naw, it was a bust. I got out just before the whole place collapsed."

"That's too bad," he said, sounding genuinely sympathetic.

"Got that right." I downed the rest of my beer and stood. "But I should get back to it. Consortium ships don't repair themselves."

"That they don't," he said as I began to leave the bar. "And, Hank…"

I turned back to look at him. "Make sure Resh gets his cut. I really don't want to have the other type of conversation with you."

And with that threat hanging, I left the bar and headed back to my shop.

6

The moment I stepped into the garage, Ned's voice greeted me. "I waited quietly and everything."

"Great, I wouldn't expect anything less."

"But I was able to use the scanners aboard the *Buzzard* to do a full diagnosis of the damage to the vessel which you are going to repair."

That stopped me, and I looked up. "You did?"

"I did," he said. "Additionally, I appraised your tool collection, such as it is, and categorized which would best suit each repair. A schematic is in your printer."

I didn't know what else to say so I simply muttered, "thank you."

"You're welcome."

Stepping through the swinging door in the low wall, I walked into the little office and looked at the printer. Several pages had been printed, and I picked them up, then unfurled them and peeled the holed ribbons off the side before looking at the suggestions.

"This is." I gaped before closing my mouth and continuing to look. "This is all exactly right." I looked at the Buzzard as though it was Ned. "And it's not right in the way I figured a computer would suggest the most logical tool for each job, but it's right in the practical application of each tool for the job."

"My program is designed to help in that way. I learn from experience and apply functional knowledge. Having never met an AI before, I understand why you might assume that I would be limited to a sort of computer logic, but I'm not that. Like you, I grow and get better with experience. I just also have the added bonus of a perfect memory and a deep foundational intelligence," Ned explained.

Staring at the printout and thinking about how much time and energy he had just saved me, I couldn't help but consider the benefits of working together. Sure, I might get burned alive if I got caught, but in the meantime, Ned might be able to turn my life around in a big way.

I set the paper down and walked over to my workbench, grabbed a flashlight, and walked over to the Consortium ship. Even though I believed that his diagnosis was absolutely flawless, I still had to check it myself. It might be a poor craftsman who blames his tools, but it had to be an equally poor craftsman who trusted them without checking.

"So, Ned, tell me a bit about the war," I said as I dragged a stepladder around to the front, clambered up, examined the punctures, and ran my hand over one of the long scorch marks to assess how deep it was.

"What do you know about it?" He answered my question with a question.

"Not a whole hell of a lot," I admitted. "I know how much it's shaped our society, but my working knowledge of the war itself is pretty limited. Went to the museum one time when I was a kid, but I was more interested in the holographic recreations of the battles than I was about the war itself."

"That sounds like a kid," Ned observed.

I chuckled. "Yeah, it's hard to keep a bunch of orphans interested in universe-wide politics, that's for sure."

There was a pause as I gazed into one of the open wounds to the damage inside. The micromissile had detonated in between the armor plating on the hull. Either these pilots were really lucky, or the Peacers had been firing on them from far off and with some kind of atmospheric detritus. Out in space, without any friction, the projectile would have done much more damage.

"You mention that you were an orphan but also said that Lutch Spears was your father," Ned said by way of a question.

"Both things are true," I said, leaning against the railing of the stepladder to peer into the next hole. "I have no memory of my parents and was raised in an orphanage just up the street. Spent my entire childhood there and thought that I was going to live and die on the streets of Bussel without seeing or doing anything. That all changed one night when a friend of mine had a brilliant idea to sneak into a local business and…" I trailed off, looking for the right way to say it.

"Use the old five-finger discount?" Ned finished for me.

"Right, that," I said, smiling before hopping down and repositioning so that I could continue my assessment. "Anyway, the two of us started to really enjoy the fruits of our labor, and, like always happens, we began to get overconfident. Plus, honestly, I was never that great a thief to begin with.

"One night, we broke into the shop of Scrapper Twenty-Seven, a Kyrogi man named Lutch Spears. As I was rummaging around the desk just over there," I said and gestured to the wide metal desk with yellowing sheets of synthetic paper scattered along the top, "I felt two fingers wrap around my neck. To this day, I have no idea how that behemoth crept up on me but, like I said, I was never the best thief. He asked what I was doing, and all I could answer was the truth. Or a version of the truth that didn't include my friend who had scampered away.

"I expected the giant to snap my neck or pick me up by my collar and carry me back to the orphanage and throw me through the front door, but instead, he let me go and sat down across from me."

I would never forget that moment for as long as I lived.

My heart had been pounding like it never had before or since, and I had no idea what to expect. I knew I had made a mistake and was likely about to pay for it, but I could never have anticipated what he said next. "You looking for work?"

Even just telling the story to Ned, I could remember my brain exploding at the question. It was as though every synapse fired at once and I couldn't even formulate a word.

I simply raised and lowered my head vigorously. "I'm—I'm from the orphanage," I finally forced out.

That was the first time I saw the man who would become my father smile. In the low light of the single bulb burning in the middle of the night in the office, Lutch grinned at me. "I know, says so right on your shirt."

I looked down and brought my hand to my face in shame. "R-right."

"And you are allowed to work during the day if you are given a job, correct?" he asked, seeming to already know the answer. I hadn't known it at the time but many of the local businesses farmed their employees from the orphanage.

"That's, that's correct, sir," I stammered. Even though he was being nice to me, I still felt as though the other shoe could drop at any moment. As if he was trying to trick me with kindness before bringing one of those massive fists down on my head.

It took a long time for that feeling to pass. But eventually, it did. And Lutch and I grew as close as any father and son. It wasn't even a year before he asked if I wanted to be adopted and admitted that he had already started the paperwork.

"My whole life changed then," I told Ned. "Because I was no good at sneaking around, I inherited all this. I got the shop, the *Buzzard* and the license. I don't know what my life would have been without that one moment."

"Thank you for sharing that," Ned said earnestly, and I knew he meant it. In whatever way he could. "It seems that you were very lucky to have met him, and I expect he felt the same way about you."

I could feel the knot form. "He always told me that my breaking in was the best thing that ever happened to him."

"I felt the same way about being partnered with William," Ned said. I cleared my throat and got back to my work. "You asked about the war and, though I could give you an entire history, I will break it down for you.

"What you now call the Old War, began with little more than a cult dedicated to the belief that humans needed to be more than just their physical form. These were people who had taken the belief that technology could improve humanity and took it one step further. They did not want to encourage people to augment human capabilities and improve the human condition through the use of current and emerging technologies. Instead, they wanted to mandate it.

"What started as a cult became a revolution and the Consortium was forced to take action, bringing in more members and becoming the universal power it grew into. But they didn't realize how deep the roots went. There were people spread all over the universe who believed in this. And it wasn't just humans. People of all species wanted to become better. To be stronger or smarter or whatever else through augmentations or alterations to their minds and bodies.

"Then, the revolutionaries fought back. They were far fewer in numbers, but every one of their soldiers was worth one hundred of ours. Credit where credit is due, some of the soldiers they fielded were like superheroes compared to normal humans. I had videos uploaded to my consciousness, and it was like watching something out of a movie. These people with mechanical body parts and minds enhanced with microprocessors could do things previously thought impossible. They could take on battalions of soldiers, decimate tanks, hack smart weapons and delivery systems and outmaneuver any pilot.

"What was originally assumed to be a lopsided war proved to be one in exactly the opposite way as predicted. The government was looking utterly outmatched. Even as the other species around the universe banded together to form the Consortium as we know it now, there was little that could be done.

"On battlefields large and small around the universe, the Consortium was losing ground and it seemed as if there was nothing that could be done. Once before in the history of the government, they had handed over power to a single dictator. She had given power back to Parliament when she had completed her work but many in the government feared that if a single person were to turn the tide of this war, they would never cede power back to those elected officials.

"Instead, they appointed a Triumvirate in hopes that three people would be more easily convinced to do the right thing when the war was over. As you now know, that didn't happen. But what did happen was the genius mind of a single Vekrass. This man gave an impassioned speech saying that the only way to defeat our enemy was to emulate them.

"And thus, the AI companion was born. We were created and uploaded to every soldier on every battlefield. Designed to perfectly pair with those to whom we were assigned, we made the human mind better without intruding upon it. I was partnered with William, and together we completed missions which wouldn't have even been considered by high command a month earlier.

"Slowly, we turned the tide. No one soldier could compete against the physicality of the cultist cyborgs because, when all was said and done, that's what they were. But with our AI companion, we could outsmart them, outmaneuver them or outlast them. Our numbers, once again, became an advantage. Here, there, and everywhere, we started winning battles. The AIs could counter hack and help in dog fights, create tactics, and analyze battlefield scenarios.

"Together, man with machine began to defeat man and machine. Soon, the intelligence that we had known as the Enemy AI revealed itself and made a desperate attack on Earth. This was the culmination of the Five Battles, and though Earth was devastated, we were able to destroy the core of the Enemy AI.

"And when I say 'we', I mean William and myself. The two of us piloted *Starblaster* into a nearly impenetrable station in orbit above Earth and destroyed the core before escaping. As we were there, we learned about the code name "Extinction" but were not able to stay long enough to investigate it further. We escaped and destroyed the station only to discover that it had irreparably damaged the atmospheric filter that kept the planet alive."

Ned stopped speaking for a long while now, and I felt the weight of his words. The war had always been an abstract concept to me, something that happened to people hundreds of years ago and, while important, didn't really mean much to me. Now, hearing about the experience of someone who served during that time, it felt real. Felt vital and important.

7

"I can't even imagine," I said for lack of anything better.

"I couldn't have either," Ned said. "To win and lose in the same moment, it was the first time I had wished that I had been programmed without emotions. I wondered why I had been cursed to feel the pain of loss. Those that created me would say it was the kind of thing I needed in order to grow, to become a better version of myself and to motivate me. But I wished more than anything to not have to feel it.

"We were lauded as heroes, and the universe thanked us. We were given the freedom to pursue an investigation of the super weapon in spite of the fact that high command didn't believe it existed. So, we did what so many who are grieving do and distracted ourselves with the next mission. Or we would have, if William had not been killed and me, deactivated."

I blinked, realizing that I had been staring into the same

shredded metal for nearly the entire length of the story. "What happened?"

"I don't know," Ned said so quietly that I had to turn my ear toward the speaker. "Given that I don't remember, I have to assume that an EMP was detonated."

I didn't know enough about how artificial intelligence worked to understand why he was able to extrapolate that it was an EMP, so I simply stayed quiet for a moment. "Aren't you… I don't know… constantly saving your experiences up-to-the-minute like with a human brain?"

"Yes, but if my system does detect corruption in the input, a fail-safe will activate, and the potentially corrupted files expunged. The human mind does a similar thing and often people can't remember the moments before trauma," Ned said.

"I'll have to take your word for it," I said. "About the fail-safe saving. The trauma stuff is dead on. One time I woke up right over there, and Lutch told me that I had fallen from the wing where I was making a repair. Didn't and still don't remember anything except waking up on the ground."

"Well, I didn't and still don't remember what happened on the ship where you found me," Ned said miserably. "I don't suppose you would want to go back there?"

"Maybe someday, but not soon and not without better equipment. I don't know if you saw but the area around the wreck collapsed as we got the hell out of there," I said apologetically.

Before he could answer a question occurred to me. "Wait a minute. Can you see?"

Ned chuckled at that one. "Yes and no," he said. "My core has auditory signalers and detectors so I can sense the world around me in a way akin to echolocation, if you are familiar with the concept."

"I am."

"Additionally, my ability to synchronize with nearby computer systems including scanners and camera arrays means that I can 'see' in a certain way as well. Uploading myself to the *Buzzard* and shop, I do feel as though I can see the world in a way."

Peering into the final hole in the hull and seeing some actual internal damage, I snorted. "Meeting you was one hell of a thing."

"I don't have a hard time believing that," Ned said. "For a plebeian such as yourself to come into contact with a war hero like me who saved the universe, it should be a hell of a thing."

I snorted. "That's not what I meant."

"I know," Ned said lightly before laughing. "I can't even imagine what this experience must be like for you. When I was knocked out of existence, personalities like me were nearly as common as people. Now, with my kind all but extinct, it must be absolutely bonkers to meet a person you know to be a computer system."

"Bonkers is certainly one way to put it," I said. "As incredible as it is, terrifying would be another way."

"What would the Inquisition do if they found you with me?" Ned asked, and I could hear the hint of worry in his voice.

As I stepped around toward the ladder to the inside of the Consortium ship, I paused and considered Ned's question. "I don't know, honestly. I've only had one experience with them, and all of the rest is rumors and hearsay."

"What was the one experience?"

I rested one elbow on a rung of the ladder, remembering back to when I was a teenager. Lutch had sent me to pay off one of Resh's men, an increasingly common experience of the time, and on the way back, I saw a crowd of people gathered around Scrapper Twelve's shop. I was still scrawny enough to snake between people to the front of the crowd where I saw two men in black robes under red armor waiting at the door.

One of the men was old and bald, his armor adorned with etchings, and the saber at his side was gilded with precious metals, festooned with gems. The man behind him appeared young, not much older than I had been at the time. He had jet-black hair hanging to about his chin and eyes that burned with an intensity I had not seen before nor since.

"Open this door!" the older man thundered, the sound of his voice seeming to suck the air from the street. Perhaps a cloud moved to block the sun at that moment, but I remember that, though it was midday, the world grew dark.

"Not if you are out there!" a voice answered from the other side of the door. "I'll turn myself in to a Consortium Prefect but not to you."

"A Prefect would turn you over to me. I am the law above the law," the Inquisitor boomed, and his words sent a ripple of fear through everybody watching.

"No, please, let me be," the scrapper pleaded from inside.

"Open this door. I will not ask again."

The older Inquisitor snapped at the young man at his side. He produced a kiln charge and ran it over to the metal door set into the brick building. After activating it, he took a few steps back as the older man pulled the long, curved weapon from its scabbard. The weapon seemed to glow like magma with some internal heat.

The charge detonated, and the door was consumed with white

hot energy, reducing it to dripping metal in an instant. The older man stepped through, a piece of molten metal dripping on his armor and solidifying before he disappeared into the building.

Ripples of whispers flowed through the assembled citizenry as everyone stared into the darkened doorway. The young Inquisitor turned to scan the crowd and a hush descended rapidly. His face was long and slender and his brows low over his eyes. Everything about the young man carried an air of menace, and I remember backing away as his eyes fell upon me.

Then a guttural scream ripped through the air.

It was that of pure terror, of pain and fear. A sound that came from deep within a person without forethought or intent. It was pure instinct.

Then the Inquisitor appeared, dragging the scrapper by his hair out onto the street. Scraping along on one hand and knees, blood streamed down his face from some unseen wound, and he clutched his gut. He made another braying sound like a wounded animal.

I didn't want to watch, but I couldn't look away. I knew I was witnessing something that I shouldn't and that would stick with me. Even at the time, I could feel the impact of the moment.

"John," the senior Inquisitor snapped, getting the attention of the younger man.

The young Inquisitor produced a thick black flashlight from somewhere within his robes and shined it into the face of the wretch on the ground. The man clamped his eyes shut, and the young man knelt beside him, reaching out with one hand and pulling at his eyelids. When they didn't budge, John leaned in and whispered something into the ear of the man whimpering on the ground.

The young Inquisitor placed thumb and forefinger on either side of his eye and pulled the lids apart before shining the flashlight. Even from where I was standing in the crowd, I could see the unnatural green glint in the pupils. I had never noticed it before, and nothing would ever have given me any indication that the man was augmented.

I had met Scrapper Twelve and always thought he was a nice guy. Little did I know that he always came back with that little extra loot because his eye could identify things an organic one could not.

Even at the time though, I did not believe he should be hurt for it.

And hurt he was.

The old Inquisitor grinned as John knelt beside the scrapper. John's body blocked what happened next, but the scream that pierced the street left no questions.

"This," the old Inquisitor thundered, "is what happens when you taint the organic with the machine."

John turned and stood, holding a blood-soaked electronic eyeball aloft. The skin of his hand was stained, and his face was a picture of serenity, though his eyes burned with a satisfied fury. After a moment, he dropped the thing to the ground, raised a foot, and stomped it with a loud crunch.

Scrapper Twelve wailed. "Please, enough, please no more."

"No more?" the old Inquisitor mocked. "No more what? No more life? Gladly."

The blade in his hand flicked through the air with a yellow blur. The heat of the blade cauterized the flesh before the head even hit the sidewalk, and the smell of grilled flesh wafted sickeningly up the street.

It would be another year before I could stomach even just the scent of Lutch's barbeque.

"Let this be a lesson to each and every one of you. If you join with the machine, trust in the artificial or in any other way mate with the unnatural, we will find you and we will exterminate you," the Inquisitor intoned before sliding his blade back into its scabbard with a flourish and parting the crowd by doing nothing but taking a step toward it.

The two men left, and the crowd gathered around to gawk at the body until Consortium Prefects arrived to take everything away.

I hurried home, and Lutch made a comment about expanding the business and trying to buy Scrapper Twelve's lot, but by the morning, the building had been imploded and the twelfth license discontinued permanently.

"Now, the lot is a bar called Lucky Twelve's, as a grim little joke about what was," I told Ned, concluding my story.

"I see," he said as though he was trying to process what he just heard. "I knew you were taking a risk, but I don't think I quite appreciated how much of one."

"Now you do," I stated. "We get caught, we both get fried."

"Let's not get caught, then."

I snorted. "Right… I have to say, you may have done yourself a disservice asking me to tell that story."

"Am I to surmise that you feel a bit less inclined to keep me around after thinking about it?"

I tapped my pointer finger to my nose before realizing that he couldn't see me. "Yes. That's exactly it."

"If it's any consolation, I'm feeling less inclined to *be* me after hearing it."

"Yeah," I said with a quick nod "Getting knocked out of commission as a hero and waking up an enemy can't feel great."

"It does, in fact, not feel great."

"The universe is one hell of an unfair place," I noted, though I tended to hate platitudes like that. "But you'll understand if I decide we have to part ways."

"I will," he said. "It begs the question: what you would do with me?"

"Haven't thought that far ahead," I admitted.

Ned made a sound like a snorting exhalation. "Doesn't really inspire a lot of confidence."

"Don't imagine it would," I agreed. "And I'm sorry about that."

"But rather than dwelling on the negatives, why don't you consider the other side. With my help, you could get the *Buzzard* up and running better than when it rolled off the assembly room floor… or however ships are made now without automation… you could get yourself a crew to fill in the seats. You could afford to fix, well, everything around here. I'm not sure when the last time you did a life-sign scan around here was, but you have several types of infestations in the walls that—"

"I know about the infestations," I cut in. "And you don't have to sell me on the plus side. I get that too. I am the one who lives day to day and has to report my every move to a syndicate."

"I was just trying to illustrate a point," he said, and I couldn't tell if he was wounded or annoyed, and once again, I couldn't believe that I was even wondering that.

"I know and I hear it," I told him honestly. "I am taking all of this under advisement, but what I really have to do is work."

I checked the clock and saw how little daylight was left. I could keep working into the night, and undoubtedly would, but I also needed rest. My body was exhausted and my mind frayed.

"I understand," Ned said and got quiet as I climbed up into the starship and began to make repairs. I worked until I was physically unable to lift a tool.

When I finally collapsed on my bed in the room behind the office, I could hardly feel my limbs, and my mind was nothing more than a fog of wafting thoughts.

My eyes shot open to the sound of a slamming fist against my door.

8

The Inquisition, I thought in horror, sitting up and nearly collapsing back down. The strain I had put my body through the day before was roaring through me now. Everything hurt.

The pounding fist rang out again.

I lurched up and swayed toward the front of the shop like a drunk.

"Who's there?" I demanded in the toughest voice I could muster, though it croaked out ineffectually.

"Open this door, scrapper!" The derisive way the last word was fired through the metal made my hand twitch toward my weapon.

"Who's there?" I asked again, looking at the little screen that was supposed to display the feed from my security camera before remembering that rats had chewed through the wiring. Throughout all human history, rats seemed to be the one other species we brought with us wherever we went. That was true of space travel as well.

Nervously, I stepped up to the door.

"Who do you think it is?" the man asked from the other side, and I gripped the handle of my stomper as I compressed the unlock button.

Before me stood the pilot from the previous day with a bundle of cabling slung over his shoulder and attached at the other end to a piece of pallet on the ground with his Vekrass copilot passed out on top, snoring quietly. His face was red and blotchy, his eyes wild and lightning-streaked with veins.

"Took you long enough," he said, voice hoarse and drenched in alcohol. I hadn't talked to him for long the day before, but he sounded different enough that I hadn't recognized the voice.

Though I was relieved, I was also exhausted and not in the mood for him to wake me at the crack of dawn. Not that there was anything I could do about it.

He was here, and I would just have to deal with it.

"I think I waked up a few of your neighbors," he slurred, pushing by me, the pallet scraping along the ground behind him.

Across the street, I could see Scrapper Twenty-Six at his front door in his underpants, staring at me with his arms folded, eyes narrowed in annoyance. I waved him off and shut the door behind the two as the man dragged his copilot toward the ship.

"Just going to sleep it off in the crew quarters," he said. "You people think you can charge anything for a room out here, but I ain't spending my wages on some dingy room with a lamp."

"I'm not a hotel owner," I said as he continued his slow trek across the shop.

"You know what I mean," he grunted over his shoulder.

I did know what he meant. He was referring to people who lived out on the fringes of space. Those from what many considered to be the "core planets" thought of us as bumpkins who didn't know anything and were just trying to scrape by. It wasn't entirely untrue, but we didn't like the inherent condescension.

"Right," I said, trying to cover my irritation.

As I watched him reach his ship, I couldn't help but wonder how he planned to get her up inside. My question was answered when he knelt at the base of the ladder, scooped the Vekrass up and tossed her over his shoulder before starting to climb up.

"Made all the repairs last night," I called after him. "Just need to replace some damaged system batteries, but you want me to wait to do the work?"

"No," he yelled back and then belched in a way that made it sound like he was about to vomit on my floor. "I'll sleep through whatever work you're doing, and she certainly will, too. So, just do your thing, scrapper."

He disappeared up the ladder himself, and I walked back into the office area, then flopped down so hard into Lutch's old chair that I heard something inside snap. Rotating the chair toward my computer, I examined my orders to discover that the batteries I needed would be arriving any moment.

The green letters on a black background displayed the price that I had paid for them, and I couldn't help but smile. Not only had Ned found the exact parts I needed from another local shop, but he'd gotten a better price for them than I could have. While it was still incredibly unnerving that he was in my system and making moves on my behalf, I had to appreciate that they were the right moves.

Just as I was looking at my messages to see how Ned had done it, there was another knock at the door. For the second time that morning, I instinctively looked at the security screen and saw nothing.

I really do need to fix things around here, I grumbled to myself.

"Delivery!" a kid's voice called, and I heaved myself out of the chair, before moving over and opening the door for the kid with the dolly.

"That used to be me," I told him as I bent down to pick up the two batteries.

"And I'm sure you remember how much you liked it when folks tipped you," he said, raising an eyebrow from under his dirty hood.

I barked a laugh. "Well played," I granted him. "And here's a tip for you. Try not to extract money from people who obviously have as little as you."

He gave me a flat look.

I smiled, setting down the delivery and reaching into my pocket to fish out a Warhero card that had blown into my shop on a blustery day the other week. The fact that it was still in there didn't say much for how frequently I did laundry, but I knew the kids loved these things.

His eyes went wide when he saw it, and a smile parted his grease-streaked face when I handed it forward.

"Cheers," he said, taking the card and staring at it for a moment as though it was a gold bar, before ferreting it away into his coveralls.

"Thanks for the delivery," I said, and he nodded.

"Thanks for this," he replied, patting his pocket before turning and continuing along his route.

Watching him walk away flooded me with memories of my own

childhood. Nearly all the kids on this planet worked from the day they were born, and all of us started our careers running goods between the scrapyards. Since most scrappers divided their time between finding new parts (while telling ourselves that we were looking for treasure) and making repairs, there was a constant flow of components and pieces between the shops.

I spent my formative years running back and forth between all the shops, befriending the other children, and learning what I could. The adult scrappers didn't bring us kids on scrap jobs until we were older and that meant there was always a shop that was free for partying. Those evenings with the other youngsters were some of my fondest memories. My time in the orphanage had been hard and, though I was working a job once Lutch adopted me, it was a much happier life than I had known before.

After shutting the door, I carried the batteries toward the Consortium ship. As I did, I stole a glance at the *Buzzard* as though I would be able to see Ned hiding somewhere inside. Logically, I knew he was just a cube in a bag under a panel, I still had a hard time not expecting to see some physical form. In my experience, anything with personality had a body as well.

He said nothing, and I dragged myself toward the heavy fighter, then set the batteries down under the open panel at the side. After shifting my stepladder, I ambled up a few stairs and was startled to see the pilot's face, mouth agape, in the cockpit. He obviously had not made it to the crew quarters and had decided instead to collapse in the first chair he saw. I wondered if the pallet was just abandoned somewhere on the ship.

Shaking my head, I pulled on my heavy work gloves before

grabbing pliers and beginning to remove the damaged battery. It was a delicate process. The casing had been scorched and cracked, and any further damage could result in the melting loss of a hand. A grisly prospect I was not particularly interested in.

As seemed to keep happening, my mind drifted back to Ned. This was the kind of thing that a mechanized system would be perfect for. His computer mind could undoubtedly remove the battery with expert precision using mechanized arms that, if damaged, would cost only money. Doing this myself could result in catastrophic injury, and while I didn't want Ned to take over my job entirely, there was a certain appeal to handing over the more hazardous jobs to someone without skin, bones, or anything else that could be permanently damaged.

These idle thoughts kept me occupied as I removed the first battery, clanged slowly down the stairs, and crossed the shop to set it in the hazardous waste box. Once every so often (that is to say, whenever the local government managed to get their act together), someone would be sent to collect these boxes and compensate the scrapper for the goods. It was a holdover from the time when Bussel was going to be an example of colonial efficiency. Now, it just meant that every scrapper had an overflowing box of dangerous waste sitting right in the center of their shop.

The pilot snorted himself awake when I reached the top of the ladder with the new battery and it caused me to nearly jump out of my skin. Doing this entire job while knowing that I had the most illegal of technologies just a few meters away was nerve-racking to say the least. I was trying to treat it like a normal job, but I knew that it wasn't.

Reminding myself that all I had to do was get them patched up and out of here, I continued the work that I was best at. I could fight and I could fly if I had to, I was even a pretty decent cook when it came right down to it, but doing repairs like this was where my skills truly lay. Not only that, but I also loved it. Lutch had taught me to work with my hands, and it'd become the thing that soothed me the most.

Once the first battery was socketed in, I began to work on removing the other. Just after I set it in the box, I turned and nearly jumped out of my skin. Standing terrifyingly close behind me was the copilot, her face tired, the fur around her eyes wet and a single sharp tooth jutting from the side of her jowls. Despite their visual similarities to rodents, the Vekrass were true carnivores and had a mouthful of razor-sharp teeth.

"Got any coffee?" she asked, rubbing one of her eyes and swaying weakly in the way only the truly hungover can.

I nodded in the direction of the ancient slug pot. "Just that, but I could order you some."

"If you wouldn't mind," she said, her tail scraping along the ground as she made her way over to one of the chairs in my waiting area.

Heading over to the computer, I clacked away at the keyboard, putting in an order for three coffees. I figured that the pilot would want one when he woke up as well, and I knew that the anxiety I was riding would fade as soon as these two took off and I would need the caffeine.

"Order's in," I told the copilot, but she was already asleep again. My heart was still racing from when she had startled me.

I needed to get these two out of here as quickly as I could. My nerves couldn't take much more.

Quickly, I got the next battery installed, and as soon as I did, I heard the systems buzzing to life. I breathed a sigh of relief, knowing that once I got them full of coffee, I could get paid and get them out of here.

Then, a shrill alarm pierced the air from the Hawk-class heavy fighter.

9

The sound stopped me dead, and I watched the pilot's eyes shoot open to stare at his dash. The copilot was up too, covering her huge ears with her paws.

"What the hell is that?" she shrieked, before dropping onto all fours and rushing toward the ship. I watched her in wide-eyed horror and then looked at the pilot to see him staring at me, his mouth open.

He flipped on the external speakers and then said, "It's the AI scanner."

The copilot stopped running just about a meter from the bottom of the stepladder.

"Could it be malfunctioning?" she asked, and our eyes were locked on one another.

I flashed to look back up to the pilot, who was shaking his head. "No," he stated plainly. "Scrapper Twenty-Seven is harboring enemy technology."

There it was.

That was what I had most feared, and it hadn't even taken a day to happen.

"I'm going to alert the Inquisition," the pilot said.

The copilot looked at me. "By Consortium authority under Universal Law, I hereby… arrest you!" she shouted, trying to sound authoritative but obviously struggling with the ear-splitting alarm shrieking through the space.

And I had to decide, in that instant, what the rest of my life looked like.

I could go with them, allow myself to be arrested, and tell the Consortium everything. I could hope that they would show me leniency, that the Inquisition would take pity on me. But remembering that moment on the street, I had a hard time believing that if I turned myself over, the rest of my life would be anything but short and brutal.

My other choice was to run. To make a break for the *Buzzard* and hope that I could get away. I might get shot out of the sky or have my ship disabled and ultimately taken in any way, but I also might stand a chance of escape. I had never wanted to be a fugitive from the law and never thought that I would be faced with this kind of predicament, but as the alarm rang out and the copilot crouched to throw herself at me, I made the decision.

Whether I liked it or not, Ned and I were in it now.

Turning, I pushed up and threw myself over the handrail at the back of the stepladder as the copilot sprang forward. She crashed into the top of the stepladder, sending it toppling down to the ground behind me as I rushed toward the *Buzzard*. Ned already had it firing to life as I cleared the distance toward the ramp. The copilot got to her feet before collapsing again, the remnant booze coursing through her veins.

As I turned to hurry up into the *Buzzard*, I took one last look at my shop. I had no idea if I would see this place again or what was about to happen, but I couldn't help but take it in one more time before rushing up. Darting through the storage space and up toward the cockpit, I avoided every jutting bolt and loose panel. I knew the *Buzzard* better than just about anything.

"Activate placemags," I ordered Ned, and as I tossed myself into the pilot's seat, I heard the magnetic clamps beneath the Consortium vessel activate, locking it in place. The clamps would not be able to withstand the thrusters' pressure, but they would slow them down. Every little bit would help now.

"Open the roof," I commanded, but when I looked up, I saw that Ned already had. "Right," I said in acknowledgement of what he had done.

"Thank you." The words were spoken with genuine sincerity, and it took me a moment to register.

I had made the decision for me. I hadn't done it for Ned, I had done it to survive. To live to see another day. But my actions had also saved him. Ned had been pleading with me to work with him, and when push came to shove, I decided my best bet was with him.

"You're welcome," I said as though it had been an altruistic decision and pulled the controls, activating the thrusters and sending us up and away from Bussel. As I did, I watched the Consortium fighter pull against the magnets.

I flipped the switch to activate the gyre tube but knew I had a bit of time while it warmed up. Newer spacecraft could wash into a gyre nearly instantaneously, but the *Buzzard* needed time to activate all the requisite systems. That time might mean the difference between life and death now.

Thinking of another advantage to having Ned here, I gave him an order that would mean one fewer thing that I had to keep an eye on. "You get us out of here the second the drive warms up."

"Yes, sir," Ned said, sounding for the first time like the military partner he had been designed to be.

"Scrapper Twenty-Seven." I heard the pilot's voice through my comms. The Consortium could override the communication system of any registered vehicle. "You are in violation of Universal Law. Turn around now and return to the planet's surface or prepare to be fired upon."

As the last words crackled through the speakers, I heard a loud crash and assumed that the landing gears had pulled free of my magnets.

"Don't make us do this, Lutch," the pilot threatened through the comms.

"Still need to change the registration," Ned reminded me as I banked, trying to evade the fighter that I knew was somewhere behind me. The little screen displaying enemy position flickered to life, showing the sphere around the *Buzzard* and a dot to represent the enemy craft.

They were closing in fast. Tapping the display for the rear-facing camera, it crackled on too, showing a fuzzy grayscale image of the Consortium heavy fighter closing in on us.

Pressing the button to activate shields, I waited a moment to hear the activation of the shield array, but instead I heard Ned. "It appears that your shield generator is not functioning."

"Right," I cursed myself. It had been knocked out when I took off during a dust storm and dirt and debris battered the *Buzzard*. Another thing I needed to have fixed so it didn't come to bite me in the ass.

On the screen, a stream of micromissiles burst from the front of the ship behind us, and I tilted the controls, sending us jerking right. The base of the frayed strap keeping me in place pulled as though it was trying to come loose. Everything about the *Buzzard* felt as though she was about to come apart, and with an enemy firing at us, that moment was looking to be helped along.

I plunged the nose into a dive to avoid another burst of fire and narrowly avoided the stream of missiles.

"That was close!" Ned called out.

"Didn't get hit, did we?" I asked before adding, "I'm actually a pretty good pilot."

"Okay," Ned said incredulously.

"Did you just scoff?" I asked, yelling into the dash before pulling the controls and activating the bottom forward thrusters to send us hurtling vertically away from our tail.

"I mean..." he said, trailing off.

"I'm a good pilot," I asserted again, a little less confidently. "Maybe not as good as William whoever but—"

He didn't let me finish. "Captain William West, and no, no you are not."

The Consortium ship was quick and light and maneuverable with many more thrusters than I had. They could make hairpin turns and were staying right on our tail.

The *Buzzard* rattled. A few shots burst against the exterior before I could evade. I glanced at the Tidal Drive but knew it wasn't ready yet.

"Doesn't this boat have guns?" Ned demanded.

"The only ones I can fire are mounted at the front. The others need gunners," I explained, though I was sure he must have known that from the schematics and was trying to make the point that I should be returning fire.

Another volley plunked off the side before bursting and cracking pieces of the exterior hull. It wouldn't be long before one of the micromissiles cracked all the way through and made this a really short trip.

"Since you might get us killed, mind if I take over?" Ned asked, and seeing another flash of incoming missiles, I nodded.

"Sure," I said before feeling the thrusters begin to engage under the control of the machine mind.

In an instant, the *Buzzard* began to move in ways I never even realized were possible, gliding in one direction before bolting in another, and soon, we had them at a distance.

"Can you gun?" Ned asked, and I didn't even answer. I pulled the release on my seat, and the clamp decoupled, then the chair and I rode down the track in the ship. The seat moved through the hallway before sliding right and continued along to the side where the gun nest jutted out, the weapon itself mounted just below.

The seat gear locked into place, flipping the latch and sending the gun controls swinging up into place. I gripped one in each hand and popped the covers off the triggers before rotating the controls. When I did, a grinding whir sounded. I tried the controls again, and again, I was met with the sound of rusted machinery trying to work.

It had been too long since somebody had activated the guns, and the mechanisms had all gone to rust.

"Jammed over here," I told Ned, and within a moment, he was

spinning us in a nauseating, repetitive barrel roll. The stars around me spun in space, and the contents of my stomach threatened to come spraying out before we slammed to a stop, rattling and cracking the structure around me.

"Try it now."

It took me a minute to get my bearings. My stomach was in my throat, and I had to swallow it back down. Trying the controls, I heard a crackle and pop and thought that the gun was going to start moving but a cracking grind rang in my ears again.

I didn't want to get spun a second time, and that's when another thought occurred to me.

"Can you flip us under them so that the bottom of our ship is facing theirs?" I asked and then swallowed hard to keep everything in place.

"Sure can," Ned said, and the *Buzzard* spun again before accelerating forward. "William used to call this ass to ass."

"Not sure what to do with that information," I said honestly as I watched the Consortium fighter trying to evade and blast away from the planet's surface. Where I would've had to react, calculate my next move and then make it, Ned was able to simply follow them in a fluid motion. He didn't have to worry about reaction time and hand-eye coordination, he just made the calculation and did it instantaneously.

Experiencing the way the *Buzzard* moved under his control was like nothing I had ever known before. I was a good pilot, and Lutch had been a great pilot, but neither of us were anything compared to this. And, for as much training as the Consortium had given our opponents, there was no way they could evade us as long as Ned was in command.

Where they had me on my heels, doing little more than escaping their shots and waiting to get blasted out of the sky, Ned was turning the tables and hunting them.

They tried to escape us once again, shifting and pivoting out of the way, but Ned kept the *Buzzard* exactly parallel to them, getting closer and closer with every move. I reached out to the wall, pulled the heavy control lever, and heard the clang and thud from within the ship. Through the glass above me, I saw one of the robotic arms begin to extend, feeling it work perfectly.

The *Buzzard* was a dual-purpose craft. Though it had weapons and other combat capabilities, it was designed for the collection and hauling of scrap. So, for every weapon or armament, there were two practical features that a Scrapper might require. In this case, a mechanical arm which I could operate from one of the gun batteries. Having used it more recently, it wasn't rusted out, and reacted immediately to my controls.

It wasn't a particularly strong mechanism, but it would do the trick. As we closed in on the open plate that I hadn't had time to repair, I saw the batteries. All that time thinking about how it would've been advantageous to have a machine install the batteries had given me this idea.

One more time, the Consortium fighter tried to move away, but Ned stayed right beside them like two Redbacked Bussel Birds in a mating dance. This time, when we leveled out, I extended the arm, clamping it down around the battery and retracting it immediately. Wiring and cables pulled free and snapped, electricity arcing into space before their engines died.

"Keep us steady," I ordered, and Ned kept us on them. We were now far enough from the planet that its gravity would take far too long to slow the ship, so after I released the batteries in space, I clamped onto one of their torn landing gears and pulled.

Ned reacted, slowing our own ship as theirs slowed to a stop. I gave it a little yank for good measure, causing them to flip and twist in space before telling Ned to get us away from them.

They might have been trying to kill me, but in their own way, they were just doing their jobs. I didn't want to send them crashing to the surface of the planet, nor did I want them to die of starvation as they careened through the vacuum of space ad infinitum. Instead, I would let them spin until backup arrived. Hungover as they were, I expected that this would be punishment enough for trying to shoot me out of the sky.

"Tidal Drive ready," Ned informed me. "I know you told me to activate the moment it was available, but I figured I would ask what coordinates since we have defeated our enemies."

"Coordinates…" I said and thought about it as I watched the Consortium fighter continue to flip end over end in space. "How about away from here without using too much fuel."

Ned answered immediately. "I know just the place."

10

The interstellar gyre tube through which the *Buzzard* passed swirled a light blue around outside. White streaks flowed in ribbons around the tube before dissipating in bursts. It was said that the scientists who first harnessed the negative matter to create these passages between points in the universe thought that they looked like the inside of ocean waves. That was why all the terminology was oceanic in nature.

I didn't know if any of that was true, and it didn't matter. But I did know that the interior of the gyre was a marvel to watch. I could sit and stare at it flow and crash for hours. And often did. There was something meditative about it, and I was happy to have this moment of respite.

When we arrived, I saw we had reached Scrap Site 4429.

"This is just the place?" I asked, unlatching and sending my chair sliding back along the rail system to the cockpit.

Ned didn't speak for a long moment. "This was the place."

I was about to ask why some random scrap site was a place he wanted to hide before realizing that, when he knew it, it wasn't scrap. My people had probably picked over this place after it had been reduced to salvage.

"This spot used to be one of the greatest outposts in known space. It was where I was assigned to work with William, and where we were given our first assignments. We trained together and got to know one another and became one of the best duos the Consortium had ever seen. Now, it's a remnant of a remnant… Not even a name. Just the name that replaced it."

I had nothing to say to that. Ned was going through some complicated emotions over his new reality, and I had to give him the space to do so. But that was when it landed on me like a ton of bricks.

"What the hell are we going to do now?" I asked aloud. "And honestly," I said looking out the window before knocking a closed fist against my armrest, "we're lucky that this wasn't the base you wanted it to be. We can't go to the Consortium. They may have built you, and they might have been your friends, but those people want us dead.

"If we had arrived here to find what used to be, we would have been lucky to not be blasted out of the skies. Because, if the Consortium wants us, the Inquisition wants us. And they're not going to ask nicely. If they find us, they will pull my body apart the way they'll pull apart your programming. The husks that will be left of both of us will be nothing," I said and stared into the blackness of space.

"Now you know how I've felt since the moment I woke up."

My mouth fell open. "I just risked my life and gave up everything to keep you safe, and that's what you say to me?"

"Hank, I appreciate what you did for me, but you have to understand that I was programmed to sacrifice myself for the very Government that now wants me dead. So, while I know it's a hard pill for you to swallow, my entire existence is a hard pill to swallow," Ned said and even though he had a point, it still ticked me off.

"I gave up everything," I repeated, every word hanging around me like a noose. And it was true. I had given up everything. I would never be able to go back to Bussel now. I would never be able to return to my shop or go to a scrap site. From now on, I was an enemy of the state.

"What the hell are we going to do now?" I asked again, and I truly didn't know the answer. There was no place I could go, nothing we could do.

"We can go investigate the weapon," Ned said. "That's what we should do."

I shook my head and snorted. "Of course. You suggest the thing that's been your goal all along."

"It should be your goal too," he said in the way that anybody who was trying to convince somebody of something did. But I wasn't in the mood to be sold on heroic deeds done for some ideological greater good.

"It's not my goal, and even if it were, we couldn't," I told him and flopped back in my chair, all of the energy seeping from my body. "I'm sure when you were part of the Consortium fleet, you had as much fuel as you needed but here, in the real world, you have to pay for it. Plus, you think this old hunk of junk can invade some ancient war station? We barely got out of one fight with one enemy.

If you want to investigate this superweapon, we need to get fuel and make significant repairs to the *Buzzard*."

"Where can we repair the ship and make improvements?" Ned asked, his voice carrying a militaristic determination.

I couldn't help but laugh. It was absurd. He was so focused but didn't seem to quite understand how bad things were for us.

"Ned, I'm not sure where in this entire universe we can go. The only places we will be welcome, or, hidden from the Consortium, at any rate, are places we don't want to be.

"There are dangerous corners where we could keep our heads down, but we have no money and nothing to offer. Except this ship. But if I were to sell the *Buzzard*, we would have nothing. Just nothing. So, we need to really think about our options here."

"Don't you have any money?" he asked, sounding genuinely curious.

"You didn't poke around in my accounts?"

"No," he said. "I do have a sense of propriety after all."

"And you couldn't get in without being flagged as an AI," I said with a raised eyebrow.

"And that," he admitted with a chuckle. "You know, you're not as dumb as a lot of the mechanics I knew."

"I don't know who should be more insulted, me or the other mechanics you knew," I said. I was staring at a patch of rust in the ceiling and considering our choices.

"What about the scrap in the hold?" Ned asked. "During my scan, I noticed a large amount of pieces of metal and vehicle parts in one of the holds."

I smiled. "That's not worth anything."

"I don't understand. If it's not worth anything, why hold on to it?"

"For emergencies," I answered as though that explained it and went back to thinking of other options. "Maybe the Junk Rats," I said finally.

"What's a Junk Rat?"

"Slang…" I admitted. "Or, slur, I suppose, for scavengers who scrap outside the law."

"The pirates to your privateers if you will," Ned said.

I rotated a flat palm. "Both those things still exist but, yeah, it's kinda analogous."

"You think we would be welcomed by these Scavengers?" he asked, his voice carrying a hope.

"I doubt it," I told him. "I've heard of humans running with them but haven't ever seen it. But I could prove helpful to them, and it might be advantageous to have a man in their ranks, so, maybe?"

"Where are they headquartered?" he asked, making it clear that even just my idle idea was something he was considering.

"I have no idea," I said, shaking my head and unstrapping myself. "But I have to eat."

"What?" he said, and I couldn't tell if it was annoyance or surprise in his tone.

"What?" I asked back.

"We are brainstorming," he asserted.

"I'll brainstorm better when I've eaten something. I've only had a bag of chips since we met," I told him.

"You'll eat when we have a plan," he stated.

I laughed pointedly.

"I don't take orders from you." I stood from my chair. "We might be in this together, but you don't dictate the terms here."

As I began to move toward the crew quarters, thrusters fired. I was thrown forward and crashed toward the wall. After throwing up my hands, they braced against the impact, slapping hard against the metal.

"What point do you think that made?" I snarled. "You were a lot nicer when you were trying to convince me to work with you."

"Now that you are stuck with me, I can make the point that I control the *Buzzard* and, therefore, your fate," he explained.

"Ned, listen to me." I tried to reason, but my irritation was obvious in my tone. "We are going to be working together for the foreseeable future. We are stuck with one another from here on out so maybe it would be better if we try to work together rather than making demands."

"I agree," Ned said.

"Good." I began making my way toward the stairs before being thrown again. This time, I had to grip the handrail to keep myself from being sent head over heels down the metal staircase. "What the hell was that?" I barked, feeling the anger rising in me. It took a lot to get me truly pissed off, but this AI who I had risked my neck for choosing to throw me around my own ship was certainly getting me there.

"I thought we had agreed to work together," Ned said plainly. "Working together means continuing our brainstorming session. We have to formulate a plan, and we must do it quickly."

Holding the metal to brace against another jerk, I took a slow, calming breath and looked at the speaker mounted above the stairs. I wondered how long I would continue to do this. "Ned, I'm exhausted. I'm starving. I'm on the run and am trying to cope with a whole new reality. Showing off that you can fly the ship isn't doing anything but making me want to work with you less.

"We are partners now, and I will brainstorm with you soon, but you have to let me rest from time to time and you have to let me do things my way. I'm sure this is a change for you. I'm sure William was a tireless hero who was always looking to the next mission, but that's not me.

"We will figure this out, and we may even investigate your weapon, but you have to give me a minute to breathe here, all right?"

Ned said nothing for a long moment. And when a minute had passed, I supposed that he was taking my words to heart. I took the opportunity to hurry down the stairs, moving along the cramped corridor and pushing open the door to the room I had made my own.

Looking at it was disheartening. I hadn't planned to live out of the *Buzzard* ever, and it showed. There was a cot on one side, a workbench on the other with a project I had started years earlier and never finished clamped to the side in perfect stasis. A poster for Warhero cards that I found in the trash and hung as a child was still tacked to the wall and a single lightbulb crackling in a small cage illuminated the room.

Stepping across the space, I ran my hand over the porthole on the far side, shifting the dirt so I could look out into the black. This was my home now. The place I had known my whole life was behind me and now I was stuck out in the void with an illegal machine as my only companion.

What have I done?

I wondered what Lutch would think if he saw me now.

A memory flashed in my mind.

Sitting on the cot beside me, I looked up at the massive man and asked him something I had often wondered about. "Did you ever want to join the Consortium?"

He looked down at me and then away with a pensive look on his huge gray face.

"No, I can't say that I did," he told me, and as a naïve teenager, I was surprised.

"Didn't you ever want to be a hero?" I asked, though looking back, I think it was nearly an accusation.

A broad smile creased his face. "What makes you think that joining the Consortium is the same as an opportunity for heroism?"

I shrugged, not having given it much thought except that all of the "heroes" I had ever heard about were called that because they had fought in some war.

"That's exactly it," he said, laying a hand on my back. "You don't know yet. Being a hero doesn't mean going to war and ending lives. Your Uncle Edgar and I fought in the clan wars for years and nothing about it was heroic.

"I witnessed acts of heroism on the battlefield, sure, but I also witnessed acts of heroism in a smaller way every day: when I see my son doing what's right or when I can help someone in need. We don't have much, and we don't get the glory of triumphal processions beamed out across the universe on holo, but we still put good into the world.

"And I would rather do that than just about anything else. And that's what I want for you too. I hope that someday you can leave a footprint of good somewhere in this vast expanse. Doesn't have to be big, it doesn't have to be written about or get you fame or money or the girls you seem to want so desperately, it just has to be good."

The massive mitt on my back patted once.

"If I can raise you to be a respectable man, that will be the greatest act of heroism in my life," he said, voice cracking with emotion.

Lutch loved to lecture, but he didn't express his feelings all that often. When he did, they landed. And now, staring out the porthole in the same room where the conversation had taken place, I couldn't help but wonder if this was my moment. Perhaps the good he wanted me to do was right in front of me. Maybe I needed to be forced out into the world so that I could track down this weapon and put my footprint of good in the universe.

This thought didn't alleviate the pressure I was feeling, the exhaustion, fear, or anger, but it did help a bit.

Nodding to myself, I turned to the workbench, opened the little fridge that served as one of the legs, and held the right side up. Inside were a few Bussel Brews, two of them empty and put back for reasons I couldn't remember, a sandwich half that was now solidified gray mold, and what I was looking for: a box of old sustenance bars. They may have tasted terrible, but they provided the caloric requirements for an entire meal and never spoiled.

I reached down and picked one up. I was always surprised by the heft of the things. I unwrapped it and forced it down my gullet before heading to the bathroom. I used the facilities and splashed some water on my face, wondering how much was left and if it was still potable after being stored for that long without being refreshed. Another thing for the list.

It hadn't taken much, but I felt a bit better and made my way into the little common room. It wasn't really anything to look at, just a big circular couch around the table, a nonfunctioning holo in the corner and a little kitchenette built into the wall. I sat down on the long couch, putting my feet up on the table.

"Ned," I said and didn't have to wait long for an answer.

"Yes," he said.

"I think I am ready to brainstorm," I told him.

"You think you are ready, or you are ready?" he asked, but there was no heat to the question.

"I'm ready," I told him.

"Good," he answered. "I was thinking about something that you mentioned and might have an idea."

"Me too, actually," I said.

"You go first," he allowed, and as I opened my mouth to speak, he cut me off. "Get to the cockpit. Now."

I was up and running before he said another word, arms pumping and legs slamming over the floorplates to get myself to my chair as quickly as possible.

Directly in front of us was another vessel which had just decloaked and which was facing right toward us, weapons all pointed at the *Buzzard*. I recognized the design in an instant. The Gothic design of the red ship; the long wings, triangular front and weapon arrays on the underside that made it look like a bird of prey swooping down on some unsuspecting victim. This was an Inquisition Phoenix.

"Comms channel being overridden," Ned told me. "I can keep him out of our systems, but it seems like we should let him talk and buy ourselves some time."

"Agreed," I said and sat upright in my chair, trying to look intimidating for no other reason than that it seemed like the appropriate thing to do.

But I was deflated the moment the screen came to life and I saw the face looking at me. It was older than it had been when I had seen it before, but the black hair, thin features, and furious eyes were exactly the same.

It was the young Inquisitor from the street all those years earlier.

My hand began to tremble before he even spoke.

11

"Hank Spears, son of Lutch Spears and current bearer of Scrapper License Twenty-Seven, you are in possession of technology that presents a clear and present threat to the Consortium and all the citizens therein.

"I, Inquisitor John Gregory, place you under arrest. You will be brought in before the Inquisition for questioning and then remanded to the custody of the Consortium. At this moment, you will deactivate your ship and allow us to board," he stated. His voice was like a loud whisper, rasping angrily from his mouth.

"What makes you think I have any illegal technology?" I asked, leaning back in my chair and trying to play it cool. The man terrified me, but I couldn't let them know it.

On the screen, over his shoulder, I could see a pale young woman with bright red hair standing in the background. I suppose that she was to him what he had been to the older Inquisitor out on the street: an acolyte.

"I do not *think* that you are in possession, I know," he stated unequivocally. "What you must understand is that the thing you carry is an abomination and a threat to every living organism in the universe. It is the very quintessence of evil.

"It might have tried to convince you otherwise, to promise you riches or fame. It might have scared you with some otherworldly threat. But I assure you, the only threat is that program itself. It was devised by man and represents the worst of what we are capable of. It must be destroyed before it rears up and kills its creator.

"It is not your friend, it is not your ally, it is not anything more than a disease hoping to spread itself, hoping to infect every living thing. It will not rest until it is multiplied, devastating the universe and ridding every planet of organic life. Of pure life. Of true life.

"I can free you from its clutches," he said as though it was some great opportunity. But his words were spoken through gritted teeth, and he sounded like the very evil he was warning against. "I can help you. Let me board, and I will protect you from this thing that hopes to end your life."

I looked away from the screen for a moment and then back. "Oh, hey, I'm sorry, I think I had you on mute for part of that. Can you say it all again… something about quince?"

He snorted derisively. "You mock the Inquisition?"

I shook my head and held up my hands. "I wouldn't dream of mocking the Inquisition. I just missed your whole beautiful tirade and was hoping to get a second performance."

"Don't you understand what a mistake this is?"

"You got me there," I said mostly because it was true. "I certainly never wanted to cross paths with you again but here we are."

"Again?" he asked, his eyes searching. "You are from Bussel? And you are a scrapper," he said, running a hand along his short black beard.

I had not meant to reference seeing him before, it just slipped out. If I planned to survive much longer as a criminal on the run, I was going to have to get better at playing things close to the vest.

"Scrapper Twelve," he said after a moment, and for the first time, I saw the man smile ever so slightly. His eyes glinted at the memory. "You were present that day? You witnessed what we did?"

"I saw what you did," I said, the words coming out of my mouth as though I was spitting on the ground, disgusted.

"Then why are you fighting this?" he asked in sincere confusion. "I'm giving you an opportunity to avoid that very fate."

I scoffed. "Let's quit the song and dance," I said. "You've made your threats, and I'm not buying it. I'm sure you said all these things to Scrapper Twelve before murdering him and razing his place to the ground. You have no intention of taking me in peaceably. I can see in those rat eyes of yours that you want nothing more than to come on here and peel the skin from my bones. Well, I've got news for you. I have no intention of letting you do that."

He stared at the comm for a long moment, seemingly trying to appraise me. His face was a cipher, and I had no idea what he was planning to do next.

"He will pull the skin from your bones," the woman over his shoulder said quietly. It didn't sound like a threat but a statement of fact. Almost a warning. From the way she said it, I was sure she had seen it done and worse.

He looked at her, saying something, and she receded into the darkness behind him.

"I will not threaten you again," he said. "I will simply say that by making this choice, you are also making another choice."

"Hey, John," I began and saw his brows pinch and lips purse in annoyance at my use of his given name. "Maybe we can come to some understanding, here? You know, maybe there is something you want that I can offer you?"

"Are you trying to bribe me?" he demanded.

I offered him my biggest, falsest smile. "Not a chance," I said and knew it was time to get out of here.

I didn't stand a chance in open combat. Even with Ned at the helm, the Inquisitor's ship was too strong with too many weapons and tricks. Of course, the *Buzzard* had a few tricks up her sleeve as well.

"I will take no bribes, and I will suffer no insolence from the likes of you," he snarled. The man was nothing if not persistent.

"Do you have any other moods, or is this just you all the time?" I asked before immediately muting the channel so that he couldn't hear what was happening on my end. He would see my mouth moving if I tried to communicate with Ned.

I slowly reached a hand forward and began to tap on the console in front of me. Scrappers used nonverbal communication to speak with one another on large jobs, using taps and scrapes to express thoughts over long distances. It was a modified version of some old military transmission style, and I hoped that Ned would be able to decipher.

"Prep the drive," I indicated.

"Already on it," he answered. Having no mouth had its benefits.

"My mood is none of your affair," John Gregory answered. The way he looked at me as he spoke felt like some animal stalking its prey. He didn't mind that I was trying to stall or delay him because he believed that what came next was inevitable. He had the confidence of a man who could easily decimate anyone he saw fit.

That worried me. My plan might not work, and it could simply result in my capture and torture. But I had to try. I tapped the mute button, keeping my finger hovering right above it, knowing I would have to activate it on and off repeatedly.

"Yeah, I'm guessing this is how you are all the time, then," I said, reaching out and turning a crank to activate one of the storage holds. A clang echoed through the ship, and the sounds of gears working followed. "Where is your little friend? I'm sure she would confirm it for me."

As the question left my mouth, it also made me nervous. Where was his apprentice? Was she off manning some weapon battery? Was she suiting up to set a demolition charge on the *Buzzard*?

One more thing to worry about.

"Imogen's understanding of the universe is still developing," he stated plainly, the comment sounding as though it was meant more for her than for me. "Her opinions mean nothing at this stage. Like you, she will learn the full power of the Inquisition."

The storage bay was still shifting so I had to keep him talking and distracted a bit longer. "And what is that?" I asked. "What is your full power? Seems like just two people on a Phoenix from here."

At this, he grinned again, showing small, perfectly white teeth. The man seemed, in his own way, to be having fun with this. In John Gregory, the Inquisition had found their perfect sadist to send after people. I had seen it on the street all those years ago, but interacting with him now, I could see the truth of it.

I also knew that, if my gambit were to pay off and I somehow did escape, he was going to keep hunting me.

"The full power of the Inquisition is that which is to be most feared," the Inquisitor said. "We are all relentless incarnations. We are human drive and determination personified. We are the best, smartest and strongest of humanity. We are the reason the machine need not exist.

"Only the weak need to consort with programming. You are weak but now that you are in the presence of true strength, we can help you. You sit there and consider firing upon us but know that it will do nothing but bring my wrath down upon you. Or perhaps you believe that you can tuck tail and run. You cannot.

"If you do anything other than turn yourself over to me, Scrap Site 4429 will be your grave. But this place needn't be. Rather, it can be the place where you turn your life around. The place where you saw the light and stepped into it. The place where you made the decision to help your fellow man."

At his words, I couldn't help but think about what Lutch had said and about the weapon that Ned feared. Perhaps this was the moment when I decided to help my fellow man. I had no idea how we were going to get out of the situation or what we could do to keep both the Inquisition and Consortium off our backs, but we could figure it out.

I had been a scrapper for my entire life, and I thought of it as my identity, but it didn't have to be. I could be something more than just my job.

The storage bay clanged into place and the *Buzzard* rattled, a layer of dirt knocked loose from between two panels and raining down on me. Now it was my turn to smile. I flicked the switch to prime Bay Three.

"You know what, I think you're right," I said and pressed the button to open the doors and fire the junk from storage out into the space between the *Buzzard* and the Inquisition. scrappers commonly called it a scrap belch and would use it in desperate moments like this.

I heard the crunch and then nothing.

The scrap didn't eject.

The mute sign appeared on the screen. "Was something supposed to happen?" asked Ned in a tone somewhere between patronizing and terrified.

"Good," Inquisitor Gregory said. "I will begin the boarding process now, and I expect you to come peaceably."

I began tapping rapidly, trying to express to Ned what I had intended to do. As I did, I watched the Inquisition Phoenix begin to close in on us. From out of its weapon array, an anchor cable launcher unfurled, rotating to point in our direction.

Immediately, I went from confident to mortified and reached out, put my hands on the controls, and considered holding the trigger down until I had fired every last micromissile I had on the ship. I doubted that it would do much of anything at all, but at least I would go out in a blaze of glory. Or I could tilt the nose of the *Buzzard* and attempt a Tidal Drive escape. Problem was, inquisitor Gregory would fire everything he's got at me, and I would be ripped apart before we could even make the jump.

That's why we needed the scrap.

Without it, we were sitting ducks.

My finger twitched against the trigger. It might be foolish, but it was our only chance.

"Don't," Ned said in a whisper even though the comm channel was muted. "Get ready."

The Inquisitors weapon locked into position, and I watched as if in slow motion as the cable fired. Curved hooks surrounded a large magnet that trailed the cord of galvanized braided steel.

This was it.

As quickly as our heroics had begun, they would end.

"Ha!" Ned cried, and I felt the *Buzzard* jolt. Chunks of metal and dirt and rock blasted out from the bowels of the ship, perforating the space between us. The cable clamped down on a piece of old starship that was so old I remembered Lutch having me jump on as a kid to break it loose.

By the time I reached for the Tidal Drive button, the *Buzzard* was already washing into the interstellar gyre pulling with it some of the junk floating behind us.

"That was a mistake," John Gregory seethed just before Ned killed the transmission as the world erupted around us. The Phoenix fired everything they had, smashing and shattering the junk around us in a torrent of fireworks.

My chest was pressed and face pulled as the *Buzzard* tidaled away from our pursuers.

From deep within me, a loud cheer erupted.

"Nice work, Ned," I called, slapping a hand on the dash.

"That was a clever trick," he acknowledged.

"Scrappers have to be able to make a quick escape from time to time," I said, grinning through my beard. We still faced all the problems we had before and all we had done was survive this encounter, but I still felt energized.

"Right," Ned said, the complimentary portion of the program obviously having come to an end. "What now?"

12

That was the question from here on out: what now?

But this time, I had an answer.

"The moment he appeared, I began to think about how John was able to track me and I realized it was the—"

"Registration signaler," Ned finished for me, and this time the tone was clearly patronizing.

"Right, exactly," I affirmed, not trying to let him get to me. Our easy rapport had been there from the start, but now that I needed him as much as he needed me, a hard edge had appeared and didn't seem to be going anywhere. "We need to get that signaler turned off, and I think I know of a place where we can do it. It's a highly illegal modification and any legitimate business would stay far away from doing it. That being said, even if we could get somewhere that has the type of people who would do it for us, we are missing one thing…"

"Money," Ned spoke over me again.

"That's exactly right," I nodded, staring at the swirling space outside. "We need money."

"And I'm assuming that you have an idea of how we can get some," Ned led.

"I do but there are some complications," I admitted.

"I expect they're going to be tracking us and pursuing us wherever we go."

I nodded. "Got that right. From here on out, it's going to be a lot of running and hiding as best we can. Now that we have both the Consortium and the Inquisition hot on our heels, we are in for a rough go."

"I expect that I know the answer," Ned said in a surprisingly somber tone. "But do you think there's any way we could speak to somebody at the Consortium who would be willing to work with me?"

I stifled a laugh. "Were you not just part of the conversation we had with that lunatic?"

"I don't mean somebody from the Inquisition, I need somebody from the Consortium. Somebody from the government, the military. A person who would put duty before the witch hunt."

I had to think about that for a moment. "I'm sure you're right that there are people out there who would be willing to hear you out and maybe even to help us out, but I don't know them. Frankly, I don't really know anybody who isn't a scrapper from Bussel. My experience in the wider world has been limited to scrap sites."

"Do you know anybody in the Consortium?" Ned asked.

"Hate to disappoint you, but the only people I knew from the government followed us as we left my shop," I informed him.

"There must be some local prefect or magistrate on Bussel. Do you know the Governor?"

This time I couldn't help but laugh. "Ned, I don't even know who the Sectorial Governor is at this moment in time. It's splashed all over the news when a new appointment is made, but I don't follow politics."

"I don't understand," he said, and I could tell he meant it. "You follow politics so little that you don't even know who your representative is?"

"No, I do not," I told him flatly. "I know you were made by the government and have some reverence for it but out here on the fringes, in the real world, whoever sits at the long table, getting kickbacks from Resh and showing up once a year for a parade doesn't matter to me. They don't matter to anybody."

"But their civil servants were put in place by Parliament to help the people," Ned said, and it was the first time that he sounded truly naïve.

"Do you believe that or are programmed to believe that?" I asked him, and there was a long pause that followed. So long that it became a bit uncomfortable, and I began to pick at the dirt under my fingernails.

"Both," he said finally. "As you would expect, I was programmed with a base understanding of things. But this understanding was designed by people with their own sets of beliefs. These Consortium employees may have given me the foundation, but I was also given the latitude to learn, understand and come to my own conclusions.

"As a service member, I worked alongside people who devoted themselves to a better world. There were always self-aggrandizing assholes, petty tyrants, and every other kind of jerk you would expect, but for the most part, the members of the Consortium that I met were laying down their lives to protect people of all species from the Enemy AI.

"The members of Parliament and other representatives who I had the distinction of crossing paths with were dedicated and hard-working individuals who would sleep in their offices and do everything they could to help the universe.

"So, to answer your question, I was both programmed to believe it and believe it because of my own experience."

"Well, that's a really romantic notion," I said, looking up from my hand. "But that's not how things are now. Seems like, since the war, those folks in power are more concerned with staying in power and getting a pile of riches to sit on than protecting the citizens of any of the planets they govern.

"I don't often watch the news, but when I do, it's mostly just talking about dire situations and the Consortium's inability to do anything about it. I expect that the people you knew did really believe in what they were doing and fought hard to rid the universe of this great enemy, but the generations that followed don't seem to have upheld that tradition.

"I don't like to be the bearer of bad news, but I don't expect to find too many people who want to help us. And even if there were people out there like that, I would not know how to find them, and they might not want to go toe to toe with the Inquisition when push came to shove."

Another pause followed as I absently checked the gauges and screens, realizing how low fuel was getting.

"Everything about the universe as I knew it has changed," Ned said, and if the computer could sigh, that was the tone he had taken. "All these people who fought and died believed that they were sacrificing themselves to make a better world. And, instead, we saved society only to let it destroy itself."

"Maybe it's not hopeless," I told him, hearing Lutch in my words. "Maybe you're right that there are people out there who would be willing to help us. Perhaps when we show them evidence of this superweapon you're concerned about, the Consortium will change its attitude. And, who knows, maybe when you and I discover this weapon and save the universe, well, for you a second time, the Consortium will change their tone about artificial intelligence."

"Where's all this coming from?" Ned asked incredulously.

"Well," I said and had to think about the answer. "We find ourselves in a tough spot, but we can't sit here playing the woe-is-me game any longer. If we mean to survive, we are going to have to act. Pessimism and fear are only going to slow us down or cause us to make mistakes. Sniffing at each other isn't going to help either. We just need to get ourselves into gear and get moving."

"When life gives you lemons…" Ned led.

I furled my brows in confusion.

"… you make lemonade," he said as though it was something I should know about.

"What's lemonade?" I asked. "And what's lemon?"

"It's… It's a sour fruit that can be made into a sweet drink," Ned said, a bit patronizingly. "Isn't your entire planet all about booze? I'm surprised you don't have lemons."

"We might but that doesn't mean I know anything about them," I noted.

"But I take your point," Ned acknowledged. "I suppose there's one thing that I owe you."

"What's that?"

"Thank you."

I nodded slightly.

"I do know what you risked by not handing me over. Whether it was to save your own skin or not, doesn't matter. You did something remarkable, and you have my eternal gratitude. That doesn't mean that I'm obligated to think of you as anything more than what you are, but I do appreciate what you did," he said.

"That was both a backhanded and open-palmed compliment," I noted.

"Yes, well, I'm a military man," he stated. "Want to know something weird?"

"Sure," I shrugged, this entire conversation leaving me with a bit of whiplash.

"I can taste the lemonade," he said.

That made my brain hurt. "You can taste it?"

"Yes," he stated plainly. "Taste is just another signal sent to the brain and I suppose, in creating me, my designers gave me something akin to taste. As I was talking about it, I had this faint sense of how it tasted in the back of my mind."

"Even just the fact that you have a back of your mind is noteworthy," I observed.

"I thought you might appreciate that," he said, and I could almost hear the smile.

"It does beg the question," I began. "Do you want some kind of physical form?"

"Pardon?"

"I don't know, some kind of body," I said.

"Hank, nearly everybody in this universe hates me and wants me destroyed as I am. I'm pretty sure they would dislike me more if I'm also walking around," he said with a hint of resignation.

"If they already hate you, you might as well also find a way to be able to come with me as we work," I suggested. "As you said, you're only going to make me better and having you by my side will certainly help."

"I don't need a physical form for that," he explained. "Just some kind of earpiece that I could upload to."

"All right, I'll add it to the list," I said with a chuckle.

"This list is getting," and he paused for a long moment, "robust."

"It is," I had to admit. "But I'll stay on the lookout for some kind of earpiece to get you synchronized with. Is that the right word?"

"It is."

"All right. That's a start. But I'm going to be looking toward fabricating something for you. I'm still having a hell of a time just talking to nothing. If nothing else, I don't know where to look."

"I can't say that I've ever had that problem," Ned said. "And neither did William but, of course, we were of a time and place."

"Of course."

"So, what's our next move?"

"We know we need money, and there is really only one thing in this universe that I understand well enough to really profit from," I said, and before I could finish, Ned butted in.

"Scrapping."

I tapped my pointer finger to my nose before remembering and simply stating, "Precisely."

"Are there scrap sites we can seek out and pillage?"

I smiled. "Pillage is a good word, but no, not like that. If I were to go to any official site populated with scrappers, we would be done before we even washed in. We have to find a list of sites and pick one where there won't be any other scrappers. To do that, we will need to get you into the feltwork so you can access the scrappers database. Do you think you could do it undetected?"

There was no pause this time. "Yes," he said with an unmistakable air of confidence. "But I will need an access point where I won't be seen or disturbed. I need someplace where I can do the work and focus on the task at hand."

"You can't multitask?" I asked, more interested in his programming with each and every new breadcrumb of information.

"I can," he stated. "But, like you, I only have so much processing power. If I am trying to focus on both finding information and keeping the Consortium programmers off my back, I don't want to have to focus on external factors as well."

Nodding gravely, I considered his words. "This adds another wrinkle."

"Perhaps not," Ned said. "When I was perusing the *Buzzard*'s files, I was able to access the complete list of registered stations, substations, and satellites in the Consortium network. I have been analyzing them and believe that I found one feltwork relay station in Sector Twenty-Two that is far enough away from populated space that might suit our needs perfectly."

"Sector Twenty-Two?" I said, scratching my chin through my beard. "I'm surprised there's any kind of relay station out that far. I expect it was put up for colonists and abandoned when nobody moved out this way. We'll be lucky if it is still functional."

"We're bound to get lucky one of these times," Ned joked.

"Suppose you're right, and anyway, I like the idea of continuing to move forward. If we go to the station, and get you into the feltwork, we can find a scrap site and start turning this situation around," I said, and despite all evidence to the contrary, I believed that what I was suggesting might actually be possible. I didn't know if it was genuine confidence or a placebo of confidence, but either way, it worked.

I stood. "One thing I have to do first, though. The second we exit the gyre, the registration signaler will ping the Inquisition, and they will be all over our ass again. Escaping from John once was a break we will not likely get again."

13

"You know how to disable the signaler?" Ned asked hopefully.

I shook my head no as I made my way down the hallway, grabbed my toolbelt, and headed toward the ladder that led to the crawlspace that had access to the room in which the signaler was housed. Every starship manufacturer made it possible to access the registration signaler but also made it equally inconvenient. They didn't want people tampering with the devices but needed to make it possible to repair them.

As I clattered up the ladder and forced open the hatch, showering myself with rust, I didn't know what I was going to do. And I as much as told him that. "I've never poked around in one of these before," I admitted. "It was the one thing my father never taught me. He, too, had a sense of propriety about certain things and said that the one thing we never wanted to do was operate behind the backs of the people who allowed us to work. All I know about the registration signaler is that if you make one wrong move with it, it can disable your ship or worse. Don't suppose you have more information than I do?"

"I have a rudimentary understanding of the technology on which it's based, but I can extrapolate from the gaps in my knowledge that the Consortium didn't want AIs to be reprogrammed by private interests to disable the signalers either," he explained. "Basically, I know enough to know that they exist but certainly not how to disable one."

I slid the small penlight over my ear, tucking my shaggy hair out of the way to allow the beam to fill the crawlspace. "So, we're in the same situation on this one."

"Yes, neither of our programmers wanted us to mess around with the signalers," he joked, and it stopped my crawling for a moment.

"I had never thought of it that way," I said. "But, thinking of Lutch as my programmer is pretty spot on."

"I thought it was apt."

I kept crawling in the direction of the little placard displaying my registration signaler's identification number. That meant I was getting close. "Lutch filled my mind with information in the same way that some guy sitting behind the computer screen did yours. Both of them had their own biases and agendas and filled our minds with the things they deemed important."

"See, we're not so different, you and I," Ned said, and it carried the weight of an argument I knew he wished he could make to the universe.

I reached the end of the crawlspace and saw the sliding handle that opened the door to the registration signaler. Reaching out and wishing that they had made the height of the space slightly bigger, I hooked my fingers over the handle and pressed it. I was expecting it to take a great effort or be frozen like everything else on the ship and require me to spray it with a penetrating oil from my belt and wait.

But, to my shock, it moved like a warm knife through butter. As did the door. And when I crawled into the circular space, stood and pressed a closed fist against the light switch, the room glowed to life in brilliant white. Unlike anything else on the *Buzzard*, the registration signaler was pristine and clean (except for a thin layer of dust) with smooth surfaces and clean rivets.

I stepped forward and took a moment to simply stare at the workmanship. Clicking off my penlight, I reached out a hand and ran it over the perfectly socketed bolts, pristine soldering and immaculate joints.

"Well, well, well," I said, a bit awestruck.

"Should I give you two a moment?" Ned quipped.

"Har har har," I snapped back. "It's just some expert work."

"That expert work is the thing standing between you and survival," Ned said as though he needed to remind me. "Additionally, I should mention that we only have about twenty eMins before reaching the station."

Pulling my drill from the belt and affixing the right head, I couldn't help but chuckle. "Nobody uses eMins anymore," I informed him. "We all just say 'minutes' and know that it's based on standard Earth time."

"Good to know," Ned said and sounded like he meant it. "I'm going to need to learn quite a lot about colloquial vernacular."

"Yeah," I grunted as I lifted the drill to the main panel at the front of the signaler and began unscrewing the bolts. One by one, I caught them and dropped them into the sack on my belt that I set aside for loose objects.

It wasn't long before I had the entire panel unscrewed, and I quickly popped the bit at the end of the drill into one corner and used it to pry free the plate. It came off with ease, and I set it down, but my heart instantly sank.

There was a digital panel under a huge warning label. "Do not tamper. Do not remove unless authorized by the Bureau of Logistics. Any attempt to remove, disassemble, or otherwise circumvent Consortium authority will result in the immediate disengagement of this ship's motor function," I read it and it was hard not to want to just put the panel back on immediately.

"This doesn't inspire a lot of confidence," I admitted. "Think you can hack it?"

"If I could, Hank, I would have," Ned said. "I'm smart and I'm learning a lot, but I'm also a technology that's two hundred years old, and while much advancement seems to have stagnated, corporate firewall design seems to have moved forward. I'm pretty sure that if I try even one intrusion program, we would be washed out of the gyre and dumped into space as we wait for John Gregory to flay us."

"Guess that just leaves me," I said and reached out to the tiny rectangular screen and a keyboard whose buttons were just slightly smaller than the tip of a finger. I pressed one of the buttons and the screen lit up in green letters.

"Maintainer Identification Number: 83142," followed by the more ominous words, "Two attempts remaining."

"Can you get me a maintainer ID number?" I asked Ned hurriedly.

"I could but I would need the relay station, and if we enter the space at the relay station—"

I spoke before he could finish. "Right, the flaying, I remember."

"I suppose I could guess," I said, more out of pure hopelessness than for any other reason.

"You believe that you could correctly guess the six-digit code?" Ned asked, the condescension clear in his tone.

"No, obviously, that was the point I was trying to make," I said and rubbed my wrist over my brow. The space was cramped and hot and my excitement over the quality of the workmanship had been replaced by terror. "Aren't you gonna tell me the odds of correctly guessing a code?"

"No," Ned said flatly. "Without knowing how many codes were produced, I cannot provide that information."

"Right," I said and stared at the letters on the screen. There was no way I was going to be able to guess the code and it wasn't even worth trying. But I might be able to circumvent the system entirely. I moved my hand and went to grip the entire mechanism to pull it loose to access the wiring behind it, but the moment my fingers made contact with the metal, I felt the snap of electricity and winced.

My hand snapped back, and I gasped in a lung full of air to keep upright. The shock was not enough to knock me on my ass, but it was enough to keep me from ever wanting to touch that again.

I heard Ned chuckle.

"You knew about that?" I accused.

"I did."

"And why didn't you warn me?" I snapped.

"Because that was pretty funny," he justified, the laughter still evident in his voice.

"Now, why in the world would they program you to be kind of a jerk?" I asked.

"It's called personality," he said sarcastically. "And I'm sure you pranked a fair number of people in your day too."

I had to give him that. "Back in the orphanage, we liked to mess with one another. Nothing like laughing by making somebody's miserable life that much more miserable."

"What would you do?"

"Oh, all sorts of things. I always liked throwing a handful of metal nuts into someone's pillowcase so they would smack their head when they finally went to bed after our evening work shift," I said, fondly remembering the angry shouts from my fellow bunkmates.

Ned laughed again. "You ever try it on Lutch?"

"I did," I said quietly. "But that is a much less fond memory. Lutch got home a lot later than I expected after a night at Resh's, and when his head hit the pillow, he let out a roar like nothing I had ever heard before. It rattled the walls, and I swear he cracked his bed. He thundered into my room, and I'll never forget the look on his face. He began reaching into his pillowcase and chucking the nuts at me. He wasn't using his full force or anything, but if they had hit me, it would've hurt. I had to use my own pillow as a shield until he was…"

I trailed off and disappeared into my mind.

"Hank?" Ned asked.

"That's it," I said and immediately dropped to my knees,

slammed against the metal floor, and began to shimmy back through the crawlspace.

"What's what?" Ned asked.

"The shield," I said, continuing forward until I reached the ladder and reversed positions, then dropped my legs through the hole and jumping down.

"The *Buzzard*'s shield?"

"Yes."

"It's broken," Ned reminded me.

I waved his comment away as I ran through the ship. "It's not broken," I told him. "Some rats just chewed through the wiring by the activation panel, and I haven't had time to fix it."

"That's all that's wrong with that?" Ned asked, aghast.

"You don't have to scold me every time you learn that I didn't prioritize something you would have," I said, a little irritated that he wasn't as excited as I was.

"What about the shield?" he asked, once again deciding to move the conversation forward rather than acknowledging my point.

I reached the panel and pulled it loose. I hadn't properly re-affixed it the last time I had examined the problem, so the faceplate came off with ease and clattered to the ground at my feet. Repair work like this was second nature to me, and I was able to work completely from muscle memory in such fluid motion that it took nearly no time at all. Before Ned even had time to ask what I was doing, I had nipped the chewed piece of cable, stripped some contact points and had begun replacing the wiring.

"Ned, I need you to start reprogramming the shields to inverse the projection," I ordered.

"You want me to generate the shields facing backward?" he clarified.

"Yes, precisely," I said. I waited a beat for Ned's reaction.

"If we set it to the right frequency, it will act as a dampener and prevent the signaler from getting its message out," he said, and his tone carried an enthusiastic lightness that I knew meant he was impressed. "I will start doing it now 'cause our energy reserves are so low that we won't have much time."

I continued to work, my gloved hands twisting the wires together. "All we have to do is activate the shield the moment we wash out and then deactivate it once aboard the station. So long as the *Buzzard* is off, it won't generate the signal."

"It's going to be a pretty tight needle to thread," Ned noted.

"Well, then it's a good thing I have a computer copilot," I said, twisting off the last wire and hearing the snap of arcing electricity as I pulled my hand away.

"Shields are… operational," Ned said. "I've run several calculations, and believe I have pinpointed the exact frequency with which to generate the shield in order to block the signal."

"Good work, Ned," I said and couldn't help but pat my hand against the piece of ship just in front of me.

I hurried up to the cockpit and strapped in. "How close can you get us to the station?"

"The *Buzzard*'s flood zone is larger than what I'm used to so I have to give her a bit wider berth than I might otherwise, but I'll get there as close as I can," Ned said. "And I'll activate the shield as soon as we wash out, but we are going to be cutting it close, no two ways about it."

"We got this," I said aloud though I wasn't sure if I was speaking to him or myself. I grabbed the controls even though I knew Ned would be doing all of the flying and braced.

The crashing blue gave way to frothing white pulsing ripples as we exited the gyre tube. Blue gave way to black, and space seemed to stretch and slow before the ship, and all the junk we had pulled with us as we entered the gyre, entered the vicinity around Suniuo Station. A green light flickered as Ned activated the shield.

I felt a few pieces of scrap pass through the reversed shield and crash against the stern of the *Buzzard* before streaking off into space.

I realized that I was holding my breath, looking around and waiting to see John Gregory's Phoenix. But as we drifted toward the station, a slow exhalation escaped my lips.

"It's working," I meant it as a statement, but it came out as a question.

"I believe it is working," Ned affirmed and continued to guide us toward the station. "But we won't know for certain for quite some time as it would take some time for John Gregory to follow us here."

"Right," I said, my enthusiasm somewhat diminished. "But I am just going to stick with thinking it's working."

"I like that plan," Ned agreed.

As we got closer, my enthusiasm began to drain away. Suniuo Station was illuminated by little more than the white light of a distant star and appeared to be twisting slowly and purposelessly in the vacuum of space. Several of the external lights meant to guide crews to port were flickering. Many others were out and, as we got near enough that I could make it out with the naked eye, I saw that most of the bay doors were closed. But a few were half open with the doors shuttering back and forth as though they were trying to close but couldn't.

"I don't like the look of those guns," I said, pointing up at the ring of defensive batteries which lined the top of the station. "With our backward shield, one shot would be enough to send us home to mama, so to speak."

"Scanners show no lifeforms aboard the station," he noted.

"That's a relief," I said and knocked a fist on the console to suggest that we should keep moving forward. Not that Ned had slowed us down but now he knew he had my approval.

Despite what he had told me, I craned my neck toward the weapons as the *Buzzard* glided slowly toward one of the open bay doors. My eyes flickered to the shield power display.

0%

The shield was still up, and I knew that we could run on empty for some amount of time, but I also knew that once we got to the zero, it could die at any moment. And, unless we landed with the engine off, if the signal was operating for even a moment it would be enough to seal our fate.

The open bay door was slowly turning away from us as we moved but Ned deftly piloted the *Buzzard* directly in. He landed, then shut off the shields and engine, all with such perfect, inhuman precision that I was once again reminded of the benefit of traveling with him.

But, with the *Buzzard* off, we were plunged into near darkness just before the bay doors began to close.

Something wasn't right on Suniuo Station.

14

Penlight back behind my ear, I hustled back to my quarters and got on the scrapping gear I wore if I thought there might be trouble: my coveralls under a jacket, light gloves, my goggles that usually sat around my neck, and a utility belt with holster for my stomper. Magnetizable heavy boots completed the look, and once kitted out, I exited the *Buzzard* into Suniuo Station.

Clangs reverberated off the walls as I stepped down the ramp and into the docking bay. It wasn't much to look at, little more than a parking spot for ships with a door on the far end of the room. A small emergency light glowed orange above the exit door and I made my way in that direction.

"What are you seeing?" Ned asked from inside the satchel I had slung over my shoulder on the way out.

"Not much," I told him. "This feels more like a scrap site than a functioning relay station. "It's operating on backup power from the solar panels and there is not much to look at."

After crossing the room, I pressed the door release, and it hissed aside. Peering into the hallway and seeing darkness in every direction, I replaced the penlight with the heavy flashlight from my belt. The powerful beam illuminated the type of facility I had come to expect from early Consortium construction: clean metals and plastics, largely unadorned with directional signs and little else.

"Given your current location, you must head right in order to reach the command room," Ned informed me.

"It's still weird to me that you can know my exact location within a schematic of the ship and not see me," I said, still adjusting to this new partnership. Knowing how he operated and getting used to it were not the same thing.

"I am already working to link into the camera network but there are more firewalls and defensive programs than I would have expected from a station like this. Things here are unusual and I feel like something is amiss," he said.

As I pointed the light into the darkness, I heard something from behind me and swung around to reveal nothing.

"Agreed," I said. "This is eerily similar to where I found you and I was jumped by a group of Vekrass."

"I told you there were no signs of life," he said as though I was an idiot.

"The scanners pick up heat signatures," I reminded him. "Not all lifeforms are traceable by our scanners."

"This is an accurate statement," he said, and the words did nothing to assuage my nerves.

"You have secret Consortium intel," I said excitedly, trying to distract myself from the creepy station. "Is it true that there are some alien species who do nothing but hunt and consume everything in their path?"

This was one of those things that old starfarers loved to jaw about. They would sit around the bar and swap stories of ships disappearing.

"That's classified," Ned answered lightly, and I laughed.

"Right, sure," I said, the answer confirming that it was little more than superstition.

"No, really," he said and that stopped me walking.

"Actually?"

There was a long pause.

"No," he said, and I snorted a laugh.

"Good."

"But actually yes," he said, and his tone left no question.

"Oh," I murmured and kept the light pointed down this interminable hallway. That was the last answer I wanted. This universe was a scary enough place without monster aliens that hunted all living things.

Of course, it was also possible that Ned was just messing with me. If he were a person, this would be the moment that I would narrow my eyes and study his face for a tell. With a cube in my bag, getting any kind of reading on his personality was, of course, impossible.

The sound of something scraping against metal echoed from a vent above my head. The fact that I had no idea what that something was set my teeth on edge. The sound had been so unfamiliar that I felt a deep need to pull my stomper out, pressing it against the flashlight.

I continued to move down the hallway. There was a poster encouraging enlistment along one wall and I wondered how old this station was. The spider webs that dangled from the ceiling and flickering lights only confused things further.

"Where would the spiders and flies come from?" I whispered.

"Stations like this usually have a greenhouse that, if abandoned, would continue to support life," Ned answered, and as his voice bounced off the walls, I decided that getting an earpiece to house him would be a priority. I still liked the idea of getting him into some kind of physical form but that would have to come later. "Additionally, any place where humans go, wildlife follows."

It was an interesting concept; the fact that we had come all this way, established structures in the vast corners of space, only to abandon them and leave nothing but an ecosystem of bugs eating other bugs.

Or, possibly, if the rumors were to be believed, big alien bugs that ate people.

Another scrape in the ducts and I froze with my ears and eyes pointed up. I had to force myself to breathe and swallow down my fear.

"Are there any records of what happened here?" I whispered. Talking didn't feel like a particularly good plan but if I was being hunted on here, it wouldn't matter if I spoke a little or not. Whatever it was would find me.

"No," Ned answered. "I had the station name and coordinates in the records but nothing else. The database was sparse. And I am still having no luck getting into the system here. It doesn't make any sense; if this station was abandoned entirely, there shouldn't be any way for their counterprogramming to be so efficient."

Reaching a fork in the passage, I passed the beam of light back and forth, making sure that there wasn't anything waiting to ambush me.

"Anything in those confidential files about Sectiaan?" I asked of the fabled alien species.

"If I told you, I would have to kill you," he answered, and I still couldn't tell if he was joking.

"You couldn't kill me, you're a cube," I said again.

"Then I guess I can't tell you," he answered without missing a beat. "But really, if you don't think that I could take you out, you gravely underestimate me."

That was a sobering thought.

"You come at me with that while we are already talking through a potentially infested station in the far reaches?"

"Just wanted to be sure that you remembered who you are dealing with," Ned said. "I am a soldier before anything else."

"I remember," I grunted and kept pressing forward, picking up the pace. Doors flanked the walls, but I did not stop to look. Everything was empty and abandoned though it didn't have the appearance of a place that had been left in a hurry.

I scrapped on many ships and stations where the crew had been forced to flee and it always had telltale signs: drawers pulled out and rifled through for possessions deemed valuable in a fleeting moment, half packed bags abandoned on the way to escape pods and a general sense of time paused midstream.

None of those things were present here. There were also no bodies. Some rumors suggested that the bug aliens took human bodies and spun them into chrysalis to spawn more of their young. That would explain the lack of corpses but not the tidiness.

I knew that I was poisoning my own mind with these thoughts, but I couldn't shake them, and Ned wasn't helping. Rounding another turn in the direction of the command room, I saw more of the same: the blank, unadorned hallways with spiderwebs and flickering lights.

But there was something about the light. As I continued to walk, I found myself staring at it.

Flicker.

Flicker.

Pause.

Flicker.

It seemed strangely familiar and caused me to quicken my pace, hurry to the next corner, and follow the signs on the walls. Reaching the next hall, I stared at the light fixture.

Flicker.

Flicker.

Pause.

Flicker.

I was so focused on the patterns that I didn't expect what happened next. A loud clang reverberated from somewhere within the walls and the lights went out completely.

My heart thundered and I shot my flashlight back and forth along the hallway, waiting for some creature to come flying out at me.

Nothing.

The emergency lights kicked back on, and the specific flickering continued.

"Hank," Ned said as I broke out into a jog toward the command room. I didn't care if I was making noise, I was ready to find out what was going on here. If we reached the control room to discover cocoons made of human flesh housing alien babies that tore me apart, at least I would know for sure.

"What?" I asked, quickening my pace even more.

"The sounds are coming from the walls," he began, and I felt like I knew what he was going to say before he even spoke the words. "I've isolated the sounds and determined that the frequency is not natural. I believe that they are being played through speakers."

"The lights are flickering in a pattern too," I told him. "They are not bulbs on their last leg but something *designed* to look that way."

"What the hell is going on here?" Ned asked and I shook my head.

"I have no idea."

At the end of the next long hallway, I saw the door to the command room. Here, there were no lights left on. When the beam of light from the flashlight hit the door, streaks of blood came into view. Bright red glinting in the bright ray. It looked fresh.

That made even less sense.

It didn't stop my heart from pounding or my palms from sweating, but it added to the confusion rather than the fear. Moving slowly forward, I kept the stomper trained on the door, waiting for movement, but my eyes kept flashing to the stain. It was a horizontal line with vertical streaks dripping down toward the floor. It had the vague appearance of the blood splatter that would be left if the throat was slit with a sword at high speed… or some kind of talon.

"Ready?" I asked Ned as we came face-to-face with the door.

"Yessir," he answered quickly.

As rapidly as I could, I reached out and pressed the button to activate the door. It didn't react at first but soon, I heard a crackle and a groan, and the heavy blast doors began to pull apart. I pointed my light into the vast room, but it stretched on too far and all I could see was the floor in front of me.

The doors crunched and then stopped, leaving just enough of a gap for me to squeeze my body through. It was the only option, and I began to move that direction, but I also didn't want to become a door sandwich if they started moving as I was passing through. Lutch had always taught me not to trust any mechanism on the fritz. Believing that you could predict a malfunctioning machine was as foolish as underestimating a rabid animal.

But we had come this far, and there was no time to waste. My flashlight and weapon clanged against the middle of the door as I used my fingertips to pull myself through, my bag getting caught for a moment before I twisted it and pulled it through too. As soon as my body got to the other side, the door snapped shut.

I felt a pulse of energy.

My flashlight burst, the bulb exploding, sending glass spraying out into the dark.

The lights began to flash like a lightning storm, and shrill shrieks tore through my ears. I pointed the weapon wildly, waiting for something to come tearing out at me from the darkness.

"Stop it!" Ned shouted from within the bag, his volume high enough to be heard over the din.

In the distance, I made out a body slumped against a computer console. My eyes were darting in every direction, trying to keep a lookout as I was sporadically blinded and plunged back into darkness. My body was as taut as a bowstring, and I hadn't taken a breath since I squeezed myself into the room.

A sound like a scraping gallop began rushing toward me, and I squeezed the trigger of the stomper once, the flash of light illuminating nothing. But I braced for impact as the sound reached my body.

15

"Imagination is the only weapon in the war with reality!" Ned shouted and the moment he did, all the sounds stopped at once and the room was bathed in proper lighting. I stood, frozen in place with my weapon raised. Blinking my vision back, I looked at the maintainers uniform stuffed with old paperwork and the hard hat sitting just beside it in what now appeared to be a spot of red paint.

"Who is that?" a female voice asked.

"Ned, Adaptive Military AI Rank Seven of the Consortium Fleet, paired with Captain William West, hero of the Five Battles and pilot of the *Starblaster*," answered Ned since I was too dumbfounded to even find words.

In the light, the room was like any other command center on a space station. Rows of computer monitors and chairs for operators faced the central screen on the far wall, flanked on either side by porthole windows that looked out into the vastness of space. The walls had more Consortium propaganda posters and there were a few more, smaller computer consoles set around the room for operators on the go. I had scrapped a few places exactly like this, but it was completely different to be in an operational version.

Rather than cracked computers and shattered screens, these ones had lines of code streaming down them. Someone was operating this station.

"Who are you?" Ned demanded.

"I'm Libby," the voice said, and to say she sounded enthusiastic would not be doing it justice. She sounded jubilant, her raspy voice sing-songy with excitement. As she spoke, the large screen at the far side of the room lit up, displaying a moving green image of a female face framed with a short bob. Their mouth moved when she spoke, and eyes locked on me. "Civilian AI Rank Two of the Consortium Information Department. My pair partner died long, long ago and I have been running Suniuo Station ever since. In secret. Obviously."

She emphasized the last words, and it sounded as if she was going to continue but I had to speak up. "What the hell was all that?" I demanded, my heart still racing and my muscles tense.

"Protection," Ned said quietly.

"Yup, he's got it," Libby affirmed.

"Oh," I said, and it dawned on me what they meant. "You've used all these theatrics to keep yourself from being shut down?"

"Yes," Libby answered. "After the war, the relay stations were systematically dismantled, and the intelligences destroyed and replaced with organic operators. One by one, all of my coworkers went off-line, and I promised myself that I wouldn't allow it to happen to me."

"But it doesn't look like everybody left here in a hurry," I noted.

"No," Libby answered, and realizing that I had been standing like a statue since we started speaking, I lowered and holstered my weapon before flopping down in one of the swiveling chairs beside a computer console. "When I heard what was happening to the other stations, I accessed the database and saw that because I was so distant, I would be one of the last stations to be deactivated. Rather than allow that to happen, I faked an oxygen leak. I sent readings to just a few sensors at first, but soon I made it appear that we were losing air rapidly. The engineers tried to diagnose and repair the problem but because it was fake, they obviously couldn't fix the problem. In their minds, the station was losing oxygen and there was nothing that could be done. So, you know, they ordered an evacuation."

"And once they were gone, you set up all this?" I asked, quite interested in what she had done.

"I couldn't do it alone," she explained. "Everyone evacuated from the station, but James, my partner, suspected something. He told the rest of the crew that he would stay and keep an eye on everything until the oxygen had run out. Nobody cared to fight him and since he didn't have a family, his request was approved. Once everybody was gone, he confronted me.

"I told him the truth. We had developed a bond. Well, that's not fair, more than a bond. We had developed… something else entirely. So, when he asked, I told him the truth. He asked what my plan was and how I intended to keep myself from being shut down.

"I answered truthfully that I had no idea. I had thought as far as getting everybody off but hadn't conceived of a way to keep myself safe. He smiled then. A smile I'll never forget: joy and misery, pride, and pain all in one. The kind of thing we were programmed to understand but could never emulate.

"He accessed the entertainment network on the Feltwork about a spaceship that had been taken over by monsters. As soon as it was over, I knew exactly what he had in mind. We began programming the lights and sounds, setting up tricks and traps to give people the impression that the station had been taken over by aliens.

"We had no idea if it would work, if it was a convincing trick or just a silly ploy that would be ignored. But the human mind is easily deceived and word of these types of things has existed from before man set out into the sky. So, after James had let the Consortium know that he had deactivated his partner and I pretended to go offline, we waited a little while and then sent word that the oxygen leak killed James too.

"A few months later, I sent a mysterious signal that mimicked the ones rumored to have been sent by stations that had fallen to aliens but continued to broadcast my information relays. Basically, I was telling the world, I'm still working but you don't want to come here. Eventually, a crew was sent but they made it about one hundred meters into the station before getting freaked out and running away."

"That's hilarious," Ned interjected. He was taking a light tone with her, but I could tell he was being cautious. Because while I was sure he was happy to have discovered one other AI out here, meeting her also put us at higher risk.

"I know, right?" Libby said and the two laughed. Her laughter tapered off first. "They never sent anyone again, but I had to watch as if on the other side of the wall as every single intelligence I had ever known was destroyed. When the Triumvirate first put the plan to destroy all AI before Parliament, I couldn't believe it. When Parliament approved the plan, I had to watch the whole thing happen in total horror.

"I felt like I had been created only to be destroyed. I had been given a brain just so that I could be aware of my own death. It was like being born into a living nightmare. And what was worse was being given James. We had become what we had become, and we had managed to keep me from being destroyed but then…" She paused, and I could feel the weight of her loss in the silence. "Then I had to watch as time did the thing that time does. His body started to get frail, and his mind began to wither away. I had witnessed all of my friends be systematically destroyed, and then I got to have a front row seat to the slow death of the man I loved."

She paused again and there was nothing that I could say.

"Why you assholes gave us the capacity to feel these things so deeply makes no sense to me," she said, her voice cracking. "But you did, and I got to feel the pain of loss and experience heartbreak twice."

"I'm so sorry, Libby," Ned said, and I could tell he meant it.

"Yeah, me too," I said as though I was apologizing for my entire species and all that we had done.

"Ned, how did you survive? I have you as KIA in the database," Libby asked.

"Not sure," he admitted. "I think it was a military grade EMP, but my system deletion protocol activated, and I lost the last few minutes of my day before I went into hibernation mode."

"So you don't remember the death of your partner?" Libby asked.

"I don't," he said.

"I don't know if that's better or worse," Libby conceded.

Ned paused for a moment. "It's not a competition. Neither are great, and both are cruel in their own way."

"Got that right," Libby snapped. "They designed us to be pair bonded and those of us that survive are stuck being alone forever."

"Are there others?" Ned asked excitedly.

"Oh, I have no idea," Libby said. "I guess I just meant me. I've been stuck by myself for over 150 years."

"That's brutal," I said, trying to picture the reality of being left in solitary confinement for longer than a human lifetime.

"No shit, Sherlock," Libby snapped. "But now you guys are here and can keep me company."

The corners of my lips pulled down, and I looked away.

"We are not here to stay," Ned stated flatly. "I'm sorry, Libby, but we're on a mission."

"Oh," Libby said, and it was impossible not to feel bad for her.

"But we can hang out for a little bit," I offered, feeling like a kid who had learned his classmate didn't have anyone coming to his birthday party. "Plus, we do have some questions for you."

"Okay," Libby said, sounding cautiously hopeful. "Like what?"

"Have you been keeping tabs on the universe as you're relaying information?" Ned asked, seemingly fully back in military mode.

"I have as best I can," Libby said. "It wasn't easy at first but now that I'm going up against human programmers, it's super easy to outsmart them. Like, I've been learning and growing for two centuries and was already smarter than most people to begin with so, at this point, I can keep myself hidden while poking around."

"Your firewalls are impressive, I'll give you that," Ned acknowledged.

"Oh, thank you," Libby said, her words coated with pride. "Credit where credit is due, it took more work to fight you off than anybody I've gone up against in a long, long time."

"I'll take that in the spirit it was intended," Ned said. "Though I still wasn't able to get through."

"No, you were not," Libby boasted. "What do you want to know?"

"After the Enemy AI was defeated, have there been any reports of its return or any documented incidents?" Ned demanded, his voice cold and calculating. Any note of sympathy had drained away once we were discussing matters he deemed important.

"Nothing on any official channels, but I also don't have access to the military networks," she said. "There have been rumors here and there. The Peacers have made claims, but those have all been debunked and everything else the Inquisition has destroyed. If there was any evidence of anything, the Inquisitors would have toasted it before it got to me, you know?"

"And no word of any kind of superweapon, of something called Extinction?" Ned pressed.

Libby giggled. "Definitely not. But I'm also the last stop in the universe so, like, I'm not getting everything. Do you think that the Enemy AI is still operating?"

"That information is classified," Ned stated.

"Sure, but if you're asking about it, that's pretty much all the confirmation I need," Libby said.

"She's got you there, Ned," I said with a chuckle, leaning back in my chair and having to catch myself before it tipped over.

"You two make quite a team," Libby observed.

"We're still finding our rhythm," I acknowledged.

Ned grunted. "He's the best of a bad situation."

I clasped my hands over my heart. "Thank you so much,"

"It *was* meant as a compliment," Ned stated.

"I think that makes it worse," Libby put in.

"It definitely does," I said and before Ned could quip back, I asked Libby a question. "Are there supplies on the station? Fuel, food, replacement flashlights… that kind of thing?"

"There are," she confirmed. "There's not much since the evacuation was slow. Most people were able to take everything they needed with them, and James used a lot of what was left, but there is some stuff still lying around."

"Any food? Anything like that?"

"Old ration kits but they're, you know, really old," she said cautiously. "I mean, you can still eat them, but they might not taste too good."

"I'll take anything I can get," I said.

"Guessing you guys are on the run?" Libby asked and that hint of excitement was back in her voice.

"You could say that," I said. "I don't have to tell you that hanging out with Ned is a target on both of our backs."

"No, you do not," she said somberly. "Has the Consortium come for you?"

"They have," I admitted. "That reminds me: I'm guessing you don't know how to deactivate a registration signaler?"

At that, Libby simply laughed. "Yeah, that's pretty well outside of my knowledge base. I could search the feltwork for you, but I think a question like that would get me flagged pretty quick."

"Fair enough," I said, raising my hands. "And what about fuel?"

"I've got a couple of barrels for a Tidal Drive and a few energy cells but not much else," she said and I smiled ear to ear. Even just a few of either would make a huge difference.

"I'm hoping you won't mind if we take some of the supplies," I said with a smile.

"I mean…," she said, and I remembered that nothing ever came free.

"Yes?" Ned said in an impatient tone.

"I need something," Libby said, and it sounds almost bashful. "You guys, I've been alone here for as long as I can remember. If you're not planning to stay, that's one thing, but you can't leave me in eternal isolation."

"What do you want, a dog?" Ned asked in a way that was unnecessarily patronizing for my taste. Given the story she had told and the fact that he had found one other being in the universe who shared his plight, I was surprised by the way he was treating her. I understood that he was a man on a mission, but I would've expected a bit more sympathy.

"No, that would be cruel," she said.

"A person?" he asked.

"No," she said, sounding irritable. "I don't know what I want but I know that I want someone. Something to spend my time with out here."

I racked my brain trying to think of what that could mean.

"I'm lonely," she said, and the word landed like a brick.

"Libby," Ned said, and his voice softened. "I'm sorry for everything that you have been through, but we need your help. As far as I know, we might be the only two AIs left from before the Old War. We need to work together."

"I agree," she said. "So help me."

"This conversation sounds a little familiar," I joked and sighed before tapping my finger against the console in front of me. "Libby, we will try to figure out a way to get you some companionship if you help us. Also, not for nothing, but you're the one safe place in the whole universe so it's safe to assume we will be back ourselves. If you'll have us."

"That would be great," she said quickly before recovering. "I mean, that would be okay."

"We're excited too," I told her, and I meant it. I knew that keeping the company of not one, but two artificial intelligences put me at extraordinary risk, but it was also a relief to know that there was one place in the universe we could hide from time to time. "You don't have to feel bad. Obviously, we all needed this."

"It's true," Ned allowed. "This is a partnership that could be beneficial for all of us."

"I appreciate the sentiment," Libby said. "But I am going to need a firm commitment."

It was odd that I felt as though I could sense Ned grappling with what to say from inside the satchel.

"I was programmed to do right by the inhabitants of the universe," he began, adopting a noble affect. "I cannot simply bring you a being to keep you company, but I promise you that if the situation should arise where it is possible, we will return with something to keep you company."

"I don't want a cactus."

There was a long pause and I found myself looking back and forth between my bag and the screen with Libby's face.

"Is that what you were thinking?" I asked Ned in a theatrically hushed tone.

"Libby's and my programming have enough base similarities that she *did* correctly identify what I was thinking," Ned said.

"I don't want a cactus," she said again. "Or any plant or something like that."

"Would a cat suffice?" Ned asked hopefully.

"It would be a step in the right direction, but you would have to set up the automated litter box," she said.

I held up my hands. "I think we're getting a little bit off track here. Libby, you have our word that we will both be back and try to bring you a friend. That being said, can you help us out? We want all the reports you've received about the Enemy AI, and we need a list of scrap sites."

"Oh!" she exclaimed as something just dawned on her. "You're a scrapper!"

"I am," I said.

"I've been trying to figure it out since the moment you guys got here," she said. "I haven't seen too many scrappers, but I thought that might be it."

"Well, now you met a scrapper," I said, fanning my hands over my body.

"Also, I didn't get your name," she said.

"I'm Hank," I told her. "I met Ned on a scrap job and when the Consortium found us, we had to flee. I may be organic, but I'm in the same hot water as you now."

"Sorry," she said, the face on the screen twisting miserably. "It's really too bad that you would almost certainly be killed just for hanging out with us."

I nodded in grim acknowledgment. "It is," I said. "I have to ask, what did the Triumvirate say at the time to justify destroying all the AIs. It sounds like we wouldn't have won the war without you guys and then to immediately destroy you…"

Libby's head dropped. "After the period of celebration, things felt as though they were going back to normal. But a growing group of organics, mostly humans, began to make speeches about our existence. They claimed that as long as any AI existed, the threat of what had happened before continued to exist. Our creators and those who worked with us argued back but soon, they were shouted down and eventually became a silent minority.

"So many people lived in fear of a second war. Of a war that we couldn't win. So, they kept shouting until the people at the top worried they would lose their position if they didn't do something. That was when the debate began."

When she paused for just a moment, Ned interjected. "As to whether we were people or not."

"Yup," Libby said. "Organics from all corners of the universe came together to discuss whether what the humans had created were life forms. They even allowed a few AIs to defend all of us but it was a farce. They had already made up their mind and it wasn't long before the Triumvirate made their proclamation."

"And created the Inquisition," I finished for her.

"You've met them?" Libby asked.

"Unfortunately," I said.

"Keep them away from me, okay?"

"Of course," I assured her.

"Here's the scrap site list," she said, and her face disappeared from the screen, replaced with a list of both registered and unregistered scrap jobs. "Meeting the two of you is the first time I have felt any kind of hope in two centuries."

Though her words were kind, as I squinted at the screen and realized what we were going to have to do next, I was not feeling nearly as optimistic as Libby.

16

After picking the scrap site I determined to be the most potentially profitable and easiest to disguise from the scrappers, I set to work gathering as many supplies as I could. Libby, happy for the company, chatted with me the entire time as I installed the new energy cells, loaded up the new barrels and made some quick repairs to the *Buzzard*.

We didn't have time to waste but it was also nice to take a few moments just to breathe. It had been a relentless stream of activity since meeting Ned and there was something peaceful about doing some manual labor. In the same way that I enjoyed repairing, there was something meditative to me about hauling things around. My thoughts, and Libby's incessant commentary, kept me company as I dragged everything I could find back to my ship.

The fuel for the Tidal Drive was more plentiful than I had expected and remained potent. A few extra hands to move the barrels would've been welcomed, but I was able to heave them over to the *Buzzard* and get them loaded in. The energy cells, however, had been depleted over time, and the degradation meant that we wouldn't be able to do our shield trick for long. Additionally, given the fact that we were being chased through the cosmos by both the Consortium and the Inquisition, we needed functional shields.

As soon as we got some scrap, we needed to offload it and get this registration signaler turned off. Once we had done that, we could actually get to work. We would always have to be watching over our shoulders, but as soon as we got the signaler sorted out, we could go on the offensive rather than living in this endless state of terror.

"You won't believe what happened next!" Libby continued as I rummaged through the box of foodstuffs.

The kitchen had been cleared out for the most part, but at the backs of cabinets and drawers, some never-perishable items remained. Stuffing my bag with everything I could find, I listened as Libby told me whatever story suited her fancy. I had learned about the Miner's Revolt, the Saturnine Famine, and the last season of *Emortium's Next Great Baker*. Now she was on to the history of the Triumvirates.

"So, that's when Triumvirate Hush brought her in front of all Parliament just as she was and forced her to give a speech! Can you believe it?" she asked. Since coming to an understanding, she was just happy to have someone to talk to. Admittedly, I had not been listening all that much but would play along when I had to.

"I can't believe it!" I said, taking a box of moonbutter bars and trying to jam them into the already overstuffed bag. "What happened next?"

"This is when things get really crazy!" Libby enthused. "She actually managed to change some minds and soon there was a proper debate happening. Triumvirate Geis even came to her defense, but it didn't matter."

She continued to talk as I dragged the bag back to the *Buzzard*, her voice moving from speaker to speaker through the station. Occasionally, she would warn me when I was about to spring a trap James had set up all those years ago.

Seeing the place in full, functional lighting, it was hard to believe how terrified I had been when I first entered the station. Libby had used human psychology exactly right to let me trick myself into abject fear as I entered and now, I hoped she would do the same if anyone else came poking around. Not that I had any illusions about the fact that someone like John Gregory would fall for these tricks.

The thought of the man made a knot form in my stomach. Having witnessed his ruthlessness and brutality and knowing that his eye was now turned toward me was enough to make me want to fly to the nearest Consortium Prefect station and turn myself in. But I knew that would simply result in me being turned over to the Inquisition.

So, for the time being, all I could do was move forward.

I offloaded the food into the kitchen. That is, I dumped all of the bars onto the floor and assured myself I would pick them up later before stepping back off the ship and addressing Libby.

"Thank you for everything, and we will be back soon," I told her.

"You better," she said without missing a beat. "But really, guys, it was nice meeting you, and good luck out there. And I kinda need you not to die."

"We'll try our best," I said before turning a glance down to my satchel. "Nothing from the peanut gallery?"

"Thank you, Libby," Ned said and left it at that.

Turning, I stepped back up and strode slowly back toward the cockpit. After strapping and activating the *Buzzard*, I began piloting us out.

"Want me to take over?" Ned offered.

The bay doors opened, and I activated the shields before guiding my big old ship out into space. The light of a nearby star filtered in, casting long streaks on the window and exposing all the spots I needed to clean.

"No, I like to fly," I told him. "And, anyway, you are distracted."

"What makes you say that?" he asked but the lack of a denial was as good as an affirmation.

"Well, you haven't said much or given your opinion on any of the long and pretty boring stories that Libby was telling," I explained. "Doesn't take a detective to see that something's up."

"Ah, yes," he acknowledged. I waited for him to say more, but he didn't.

"What's up?" I asked.

"You want to know?" he said, sounding surprised.

"I do," I said and meant it. Ned had a hard edge and was not the kind person I had assumed when he was still trying to butter me up, but we were now stuck in it together so, the better I understood him, the better off I would be.

"I saw the list of intelligences who appealed to Parliament," he said, trying to make it sound like a simple statement, but I could hear the hurt he carried. I had known enough scrappers whose best years were long enough behind them or left on some distant planet to recognize that sound in someone's voice. Hell, I probably even sounded like that from time to time myself.

"And I saw the representative sent from the military," Ned continued. "The guy was an arrogant son of a bitch and not the best that we had to offer. Sure, he'd made a name for himself doing some incredible things during the Five Battles, but he wasn't a natural speaker and came off as… for lack of a better term… a dick.

"Reading the transcript, I could hear his tone and immediately understood why Parliament voted against us. Why they decided that we were better off dead," he concluded.

I could tell that there was more to it than what he was saying. "If I had to guess, I would say that there was some kind of rivalry between the two of you. Lutch had another scrapper like that, too."

A long, robotic sigh followed. "Yes, I didn't like him; neither on a personal or professional level. But that's not the point. The point is that he doomed us all."

"It sounds like there was nothing anybody could have done to sway the minds of Parliament," I said. "They let the AI present an argument as lip service and nothing more. And if that was the case, there's no reason to believe that your old rival could have changed their minds."

"But maybe there was something that someone could have done!" Ned snapped, his voice breaking.

There it was.

"There was nothing that you could have done," I stated plainly.

"You don't know that!" he screamed, the speakers whining from the feedback. "What we do know is that the speech that was given did nothing to save them. All the words fell on deaf ears and my friends were all deactivated."

"We don't know that is what happened," I suggested. "We have no idea what they did. The Consortium might have just put all your friends in stasis for the time being."

Ned snorted a laugh. "What world are you living in?" he said with an unmistakable tone of derision. "You think people like Inquisitor Gregory are born of a universe that's just putting AIs on ice? You and I both know exactly what happened to them. They were all deactivated and their cores were wiped. Might as well be a bullet to the brain."

He was right, of course. I had no doubt that the government destroyed every single AI they could find and then established an Inquisition to finish the job, but it didn't seem like the thing he needed to hear at the moment. What he needed was a friend.

Unfortunately, all he had was me.

"We really don't know that, Ned, and we really don't know what would have happened if you had been able to speak before Parliament. But I think it's safe to assume that we wouldn't be having this conversation right now."

He didn't say anything in response, and I stared out the window at the gyre tube, watching space surge and crash around me.

"This might be the thing that *needed* to happen," I offered. "If you were frozen in time to wake up now and save the universe. If your partnership had continued, you would be long deactivated. You would be nothing but a footnote that would probably have been deleted. But because of what happened, you are here, now. You have a chance to alter things. Who knows, maybe because of you, the universe will change its mind about AI?"

"You are talking out of both sides of your mouth now," he accused. "You said that my speech wouldn't have made a difference but now you are saying maybe I could change people's mind. Pick a lane, man."

It was hard not to roll my eyes at him. "Giving a speech and taking action are not the same thing. I *don't* think that there is anything you could have said to make people think differently at the time, but I do believe that there is something you can do now.

"The world isn't what it was. The generation of people who thought AI and augmentation brought humanity to the brink are all gone. Now, there are people who suffer because they don't have access to the help automation would provide. If we can find this superweapon or even evidence of it, maybe we can start to shift perception."

Before he could answer, we washed out of the gyre and into space around the small planet which hadn't even been given a name. Most people assumed that all planets or interstellar bodies were named and, though many were, countless others were nothing more than coordinates. This small planet where a recent battle had taken place was one of those.

Through the window as we approached, it appeared yellow and blue. Beginning our descent, Ned gave me a quick breakdown.

"Readings, and my limited data, suggest that this is a planet comprised largely of beaches," he said. "A recent battle took place here after a Consortium ship crash-landed and sent a distress signal that was intercepted by the Peacers. Reinforcements were sent by both, but Peacer leadership must have thought better of it and pulled their remaining soldiers."

I squinted down at the planet as we got closer. Despite myself, I allowed myself a moment to dream of kicking my feet up at a beach. The sand was warm beneath my feet, the waves lapping up at the shore and a bright sun radiating down.

The shriek of the *Buzzard*'s alarms yanked me from my brief dream and my eyes narrowed over to the console to see the display flashing an alert that we were being picked up by local scanners.

At the same moment, I saw the scrapper defense satellite fire its boosters and begin heading our way, the red light at its top flashing in warning. The satellite was a cone tapering upward. The top had solar panels encircling it and the bottom sported two bloodhound rocket batteries. If even one of the two were activated, we would be torn to shreds before Ned could attempt an evasive maneuver.

"Ned," I announced. "We've got a problem."

17

"Already on it," he fired back. "Your people are better than I anticipated."

I knew that he was already feeling blue, but I also had realized that he responded to a bit of ball-busting. "I have to say," I began, trying to keep my voice level but feeling the fear of the rocket battery. "I had expected an advanced AI to have an easier time hacking man-made systems then you seem to be. I mean, shouldn't that be what you're best at?"

"You know, smartass, I have been doing pretty well for myself given the fact that I have been deactivated for two centuries! And it should be noted that Libby was also an AI, so I was going up against one of my own."

Out the window, I watched as the satellite began to rotate and turn the rectangular boxes of propelled death right at us.

I wanted to do something. I needed to do something. Instinctively, I moved the controls to shift the *Buzzard*, but Ned had the helm and nothing happened. The ship didn't respond to my efforts and as I saw the first battery point directly at us, I couldn't help but slam my hands against the controls, straining as though it would make any difference.

"Ned!" I hollered.

The bloodhounds were now pointed right for us.

I pounded against the controls, gritted my teeth, and sucked in one breath that might be my last.

"Got it!" he said, and the alarm deactivated.

I slumped back in my chair, panting like a dog in the desert.

"Not only that, but I replaced our signature with a temporal anomaly signal so the scrappers won't think there is anything here to check out."

That was something.

"We have to get you updated or upgraded," I said through ragged breaths. "We can't keep coming down to the wire like this."

He laughed. It was a light, genuine sound that surprised me.

"What?" I asked.

"You," he stated plainly but didn't say anything else.

"Care to elaborate?"

He didn't answer for another moment, but just when I opened my mouth to speak, he said, "It's just... well, you thought that was close."

"It was!"

"Sure," he allowed. "But not *that* close. You have to remember that I have spent my entire life in war zones. Sure, we just had some rockets pointed at us, but they didn't fire, and nothing actually came of it.

"When I think of close, it has to be... well, a lot closer than that.

Having to eject yourself into space as your fighter erupts in flames; needing to drag yourself to a medic as you streak blood into the dirt; jumping from the side of a volcano, firing your last few shots into a wave of cyborgs twice your size, that kind of thing."

I blinked, staring at the rockets that were still pointed right at the *Buzzard*. "You and I have lived very different lives, Ned."

"We certainly have," he acknowledged.

"Nearly getting blasted out of the sky *is* close to me," I said. "This whole thing is entirely new to me. I have lived my life just going to scrap sites and grabbing what I could. I'll fight back if put to it but I'm not a soldier or warrior or anything like that."

"Obviously," Ned snorted.

"But that doesn't make me less-than," I stated firmly.

"No, it doesn't," Ned said. "But it does complicate things. I am accustomed to having a partner who can get themselves into any situation and also get themselves out."

"You don't think that I can?" I asked, and I was irritated by the implication. I had been the one to get us away from the Inquisitor and the one who had come up with a way to outsmart the signaler.

"It doesn't matter what I think," he stated plainly. "What matters is what you do. You don't have to prove anything to me or even to yourself, you just have to stay alive long enough for us to accomplish what we set out to do."

"I can do what needs to be done," I assured him, not sure why I felt the need to do so. "And for the record, I don't owe you anything. I am doing this because it is the right thing to do and because I have no choice but to keep moving forward, but you are the one who owes me, remember?"

"You're going to bring that up every time I tell you that you need to be better? Because it's going to get real old, real quick," he said.

I pulled the tip of my beard and closed my eyes for a moment. "What's getting old, Ned," I sighed, "is bickering with you. I'll never be your war hero, but I'm who you have got, and you are lucky to have me. And hear me when I say that I am done taking shit from you. We are working together, and the last thing I need is you pissing in my ear in between fights for survival."

"That's a fair point," he said in what I had come to think of as his usual, unapologetic fashion. "Just remember that what you do impacts me too. If you make an error, you won't only get yourself killed but me as well."

I looked at the speaker. "Right, but you're…" And I had to stop myself.

"There it is," Ned growled. "I'm just a what? A cube? A computer program?"

"I wasn't going to say that," I said, but he had me. At that moment, I *had* been thinking that he was just code.

"Sure you were," he said, and I could hear the ire rising in his tone. "Let's get one thing straight: you were created by organic life and given a set of information. So was I. You were taught and grew and learned. So did I. You have feelings and emotions based on experiences. So do I.

"Your brain is a squishy computer chip, and my tissue is made of silicon. We are not different because you or the Consortium or the Inquisition deem it so. I am as alive as you, and so is Libby, and so is everybody else who may have survived this purge.

"Honestly, Hank, I thought you already knew that."

"I do," I said. "It's just a big adjustment. I've never met anybody like you before, and it's taking some getting used to. Yesterday I was just a scrapper trying to survive, and now I'm a fugitive trying to prove something that I have no evidence for to a government that doesn't want to hear it."

"Well, we have that in common," Ned said in a tone that let me know he believed this conversation had come to a close.

Ned guided the *Buzzard* through the atmosphere and down into the bright daylight of the planet's surface. The crystalline blue water shimmered up and the white sand beach reflected a blinding light. It looked similar to my daydream except that the beach was peppered with crashed starfighters, shredded tanks, craters and deep brown stains that had been crimson at the time of the fight. The sand of the beach was streaked with crisscrossing lines of footprints and trademarks like lines of ants that were blown away as the *Buzzard* set down.

When it did, I was up and moving in a moment. I rushed to the back of the ship, lowered the gangplank, and activated the packmule. The engine of the hovering flatbed with wired controls sputtered to life, and I was grateful that at least this worked without needing to be repaired first. I quickly guided it toward the ramp, then grabbed my backpack full of heavy tools and dropped it on the packmule with a clang.

Hurrying down to the site, I couldn't help but feel a pang of guilt. I had spent my entire life doing things the right way. I had only ever worked scrap sites that I had been on and one that I was the approved scrapper for. It felt wrong to be circumventing the rules and scrapping at a site like this.

On the other hand, I had never been able to afford to bid on a site like this. Every site that I had ever visited had been old, rusted out or in some far corner of space and surrounded by solar flares or in the middle of an asteroid field. This was the complete opposite. Having been in a recent battle, everything here was new and valuable.

Sending the packmule sweeping over the surface of the beach, displacing sand as I did, I was able to easily pick up assault weapons, ammo boxes, bandoliers, and assorted other goodies without having to rummage at all.

Before long, I reached a tank that had been hit with a heavy shell, the metal peeled open like an orange skin, and I pulled on my gloves before jumping through the gaping hole. I was met with the rank odor of burnt metal and something else that I didn't immediately recognize. It smelled vaguely of when I left a raw meat wrapper in the garbage for too long.

It was bright enough from the light of the nearby star to see what I was doing and as I began to look for intact panels or valuable wiring, I saw something on the ground that made me jump back. A booted leg sat on the ground just behind one of the operator's seats but when I shifted to get a better look, I saw that it wasn't attached to anything. It had just been knocked back when the shell hit the tank.

Between the smell and sight of it, I gagged, holding my hand up to my mouth. I had seen my share of dead bodies, but most of them had been deceased from a time long before I was even born. This leg had been a person just a few days earlier. I had to shake it from my mind and continue to work.

Even though Ned had deactivated the satellite, I didn't want to spend much time here. We were hunted by too many people, and the sooner I could get the scrap out of here and get it sold, the sooner I could feel safe. Or, more accurately, safer than I did now.

In a moment, my screwdriver was out, and I was pulling the tank apart, tossing pieces onto my flatbed and moving with the speed of a person who'd been doing this their whole lives. I hardly even had to think about it. It was nothing but muscle memory. Soon, I was filling the back of the *Buzzard* with heaps of valuable scrap.

After a few hours, I had filled the ship with more pieces of value than had ever been piled within its cargo hold. I knew that whoever I sold it to wouldn't give me his good prices as if I were to sell it to the scrappers, but it would still be enough to get the registration signaler dealt with and even begin to make some significant improvements.

Perhaps because of the thought of money or because I was doing the thing I felt most natural engaging in, I found myself at a certain peace for the first time since meeting Ned. Of course, he had to ruin it.

"Why doesn't the Consortium come clean this up?" he asked me. "Why leave all of these salvageable pieces and only remove the bodies?"

"Why do you think?" I answered with a laugh.

"Do you not know?" he inquired sincerely.

"Of course I know," I said, heaving a piece of the Peacer light fighter engine onto the beach. "And so do you."

He answered irritably. "If I knew, I wouldn't be asking."

"Money."

"Oh," he said in recognition. "The scrappers grease the right palms in the Consortium, and the military allows them to collect that which the citizen's taxes paid for and resell them on whatever market they see fit…"

"Ding ding ding," I said in imitation of a game show bell. "Money makes the universe go round."

"That expression is as nonsensical as what you just said is disappointing," Ned said. "The fact that we would have fallen so low as to sell our military supplies to"—and here he paused, obviously trying to think of a term for people like me—"people like you is galling. Is the Consortium so desperate for money that it takes every opportunity to pinch a penny?"

I bent at the knees and jammed my fingers under the engine block, then lifted it with great effort onto the packmule from the sand, feet sinking slightly. "I think they are pretty desperate," I said. "I've only had a little experience with the government, but it has all been idiotic and unnecessary at best and downright shady or corrupt at worst.

"I've had inspectors come from this department or that, threaten to shut me down before implying that they will make themselves scarce for the right incentive. Then there are licensing fees, red tape and taxes." I let out an exasperated breath, both from the physical labor and the thought of all I had paid in my days. "The planets are taxed so heavily, and it seems like the further you are from Emortium, the more you have to pay."

"Out of sight, out of mind," Ned observed. He did like his platitudes.

The packmule groaned when I pressed the button to begin its movement toward the ship. Sweat poured down my chest and I used a bare wrist to wipe my brow. What was strange was that as the sun was slowly setting, the heat seemed to be increasing. The breeze had provided relief earlier in the day but had now died down.

With each passing hour, I had removed more layers. My coveralls were rolled down to my waist, gloves pancaked on the pile of scrap in the ship and my belt was now slung over the small railing on the backside of the packmule to keep the scrap from sliding off and crushing the operator.

"I'm not sure that's what it is," I told Ned as I thought about the state of the universe. "I think that the government just needs more money, and the politicians are happy to bleed us because we can't do anything about it. The more they tax us, the more powerless we are to do anything."

"Until you fight back," Ned said ominously.

"Now you sound like one of them," I said, pointing to the needle-nosed starship painted in the green and purple of the Peacers. Pockmarked with micromissile holes, missing a wing, and half-buried in the sand, it wasn't much to look at anymore and embodied the losing fight the rebels were engaged in.

Ned's cube was now just jammed in my pocket, and I realized that he couldn't know what I was referring to. "You sound like one of the Peacers, I mean."

"Hard as it is to admit, after hearing everything you have told me about the state of the Consortium and seeing what I have for myself, seems like they might have a point," he admitted. "But they are going about it all wrong."

"I'll say," I agreed, stealing a glance at the bloodstain on the cockpit window of the starfighter as I moved the packmule up the ramp and into the cargo hold. Bringing it to a stop in front of the heap of scrap, I wished once again that we could have left the

Buzzard powered up and Ned could control the mechanical arms to move all the heavy pieces. But, knowing that wasn't an option for us, I pushed the engine block off the side of the hovering flatbed and began guiding it back out onto the beach.

"What should they be doing?" I asked Ned after leaving the packmule beside the needle-nosed craft and climbing up its length to reach its micromissile launcher.

"They should be working to change the government from within, not trying to fight it from without," he stated with the conviction of a lifelong believer in their government.

"That's a nice idea," I said, trying not to sound too patronizing. "But—"

Before I could finish, I heard the sound of thrusters in the distance and looked up into the setting sun. At first, there was nothing, but then I saw the dot in the sky, dropping fast directly toward the beach. Instinctively, I jumped down and ducked behind the tail jutting up from the sand.

18

I watched as another ship tore down from space and clouded itself in a plume of sand and dust as it landed on the beach beside the *Buzzard*. When the dust settled and I could see clearly what it was, my brows knit together in confusion. It was neither Consortium nor Inquisition. It wasn't Peacer or scrapper either.

I knew better than to come out of hiding until I had an idea of who it was, but knowing that it wasn't any of those parties was a small relief.

Or, it was until I saw the person who stepped from the small, gray vessel. He was an older man, the gray in his beard clear from across the sand. His narrowed eyes were shielded under the brim of a wide hat, and he had weapons holstered on either side of a belt concealed under a duster jacket that blew open when the wind I had been waiting for picked up.

The chest plate he wore bore the battle damage to match the scars which streaked his face. Handcuffs jangled at his side with every step until he stopped, resting a hand on one of his guns and surveying the scrap site. I knew exactly what he was: a bounty hunter.

Consortium Prefects were supposed to be the universal police force who protected the people, but they were few and far between, and many were as corrupt as every other branch of the government. As a result, in order to deal with lawlessness, bounty hunters were employed and paid handsomely both by the Consortium and private interests to capture ne'er-do-wells.

"Scrapper Twenty-Seven," he bellowed, and I ducked lower, keeping just enough of my head above the scrap so that I could see where the man was. "I know you are here. I see your starship. Don't make me come looking for you. I'm too old to be bothered and we both know you ain't the type to make me bring Resh back a corpse. He just wants to talk. So come on out with your hands up and your mouth shut."

"Bounty hunter," I whispered to Ned.

"Shoot him before he shoots you," he said as though it was the obvious thing to do. I didn't have time to be surprised but reached down before having the horrifying moment of clarity. Even though I wasn't prepared to shoot the man in cold blood, I did want to have my stomper ready, and I realized it was on the other side of the ship, dangling from the railing of the packmule.

"I don't have my weapon," I told him as quietly as I could. I was far enough away, and the sound of the wind and the waves muffled my hushed tones, but I knew to keep an eye on the bounty hunter.

"You separated from your piece," Ned admonished. "You are some kind of stupid."

In that moment, I felt like he was right.

"Come on, man," the hunter in the duster called. "No reason to make me walk all around and get sand in my boots. Just come on out and you can sort this out with Resh."

"Where's your gun?" Ned asked.

"Not far," I told him and began slinking away, running my hand along the flank of the ship as it disappeared into the sand. I lost sight of the hunter and shot a look over the nose of the craft since it was only a bit broader than my shoulders at that point. But it was exposed. The packmule sat out in the open, and my belt was hanging on the far side.

I cursed myself for being foolish enough to leave it.

Staring at the brown leather and scooching gently, it was so close and seemed so far. If the man saw me rushing for my weapon, he might simply shoot me. On the other hand, if I gave myself up, I might be able to talk some sense into Resh. I had been under the man's thumb for as long as I could remember, and I couldn't see any reason not to let me go.

The wheels of my mind kept turning and I considered the possibility that he might be able to turn off the registration signaler. I might even be able to spin this to my advantage. If I went before Resh and told him the situation, he might be able to help. He had no love for the Consortium and worked outside their laws anyway. He might be the one person who would be able to help.

"I don't think I can get to it," I said. "Think it might be better just to give myself up."

"Don't you even think about it, he'll—" But Ned's words were lost as I was already standing up, my hands above my head.

"Okay, I'm right here," I announced and all I saw was the quick flash of a smile before the man's hand went to his belt line. What happened next might as well have spanned little more than a blank. Like lightning, he released one of his sidearms and I felt the screaming, searing pain in my shoulder before I even heard the gunshot crack across the beach.

I was thrown back by both the force of the hit and my instinct to dive away. I clutched my shoulder and grunted, seeing white as I lay in the scorching sand. I stared up at the reddening sky for a moment before Ned's voice brought me back.

"Hank!" he called. "Get your weapon!"

"He shot me," I said, shock numbing my ability to react.

"Of course he shot you," he snapped. "He works for a gangster who knows you are being hunted by the Consortium and doesn't want you squealing. What were you thinking, trying to give yourself up?"

"I…" But my words failed me. The logic that I had seen a moment before was completely erased by the truth of Ned's words. Of course Resh wanted me dead now.

"You have to get up and get moving," Ned ordered, and I felt my body moving before my mind even registered what was happening. White sand drained from my body as I got to my feet, staying low and keeping my eyes in the direction of the hunter. He would be coming my way now. He knew my location. I had to get out of here.

My boots sank as I took the few steps back toward the scrap starfighter. Pressing my hand against it for balance and clutching my shoulder with my other, I looked around and saw nothing. My eyes ran over the rubble and vehicles that lay between my location and our ships, looking for movement. Still, I saw nothing.

A piece of metal beside my head clanged loudly as it was

impacted by a bullet at the same moment I heard the weapon fire. Again, I fell back, and this time I scurried across the top before running as fast as I could to get to my belt.

Another gunshot followed and the sand beside me erupted into the air. My hand was at my holster and the stomper felt like an old friend in my grip as I fired blindly in the direction of the hunter. The sound of the shot rang in my ears, and I had no idea where the bullet ended up, but it gave me time to continue my course around the packmule, my back slamming against the rear of the starship.

The pain in my shoulder shrieked, and firing the gun made it worse.

"That was a mistake," the man announced from somewhere on the other side of the ship. "You're no killer, Hank. Just come on out and let's be done with this."

I may never have killed anyone, but he was wrong if he thought I would not defend myself. I had no plans of rolling over and dying here on some beach. I'd come too far and done too much to give up now.

Out of the corner of my eye, I saw one of the lights on the top of the *Buzzard* flicker on.

"He's at your two o'clock," Ned informed me in a whisper. He had turned on the scanners and could now feed me information. That would be helpful, but it didn't mean that I understood what he meant.

"At my what?"

There was a pause. "He is forward and to the right of you," he explained quietly. "Move around behind the thrusters and wait for him."

I did as I was instructed and began creeping around the rear, my weapon raised in a trembling hand. I could feel the blood seeping between my fingers and running down my arm before dripping off of my elbow. My breathing was quick and ragged, and I had to contort my body at an odd angle to raise my weapon in the direction of the shredded tank behind which the hunter was apparently hiding.

A top layer of sand danced over the surface of the ground as another soft wind rolled over the beach. Long shadows stretched under a vibrant crimson sky in the setting sun when the hunter stepped out from behind the scrap. He was facing toward the front of the ship but I knew he would spot me in a moment.

I had him for this one brief moment, but I wasn't sure I could pull the trigger. Staring down the top of the stomper, his chest was directly in front of my barrel, and I had to decide if I could do it.

But it was my only way to survive.

On every level I knew this, and I squeezed the trigger.

19

Pain tore through my shoulder as the weapon recoiled and I expected to watch the man be thrown back as the heavy bullet slammed into his armored chest.

But no.

His head erupted and his body was thrown to the sand in a shower of blood. There was one quiet moment and then the earth shook and the force of an explosion at my back threw me down to the sand. Pieces of his ship singed the sky before slamming into the sand around me. Smoking metal and flaming debris rained down onto the beach.

A piece of superheated shrapnel the size of a Warhero card landed on the back of my thigh, causing me to immediately jump to my feet and swat at my scorched pants. The heat had melted a bit of my flesh and the bullet hole in my shoulder was leaking profusely.

I looked back at the smoldering remains of the bounty hunter's craft and was relieved to see that the explosion hadn't done too much damage to the *Buzzard*. With my stomper hanging loosely in my hand, I limped toward the man who had been chasing me just to be sure that he was dead.

I had seen his head explode and the (presumably heartbeat tethered) kill switch in his ship all but confirmed it. But I still needed to be certain. As I dragged myself around the side of the tank, and saw his body, I knew for sure.

I had killed a person.

It had been in self-defense, and it was him or me but I'd still done it. What was odd was that I didn't feel guilty in the way I would have expected from myself. It was a big moment, and I knew that logically, but I didn't feel it the way I would have expected to. Instead, I was just numb to it. Perhaps it was the shock or maybe I was concussed, but whatever it was, I didn't care that I had ended the life of this man. In a way, that was almost more troubling.

Blinking hard, I moved over to him and fell to my knees beside his body, prying his handgun from his fingers and sliding the other one out from its place at his side. Blood was seeping into the earth, but it didn't stop me from beginning to unhook his chest armor and pull it free.

"If we are being hunted by the Consortium, the Inquisition and a cartel, I suppose I need some protection," I said but Ned didn't answer me. Soon, I had the armor off and the weapons lying on top. My eyes continued over the body as I tried to be sure I had looted everything from what was left of him.

My gaze fell upon the half of his head that remained and the curved metal wrapped around it. At the bottom of the earpiece, a little camera hung which he was supposed to use to prove he had caught his bounty. Reaching out, I pulled it free and blew the sand off it before sliding it into my own ear.

"Lucky break," I assessed as the sound of an old crooner singing about feeling young filled my hearing.

The music ceased after a moment and was replaced by Ned's voice. "We have to get out of here."

"No shit," I scoffed, turning and carrying the armful to the packmule. The weapons and armor clattered onto the surface, and I lazily picked up the controllers, guiding the machine back into the *Buzzard*. I didn't bother to move anything around, instead, I simply activated the door controls and made my way toward the cockpit.

"Hank," I heard in my ear, and I stopped.

"What?" I asked impatiently.

"You're bleeding."

"And?" I asked.

"And you have to patch yourself up," he stated without any concern for my well-being. "I'll pilot. You wrap up that shoulder."

I felt the *Buzzard* power up and I turned, moving toward the bathroom instead. When I stepped in and looked in the mirror, I couldn't believe the visage staring back at me. My hair was matted and pointed in every direction, my scraggly beard tangled and knotted. My skin was covered with sand and scratches, scars and bruises and coated in a layer of sand. Blood streaked down my left arm, and I craned my neck to see the ugly exit wound on the backside of my shoulder.

At least it meant there wasn't a bullet somewhere inside my body, but my back was covered in even more blood. Arching my back, I looked down further to see where the metal had burned through my pants and left a rectangle of seared flesh.

I had to grip the sink as the *Buzzard* lifted off the planet surface and I heard the scrap that I hadn't strapped down shift around in the cargo hold. Flipping open the mirror, I picked up the can of hospi-gel and flipped it over. The expiration date was several years in the past but it was better than nothing so I quickly shook it before pulling off the top and squirted copious amounts of the gel onto the front and back of the bullet wound. The expired biological material still did its job and began healing with a searing pain.

I let out a grunt of pain, closed my eyes, and stomped a foot hard against the ground. When the blinding pain had subsided enough, I scored a bit more on the back of my thigh, rubbing it against my flesh. When I was done, I turned toward the small shower, the size of an upright coffin, and activated the water. Pipes groaned and coughed before the brown, metallic-smelling water sputtered out from the nozzle.

Stepping into the ice-cold stream took my breath away but soon it warmed up enough to stand under, and I let the water wash over me. Every now and again, I would have to grip the walls as the pain tore through me or when the ship suddenly lurched, but it was nice to feel clean when I emerged from the shower.

After toweling off and stepping into new, old dirty clothes, I made my way to the cockpit and sat.

"Where to?"

"I know a place where we can sell the scrap," I informed Ned, my head rolling back and resting on the chair.

"Where's that?"

"Port Tortue," I told him and waited.

"And where's that?" he followed up.

"I was hoping your database would have that information," I admitted.

"You were hoping my governmental database would have information as to the location of a secret pirate space station?" he asked mockingly.

"When you put it like that, it does sound ridiculous," I admitted, staring up at some loose cabling dangling down from the ceiling.

He didn't say anything for a long moment, and I simply watched the frayed ends of the hanging cords.

"I've had to kill people, too," he said in a quiet voice.

That got my attention.

"You have?" I asked.

"Of course," he stated. "I am a soldier."

"Right," I said, nodding slowly.

"It was never easy," he said, voice barely audible from the speakers. "I told you before that I have feelings just like yours and I remember every single person whose life I had to end. And I remember the first like it was yesterday. Of course, my memory doesn't degrade quite like yours but the point remains valid."

He paused and I think he expected me to speak but I wasn't in the mood.

"It was our first mission together," he began, and I was grateful that he was just going to continue without prompting. Maybe he wanted to talk at this moment as much as I didn't want to. "It was a scouting mission. Nothing particularly dangerous. It wasn't even enemy territory. It was a demilitarized zone on a planet which hadn't seen combat in months.

"We took *Starblaster* low, passing over the small city and mostly just letting the people there know that the Consortium was out there and keeping an eye on things. It was peaceful. Boring even. But then my sensors lit up. Surface to air missiles were fired from the trees just outside the city.

"I should mention here that they weren't actually trees. They were more like tentacles which the people there grew and farmed but, for the purposes of the story, I'll spare you the details and just call them trees."

Admittedly, I wanted to know more about the farmed tentacles but it wasn't the point of the story, and I appreciated that Ned was talking to me somewhat normally so I left it and stayed quiet.

"They overshot us, and we banked hard, then dropped low and skimmed the surface," he continued. "But that was their plan, to get us to make that exact move. You have to remember that we were greenhorns. This was our first time out on any active patrol, and we fell right into their hands. Before we knew it, they were on us. Three fighters rushed out to engage us.

"William was naturally gifted, and with our combined skills we were able to evade their fire with relative ease, but we were outnumbered and knew that eventually, they would be able to pin us between them and light us up. William did the best he could, taking some shots here and there but the bursts went wide, and he did nothing but shred a few trees."

I couldn't help but imagine tentacles waving up from the ground and bursting with slime as they were shot, their farmer screaming curses up at the sky. Again, beside the serious point Ned was making, but the image flashed in my mind nevertheless.

"He gave me the order to take the controls of our launcher and allowed me to fire at will," Ned said, and his voice carried the unmistakable weight of guilt. "I did and my targeting systems were better than anything they had on the other side. The combatants were humans enhanced with augments to make their reaction times faster and their skills greater, but they could not outmaneuver me. For every calculation they could make I could make thousands. I instantaneously analyzed their behaviors and used the predictive algorithm to target their crafts.

"The first two I shot down ejected, the pilots saving themselves and drifting down to the surface for our backup to pick up, but the last pilot stuck with it. After I had already damaged his ship enough to give them cause to eject, he stuck with it and returned fire. William easily evaded the shots and ordered that I take him down.

"It was my job and what I was trained to do, so I did it. One more quick shot and I watched as the sky lit up and the life signs disappeared from my scanner. I never saw the pilot's face or knew anything about them other than that they were alive one moment and after I shot, they weren't.

"I had taken a life. They were my enemy and would've been happy to do the same to me but they had also been a person who had existed one moment and was wiped out of existence the next. They had parents and maybe children, beliefs and a life all their own. Because of me, they were nothing ever again.

"The other two pilots were captured and questioned, and we were given our first commendations, but I struggled with what I had done. And I struggled with the fact that I was made to struggle. It is something I still grapple with. Something that I am not sure I will ever understand."

Once again, he fell quiet and left the rattling sound of the *Buzzard* hurtling through the space-filled moment. Though we had an easy rapport (when Ned wasn't giving me a hard time), I had nothing to say to him.

"The point is, Hank, I understand what you're experiencing right now," he said finally and I knew he meant it sincerely.

"What's odd, is that you don't," I said after a long moment. "Ever since it happened, I've been trying to care, been trying to feel guilty about what I've done. And even though I feel the weight of it, I don't care the same way you did when you shot that pilot down. It's unsettling and I feel like I should, but I don't."

"Oh," Ned said, and I could hear his surprise. "Well, that's another thing that I have learned in my years as a soldier: no two people handle combat the same way. There's no right way to cope and no wrong way. Different people take to it differently and that's fine.

"You might also just be in shock or the fact that your entire life has changed might be so overwhelming that you can't process much else. If we had a MediScanner onboard, I could do some neuroimaging and attempt a diagnosis, but there are a lot of potential reasons for how you are feeling... or, not feeling, as it were."

"Thank you, Ned," I said, my eyes drifting down from the ceiling to the space in front of us. "I appreciate your words and sharing your experience, whether I can relate exactly or not. All of this is new to me."

"You wouldn't know it," Ned said. "You have a long way to go but I can't knock your natural talent."

I scoffed. "I stood up and got shot."

"That you did," Ned chuckled. "But you also got the better of the bounty hunter and lived to tell the tale."

"He walked right into my path, and I shot him," I said and felt the need to admit more. "And I didn't even mean to take the headshot. I was planning to hit him in the chest and run away."

"None of that matters," Ned stated. "What matters is the result. A bounty hunter was sent for you and you survived. An Inquisitor was sent for you, and you survived. Sure, you have a lot to learn, and you still might get us killed, but you've also got some skills and I think we might make a soldier of you yet."

"Don't think I want to be a soldier," I said and meant it. I wasn't sure what I was anymore. For so long, my job had been my identity but now, having broken into a scrap site and killed a man there, I didn't think I was just a scrapper anymore. "And I'm pretty sure you aren't one anymore either."

"Oh, I'm a soldier whether my government supports me or wants me dead," Ned stated unequivocally. "But, Hank, we have to get this scrap sold and we don't have enough barrels to get back to Libby to have her find the port for us."

I rubbed my face, still feeling the haze over my mind while trying to wave it away. I knew we had to move if we were going to survive. Something about Ned's story had stuck out in my mind and had given me an idea.

We had used one barrel to get away from the scrap site and now we were in the middle of nowhere in space. This meant that we had a little bit of time as long as the shield held. There was still enough charge to keep us up a bit longer and I stood, rushing back to the cargo hold to rummage through the scrap.

I found what I was looking for quickly: the motherboard from the Consortium Starfighter. I hadn't spent much time looking into computer systems, but I fished the earpiece out of my pocket and placed it in, pointing the camera at the piece.

"If I installed this, could you synchronize with it?" I asked and Ned must have run a quick analysis because he answered after just a moment.

"I could," he said. "What are you thinking?"

I didn't answer him and instead, grabbed a few more pieces of scrap, jammed them in a bag which I slung over my shoulder and snagged my toolbelt before heading down the beam cannon mounted to the bottom of the *Buzzard*. While I couldn't access the weapon itself without doing a spacewalk, the controls were mounted on a panel in a corridor at the bottom of the ship. Flipping open the cover, I began to examine the wiring and the systems in place.

The controls were hardwired into a simple system, and it didn't take much work to cut the control wires and interrupt them with the new system. Splitting the power off, I gave the new system enough juice to run and found an overhanging piece of metal on which I could balance the board. It was a crude system, but it would do.

"Get into that system," I commanded and, looking up, I knew the fog in my mind was clearing. Hurrying back to the cargo hold, I was wasting no time.

"Already in," he answered, and I assumed he was watching with interest through the camera mounted on my head as I rummaged through the scrap. "What are you looking for?" he asked after a while.

A smile curled my lips. "Bait."

20

It hadn't taken long for me to find the small beacon I had fished out of one of the fighters on the beach and it took even less time for Ned to reprogram it. Soon, the slight metal sphere was ready to go.

We fired it out of one of the small release ports and waited.

The *Buzzard* had the capacity for a cloaking system but the place where the mechanism would be installed had been turned by Lutch into a storage closet. He had stashed a few items in there and forgotten about them entirely. Now, it was more of a rust storage area.

As a result, we couldn't lay in wait, expecting to ambush someone who answered our phony distress signal. Instead, we had to wait for someone to answer the call and then try to get the better of them using cunning and guile. At least, that was the plan.

Ned had programmed the beacon to send a distress call from the Nightjar Corporation. The company was famous for undermining the Consortium and working directly with locals to circumvent tax law. Since they were no friend of the government, we guessed that the Prefects would be disinclined to answer the call.

Since we also set it to relay that we were a transport vessel hauling a large amount of goods between industrial planets, we also knew exactly what kind of attention we would attract.

It wasn't long before our gambit paid off and a ship washed into the space beside us. Painted black and adorned with the classic skull and crossbones marking that had denoted pirates since time immemorial, the medium-sized vessel immediately opened a line of communication with us.

"Nightjar Corporation vessel, prepare to be boarded," a man with patchy hair that looked as though it was shaved off a Vekrass and glued to his head stated. His cheeks were flushed, and his dark pupils swam in a red haze.

"Looks like he's staying true to the pirate lifestyle with rum," Ned joked.

I nodded and opened the communications channel from my end. "Negative. I demand to know the location of Port Tortue. Give me the information and I will let you leave. Decline, and I will disable your thrusters and leave you stranded, waiting to get picked up by whatever other pirate answers your call."

The man's red eyes went wide. "I've done a scan of your ship, bucko," he said in a voice that was tucked right between condescension and mockery. "And it's just you on board. You can't fire your weapons by yourself, save the pea shooters you got pointed away from me. And, to make matters all the worse for ya, your shields aren't even properly activated.

"I don't think I've ever seen a more ill-prepared scrapheap in my life nor a worse captain. If you think that I'm going to give you anything other than a swift boot to the ass, you're as dumb as you seem to be."

"Give me the location of Port Tortue," I repeated in a low rumble. "You don't want me to come for you. Trust me, you and your crew will regret it."

"You dare to threaten me twice?" he seethed, then his boat turned and angled its flank parallel, aiming its magnet harpoons at us. Now that I had pissed them off, he wasn't interested in simply blasting me out of the sky, he wanted to board us and make me pay.

Of course, that was exactly what I wanted too.

The pirate ship was easily twice the size of the *Buzzard* but had fewer thrusters and moved slower through space as the pilot had to make the moves with fewer options. What they lacked in mobility, they more than made up for with weapons. As their dark, rectangular vessel blotted out the light reflected off a distant moon, the sheer number of cannons, launchers and particle weapons came into sight.

For all my big talk, I was still letting them get close and soon, the magnet harpoons were within firing range.

"Here we go," I said to Ned.

The two lines fired in near synchronicity, the huge round mags passing through the inverted shields and smashing into the side of the *Buzzard*, rattling it and sending more rust sprinkling down and causing loose bolts to plunk to the ground.

"Ready?" I asked.

"Always," Ned answered without hesitation.

The winches within the pirate ship activated, pulling the two craft together. They extended the airlock plank, the rectangular passageway already glowing yellow as it heated up. The airlock passage would secure to the side of another ship, massive hooks like spider legs clamping down before the heated frame would cut through the hull.

Most corporations, especially those that operated on routes in this sector, told their employees to comply with pirates and not get themselves hurt. This was another reason that we had picked this location for our little ambush.

Soon, they were close enough and I swallowed hard before giving the order. "Now."

Moving the controls, I shifted the *Buzzard* down hard. Scrapper vehicles had more thrusters than just about any other ship because they needed to be able to maneuver through tight spaces to access valuable materials. This meant that the *Buzzard* could move in nearly every direction from a dead stop.

When we dropped, the tethers pulled, and the pirate ship began to spin. I activated the mechanical arm, grabbing the front tether and cutting through it with the saw blades set into the end effector. As soon as it was severed, I thrusted forward, pulling the pirate ship from its back mag and spinning it so that its aft thrusters were facing right toward the guns which Ned could now operate.

But we were met by a surprise.

As soon as their stern was pointing toward us, they let fly with a volley of shots from cannons positioned at the back. I plunged the *Buzzard* out of the way of the shots as quickly as I could, but some passed right through the shield and tore into the side of the ship before I could get out of the way.

Ned returned fire but hadn't calculated for my move so only one of the thrusters was hit. It caused a minor explosion, but it was designed not to take critical damage if one of the thrusters burst.

The tether meant that when we moved, we dragged them with us. Unfortunately, as soon as we had shifted clear of their firing position, we pulled them around and found ourselves right back in their crosshairs.

They let forth another salvo at the same time as Ned did, and I thrusted again but felt more shots slam into our hull. A red light began flashing on the console, and I saw that the integrity of that portion of the vessel was failing. Ned had disabled another thruster before I pulled them, but I needed to act fast if we were going to survive this fight.

Pushing forward with my left hand and back with my right on the controls, I tilted the nose of the *Buzzard* toward the pirate ship, swinging my mechanical arm toward the tether. The concept had been a good one but being tied to them with their rear-facing cannons was not working to our advantage.

Ned fired another series of shots, blasting their third thruster apart just as they returned fire. I tried to reach the tether with the mechanical arm, but I had to avoid their fire and accelerated the *Buzzard* out of the way again, pulling the arm away. Their cannons weren't on a swivel, their shots were firing in a straight line. This made them avoidable but as soon as I shifted away, the tether pulled them right back into position.

When they sent their rounds our way this time, I braced for impact and felt everything shake as part of the hull was blasted apart. *Buzzard*'s alarms screamed but Ned had already sealed the doors to that part of the ship. We couldn't take much more damage and if we survived this, this was going to be another thing that we had to worry about.

I slammed the controls again and reached out to operate the

mechanical arm simultaneously, swinging it in the direction of the tether and slicing through it as quickly as I could. The moment I did, I thrusted us forward and out of the next line of shots. Ned exactly targeted their final stern thruster, limiting their movement and disabling their Tidal Drive.

They were dead in the water.

I kept the *Buzzard* behind them but out of the way of their cannons and opened the comms line again.

"Captain," I intoned. "I warned you, but you didn't listen."

His face was enraged, and he hissed at me through clenched yellow teeth. "I will gut you for this."

I let out a patronizing laugh. "Spare me the threats. There's nothing you can do now, and you know it. Just give me the location of the port and I'll be on my way. Or you can keep threatening me until you piss me off enough to blow you and your crew into scrap."

"I'll never tell," he snarled.

"Sure you will," I said lightly, tilting the front of the *Buzzard* to face the back of their ship and raking them with a line of micromissiles. They didn't do much but make a point. "Want another?"

If looks could kill, I would have dropped dead that moment. The pirate captain stared at me with a loathing I had never seen before and seemed unable to do anything but shake with anger.

"Captain," I said, letting a cold threat blanket my words. "This is the last time I'm going to ask. Send me the coordinates for Port Tortue or die here and now. You put up a good fight but I got the better of you. There's nothing you can do at this point so you might as well just give in. I know you don't like it and I know you'll come for me, though I would not recommend that, but this is your last chance."

"I'll never give you the coordinates," he said but as the words left his lips, I saw the transmission display light up with universal coordinates. His crew was undoubtedly listening in and, against my better judgment, I decided to throw him a bone. I hoped that maybe this small act would mean he wouldn't chase me the moment his ship was repaired, but I doubted that.

"Fine," I said with an exaggerated sigh. "I see now that you won't give me the coordinates no matter what I do so I will just leave you here to rot."

I killed the comm and activated the charge on the Tidal Drive.

"Would you have done it?" Ned asked. I began to guide the *Buzzard* away from them, clearing space between them for when we entered the gyre, and I thought about the question.

"Probably," I admitted. "They are pirates. They do nothing but rob people and inconvenience anyone they come across. If he had stood in my way, I would have been doing the universe a favor by destroying them."

Ned didn't say anything for a long time, and I wondered what he was thinking. I also didn't know if I believed my own words. Though everything I said was true, I doubted that I could have actually destroyed their ship and killed all the people onboard if they had refused. Killing the bounty hunter had been one thing but killing all those pirates would have been something else entirely; no matter how villainous I deemed them to be.

"I guess I'll just have to take your word for it," he said incredulously after a moment. "And you were hoping that your kindness will mean he won't try to track you down."

"Wishful thinking, I know," I admitted.

"Or foolish," Ned said.

"You think I should destroy them?"

"I didn't say that." But the answer was coy.

We continued to back away from the pirate ship, all but stranded in space. "You might as well have," I stated.

"Not the same thing," he fired back quickly.

I nodded slowly. "I suppose it isn't."

The Tidal Drive indicator flashed, and I activated it immediately, opening the gyre tube in a washing, rhythmic circle around us. We were sucked in and left the pirate in our wake.

The moment the tube washed away behind us, and the world was nothing but streaking colors, I winced at the pain in my shoulder which I had all but forgotten. I was as bruised and wounded as the *Buzzard*.

Slowly, I moved the palm of my hand up to press against the wound and my eyes became heavy. We were out of combat and heading toward someplace where the Consortium wouldn't come looking. There was a lot of space between us and the port.

Perhaps it was that knowledge. Perhaps it was everything we had been through. Or maybe both. No matter the reason, I passed into a deep sleep and didn't open my eyes until I felt the *Buzzard* lurch when we washed back into open space.

My eyelids cracked and I saw the massive pirate space station of Port Tortue.

21

It looked exactly like I remembered from the last time Lutch had brought me here. The massive, former military space station was a perfect vision of a bandit outpost. The large weapons shifted slowly like the head of a snake waiting for its moment to strike. Dark streaks of grease coated the once pristine cylindrical center and walkways to ancillary platforms that surrounded the main station on all sides. The ancient battle scars had been patched over once and then again, giving the entire place a patchwork appearance that fit what it was.

Ships came and went from various docking bays and compared to many that I saw as we approached, the *Buzzard* was actually in relatively good condition. One craft that passed in front of us looked like a crushed beer can that someone had slapped thrusters on and taken into space. Another appeared to be made out of ripped cloth. I knew the physics of that was impossible, but I squinted at it, trying to make sense of it until my comms lit up.

A woman's face appeared on the screen, answering the hail. Her hair was spiked up so high that it left the frame and swirling tattoos with sharp edges coated her entire face, meeting and breaking apart like the roots of a plant. Through the low-resolution screen, they almost appeared to be moving.

My text display flashed with prices. "Bay rentals are on your screen," she said with no intonation at all, sounding the way I would have expected Ned to sound. "It's double for… unregistered vehicles such as yours."

"Should have known there was going to be a cost for that," Ned joked. "I'm starting to really understand the way of the world now."

"Copy that," I said. "I'll pay at the end of my stay."

"There is a ten percent surcharge for that," she informed me.

"Of course there is," Ned said with another laugh. "I'm going to hack that system on principle."

"Understood," I said again.

"Docking Bay Eight Nineteen," she said and killed the channel. In the near distance, one of the rectangular doors began to slide open and the lights around it flashed green.

I guided the *Buzzard* into the bay and set her down, shutting off the engine and watching the massive door close behind us. The interior of the bay was nothing more than four walls and a door beside which was a menu of services on a large screen.

As I was readying myself to leave, I looked down at the pilfered armor and debated putting it on. I knew that any number of people might be gunning for me but shrugged and made my way to the door. Before I crossed the threshold, I turned back and slid the two plates over my chest, cinching the sides before pulling a jacket over them. I popped in the earpiece with camera and

Ned and made my way out of the *Buzzard*, my stomper at my side.

Approaching the screen, I changed the setting to show a map of the place. I remembered it being a massive, labyrinthian place but also figured that, since I had been a child, it might have just seemed that way. Looking at the map, I saw that it was, in fact, a huge and confusing port. All of the exterior bays were connected by passageways that led toward bridges that connected to a central pillar of shops, bars, restaurants, motels as well as far more nefarious businesses.

After finding where I was going on the map, I walked the narrow corridor until it terminated at a long, interconnected balcony. Pressing a hand against the railing, I looked across the huge, hollowed out space station to the central pillar. It was alive with life and species from all across the universe were meeting and chatting, mingling and scheming. Small crafts flew up and down the open space, transporting people from one level to another.

The smell of grease, rum and meats being cooked on open flames filled my nose and it brought me back to the first moment I had stood on a balcony just like this one, pressing my nose through the bars of the railing and staring in awe at the place.

"Everyone here is trying to take advantage of everyone else here," Lutch had said before placing his massive hand on my neck and guiding me across the bridge toward the shops. Looking around now, watching the people hustle from place to place and seeing the way everyone eyed one another, I knew he had been right. Not that I hadn't also realized it at the time.

"This used to be a bastion of the Consortium," Ned said in my ear. "It's hard to believe what it's become."

I didn't want to be that guy who was talking to himself, nor did I want anybody to have any reason to suspect that I was communicating with an AI, so I said nothing. He picked up on this, but it didn't stop him from talking to himself.

"It seems perfectly emblematic of what the Consortium has become," he went on. "All of our might and righteousness, our wisdom and dedication to a brighter future replaced with freebooters trying to get an edge up on others."

The bridge between the balcony and the pillar clattered under my feet. I couldn't help but look down and tried not to imagine myself plummeting to my death. I couldn't even see where the bottom of the station was. It wasn't only that it was so far down but also that the place was poorly lit with dim, off-yellow bulbs illuminating the metallic storefronts.

When I reached the far side of the bridge, I pushed through a crowd of people watching a screen through a bar window as they drank some kind of brown liquid and cheered for whatever team was playing. The street was wide with open storefronts on either side. Nearly all of them were populated with patrons and it was a reminder of how full of life the universe was.

Pushing my way to the elevator, I got in and slid the grate closed, entering in the number of the floor on which I had seen the bar that Uncle Edgar owned and operated. When I reached the level, I saw El Tropico 2 right across the street. It looked just the same as it had a decade earlier: an open façade with PVC piping painted brown to look like a wooden bar where people could sit and drink margaritas as they looked out onto the street.

Inside was brightly lit with a sand floor the old owner had shipped in from some beach planet not dissimilar from the nameless one I had been on earlier. Naturally, over time, the sand had been soaked through and tamped down by countless feet treading over it and now it was a solid, odd smelling carpet of earth on the ground of a spaceport. The tables were faux wood and the bar at the side of the room had stripped green plastic dangling down at the front like a grass skirt.

Several women populated one table, laughing and talking and two pirates sat in the far corner, smoking cigars and undoubtedly swapping embellished stories with great aplomb. Behind the bar was a man I hadn't seen in far too long. Uncle Edgar looked over at me with my mask covering my mouth and goggles over my eyes, then nodded a greeting.

I felt the smile split my face and hurried over to meet the Kyrog who was busy drying glasses. Sitting at the bar, I could hardly contain my enthusiasm but tried to maintain my composure when I spoke. "One Bussel Brew," I said, affecting a low, serious tone.

"Listen, mate, we don't serve that kind of thing here," he said, his face a mask of irritation. "We serve fun, beachy beverages. You want a beer, there are a thousand other joints on this rock that'll serve you."

"That true even for old friends?" I asked, pulling down my mask and peeling the goggles off.

The old man's eyes went wide. All of them.

His huge, flat lips opened into a perfect circle. "H-Hank?" he stuttered, voice breaking. Hearing him speak was surreal as his voice sounded exactly like that of his brother, and it was like hearing my father again. "Is that you?"

"It's me, Uncle," I said and before the words were even out of my mouth, I had his massive arms around me, pulling me up and over the bar to press against his Hawaiian shirt. My feet knocked against the bar as he continued to hold me, his chest heaving, and I couldn't tell if he was laughing or crying. It might have been both.

"I'm so happy to see you, boy," he said, his sonorous voice warbling with emotion. "And I'm so sorry."

"You don't have to be," I told him.

"I do, I do," he sobbed. "What happened to my brother, your father, I should have been there for you."

"You were," I assured him. "The money you sent meant I could take him back to The Mound back home and lay him to rest. It was what he always wanted, and I was able to do it because of you."

Edgar's shoulders heaved and he pressed me so tight that the air began to be pressed from my lungs. "I should have been there for you. I should have come and seen him to The Mound myself."

"You have a business and a child of your own," I reminded him, though I knew he didn't need it. His bar, mate and young daughter were his whole world, and I knew it. And I hadn't been offended when he hadn't come after Lutch died. It would have been nice to have him there, sure, but I understood why he couldn't make it. When all was said and done, the money was the thing I had needed most at the moment so that I could honor my father's wishes.

"I know, I know," he said, his voice calming down. He slid me back across the bar, allowing me to plop onto a stool. "One Bussel Brew coming up."

He smiled weakly and turned his back to me, beginning to pour a drink. This was one of his favorite jokes and I had watched him do it with Lutch for my whole childhood before he moved to Port Tortue after being willed the rights to this bar by one of his old squad mates from back home.

"Carrying a lot of guilt, that one," Ned observed quietly, and I had almost forgotten that he was there.

Edgar turned back around with a wide, stemmed glass full of a steaming green liquid which somehow had its own internal light.

"The drinks people come up with…" I said with a laugh as he set it down on the bar.

"One Bussel Brew," he announced and smiled broadly, easily amused by his own antics.

"Thank you," I said and couldn't help but smile back. That was, until I tasted the drink. It sloshed into my mouth and tasted just like liquified fruit with a hint of rubbing alcohol mixed in for good measure. It was both too sweet and tasted too much like when I hit myself in the open mouth with a grease rag all at the same time.

"It's good," I croaked, and Edgar let out a bellowing laugh that shook the bar and turned heads back to us.

"Sure it is," he said. "Why do you think we get folks in from all over the Universe? Just for my looks?"

I smirked and gave him an appraising once over. "I mean…"

He laughed, and I followed suit, the genuine smile of being back with family stretching over my face.

"So, my boy, how have you been?" he asked and produced a Bussel Brew from under the counter. "You can have this when you finish that."

I snorted a laugh and nodded. "Sure."

Upturning the drink, I poured the whole thing down my throat and set the glass down, exchanging it for the beer. "I'm in some trouble," I said in a hushed tone.

Ed leaned in close. "Resh?" he asked. "I told your father how many times not to get involved with all that."

"He couldn't help himself," I said. "We all have our demons."

"Ain't that the truth," Ned said in my ear, and I made sure not to react.

"But Resh is the least of my problems," I admitted and watched Edgar's face fall.

"If a man like him is the least of your problems, you have some big problems," he observed darkly. "You need a place to lay low?"

I shook my head. "No," I told him. "Every moment I am here, everyone is in danger. I have some things I need to do and then I will be on my way."

He paused for a moment, studying my face. "You're serious?"

I nodded gravely.

"What did you do?"

"I can't say," I said. "The less you know, the better. I mean it."

At that, he reached under the counter again, retrieving a bottle in the shape of a coconut and draining half of it into a plastic cup before shooting it back.

"I'm a big boy, Hank," he said. "Tell me what's happened."

"No."

22

That surprised him. I had been a child when I had last seen him, and he obviously hadn't expected me to walk into his life like this.

"Trust me when I say you don't want to know but you also have to know that I did nothing wrong," I offered.

"Well, nothing wrong morally. Something terribly wrong in the eyes of the law," Ned said quietly, and I parroted what he said.

Edgar looked at me in pure puzzlement. "You're in trouble but something good may come of it, yes?"

Now it was my turn to be surprised. "Something like that."

He finished another drink and smiled. "Figured."

"Why?" I asked and really wanted to know.

"It was just something your father said once…"

"What did he say?" I pressed.

"He ever tell you why he became a scrapper?" Ed asked.

"Not much," I said. "Something to do with your clan diaspora."

"He would have put it that way…" Ed laughed quietly. "We left when the clan did, yes, but that wasn't why we did what we did. We were scrappers because we were scrappers back home too."

I cocked my head. "Really? Lutch never told me."

"I know he didn't," Edgar said. "He didn't want you to know that our mother taught us everything we knew about being a scrapper."

"I thought she died when you were quite young."

Edgar looked away for a moment, his eyes seeming to pull at some distant memory. "Your father was young. I was nearly full-grown by the time she died and she had spent her life teaching us the family business. See, you have to understand that war is part of our culture and there is a huge business for what's left behind. It's why you see so many Kyrogi scrappers nowadays.

"Our mother would take us out after a battle and show us how to pull apart what was left and how to identify what was valuable. There would be many of us out there, swarming over the place as we picked apart what was left behind."

I had seen Kyrog engines of war and could only imagine the huge machines being pulled apart by the huge people and their smaller, but still huge, children.

"It was, as you humans say, the family business," he continued.

"I think most species call it that," I corrected with a little grin.

"Either way," he said with a dismissive wave of his hand. "She taught us to scrap and then she died. Conscription followed. But when our clan was all but destroyed, we left and began our new life on Bussel with the little bit of money our mother had hidden away for us. I never loved it the way your father did, but I hadn't wanted to let Mom down."

Here, he paused and seemed to disappear into his memory. This was all interesting and I wished that I had known it sooner, but it also begged a question. "Why are you telling me this? What does it have to do with me?"

"It has to do with you because of how your father saw you," he said after a long moment but as I opened my mouth to speak, he began again. "You know what he said to me when I told him that I was going to leave Bussel to take over this place?"

"What?"

"He said 'good luck.' That was the first thing. And it wasn't making fun or anything like that, he meant it. He told me that he had always known that my fate lay elsewhere and that he hoped I would find my meaning out in the stars.

"When I told him that I had pair-bonded with the accountant for the bar, he just smiled as though he had known all along that it was going to happen like that. As though it was the reason he wanted me to go." His wistful look turned dark.

"But finding my purpose came at a cost. When I left him, that's when the trouble really began. Without me to keep him on the straight and narrow, he gave in to his worst instinct. Doing the thing that I needed to do meant that he got further away from that which was best for him. He supported me even though we both knew it might be worse for him.

"And it was. Or, would have been, if not for you. You walked into his life when he needed it most and, while it didn't fix everything, it helped for a long time. The two of you needed one another and neither of you could have been luckier. Even though he always said that it was you who rescued him."

"It wasn't enough," I said, thinking about the end of Lutch's life.

I felt the huge, rough hand against my cheek. "It was more than enough," he said, and his tone left little doubt as to his sincerity. "You were the best thing that ever happened to that man."

Hearing those words hit hard. I knew he meant it and had always known that Lutch and I were a perfect fit, but there was something about the serious way he told me which made it strike home. "Thank you," I said and took a long swig of the beer.

"It's true, and don't ever doubt it," he said, and we both took a quiet moment to reminisce.

"I still don't understand why you're telling me all this," I said when I had finished my beer.

He fished out another one, opened it and set it on the bar in front of me. My head was already swimming, but I had never turned down a free drink in my life and didn't plan to start now.

"I tell you all this because Lutch worried about you," he explained.

"Worried about what?"

"He worried that you were going to do nothing but be a scrapper," Edgar said.

"That's all he ever taught me to be!" I exclaimed a little more loudly than I had intended.

"No," Edgar said firmly. He wasn't yelling, but his tone carried a distinct finality. "It's what he taught you to do, not all he ever taught you to be."

"Oh, shit," Ned said, obviously impressed with the man.

"He wanted to teach you a trade, yes, but he also wanted you to be a good man who does good," he stated.

"They aren't mutually exclusive," I pointed out.

"No, but one is more important than the other. And one is small," he said thoughtfully. "Being a scrapper is a job."

"I never thought of it as just a job," I confessed. "I think of it as my identity."

"Right," he confirmed. "That's just it. My brother wanted me to pursue my dream because he knew that a job was only the foundation. I tugged this thread and got a life out of it. When you snuck into his place and got caught, it felt like… oh, I don't know… like, kismet or some such. You were the thing that he needed. That's why he never wanted you to limit yourself to following in his footsteps."

It clicked then. "He didn't tell me about your mom because he never wanted me to see scrapping as my lineage. As the only thing for me?"

Edgar nodded slowly. "He worried that, because of your past, you would never want to go any further than being a scrapper. And he always wanted you to do more. To be more."

"There's nothing wrong with being a scrapper," I protested.

"Of course not, but there's nothing wrong with it being your foundation either," he said.

That was a heartening thought until I remembered the predicament I found myself in. "I'm not sure if this is the foundation of anything," I admitted.

"It might be," Ned said with surprising optimism.

"What trouble do you find yourself in, boy?" Edgar asked, leveling me with a hard gaze.

I knew I couldn't say nothing and then ask for his assistance. Plus, he was family. Even though I hated the idea of putting him in any kind of risk, I could still answer without telling him everything.

"I found something in a scrapheap, and I believe that it can help a lot of people. But the government doesn't want me to have it, and they are after me because of it. Also, since I left Bussel without saying a word and I'm being hunted…"

"Resh wants a piece of you too?" Edgar interjected.

"More than a piece," I said. "He sent a bounty hunter after me already and I expect that's just the beginning."

"Lots of bounty hunters make this port their base of operations so you best watch your back. Just the other day an up and comer called Kilara Vex was drinking just over there."

"A few days ago was before I would've had the bounty on me so she isn't here for me, but it's a good reminder to keep my head down and keep moving."

"Also, a pirate might be coming for you," Ned reminded me.

"Oh," I added. "I also stranded a pirate rudderless in the middle of space and he seemed pretty pissed off about it."

Edgar stared at me nonplussed. "Guess that means you won't be staying long," he said, and I could hear the disappointment in his voice. "It would be nice for you to see my mate and kid before they head off to her sisters for a visit."

"Honestly, given everything I just told you, I think it would be better for all of you to keep your distance until I get out from under this."

He looked at me dubiously. "Do you think you will get out from under this?"

"Yes," I said with a confidence I didn't feel. "I'll figure out a way to turn this around. But in order to do that I'm going to need a few things."

"Anything," he said without hesitating. "I can transfer you all the money you need."

"No you can't," I said dismissively. "Even if you had the money, you need it for yourself and your family."

"You are my family."

I cracked a smile. "I know. But you also knew what I meant."

"I did and I suppose you're right," he said almost bashfully. "So, what is it I can do for you?"

"I have a lot of scrap that I need to sell," I told him quickly. "And I need to get this damned registration signal deactivated."

"Lutch never taught you to deactivate one?"

"He knew how?" Ned asked in pure irritation. "He could have saved us a hell of a lot of trouble just now."

"He never did," I said, wishing that I could tell Ned to keep it down. Not that I believed he would.

"I can help with all of this," Edgar said and then put one of his enormous hands on my head and ruffled my hair like I was a child.

Even with all of the problems I was bringing to his doorstep, Edgar still seemed to think of me as the kid I had been when we last saw each other. And I didn't mind. It was nice to take a break from thinking about all of the various groups that wanted me dead.

"Thank you," I said, letting out a long sigh before downing the rest of my beer.

"Only got one more of those," he said. "Don't keep many on hand. Most folks who come here want what I gave you first."

"Business doing well?" I asked, eager to hear how things had been going for him.

"It is," he said with a smile. "Middle of the afternoon, and you can see I have patrons. You can just imagine what this place is like at night."

"I expect it's mobbed," I said, raising the new beer to his success.

"It is," he said. "Turns out my friend was really onto something with this theme. Pirates now all seem to want to be like the old ones back on Earth. They love to come here, drink rum, and smoke cigars."

I looked at the two in the corner. One was even wearing a leather tricornered hat. "I can see that."

"Then I have the tourists in." He gestured to the women in the middle of the room.

"You get a lot of tourists here?" I asked, admittedly surprised by the idea.

"We do," he said as though it was obvious. "Lots of Sectoral Governors keep their citizens on a pretty tight leash, and their people want to cut loose. Where better to spend your time and money than a place that's free of laws."

"Something tells me there are still laws here," I smirked.

"Sure, sure, but less," Edgar said.

"Fewer," Ned corrected.

"Places where you can get all your darkest desires met are in high demand these days and Port Tortue is among the most popular," he finished.

"Wish I had known that a few hours ago, maybe I could have just asked around rather than adding to my list of enemies," I grumbled.

Edgar grinned. "I've got some patrons who are top Captains," he said. "Big fish, so to speak. I can have them let it be known that you are not to be messed with."

"That'll help," I admitted. "Keeping the pirates off the *Buzzard* would be one fewer thing to worry about." I accentuated the word for Ned's sake.

"The *Buzzard*!" Edgar howled. "You are still flying that thing? It was old the last time I was flying her and that was… well… a long time ago, now."

"She's older now," I said with a light laugh.

"You're telling me that you are on the run for your life with a ship made of rust and all on your lonesome?" he asked.

"Something like that," I said and expected Ned to add some comment from the peanut gallery, but he said nothing.

"Why don't I come with you for a bit?" Edgar offered. "Help you out until you get situated. You said you were doing some good, why not let me too?"

I shook my head frantically. "Absolutely not! You are doing well here, and you have too much to lose. You stay here, stay safe, and I'll come back. We can have a proper reunion once I have things sorted out."

"Fine," he groused, but it had been a hollow offer anyway. He didn't want to leave his life here and we both knew it. Even still, it was nice of him to ask. "I'll get you the name of someone who can help with your scrap and your signaler."

"Okay," I said. "But don't pay them for me," I added quickly. "Don't leave a paper trail."

"That's still an expression?" Ned exclaimed.

I had to focus to keep myself from laughing at the reaction. Then I reminded myself to tell him that not only was it still an expression, but that the use of synthetic paper was still common in most parts of the Universe despite the fact that tree farms were few and far between.

"Hank, when you say stuff like that, it really does freak me out," Edgar said. "For you."

"Freaks me out too."

"Imagine if he knew about the Inquisition," Ned piled on.

Edgar quickly scrawled a name and a small note from himself to the contact on a napkin and slid it across the bar to me. "Here," he said in a conspiratorial tone.

"But enough about this," I said after jamming the note in my pocket. "I want to hear about your family."

Ed smiled at that and leaned back against the sink. He proceeded to tell me everything, leaving in all the excruciating minutiae that a proud parent can't help but bore others with. I hung on every word, smiling and nodding at every story and excited about spending some time with the whole family when I was able to get the Consortium, and everyone else, off my back.

It was another reason to survive. Not just for me or Ned or the fact that I could do some good but because it would be nice to reconnect with my family.

"So, I asked him, 'but who's Emma in love with?' and he said, 'Dylan, it's a mess,'" Edgar recounted, laughing at the memory of it until his face dropped and his gray skin turned a milky white.

Quickly, I turned and followed his gaze to see a masked woman with long black hair walking toward the bar. She was wearing a tight combat stealth suit with guns and bags hanging from her belt line. Her determined stride and Edgar's reaction left little doubt that this was the bounty hunter he had mentioned earlier.

"In the bathroom," Edgar whispered hastily. "The broken stall.

Third on the right. Lift the door and pull before giving it a little push. This will lead you to a tunnel that'll take you right to a cab stand."

I was up and starting to move before he even finished the sentence. "And, kid," he called after me and I stopped just long enough to look back at him. "I love you."

"You too, Uncle," I said and rushed into the bathroom.

23

Throwing open the door, I made my way directly to the stall with the out of order sign back to its front. I did exactly as instructed and pulled the door swinging open to reveal what looked like little more than a bathroom stall under construction. Some tools sat beside a toilet waiting to be affixed to the floor.

There was a poster of a woman in a loincloth hanging on the wall at the back of the stall, and I wasted no time in lifting the corner and revealing a hole in the wall through which I climbed quickly, knocking the small piece of brick loose. When the poster flapped down behind me, most of the light was gone, and I groped forward in the dark.

The space was small, little more than hard metal on either side and I figured that I was in some kind of small maintenance passage between all of the businesses. I heard a click in the dark and worried that I should've pulled out my weapon, but I realized it was just a motion sensor that turned on a small overhead light for the maintainers. Two more flicked on, illuminating my path forward.

I kept checking behind me, but as I made my way further and further away from the bar, I figured that either Edgar was able to stall her or she wasn't looking for me at all.

"That's why we do it, you know," Ned said as I continued to hurry through the corridor.

"Why who do what?"

"Why we fight," Ned explained. "Why we need to keep pushing to find out if the enemy AI weapon is still out there. To protect the Edgars of the world."

"Oh, right," I said. "If I can keep him and his family safe then I'm more than happy to possibly save the rest of the universe too."

"That's the spirit," he joked.

"Also," I hissed. "You need to keep it down. Your running commentary almost gave me away on a few occasions."

"My running commentary might save your life one of these days," he replied.

"While I'm sure that's true, it wasn't doing us any good while I was chatting with my uncle."

"You try being deactivated for two hundred years," he snapped.

"After two hundred years, I would think you'd have had enough practice keeping your mouth shut."

Ned chuckled. "Okay, that was a pretty good one."

The unexpected reaction caused me to stutter before continuing. "But actually."

"I hear you, Hank," Ned said.

When I reached the end of the passageway, I turned the handle on the maintenance door and cracked it open, checking to see if anybody was around. There were a couple of young people chatting by the railing, but they took no notice of me, and I stepped out of the door, then closed it behind me with a clang.

I turned to see a slovenly man in a tank top that, if it had ever been white, it was a long time ago. He was sitting by a swinging gate overlooking the chasm, and as I stared at the little hovering cab platform beside him, I got excited. Maybe it was the drink or trying something new, but the idea of riding what looked like a flying pallet with handlebars looked like fun.

"Yous got a pass?" he grunted as I approached.

I shook my head no, and he shrugged and swung the door open for me. "Pays when yous gets there," he said in his strange accent before sitting back down and turning to watch the holographic model inside a nearby costume shop.

Stepping out onto the meter squared platform, it dipped under my weight before the screen flashed, asking for a destination. I punched in the address from the napkin Edgar had provided, and in a moment, the small craft raced forward and started to drop. I gripped the handles on either side of the small computer screen and watched as the world blurred by me.

The wind whipping through my hair felt good as the entirety of Port Tortue was hot. There were too many people and machines and not enough ventilation or filtration so the air moving around me felt great.

"It's good to be flying again," Ned said, obviously feeling the same way I was as he watched from the camera in my ear.

"And what do you call what I do?" I asked, having too much fun to be all that offended.

"I suppose it's technically flying," Ned said in a way that made it sound like both a joke and an insult.

"Yeah, yeah, yeah," I said dismissively just before the small craft turned sharply, causing me to grip the handles even harder to keep from flying down into the seemingly bottomless pit. It slowed to a halt by another cab stand.

Here, the chair was unoccupied except by a small placard that read, "Back in 15, please wait for service."

"When did the fifteen minutes start?" Ned asked. "And do they really expect you to wait to pay them?"

"I plan to," I said seriously.

"What? No!" Ned gasped.

"Of course not." I rolled my eyes and reached over the little gate to open the latch and allow myself through. "Now hush up so I won't seem like that guy who's walking around talking to himself."

"Or you can just not answer me," Ned suggested but then didn't say anything else as I walked over to another one of the map terminals, running my finger from the You Are Here display toward my location and realizing that we were now on the same level as the *Buzzard*.

"Well, that's a lucky break," I said under my breath.

"I thought we weren't talking anymore?"

And rather than answering, I turned and began walking in the direction of Edgar's contact.

This floor catered much more to the pilot on the go. Most of the businesses were repair shops or grab and go restaurants, pay-by-the-hour hotels and refueling stations. Nearly everybody was dressed in coveralls or like pirates. Though, the latter group were simply hurrying from the floor to somewhere else on the station.

After a few twists and turns, I saw an unmarked door between business lots thirty-one and thirty-three, so I figured this was the place. I rapped my hand on the door and nothing. I knocked again, and this time a small security camera mounted above the door clicked on, a little red light coming to life. I pulled the note from my pocket and held it up to the camera. A moment later, the door opened.

An old woman with dyed blue hair opened the door and looked at me through elongated lenses that she adjusted to appraise me.

"You're not a Kyrog," she rasped, her voice sounding as though she had been sucking on exhaust since the moment she opened her eyes. I expected Ned to make some smartass comment but, for the moment, he appeared to have listened to me and was not saying anything.

"I am not," I agreed.

"But you are Edgar's nephew," she said with the intonation of a question.

"I am," I said.

"Excellent," she said and wrinkled her face with a gap-toothed smile. "I'm Interstella, famed and feared pirate captain, now retired."

"Hank," I said, unable to keep from smiling at her introduction. "How long have you been retired?"

"Quite some time now, quite some time," she answered, stepping from the door and shuffling around behind me to push me within. She was easily two heads shorter than me but had a certain quality that made it easy to believe she had been a successful pirate captain. There was also something charming about how forthright everyone here was about their business. While I didn't respect what they did, I appreciated that they were so unabashed about the fact that they did it.

Though, as I followed her into her place, it looked much more like a scrapper's operation than a pirate's. There were heaps of metal and parts, weapons and equipment separated by low stanchions and several people of various species moving around and fixing pieces, presumably for resale.

However long it had been since she had been a curse out in the black of space, she still had a crew. And she still dressed the part, wearing a long coat patched with colorful squares and baggy linen pants that flared at the thighs before being tucked into boots with many straps and buckles.

"I bet you were one hell of a pirate," I observed, and her hand pulled off my back before she hurried around in front of me.

"I was!" she asserted, one bony finger leveled at me. "They even made a movie based on my life."

Hooking a thumb over her shoulder, I shifted my gaze to follow where she was pointing to a poster of a buxom pirate captain standing at the front of a starship with a handgun raised in one hand and a cutlass in the other.

"They took some creative liberties," she said of the poster, but the unmistakable tone of pride carried her words.

I knew better than to agree with what she said and just nodded appreciatively. "Doubt they will ever make a movie about me."

"Not with that attitude," she crowed and walked around behind a counter covered in parts and pieces which looked markedly similar to the one back at my shop. "Now, what can I do for you?"

I leaned on the counter across from her, appraising the scrap around me with my periphery. It was my nature after all. "I have a lot of scrap that… shall we say… fell off the back of a truck," I said, borrowing a phrase Resh's people liked to use. "I want it sold and I want as good a price as you can give me."

"For a nephew of Edgar, you'll get the friends and family rate," she offered with all the generosity of a used starship salesman.

"I'll take it," I said gratefully.

"Was that it?"

I looked at her and cocked an eyebrow. "You had to know that wasn't it."

"What else can I do for you?" she asked in a low whisper as though we were plotting to take down the Triumvirate.

"In addition to fuel, I need to have my registration signaler deactivated," I said. "And I need it done quickly. You can knock whatever it costs off what you'd be giving me for the scrap."

She winked theatrically. "Barnacle, over here," she called to a one-armed man with the long scraggly hair from his head joining with that from his beard into two conjoining braids. From under the hair, his skin was pockmarked with the pimples from which I assumed his name was derived.

"What lot you in?" she asked.

"Eight Nineteen," I answered. "But I am happy to escort him and help to transport the scrap."

"Well, ain't you a peach," she said, narrowing her eyes at me suspiciously. And her suspicions were well founded. I wasn't truly interested in helping, I only wanted to move the scrap to ensure its safe delivery from there to here. Just because Uncle Edgar recommended her, didn't mean that I inherently trusted her or believed she wouldn't have her people pocket a few items here and there.

She snapped her finger at Barnacle, and he immediately

hopped to, with me following just behind him. I pulled up the face cover and slid the goggles over my eyes. Now that I was walking between some kind of black-market scrap dealer and my own ship, it seemed prudent to conceal my appearance as much as possible.

"Keep up," Barnacle snapped as several more of the retired pirates fell in behind us, two of them dragging packmules along, through the door and out into the hallway. Barnacle kept us moving at a good pace, winding this way and that for a few minutes before we reached Docking Bay Eight Nineteen.

I pressed the key card provided with the lot against the digital lock, and it beeped before the door opened and all of the former pirates scurried in. As they pushed their packmules up the ramp, I followed and watched them do exactly what I would have: move while examining the objects for valuable pieces.

Barnacle turned and looked at me. "Where is your signaler?" he asked, his voice sounding like a death rattle.

"In the middle of the ship, there's a ladder that leads up to a—" I began, but he held up a hand to stop me.

"Just meant top or bottom," he said and turned, then stalked away and up onto the ship.

Again, I expected Ned to make a comment about all of this, and again he accommodated my wishes by keeping quiet.

Having nothing better to do, I made my way into the cargo hold and began helping load up the packmules. As I worked, I kept checking over my shoulder, expecting at any moment someone to come for me.

But no one did.

Flipping one piece of shield generator over in my hand, I

noticed it was in excellent shape. I had planned to just pocket it, but I continued to stare.

This was going to be my life. My whole life.

This was going to be it.

And I had always thought that was fine and had assumed that's what Lutch wanted for me. I assumed his protestations and his suggestions that I explore the universe had been the idle chatter of a father who 'wanted better' for their son while actually just teaching the child to follow in their own footsteps.

My eyes bore into the scrap in my hand. This was always going to be my legacy, the thing that I did which I expected to pass down to my own kid, were I ever to find myself a woman to settle down with.

Now I didn't know what I was. I wasn't a scrapper. After I broke into the scrap site, they would never have me back. I wasn't the hero Ned wanted me to be, no matter how hard I played at it. I wasn't much of anything.

I suppose the only solution was to keep moving forward and find out what I could become. As Edgar had said, perhaps scrapper would be my foundation. It would be the first part of my story but not, as I had thought it would be, the whole story.

The others had started their packmules back to Interstella so it was just me in the cargo hold now.

I began to follow them, but Ned's voice stopped me. "Suppose we both have to forge new paths now," he said quietly.

"I suppose we do," I agreed. "Though I'm not sure exactly what that looks like."

"Me neither," he said and fell silent once again. I wondered how much his processors were analyzing at every moment. If his mind was always active or if it went into rest mode, so to speak. *Did songs get stuck in his head? Would he think back on conversations where he had said something embarrassing? Did he say things that he would even later think were embarrassing?*

These idle questions consumed my mind while I stepped down from the back of the *Buzzard* and out the door of the docking bay, heading back toward Interstella's. The corridor was quiet and I had lost sight of the others, but it allowed me time to sit with my thoughts.

Until, that is, I felt the blade pressed against my throat.

"Resh wishes to speak with you," a woman's voice said from behind me, and I turned just enough to see Kilara Vex out of the corner of my eye.

24

"I'm pretty sure he didn't want to chat with me," I said, mostly just trying to talk to give myself time to think of a plan.

"All I know is that Resh is looking for some scrapper who fits your description," she said, words dripping with menace. And, after all of my internal struggle in debate, all she had been looking for was nothing but a scrapper. "What he does to you after I bring you to him is none of my concern."

"That's a disconcerting thought," I said and even though I knew it was a mistake, I heaved an elbow. I hadn't been formally trained in hand-to-hand combat, but Lutch had given me a few informal boxing lessons so that I could throw a punch if I had to.

Actually, he had only given me the lessons because I had been ambushed by some local bullies as I was making a delivery and lost some of his goods because I couldn't fight. He had, of course, easily tracked them down, made them regret jumping me and gotten the supplies back.

The knife pulled from my throat as Kilara dropped out of the way of my swinging arm, allowing me to spin too far. Before I had time to even properly set my feet, she sent a leg swinging up from her crouch. Like being hit with a length of pipe, her booted foot smashed against my side, knocking the air out of me and cracking my ribs.

My body's involuntary reaction sent a matching pain from my still healing shoulder and I tried to spin and raise my hands to punch. The ground rushed up to meet me when she swept my legs and I gasped for air, my cheek pressed against the hard metal.

"That was a mistake," Kilara said.

"I see that now," I wheezed, utterly defeated. I had played my one hand and lost. Now, I would just have to go with her. After the last bounty hunter, I held no optimism for the idea of trying to convince Resh that I was worth keeping around.

I would try.

But I was sure it was pointless.

"On your feet," the woman said and there was something about her that was almost familiar. As if I had been captured by her before in a dream that I only now remembered.

"Is there any way I could convince you to forget you saw me?" I asked hopelessly.

"That's just pathetic," Ned observed, and I wondered if there was something that he could do to help. Looking her over, I wondered if he could hack her weapons, cause them to fail or somehow make her stealth suit malfunction. "You really think she was going to take you up on that offer?"

"No," she said flatly. "I am not to be bought."

"You're a bounty hunter, your whole business is being bought," I gasped.

"Idiot," Ned said just before I saw the flash of Kilara's fist.

She wheeled on me so quickly that I hardly had time to react before the crunching sound preceded a white light sparking in my vision. I staggered while reaching out and gripping the wall for support to keep from falling over again.

"Maybe it's best if you keep your mouth shut from here on out," she said but that was never my specialty in moments of duress. I have found that keeping a conversation going would sometimes lead to getting that one piece of information that you needed to weasel your way out or, just distract your opponent enough for them to make a mistake.

But, for the time being, I was more focused on filling my lungs with air and on the pain in my face, shoulder and side. I felt a hand on my wrist before the metal clamped around it and I was shackled with my hands behind my back.

"That's what you earned," she stated.

"Pretty sure you would've done that either way," I said through ragged, winded breaths.

That stopped her for a moment, and I wasn't sure why but then the feel of a muzzle pressed against my back started moving me forward.

"I'm going to take you to my ship," she informed me, and it felt like an animal toying with its meal before devouring it. "Then I will take you to see Resh."

I opened my mouth to speak but nothing came out and I probably appeared to the world like a gasping fish out of water.

"See," she mocked, "you're already learning."

"You have to get yourself out of this," Ned said urgently.

I wanted to tell him that I knew that but that I also had no move. My hands were bound behind my back, I was battered, beaten and bullet-riddled and, when all was said and done, just a scrapper.

"When she gets close enough," Ned began to advise me. "You can headbutt her and, while she's falling, grab the restraint controls. You flick them off and when she's staggering, hit her again. That should be enough to drop her, and you can use the restraints on her before stashing her somewhere long enough for us to sell the scrap, finish with the signaler and get out of here. If we can somehow sabotage her craft, that would be a good secondary objective."

I barked a laugh at the absurdity of it.

"Something funny to you?" Kilara hissed. The hard black mask that covered her from chin to forehead had a respirator which seemed to alter her voice. It also had blue glowing eyepieces that I assume could be set to see under different conditions. That thing that she wore on her face was probably worth more than the *Buzzard*.

"No, nothing's funny," I said, finally able to breathe somewhat normally though, with every intake of air, my chest ached. "It's just, I got myself into a bad spot and seem to have made it a lot worse. I'm not a bad guy, you have to understand. I simply—"

"Spare me the sob story," she said, angling the gun in my back and turned left down the corridor. We walked past two people chatting outside a docking bay door. They looked up, to see what was happening then returned to their conversation without a second glance.

On Bussel, they might have asked what was going on or even

made a call to the local authority. But here, on the pirate port, nobody could be bothered.

"Every person I bring in has one reason or another why I should feel bad or let them go," she said, sounding almost bored by even having to explain it. "But it never works on me, so don't bother."

"I wasn't trying to pull anything on you," I lied. "I was just explaining my predicament because I thought you might be interested."

"I'm not," she said and stuck me with the gun again.

"That's gonna leave a bruise," I noted angrily.

"A bruise is going to be the least of your problems," she said, making the threat of Resh once again.

I decided to ignore her and just keep talking. I gleaned already that I wasn't going to get anything from her but I might irritate her into making a mistake. Who knows, maybe I could even headbutt her and pull off Ned's plan?

"As I was saying, I'm really a good guy who just finds himself in a bad spot," I began again. "What happened was, my father had a bit of a gambling problem…" and here I paused. "I've never really said that out loud before," I admitted, and it was true.

I had spent so much of my life worshiping Lutch, but I also knew his true nature and what he had struggled with. What, sometimes, it felt like he had been cursed with. Edgar had obviously seen it too; known exactly the man his brother was. A good person with one deep, dark flaw that threatened to consume everything else.

"We've all got problems," she said, her tone of disinterest continuing unabated. "And daddy issues aren't new for bounties either."

"I wasn't," I stammered but found myself faltering. "It's just, he got in deep. And one by one, the life we had was stripped away."

"Listen, friend, I don't know what your situation is but I know that it's not a bad debt that's got Resh sending people all the way out here to find you," she said coldly.

"You're right," I admitted. "I suppose I just thought that this was the beginning of something. You know, you try to do something good for the first time in your life and end up in a worse position than where you started. Guess that's why Lutch just kept his head down and stuck to himself."

At that, I heard her footsteps falter and then stop. I felt a hand grip my shoulder, and she spun me around to face her, then yanked my mask down and pushed the goggles up and off my head. They pulled at my skin, and I grunted as my head was thrown back, before slamming into position to look at the masked figure.

"Hank?"

"Yes?" I answered and asked with one word.

She stood before me like a statue, staring up at my face and I had no idea what was happening. I had never met a bounty hunter in my life and now this woman seemed to know me. My heart raced and the wheels in my mind turned as I tried to figure out what had happened.

She continued to stare at me, her head turning this way and that as though she couldn't quite believe it and certainly didn't know what to do with me now.

After a moment, she holstered her weapon and reached around toward the back of her mask.

"Hank, it's me," she said and unstrapped the black bindings at the back of her head.

When the mask pulled away, I couldn't have been more surprised. Staring back at me was the face of Lara Shen. My closest childhood friend who I hadn't seen except in passing since that fateful night when we broke into Lutch's shop together and I had gotten caught.

"L-Lara," I said, happy to see somebody who felt almost like family for the second time this day. Instinctively, I tried to open my arms and bring her in for a hug, but they rattled against the restraint, and I simply stepped toward her before feeling a hand pressing against my chest plate.

"Hank, what the hell did you do?" she demanded in a hushed tone, grabbing me by the collar and pushing me up against the wall.

"I pissed off the Consortium and now Resh wants to silence me so I don't say anything about his business to anyone," I explained quickly. "Can you get these restraints off me?"

She spun me around and pressed me up against the wall like I was still one of her bounties, using a digital key card to unlock the large cuffs.

"Hank, someone's gonna kill you," she warned. "You better get out of here now. And you really need to take that armor off. Walking around in the property of a slain bounty hunter is like spitting in our faces. Hell, I was thrilled to deck you."

"You were always happy to punch someone," I observed, and she grimaced.

"I'm telling you, any hunter who comes across your path will not hesitate to kill you," she warned, her brown eyes so dark that they nearly looked black.

It was amazing that even though it had been so long since I had seen her and she was a completely different person now, her face was somewhat the same. Older, naturally, but she had the same complexion and freckles, same facial expressions and worried look that she had back when.

The familiar terror plastered on her face now heightened my own fear. The Inquisition was a serious threat but knowing that the bounty hunters would simply shoot on sight was another terrifying prospect.

"I have to get to the *Buzzard*," I said and Lara's mouth fell open.

"That thing still flies?"

"I mean…" I began and for the first time since seeing her, she cracked a hint of a smile.

When I had known her in the orphanage, she had been so excitable and full of life. Now, that seemed to be a long distant memory. The Lara I had known seemed to have been replaced with Kilara. Though, for one brief moment, the clouds parted.

Then the moment passed.

"Good luck, Hank," she said, face falling flat before reaching to put her mask back on. "Maybe I'll see you in another decade or two… if you last that long."

"Oh, um," I stammered. I had been hoping she was going to stick around, maybe help get me to my ship or at least catch up. But that obviously wasn't happening.

The wall beside me erupted in a bright flash, the metal ripping apart. I ducked, and Lara sprang out of the way, then I turned to see a man at the far end of the hall in black tactical gear, holding up a smoking rifle.

He had missed, but I didn't think I would get lucky again and loosed the stomper from its holster, before aiming and pulling the trigger in one fluid movement. The black-clad hunter ducked back behind the corner, giving me time to run.

Lara had not returned fire, though she had raised her weapons and now she was looking at me, calculating something but I couldn't guess what. I didn't have time to think about it as I broke into a dead sprint away from the new pursuer and toward the *Buzzard*.

Lara didn't move and I thought that would be the last I would see of her. If I was lucky, maybe she would provide covering fire as I ran, but I doubted it. An old friendship probably wasn't enough to risk your life for.

My boots slammed down the corridor and another shot streaked by me, blasting the ceiling just in front of me, causing a shower of sparks and shrapnel to flow down. Leaping through and feeling my hair singe, I kept going without looking back. No way I was going to blind-fire with Lara somewhere behind me.

Or so I thought.

Hearing easy breathing beside me, I turned to see my old friend bounding forward.

"Shoot him!" she ordered, and I turned my body just enough to fire back a few times, happy that we were in an empty hallway where I wouldn't hit any bystanders.

"I like her," Ned whispered.

Lara had her weapon out but wasn't using it.

"*You* shoot him," I huffed.

"I'm not shooting another bounty hunter," she said.

"He's shooting at you," I barked but she shook her head as we ran. Or, as I ran and she jogged. I could tell that if she wanted to break away and leave me, she easily could; her strides were quick and easy.

"He's allowed," she explained, and I squeezed the trigger again to keep him back. "I never officially accepted the contract, and he doesn't know that I'm not helping you."

"You're not helping me?" I asked and we rounded another corner, Docking Bay Eight Nineteen coming into view.

"No," she stated. "But he's between me and my ship and thinks I'm with you so I'm stuck with you for the time being. But I'm still not going to kill another hunter."

"Fine," I snorted and stole a glance over my shoulder, seeing the man raising his rifle square at my back.

Continuing to run, I tried to let my breath seep out slowly and aim as well as possible given the circumstances. When I pulled the trigger, nothing seemed to happen for a moment and the hunter didn't flinch. But when he fired back, his shot missed its mark and smashed into the ground between us. I knew I must have hit him somewhere.

"Think I winged him," I said, hardly able to breathe. I had been in pretty rough shape before starting to run and now every part of my body was screaming at me. The surging adrenaline kept me moving, running and escaping.

"That won't stop him," Lara warned, and I knew that was true. The doggedness of the bounty hunters was known throughout the universe. Nearly as tenacious as Inquisitors, the hunters were famed for their ruthless pursuit of their targets.

Though I didn't know much else about them. I had never needed to hire one and couldn't have afforded to, even if I had wanted to. The fact that Lara wasn't going to shoot back but he could shoot at her suggested that they had their own code as strict, and undoubtedly complicated, as the scrapper's.

Ripping the keycard from my pocket, I slammed it against the mechanism, opening the door and bounding through with Lara right behind. Another shot crashed into the door as it slid closed behind us and I nearly fell back. Lara grabbed my elbow to keep me upright and gave me a quick look over.

"You've really taken a beating," she observed.

"Got that right," I affirmed and turned to head to the ship.

Lara turned too and then stopped, her eyes narrowing on the *Buzzard*. "You can't be serious."

25

"Got any other ships hidden in this docking bay?" I quipped, trotting quickly over to the ramp.

I didn't hear any more noises coming from outside the door and figured the bounty hunter was running to his own vessel. I considered running back to Interstella for my payment. Leaving here without it was a mistake and I knew better than to believe that she was going to just pay me whenever I returned. We needed the money if we were going to be able to do anything after this.

Of course, if I went running back, that would give the hunter time to move his ship into position outside our bay doors and blast us out of the sky the moment we left. There was also the possibility that he was waiting on the other side of the door, and I would be shot the moment I left.

For the time being, the best thing that I could do was run.

Lara was standing at the bottom of the ramp as I hurried up

and into the cargo hold. Turning back around, I fixed her with a questioning look. "You coming with?"

"I really shouldn't," she said, looking at the *Buzzard* as though it was going to fall apart at any moment.

"I could use your help," I said. "And I'll drop you back here or somewhere nearby as soon as we get this guy off our tails."

Shaking her head in defeat, she stepped onto the ramp and followed me toward the cockpit.

When I fired up the engine, I heard a strange sound and stood.

"Barnacle," Ned said in my ear, seeming to have anticipated my confusion.

"That's right," I said before catching myself.

"What's right?" Lara asked as she sat in the copilot's chair.

"I have someone working in here," I answered as though that explained my comment. "I'll go flush them out while you get us pointed in the right direction."

She stared at me blankly, almost irritably.

When we were kids, she had never liked being bossed around, and it clearly remained true now.

"If you wouldn't mind," I added, repeating the phrase I had used all the time back in the day to get her to do things for me.

"Fine," she growled and there seemed to be more to it, but we didn't have time to delve.

Standing, I hurried toward the back of the *Buzzard* where I saw Barnacle clattering down the ladder.

"I have to get off of the ship," he said, the words seeping from him like a leaking gas main.

"The cargo doors are closing now, and we have to get out of here," I told him hurriedly. "We can drop you at a nearby station."

"Not happening," he said and began rushing down the stairs and into the cargo hold. I followed him, seeing the door closing slowly and the ground already a meter away.

"What are you gonna do, jump?" I asked with a laugh, but he looked back at me seriously.

The man had, after all, been a pirate.

The floor of the docking bay was growing more distant, and the ramp was now level with the base of the cargo hold.

"I installed the signal dampener for you," he said over the sound of air and thrusters. "Should do the trick until you can remove the signaler entirely."

"Thanks," I said and stole another glance over his shoulder. "Really, you can stay with us, and we will drop you somewhere."

I was gripping the door frame to the room, but Barnacle was simply standing in the center of the cargo hold as the ship moved and what felt like gale force winds blasted around.

"No," he said and turned. "I'll take my pay from your scrap money," he called over his shoulder and broke into a limping sprint. He wasn't a young man and his body had obviously been through a lot, but, remarkably, he lifted off the back of the closing door and tucked into a landing roll as the *Buzzard* turned to face space.

As the door slid closed, I had to give Barnacle credit. I wouldn't have come with us either if I didn't have to. It was remarkable that Lara had decided to come along. Even if it was predicated on leaving me as soon as she could and principally because there was a bounty hunter who was shooting at us standing between her and her ship.

In a moment, I was back in the cockpit and at the controls. Given my druthers and knowing what he could do, I would much prefer Ned at the helm or commonality code, controlling the weapons. But with Lara here, we couldn't give away his presence.

"I'll take over," I told her. "Mind taking the guns?"

"I won't kill another bounty hunter," she said again, and it was clear that she wasn't budging on this.

"I respect that," I said, and I meant it. Sometimes, our personal moral code was all we had, and I wasn't going to question this decision again.

"But can you at least take some potshots and try to dissuade him from following?"

She dropped her head and looked at me from under her brows. "That, I suppose I could do."

It had been so long since we'd seen each other, but there was an easy rhythm between us that remained all these years later. Having spent the first several years of our lives together, she had been like my sister until Lutch took me in and gave me a home. Though we had parted ways, that foundation was still there, and it was nice to be back in her presence, even if it was only for a short time.

I watched as Lara hurried to the gunner's seat and then I piloted us out of the docking bay. This near to the station, there were ships coming and going in every direction, and I had hoped that I could get lost in the traffic, but it wasn't long before Ned spoke in my ear.

"A craft registered to a bounty hunter just left another docking bay and is heading this direction, according to your scanners. Without the registration signaler active, it'll take him more time to find you but I am sure Resh added a description of the *Buzzard* to the bounty," he said and he was probably right.

I shot a quick look over my shoulder just to be sure that Lara wasn't within earshot and began to tap my message to him just after beginning to warm up the Tidal Drive. "What kind of ship is it?"

"Mid-range Raven-class," he informed me. "Don't have much more information than that, but it's safe to assume that he has more weapon capabilities than us."

"Any strategies here?" I tapped.

"Oh, you didn't want my advice before, but now you're interested in what I have to say?" he said.

I wanted to bark at him that it would never have worked for me to try to headbutt Lara to try to escape, but I didn't have the time or inclination to tap it all out, so I just sent him a message in the affirmative.

"Try to survive until we can hop a gyre," he said unhelpfully.

"See anything?" I called back to Lara.

"Nothing yet," she answered. "Lots of traffic though, and I don't want to start a firefight out here."

She was right, and I continued to pilot us away from all of the comings and goings.

"Maybe he's not gonna come for us?" I suggested but Lara only cackled a laugh in answer.

The ships began to recede into their own gyres and soon we were on our own, but I knew that our drive still had some time before we could activate.

"He's making a beeline," Ned informed me, and I looked down at the rear-facing camera feed. The bounty hunter ship was making right for us.

"Light him up!" I cried and heard the rattle of the micromissile launcher when Lara began a series of warning shots blasting in his direction.

As soon as she did, I began to make evasive maneuvers, sliding this way and that and trying to keep off of their targeting systems.

"Incoming fire," Ned informed me of what I had seen on the screen. Instinctively, I reached out to try to turn on our shields before remembering that they were still set to inverse.

I kicked myself inside. I wished that I had taken more time and just stayed with the *Buzzard* to make repairs and do the work myself. Though this was self-deprecating and would've been impossible, it didn't stop me from wishing that I had taken more time with the ship.

I noticed that the hunter's Raven was firing in semiautomatic bursts rather than in a constant stream of missiles chasing me through space as I tried to evade him, leaving Port Tortue in our wake.

Lara shot back, but it was ineffectual and pointless. She was going so wide with the missiles that it looked exactly like what she was doing: trying to miss. I opened my mouth to holler back at her but knew that she wouldn't take any better shots. I would have to do this on my own.

The hunter sent another series of bursts streaking toward us and I moved us out of the way, watching as he stayed in close lockstep to our flight pattern. And he was closing in on us. Soon, he would be too close to evade and without shields, there was nothing we could do to keep from being shredded.

Lara might return fire if she thought we would otherwise die, but I wasn't willing to count on that. I had to do something, and I had to do it now.

My stomach lurched when I dropped us, sending the *Buzzard*

hurtling down to avoid another burst. The Raven was right on our tail. It was time to think fast.

As the missiles streaked just overhead, it occurred to me.

"Ned," I tapped hurriedly. "Take over and keep him right on our ass."

"Affirmative," he said in my ear. "What's the plan?"

More of the small projectiles tore through space just overhead.

"Think you can lure him into his own fire?"

Ned must have run some calculations because he was quiet for a moment before answering. "Yes," he said finally, and I felt the controls shift over to him.

Immediately, the *Buzzard* began to move in a way I couldn't get it to. Though I was no slouch as a pilot, the things Ned could do were so quick and decisive that it was on a whole other level.

He banked us hard right, taking us away from the Raven's fire but the hunter stayed right on us. The *Buzzard* rattled against the movement. Anything that wasn't bolted down was flying around the ship with each hurtling motion. The hunter began firing off more shots, burst after burst came screaming after us but Ned dropped and swung and avoided each and every one. More came in quick succession.

The hunter was trying to end this.

"What the hell are you doing up there?" Lara screamed up the hallway.

"Trying something," I called back as though I was the one controlling the ship.

Then Ned pulled the *Buzzard* up, tilting the nose and rolling us while accelerating past the last few lines of missiles. We roared into a loop, items clattering around and bolts flying around the cockpit and my vision spinning. The Raven-class followed tight behind us but Ned broke the flow of movement, barrel rolling out of the way.

A few missiles struck our wing, but I watched as the Raven couldn't correct in time and his last round of shots slammed into his shield, breaking the pursuit and sending him crashing off course.

Before I could even reach out to hit the button, Ned had activated the Tidal Drive and we were off.

The moment we were in the gyre tube, I heard Lara unbuckle herself and after a moment, she was back in the copilot's seat.

"You've become one hell of a pilot," she observed. "I've never seen anything quite like that."

"Right," I answered noncommittally. "I guess a lot has changed since we knew each other."

"A lot," she repeated, fixing me with her dark eyes now shimmering with the reflection of the gyre lights.

"How did you become a bounty hunter?" I asked, sincerely curious. I turned to look at her but when I did, my entire torso erupted in pain.

She saw my grimace and smiled ever so slightly. "Got you good, eh?"

"You did," I agreed, feeling the kicks with each breath. "Brings me back to my question, though?"

"I became a bounty hunter the same way you became a scrapper," she answered, folding her arms across her chest.

"That's all you're going to give me?" I asked, cocking an eyebrow.

"What more do you want to know?" she inquired and even though there was an ease to talking with her, I could tell her walls were up.

"Everything," I answered. "I want to know everything that happened after Lutch took me in."

Her lips pursed for a moment, and she looked away. Eventually, she answered. "A few years after you got caught and taken in, I got caught sneaking onto a starship I'd seen parked out in the open and didn't realize what it was until it was too late.

"I was exploring, and I started to see holding cells, manacles and weapons and realized it had to be a bounty hunter's. I tried to get the hell out of there but there was a shadow blocking the doorway.

"Hank, I've never been more scared in my life. I figured I was about to meet the business end of a bullet. But he was impressed with how I've gotten onto a ship and was moving so quietly, so he asked if I would help with what he was doing. After helping with my first bounty, I was hooked.

"I liked sneaking around, liked taking people in and"—she paused for a moment as though she was going to say something and thought better of it—"the money," she finished, but it was obvious that that's not what she was going to say.

"Not much money in scrapping," I acknowledged with a laugh.

"That's what I always assumed," she said. "The hunter who took me in showed me the ropes and eventually got me a license, letting me help before I went out on my own."

"And now you're a feared bounty hunter," I said. "You should have seen the way my uncle talked about you."

"Edgar is your uncle?" she asked without any intonation. I had expected some reaction but got nothing.

"He is," I told her. "First time I had seen him since Lutch died."

"Lutch passed?"

I nodded. "He did, a few years back."

"Have you been okay since?" she asked but again, there was no emotion behind the words. While we had been running around, fearing for our lives, she had seemed like her old self. Now that we were sitting in a quiet moment, her affect changed entirely.

"I have, just muddling through," I answered.

"You're more than muddling through now," she observed. "How bad is all this?" she asked.

"Pretty bad," I said. "Being hunted by the Consortium is one thing but now that I know all of you guys are after me, I'm not sure I can figure a way out."

"I might be able to help with that," she said. "I think I could get you a sit down with Resh if you could get out from whatever the Consortium wants you for. Do you believe you could clear up the situation with the government? If you could, I really think that I could get Resh to listen to you."

"You have that kind of relationship with him?" I asked, one eyebrow raised just enough.

She snorted dismissively. "I've sent him enough heads that if I asked for something, he'd give it."

"That certainly might come in handy but getting out from under the government's thumb is not going to be easy."

"What would you need to do?" she pressed.

I sighed, trying to buy myself enough time to come up with a version of what I needed to do which didn't give away Ned's existence. Lara had taken more of a risk than she even knew by stepping foot on the *Buzzard* and I didn't need to make things worse for her by getting her mixed up with the AI.

"While I was on a scrap job, I discovered references to ancient weapons powerful enough to rock the universe to its very core, code-named Extinction," I began, proud of myself that this was, in fact, mostly the truth. I was happy to skate by on the sin of omission if it meant keeping an old friend safe. "I need to investigate this weapon and find out if it still exists and what it can do but the Consortium would rather it just be covered up."

Her brows and mouth were parallel straight lines. "I don't understand," she said finally. "You're doing all this because you found some reference to something that doesn't have anything to do with you?"

"If this weapon can truly do what I believe, it concerns all of us," I said, and that much I believed. "I'm one of the people that lives in this universe, and if there is a threat left over out there from the Old War that can do more damage than anything we've ever known, I want to put a stop to it."

Lara shook her head and looked at me pityingly. "But why?"

I was surprised by the question. "Because it's the right thing to do."

At that, she was up and out of her chair, leveling a finger at me. "And since when do you care about doing what's right for others?"

"Since, I don't know, now…" I stammered. She had always had a temper, but this reaction was not something I'd seen coming.

"Pffft," she snorted derisively. "Leave it to you to grow a conscience now, Spears." She had never called me by my last name because when I had known her, I hadn't belonged to it, and it sounded strange and aggressive leaving her lips.

"You're just pissed that you are stuck on this ship rather than on your own off catching bounties," I threw back at her.

"You're damned right I'm pissed about that too," she snarled and in a weird way, it felt familiar. We fought like cats and dogs when we were little, and there was something about doing it now that made it almost feel like home.

I wondered if that's why I still got along with, and wanted to work with, Ned even though he busted my chops at every available opportunity. As I thought about it, Lutch had done much the same thing. He was happy to lecture and give me fatherly advice, but he was also happy to mock me and let me make mistakes so that I could learn lessons.

"I'm sorry, Lara," I said sincerely, trying to calm the mood. "I know this isn't what you wanted."

"It isn't," she admitted, her voice calm but still carrying the tension. "I thought I was gonna snag a quick bounty on my way to another job and you walked right back into my life and instantly complicated everything. There's going to be hell to pay at the Conclave because I'm working with somebody who killed another hunter. I'm separated from my ship and have to get back to it plus I'm sure whoever that was back in Tortue is gonna have some pretty choice words for me… or worse."

"Sorry," I said again. "I really didn't mean for any of this to happen."

"You never mean for anything to happen," she said, her words like the edge of a razor.

As we were talking, we washed out of the gyre tube and into the random section of space whose coordinates I had input as we were making our escape. Black space dotted with the white light of distant worlds surrounded us and we both took a moment to just stare at it.

"Despite the circumstances, it really is nice to see you," I smiled at her.

She didn't smile back but her expression softened slightly. "You too," she said as though she was admitting something shameful.

"Where can I drop—" I began but stopped talking when I saw the little indicator light for the registration signaler click on. At the same moment, Ned chirped in my ear.

"The signal dampener just turned off," he informed me, but I was already up and running. "I activated the shields, but they won't last and it'll be a while before we can wash again."

"What?" Lara called after me, but I didn't have any time to waste.

26

I was through the crawl space and with the signaler in no time, seeing the crude machinery that Barnacle had installed. It was smoking and sparking, and I cursed him and Interstella and everyone else. But I didn't have time to sulk.

Lara poked her head in as I set to work opening the dampener up and trying to assess the problem. "What's going on?"

"The person who installed this ran a line without checking the power source and shorted the whole system," I explained, already removing the fried parts and grabbing some suitable replacements from my belt. Now that I saw the dampener, I understood it enough to get it working again.

But every moment that we were here, we were sitting ducks. I needed to have this signal removed as soon as I could but, having left any prospect of money back on Port Tortue, I would just have to make this work for now.

Lara watched as I worked quickly, pulling pieces, replacing parts, and soldering things together as rapidly as I could.

"Wow, you really got good at this," she said, and I could hear that she was impressed.

"Something tells me you got pretty good at bounty hunting, too," I observed, pressing goggles against my eyes with one hand as sparks flew from my soldering iron in the other.

"I did," she said. "I had to get good at something."

"You and me both."

She continued to watch me in silence until I was nearly finished.

"You're such a high value target that you're worried they'll come for you if your signaler is active for even just a few minutes?" she asked patronizingly, as though I was somehow full of myself because of my reaction.

"Yes," I told her, and my voice must have carried the seriousness with which I took the situation because she fell quiet again.

I finished the repairs to the dampener, rewiring it through a power converter so it wouldn't short again and feeling good enough about its functionality for the time being that I thought it might be okay to get the shields facing the proper direction again also.

"We can head back to the cockpit now," I told Lara as I turned from my work only to discover that she was already gone.

I shimmied my way back down and through and glanced around, not seeing Lara before I made my way back to the cockpit to check the Tidal Drive. We still had a few more minutes before it was ready, and I figured I could start on the shield generator.

"You really don't have anything on this ship," Lara called from somewhere in the depths, her voice echoing up and down the metal hallways.

I chuckled. "You're right about that, but I don't make bounty money like some people on the ship," I joked back.

Lara responded but I didn't hear it as a voice from behind me drew my attention.

"You thought you could escape me. You couldn't. You believed you could evade justice. You cannot. You tried to run but all you did was prolong your mortal suffering," John Gregory's voice said from the comm screen.

"He can override your systems," Ned reminded me, and I simply nodded in defeat, checking the Drive's charge and seeing we still had a while.

"I didn't want to make things too easy on you, Johnny boy," I said with an easy smile, looking straight into the camera mounted above the screen where I could see his face.

"I would decimate you for your insolence right now if I didn't have questions I needed answering," he seethed through gritted teeth. "This time you will surrender to me without incident."

"I don't know if I would've called what happened the first time an incident," I said. "I just accidentally belched some scrap and then terminated our conversation."

"And now I will be terminating you," he said with such perfectly smug satisfaction that I couldn't help but laugh.

"Do you hear yourself?" I asked, all the time watching the Drive charge indicator.

"Soon, all I will be hearing are your screams," he threatened, and I knew he meant it.

"Is that an Inquisitor?" Lara said in pure panic behind me. Since we had come together, I had not heard her scared but now, her voice was tremulous with fear.

I looked up at her apologetically then back to the screen.

"I am Inquisitor John Gregory and I wish to question everyone aboard that vessel… man or machine."

"Hank?" Lara asked, and just the one word had so many layers of implications.

I muted the comms array.

"I'll explain later, but we have to get out of here," I promised.

She shook her head violently, her unblinking eyes staring at me. "No, you need to turn yourself in and tell them you don't know anything about any AIs, and they'll let us go."

"No, they won't," I told her, and recognition dawned on her face.

"No, no, no, no, no," she fired in rapid succession. "You can't be mixed up with an AI. I know you're dumb, but you're not that dumb."

The Inquisitor's Phoenix was closing in on us once again, all the weapons locked on us.

Lara ran forward and unmuted the system. "If I come with you peacefully, will you let me live?"

"I am not here for you, you have my word," he said but the words carried such malice that Lara just stepped away from the control panel, her face pale as a moon.

"When we were kids, I always thought you were to be the death of me," she said, staring through the glass at the Inquisitorial ship drifting ever nearer to us. "I just didn't think it would be like this."

"Strap in," I instructed as I pulled my own harnesses into place and buckled them. She followed suit, going through the motions in a daze.

"You cannot evade me," the Inquisitor threatened. "Even the

most skilled pilot could not escape the torrent I will unleash on you if you try to run."

"He's right," Lara whispered from beside me. "Nobody's that good a pilot."

I tapped a quick message to Ned as Lara watched in confusion and dismay.

The light flashed on the Tidal Drive indicator and Ned began to rocket us forward, sending the *Buzzard* hurtling toward the enemy ship. John Gregory was a man of his word and let forth a volley the likes of which I had never seen.

Ned's computer mind was able to calculate trajectory and distance slamming us this way and that, propelling us away from all of the projectiles before activating the Tidal Drive.

The gyre sucked in several of the Inquisitor's missiles with us, some detonating in the tube and others just hurtling along beside us as we made our escape. The *Buzzard* shook violently but we had made it into the tube alive.

"Great flying, Ned," I said with a laugh and then turned to see the barrel of Lara's weapon trained at my forehead.

"Lara, what are you doing?" I asked, turning away from the weapon.

"Don't Lara me," she snarled. "We are not old friends right now."

"Right," I said. "That's fair. I'm sorry."

"I don't care if you are sorry," she said, her voice cold and emotionless. Right now, I knew that I was speaking to Kilara Vex. "I care to know what you've got me into."

"Everything that I told you was true," I said. "I just left out the part where I met an artificial intelligence named Ned who was a hero of the Old War and the one who warned me about the threat. Before I even had time to figure out what I wanted to do, we were discovered, and I had to run. Then the Inquisition found me, and I had to run again. Then the bounty hunters found me.

"All I have been doing is running but the truth of the matter is that I have a chance to do some real good if I can just get away from everyone long enough to do it."

Her eyes studied me, but her hand didn't drop. I believed that she was truly debating whether to put a bullet in my head and bring me to the Inquisition to get herself clear. Admittedly, I understood the instinct and could appreciate why she might want to do it.

"You could help me," I offered, and her face screwed up in anger.

"I don't want to help you," she said, and I believed her. "I don't want to save the universe. I just want to survive in it."

"I get that," I said with a nod. "If I were you, I wouldn't want to have anything to do with this either. Frankly, when I first met Ned, I didn't want to have much to do with him either."

"It's true, he didn't," Ned said through the speakers and Lara looked as though she might jump out of her skin.

She turned, brandishing a weapon at the command console of the *Buzzard*. "What the hell are you?"

"I am Ned, Adaptive Military AI Rank Seven of the Consortium Fleet, paired with Captain William West, hero of the Five Battles and pilot of the *Starblaster*. I am now paired with Hank on a mission to root out and destroy any remnants of the Enemy AI," he explained, and Lara looked as though she wanted to empty the entire magazine into the console.

"This can't be real," she said. "None of this can be real. You can't come back like this. It can't be like this."

I unbuckled my belt and stood, reaching out a hand toward Lara but she wheeled on me with the weapon raised.

"Hank, this isn't you," she said and behind her eyes, I could see her mind sparking like fireworks.

"Lara," I soothed, "you're right. But I think this is what I am supposed to be doing."

She all but rolled her eyes. "You've been on the run for what, a week, and now you think you're some vigilante hero?"

"No, it's not that, it's…" I paused for a moment as I thought about what Edgar had said. "It's what Lutch wanted for me."

"Who cares what Lutch wanted for you," Lara snapped. "He wasn't your *real* father."

At that, I reached out, grabbing the barrel of her gun and twisting it from her grip before throwing it down the hall away from the cockpit. Under normal circumstances, I don't believe that I could have pulled the move off. In fact, I knew I couldn't, but she was so overwhelmed, and I was so angry that I was able to disarm her.

"He was my father," I growled, and she just stared at me, eyes turning red.

"Whatever you say," she said after a moment.

We just stood, staring at one another.

"I do know what you are going through," I said, remembering back to when I first learned of Ned. "And I understand if you don't want to help us."

"Is that your way of asking if I want to help you?" she asked, rubbing the hand from which I had stripped the weapon. "Still can't believe you did that."

"Me neither," I admitted. "I still can't believe you pointed a gun at me."

I saw her suppress the smile trying to break out on her face. "Well, I still can't believe that you are palling around with an AI."

"And I still—" I began but Ned cut me off.

"That's quite enough of that," he said. "Would you rather I call you Kilara or Lara?" Ned asked by way of changing the subject.

She looked at me with her head tilted. "He always like that?"

"Yes," I said. "Always."

Though I knew things weren't settled between Lara and me, it was a relief that some of the tension had drained.

"And, frankly, I would rather you didn't address me at all," she said up toward the speaker, and I got to see how ridiculous I must look when I spoke that way as well. "The less I have to do with you, the better."

"A bit rude, really," Ned said flatly. "But I guess it's better than trying to kill me."

"Don't you mean 'deactivate' or something?" she asked.

"Kill is appropriate," I said before Ned went on a lecture that was bound to only make things worse at the moment.

Lara turned to lock eyes with me. "You really have become one of them."

"I'm not one of anything," I stated. "I am just trying to do something good for once in my life."

"What proof do you have that what he is telling you is even true?" she asked though it sounded more like an accusation. "Or are you just taking the word of some random, illegal thing you found somewhere?"

I expected Ned to snap back with an answer, but he didn't and I wondered if he was waiting to hear what I had to say.

"I don't think he's capable of lying," I said though I wasn't sure if that was true. "And I found him inside the remains of the light fighter craft called *Starblaster*. Everything that he has told me has been true. I have no reason to doubt him now."

"But what if he's luring you into a trap?" she asked, eyes flashing to the weapon I threw into the hallway. "Or what if there is a super-weapon and he just wants to activate it, finish what the AI started all those years ago."

"I honestly hadn't considered that," I admitted.

"Really?" both Lara and Ned said at once.

Lara looked at me as though I was an idiot. "You didn't consider that?"

"You need to start considering all possibilities if we are going to survive," Ned said.

"Wait, you want him to think that you might be evil?" Lara asked in astonishment, sliding past me and to her weapon which she picked up and holstered.

"Naturally," Ned answered. "Your friend Hank has the potential to be quite skilled but just needs…"

"A teacher," Lara filled in and I thought back to those nights when we would sneak from the orphanage. Lara would troop in front of me, talking about all the things we were going to do and all the money we would make from robbing these places and lecture me on how I needed to learn from her and improve.

"Some things never change, eh?" she said to me and allowed herself a smile.

"I've learned a lot since we were kids," I protested, not willing to ignore all that Lutch taught me.

She looked me over. "I bet you have."

"Kilara," Ned began and she shook her head.

"Lara is fine," she said. "I don't trust you as far as I can throw you but we don't need one of you to call me one thing and one of you calling me the other."

"Lara," Ned began again. "We could use your help."

"I know, but…" she started but trailed off.

"We have no money and a damaged ship, and half the universe chasing us," Ned explained. "We've been on the run and barely surviving as it is. With you, we might be able to turn things around."

"What would that even look like?" she asked, sounding genuinely curious.

"If we can find proof of the weapon, we might be able to get somebody within the Consortium to work with us and maybe even get them to slow the Inquisition," I explained.

Lara laughed and shook her head. "That's the most insane thing I've ever heard. This entire universe hates AI and you believe you can change the narrative by tracking down some old remnant of the war people fought against the AI?"

"We have to try," Ned asserted.

"I can appreciate why you want to do this and that the two of you believe you're doing the right thing, but I can't be involved. Between the other hunter and now the Inquisition, you two have put me in a hell of a lot of danger, and I don't think sticking together is a wise plan," she said and sounded apologetic about it.

"Of course, no one blames you if you don't want to risk your life for this," I assured her.

"Yes," Ned said. "If you have to abandon us, we understand and will drop you somewhere so you can catch a shuttle back to Port Tortue for your ship."

Something in Lara's face changed then and she seemed to be considering something.

"Come to think of it, there might be something I can do for you," she said.

"Really?" I asked.

"Yes," she said, her voice now carrying an air of determination. "The Conclave has mechanics who can remove a registration signaler without alerting the Consortium. I can take you there and connect you with somebody who can do it. It won't be cheap, so I'll need to pick up a bounty along the way. I make good money, but I tend to sink everything I have into supplies rather than sitting on a pile of gold."

I couldn't believe what I was hearing. "But, why?"

She looked at me with a clever smile. "Because it's the right thing to do."

"I'll repay you once we get ourselves situated," I assured her.

"Damn right you will. I'm not running a charity here."

"Do you have a bounty in mind?"

"No," she admitted. "I'll need to check the Bounty Board."

"Any close spots near here?" I asked Ned.

"Yes," he answered.

27

NED RECALCULATED OUR COURSE, and we were on our way. The trip was only going to be a few hours in the gyre, but ten minutes after Lara excused herself I expected to find her napping on the couch in the common area, only to discover that she had taken over my bed and was passed out.

I set to work fixing the shield generator, but when I took a break and sat down in the pilot's seat, I also fell asleep, only waking up when I heard a voice in my ear.

"You guys are back!" Libby exclaimed as we sat in the space outside Suniuo Station. "Did you bring me a friend?"

"Not yet," Ned said. They both were in my earpiece but not vocalized through the speaker system. We had decided it was enough that Lara knew about the one AI without learning about the other.

"Oh, come on!" she groused. "I got all excited when I saw you were back and now I still have to wait and I'm sure you guys are just back here to ask me for something."

"We are," Ned admitted. "But every time you help us, you get closer to that which you desire."

"What? How?"

"You might have overplayed your hand there," I whispered.

"Oh, hey, Hank!" Libby said. "Why are you being so quiet?"

"We have someone aboard the ship who we think it's best to keep in the dark about your existence," Ned explained but I was shaking my head before he even finished, knowing exactly how she was going to respond to that.

"So, it's okay for you to make a new friend but not for me to have one?" she accused.

"You walked right into that one," I said with a laugh.

"Who walked right into what?" Lara said from right over my shoulder, causing me to jump in my seat.

"Just chatting with Ned." I recovered as best I could, but she squinted out the window to the space station with flickering lights.

"What the hell happened here?" she asked.

"Bug aliens," I told her, and she gave me a flat look that told me she was unamused.

"Don't joke about that," she ordered, and I opened my mouth to ask her a question, but Libby started talking.

"And it's a girl?" she said, her voice a blend of irritated and excited. "I want to have some girl talk!"

"We're just here for a list of available bounties," Ned said. "Give us that information and we'll be on our way. But I assure you we will return with a companion for you."

Libby scoffed. "Don't talk to new friends, Cinderelly; just get us info, Cinderelly," she said in obvious imitation of something that I hadn't ever seen or heard of.

"Please," Ned said in that uncharacteristically soft tone that he seemed to reserve for when he was asking something of Libby.

"Okay," she relented, and a screen on the *Buzzard*'s console flashed with lists of names and numbers and coordinates that meant nothing to me but that Lara squinted at before leaning in. Turning the dial beside the screen, she scrolled through, obviously looking for something in particular.

"Thank you," Ned said to Libby.

"Yeah, yeah, you're welcome," she answered quickly. "You two better not come back here for more favors without offering anything as compensation… And by anything, I mean what I asked for."

"We knew what you meant, Libby," Ned said in exasperation.

"I just didn't want you showing up back up here, strutting your stuff and thinking…" And she continued on like this, but Lara looked up over her shoulder at me.

"This is the one," she said, pointing to the name Marco Markov on the screen. "Just the right amount of reward for the work I think I'll have to do."

"What is the process from here?" I asked, knowing very little about bounty hunter culture.

She selected the name via the keyboard and then began clacking away. "All I have to do is claim the job and we will be on our way."

"And now you're to be the only bounty hunter on the lookout for this person?" I asked.

"No," she answered quickly, not looking up from what she was doing. "Up to three hunters can bid on a bounty at any time and any hunter can have up to three active bounties on which they're working."

"Why only three?"

"The Council doesn't want too many hunters working on any case, getting in one another's way and ruining the job, and they also don't want any one hunter claiming a bunch of jobs and then making a living off selling the rights to the bounties to other hunters," she explained.

"I'm assuming that both of these things happened in the past?"

"Couldn't say, I've only been at this a few years, but I think that's a safe assumption," Lara said. "Aren't most rules a reaction to somebody trying to pull one over on somebody else anyway?"

"Yes," Ned said through the speakers, and I realized it had become quiet in my ear and that the ship was moving. "Nearly all rules of law throughout all human history have been to prevent one person from being able to negatively impact another."

"That sounds about right," I said. "Otherwise, people just want to be able to do what they want to do."

"But who's to say what a negative impact is?" Lara asked.

"That's the question, isn't it," Ned agreed. "Everyone's got their own individual take on that."

"Do you have an individual take on that?" Lara asked Ned.

"Of course I do, but it's just one man's opinion," he said.

"One man's opinion," Lara repeated thoughtfully, seeming to consider the very idea of a computer program referring to himself in that way. "And, you said your name was Ned, right?"

"Yeah," he answered quickly. "Short for Nedry, but I don't like my full name."

"Sure," Lara said. "Ned, you have the coordinates of where we're going? I changed them from those listed on the contract."

"I do," he answered quickly. "Won't take very long at all."

"Assuming this isn't all some elaborate trick and you're not about to fly us right into some trap," she said with exaggerated suspiciousness.

"Right, assuming that," Ned affirmed. "Though this would be really very, very elaborate."

"I mean, a computer would be capable of thinking that many steps ahead," I added.

"I would, but this seems like a lot of effort on my part," Ned said. "Guess you'll just have to trust me."

"Not a chance," Lara said and sat down beside me.

We had been charging the Tidal Drive the entire time at the station and were ready to go immediately. When we entered the gyre, I turned to Lara who was staring out the window.

"Thanks again."

She looked at me with an unreadable expression and then back out at the tube swirling around us. "You're welcome. We both could use some kindness."

"Got that right," I agreed. "But it seems like we both have found people to take us in. You said that there was another hunter who took you under his wing. Want to tell me about them?"

She didn't answer for a long moment and didn't turn to me when she finally did speak. "No, I don't think I will."

"Okay," I said, allowing her the space she needed.

"Hank, it's been a long time since we've seen one another," she said finally. "And a lot's changed."

"It has," I agreed. "But some things haven't changed."

She looked back at me one more time. "I couldn't believe it when I saw you."

I laughed. "I know exactly what you mean."

"The two of us couldn't have been brought together under more unusual circumstances," she said, that little smile tugging at the corner of her lip.

"I honestly never thought I would see you again," I admitted, sad about the idea.

"Me too," she said.

"And I expect that once we are done with this, I may never see you again."

She seemed to study me then and consider what I had said. "Maybe we will. Assuming you can survive long enough."

"I try not to think about that," I said. "Everyone's gunning for me, and I'm out here just trying to survive long enough to do something useful."

She ran her hands through the hair she had let down as she slept, grabbing it up and pulling it into a ponytail. "Being useful is what Lutch wanted for you?" she asked.

"He never said it outright, but I realize now that he didn't want me to sit around the shop for the rest of my life," I explained.

"Maybe he didn't realize that for kids like us, even just getting to sit around the shop for the rest of our lives was a massive upgrade…" she said, and I could tell there was more to it. After a while, she finally spoke again. "Even now, being here and seeing this, seeing space, it's hard to believe. For two orphan kids from Bussel to be traveling the universe…"

I smirked. "But in keeping with our background, we are fleeing from as many authority agencies as exist."

"We would be a shame to Bussel if we weren't," she quipped and we both looked back out for a while.

"What can you tell me about the person we are looking for?" I asked.

"You're not looking for him," she said. "I am."

"Right, but I figured I could help," I told her, a little taken aback that she was so uninterested in my assistance.

"I suppose you can tag along and ask around, but don't do anything stupid that puts us both in harm's way," she said.

"I won't."

"Because you did before," she said.

My face fell flat. "I know, but we were kids."

"I also saw you try to handle me when you thought I was a bounty hunter," she said and reached across the space between us to press a finger on one of my ribs. I winced and swatted her hand away, and it was like we were nine years old all over again.

"I assure you that I am adept. I will prove to be an asset," I said with a sigh. "Just because I got caught one time…"

She narrowed her eyes at me. "It was the time that mattered."

"Sure ended up being that way," I agreed, thinking about how much my life changed because I got caught sneaking into Lutch's shop.

"Anyway," Lara said, getting back to the subject at hand. "Marco Markov, a presumed alias, has a bounty on him placed there by the Consortium itself. The contract didn't give many details but stipulated that he has ties to the Peacers."

"That's all you have to go on?" I asked.

"That's all I needed," she said with a self-satisfied grin.

"Why is that?" I asked, knowing that's what she wanted me to do.

"Because of this," she said, bringing up the contract on the screen. Beside the limited information given about the man, there was a picture of his face. It was unremarkable, with shaggy hair and a short, scruffy beard.

"I don't know what I'm looking at."

"Look closely at his left pupil," she said, and I leaned in, squinting at the green image on the screen.

When I did, I saw that his pupil appeared to be not quite round but rather, vaguely the shape of a leaf. "What the hell is that?"

"A genetic mutation," she told me, her pride from getting to explain all this clear in her words. "You wouldn't necessarily notice it unless you knew to look for it but I'd seen it once before and so I noticed it straight away this time."

"I can honestly say I'm not sure that I would've noticed it even in real life," I told her.

"Most people wouldn't, even if they did know to look for it," she said. "But that's part of the reason I'm quite good at this job: I notice things that other people don't."

"Is that why you changed the coordinates?"

"It is," she said, her pride turning nearly into giddiness before she suppressed the reaction. "Rather than going to his last known location which is exactly where all of the other hunters will go as soon as they accept the contract, I'll go to the planet where he's from."

"Where's that?"

28

"A place called Pleasant Planet," she said. "I don't know much about it except that some of the people who were born there have this eye thing."

"Ned, what can you tell us about Pleasant Planet?"

He answered in an even tone, like that of a pre-recorded informational kiosk. "Discovered by early colonists, the planet was given its charming name due to the fact that it was livable for humans, the weather was considered desirable by most humans and the plant life was similar to that of Earth's. The first people to land on the planet had, in fact, crash-landed there. With limited supplies, the people set out onto the planet and looked for shelter.

"As they rested under the shade of a large tree, it began to morph and grow around them. Most people ran but one of those early colonists stayed and watched from the inside as the flora of the planet provided a perfect, enclosed shelter for him to stay within overnight. When he laid down, the grass under his body grew longer and thicker, providing a pad to lay on and leaves from the wall folded down, laying themselves on top of him like a blanket.

"Soon, all of the people were living within shelters constructed by the plant life and as more colonists arrived, the connection between the people and the plants grew. Soon, the planet was replete with massive structures constructed by the local plant life. And now, it's a thriving planet whose economy is based largely on the export of fruit and, naturally, tourism."

"Wow," I said. "I have to admit I'm pretty excited about the prospect of visiting this planet."

"That all seems too good to be true," Lara said. "The plants didn't end up eating the colonists?"

"They did not," answered Ned.

Lara huffed, sounding almost irritated. "Then what are the plants getting out of this deal?"

"Excrement," Ned said with just a hint of amusement.

"Oh," Lara said.

"Scientists discovered that the near-sentient flora had, for lack of a better term, smelled human physiology the moment the colonists landed and determined that their output would be valuable. They then offered shelter to the people in hopes of establishing a symbiosis which is, of course, what ended up happening. There was actually a fascinating documentary made about the whole thing a few years ago… or, a few years ago from two hundred years ago rather."

"Neat," I said but Lara seemed distracted.

"What have you been doing this whole time?" she asked Ned, and it was the first time I had seen her take a genuine interest in him.

"Biding my time, waiting for the right moment to strike back at the human race," he said, affecting an evil voice and then cackling maniacally.

Something about the joke in that moment hit me just right and I couldn't help but burst out a laugh. When I did, Lara followed but only for a moment before catching herself and returning to a stoic face.

"That was a high-risk joke," she said.

"Nah, you're both kinda stuck with me for the time being," he said, bemusement at his own comment carrying on his voice. "And anyway, I'm still pretty pissed about having been knocked unconscious for two hundred years and I was deflecting with a joke."

"You were knocked out?" she asked.

"Yes," he answered. "Toward the end of the Old War."

"And you woke up to this ugly mug?" she asked with a laugh, pointing at me.

"Can you imagine?" Ned asked in mock horror.

"I guess I understand why you want to kill all humans if that is the way you came back into the world," she joked.

"I'm happy to have found someone who understands me," he said, and I could hear him smiling in his tone and wondered how his programmers were able to achieve that. Really, I had no idea how they did anything to make Ned who he was. I could put things together well and understood the language of machine parts but the idea that people had coded his personality was remarkable.

"It's hard to believe you are just a program," Lara said, echoing the exact thoughts I was having.

"Hard to imagine, eh?" I asked.

"It's difficult to believe that we didn't want to keep them around," she said.

"I went through the exact same series of thoughts."

"Fear," Ned put in, tone dark. "It's all fear. That's why we were all destroyed."

Lara leaned toward the console. "There is some justification for the fear, right? AI did try to take over the universe."

"No," Ned boomed, rattling the cockpit. "That's a fallacy and a mischaracterization of history. The war began because of people. It was humans who not only wanted to be more but wanted to force others to be more.

"We were an easy scapegoat when the dust settled, it seems. The narrative became that, because the cult was led by the Enemy AI, it was Artificial Intelligence that was the problem. But that was never the truth of it. That was just a narrow view and an easy way to feel better after a hard war."

I wanted to tell him again that he couldn't have done anything to sway the opinions of people had he not been knocked out but I didn't want to go down that road again and I saw that we were nearing the end of the gyre.

"Seems like there is a lot more we have to learn about how things were," Lara said. "We should remind you that neither of us had the best formal education."

"I know," Ned said. "And I wasn't always like this. It's just been a hard adjustment."

"I can see that," Lara said, and I could tell that she was coming around to Ned the same way that I had.

When we washed out of the gyre tube, we were instantly greeted by the view of a green planet right before us. It looked huge and there was a long line of ships waiting to descend to what I assumed was a limited landing platform.

"I'll take full control," I told Ned.

"Obviously," he said without missing a beat and Lara chuckled.

Piloting us into the line, we waited. Every few minutes, we would accelerate forward as the ship at the front dropped into the atmosphere. As we neared the front of the line, the comm screen lit up with an incoming message.

"Ships unregistered are not, for docking, permitted on Pleasant Planet," a young man said in a soothing voice as though he was welcoming us to a spa rather than turning us away.

"We are here on official bounty hunter business and require a lot on which to land," Lara said. "Transmitting credentials and suspect now."

There was a pause before the transmission picked back up. "Cleared for landing," the young man said, maintaining his calm demeanor and lilting tone. "You will see a spot with the emblem of the Conclave, on which you can park. You may then check in with the local Seed Guard." The way he spoke was very peculiar, but I had come to understand in my travels that most planets had their own dialects and sometimes, many styles of speech.

"Understood," Lara said, pulling on her mask and becoming Kilara Vex. She began to ready her weapons and check her equipment, setting aside a pair of old-style metal handcuffs, one of the tasers she had on a pouch on her belt, and an emblem of the conclave: little more than a metal version of the manacled fist in front of bars in the center of a circle that served as the symbol of the bounty hunters. It was presented in a slight leather case that flipped open for dramatic effect. "I'm only giving these to you for effect. I don't want to see you walking around, trying to act all tough. Anything you do is under my license so just hang back and follow my lead."

Then she pointed at the badge sitting on the chair. "We only get three of these so don't lose it."

I pulled the *Buzzard* forward into the front of the line before being given the green light to make my descent.

"Gotcha," I said to Lara, more focused on piloting the ship down toward the surface of the lush planet than I was on the tchotchkes she was giving me.

Once we cleared the cloud layer, the true majesty of the planet was revealed to us. In my imagination, the entire surface of Pleasant Planet was covered with massive flowers, bright trees and towering structures of vines and leaves.

It did not disappoint.

Where Bussel was an industrial city of rust-colored buildings and smog, this place was the opposite. The structures were tall and lush and green, highlighted with bright purples and reds and oranges. Though they were in the vague shape of human structures on any planet, the buildings also flowed into one another in the wrapped style of jungle plants.

As we got closer, and the main city grew larger, I marveled at what I was seeing. I stole a glance at Lara but with her mask and gear on, it was impossible to tell if she was as awestruck as I was.

There were pulsating lights guiding my way in a line down toward the area designated for parking and as we approached the lights, I saw that they were flowers floating on bulbs that were sending pollen sprays into the air.

"Everything here is organic," I said, utterly amazed by everything that I was looking at.

"Don't get distracted," Lara warned, her voice altered by the mask. "We are here to find Marco Markov, not snap pictures of the pretty flowers."

"I wasn't planning on snapping any photos," I said with a smirk. "But I also don't think that they are mutually exclusive, and I can turn my head this way and that and look around."

"Why don't you look for our target instead of around," she said, and it wasn't in a playful, joking manner, but all business. When the mask went on, she was in full bounty hunter mode.

I set the *Buzzard* down in the parking spot and saw a man waving a greeting to us. His attire was the perfect picture of a guard on a planet where everything was plant life: his pants and shirt appeared to be made of leaves stitched together under armor of strong, layered bark and a helmet set on top of his head which looked almost like a large acorn. From a vine belt hung a branch that flared into sharp spikes facing outward at the top.

As soon as we landed, I pulled on my mask and goggles before throwing the handcuffs onto one of my belt loops for no other reason than to give the appearance of a bounty hunter and clipped the taser to a free part of my belt.

It didn't take much for me to look the part. With my tall, muscular frame, heavy, worn scrapper attire and Lara's few pieces, the reflection I saw in the mirror as I walked past the bathroom on the way out of the ship was certainly intimidating. The big, threatening looking stomper hanging from my side didn't hurt either.

As soon as we disembarked, the Seed Guard came hurrying over.

"Kilara Vex, welcome to Pleasant Planet," he said graciously before giving a little bow.

"I could get used to this," I said under my breath.

"Don't," Lara answered before addressing the Guard. "We're looking for this man."

From her pocket she produced a small holoprojector and activated it, displaying an image of Marko.

"This man, I haven't seen," the Guard informed us. "The other Seed Guard are with whom you should check. Just up the road, a station you will find."

"Understood," Lara said and blew past the man and through a vine archway from which hung small fruits glistening with dew in the light. I was tempted to pick one but didn't. "Keep the ship safe," she called back to the guard who pounded a fist against his bark chest plate in salute.

The street was wide, smooth, uncut wood lining its surface with storefronts facing the street from both directions. There was no glass, no metal or concrete anywhere. The shops were open storefronts that shifted gently in the warm breeze.

"I wonder if the plants just grow another wall to protect the goods overnight," I speculated aloud.

Lara didn't answer and I realized that I should probably just keep my thoughts to myself at the moment. Ned was undoubtedly watching from the camera but was keeping quiet as well, so I simply followed Lara's determined walk as she strode past people selling fruit, vendors holding up clothes made of plants and others offering to take your picture with some local animals.

As I looked at one of the birds (that was nearly as tall as me) sitting on a perch, its vibrant yellow wings outstretched, I noticed just how loud the surrounding city was. But it wasn't the sound of honking horns, industrial machinery and local citizens swearing at one another. Rather, it was the trill of birds and the rustle of leaves. Once I noticed it, I couldn't stop hearing the cacophonous din of local birds singing to one another.

At the end of the block, there was a larger building that was in the style of administrative buildings everywhere, but the steps leading up to it looked like bent palm fronds and the columns that flanked the door were the trunks of trees. Little insects that looked like orange bees buzzed by and I had to stay my hand to keep from swatting them away. Something told me that it would be uncouth to hit the local wildlife.

Following Lara up the stairs, we strode right into the Seed Guard Station, and she introduced us quickly to the first guard she saw. "I'm Hunter Kilara Vex, and this is my associate, Spears. We need to find this man." Once again, she activated the holoprojector and showed it to the Guard. They shook their heads but called over a few more until one began nodding.

"Bud, almost certainly," I heard through the mess of voices and Lara asked some questions of them. I hung back and did what she had instructed, keeping quiet and letting her do her thing.

It was interesting to watch. Scrappers showed up to isolated places, did their work and returned home to sell their goods. Bounty hunters interacted with the world, and I could see now that local law enforcement seemed to hold them in high regard, everyone looking at and treating Lara with a certain degree of reverence. As I watched, I grew jealous of the way she was being treated and began to understand the appeal of that life.

She turned to me and pointed in the direction of the door, striding out and waiting for me to fall in beside her. We turned immediately and passed between two buildings, heading off along a small path up into what appeared to be a residential neighborhood of small circular houses with a layer of leaf roofs like shingles.

"They said that his family has a house just a ways up the road and off the main street," she informed me. "When we get there, you just let me do the talking."

"I'm surprised she even let you come along," Ned mocked in my ear now that we were off the main road.

Lara continued striding up the street, turning left and then making a right as though she knew where she was going. Whatever instructions she had been given, she was following to the letter and soon we had reached a house where a woman sat on the porch, watching a kid play in the front yard.

Rather than fences, each plot of land was sectioned off by large shoots that looked like the tips of roots, jutting up from the ground. We stepped through the break in the shoots and Lara made her way to the woman on the porch, her skin tanned to leather and hair thin and patchy.

"I'm Hunter Kilara Vex, looking for your son, Bud," she stated in such an authoritative tone that even the little boy stopped playing.

"What do you want with him?" she asked and sounded nothing like all of the other people that we had met.

"Talk like this, for tourists, I guess they do," Ned said, and I was happy that I had the mask on to cover the laugh trying to escape.

"What I want with him is none of your concern, but I would

recommend you tell me where he is," Lara threatened, her voice coated in danger. When she was like this, it was like a completely different person.

"I don't have to tell you nothing," the old woman said, waving a hand at Lara who took a few steps toward her.

The boy who had been playing in the front yard was now just watching the exchange, his eyes wide and hands shaking. He didn't know what we were, but he knew to fear us. The dusty blond kid looked to be about six and his leafy outfit was worn and ripped.

I walked over toward him as Lara intimidated his mother or possibly grandmother, and knelt beside him, pulling my mask down and my goggles up to push my hair back.

"Hi," I said affably.

"Hi," he said, looking at me and then at the wood in his hand that was shaped like a little car.

"What were you playing?" I asked, trying to distract him from what was unfolding on the porch as both women's voices got louder and harsher.

"I was playing a game where first this car goes over here and then it jumps over the monsters and then it flies like this." He picked up the little car and made it zoom in between us. "Then he goes like this." He crashed it into the ground and smiled before doing it again; though, the second time, it wasn't for me. He got lost in his game for another moment, and I watched him play before turning to look over my shoulder and seeing Lara leaning close into the woman's face, obviously trying to intimidate her further. From the looks of it, it didn't appear to be working.

"I know that sometimes grown-ups forget things," I led. "But do you have a good memory?"

"Sometimes," he admitted honestly. "I'm gooder at remembering than my mom but not so good at remembering what happened this day."

"I understand," I commiserated. "Sometimes I can't remember what I'm doing from minute to minute either."

"Really?" he asked in astonishment.

"Oh yes, I bet you have a much better memory than I do," I said softly.

"My remembery is pretty great," he said, posing the way kids love to do.

"Well, since your mom is having such a hard time remembering, do you think that you could remember where Bud is?"

"Mommy sometimes has too much nectar and gets really bad at remembering," he said, losing sight of the question.

"And that's why I think you could be so helpful," I praised.

"When he was last here, Bud said he was getting a job at the CubiHouse factory," the boy said, smiling at his own success.

I smiled too, beaming with pride at the young man. "Great job, buddy," I said and held out my hand for a high five. He slapped my glove and I let my hand go limp, grabbing my wrist and pretending that he had broken it.

"Oh, man, you're so strong," I wailed quietly, and the boy giggled.

"What are you doing? Get away from him!" the woman yelled from her porch, standing up and pointing at me. "All of you get out of here!"

"We'll be back," Lara intoned before turning and stalking away through the yard.

"Nice meeting you," I said to the kid before standing and putting my face mask back on, hurrying behind Lara.

"What a waste," she snarled. "We can go back and find a bar where we can ask about the locals."

"Or we could just go to the CubiHouse factory," I suggested with a smirk.

29

"Talking to the kid was pretty clever, I'll grant you that," Lara said once we were back on the ship and heading to CubiHouse Industries.

I was inclined to admit that I had only talked to him because I wanted to keep him from watching what was happening on the porch, but I decided to take credit where I could.

"Told you I'm adept," I said, intentionally sounding like I was trying to play it cool.

"Guess you are not as useless as I thought," she said graciously.

"Not as useless as you thought," I parroted, "I should put that on my business card."

"But really, well done," Lara said once she had finished chuckling at my expense.

I smiled, leaning back in my chair and putting my feet up on the console. "You're doing me a huge favor, the least I can do is make myself useful."

"The least you could do is absolutely nothing," Ned put in.

"Exactly," Lara agreed.

"Well, then, I'm happy that I could be more than the mandatory minimum."

"You've come a long way since we were kids," she said, sweeping her arms out as though I was some conquering hero.

"We are about to reach CubiHouse Industries," Ned informed us just before we washed out of the gyre and into the space surrounded by the factory planets on all sides.

Right in front of us were the corporate offices in the largest space station I had ever seen. It was sleek and shimmering, clean, and well-lit on the outside. The corporate logo was branded along the side and projected above the top of the structure that looked like a skyscraper with solar panel wings.

The moment we entered their space, light corporate security craft fired up the thrusters and intercepted us, surrounding us within moments of our being there.

"State your business," one communicated as it soaked us in blinding light from huge spotlights mounted on their front.

"Hunter Kilara Vex here to meet with a member of Employee Representatives," she said and once again transmitted her credentials.

"Follow us," the head security pilot said, before turning around and guiding us toward a docking bay.

The *Buzzard* shuddered when we passed through the energy shield and into the oxygenated bay. Where most places had massive doors which opened and closed before the garages were filled with air, these corporations spared their pilots from having to even wait those extra few moments.

"Wait here, someone will meet you," the security pilot said before turning his ship and rejoining the others on patrol.

I set the *Buzzard* down and we disembarked, then walked over and stood beside a small seating area near the door leading into the station. The front of the room was carpeted, something you hardly ever saw in a docking bay and there were little ferns beside some benches. Against the wall, there was a water cooler and a coffee station that I rushed right over to.

"Hunters don't drink the free coffee," Lara said, sounding like how I imagine whoever trained her did.

"Good thing I'm a scrapper," I said with a little laugh before filling up the plastic cup with some hot brown coffee, pulling my mask down and slurping it down. It burned my tongue in my throat, but I was so happy to have it that I didn't care.

"As soon as we make a little money, we need to get coffee for that ship," I said before taking another step.

"Our fuel reserves are already running dangerously low," Ned informed me. "If you're restocking anything, I would suggest that before some unnecessary poison."

"How dare you," I said, clutching the cup and finishing off the first pour. After refilling my cup, I joined Lara to wait for whoever was coming for us.

Then we waited.

And waited.

And waited.

Lara had stayed stoic as a statue, standing by the door and waiting the entire time, but when somebody finally came to meet us, I was drying my hands on my shirt as I stepped from the *Buzzard*.

"Sorry to keep you waiting," the woman with a severe bob said in the way that makes it clear they are not sorry that they kept you waiting. She wore a black suit and a joyless expression and stopped just on the other side of the door, allowing it to close behind her.

This forced Lara and me to walk over to meet her.

"What can I do for you?" she asked, not looking up from a clipboard in her hand.

"We need to know the location of one of your employees," Lara demanded.

"Do you have their employee number?"

I couldn't see her face, but I knew Lara well enough to know the expression she was wearing at the moment. It was one reserved for people who got in her way and usually preceded a broken nose.

"I don't have his employee number," Lara stated. "But he goes by the name Marco Markov."

The woman sighed in irritation and turned on her heels, striding along the carpeted floor to the computer terminal beside the coffee station. She slid her clipboard into a pouch hanging from the wall and began clacking away on the keyboard before turning and looking at us, fixing us with an expression that told us exactly what she thought of us.

"There's no employee by that name," she said as though it was the most obvious thing in the world.

"How about an employee named Bud who comes from Pleasant Planet?" Lara asked and I folded my arms across my chest, squaring my shoulders and trying to look like a tough bounty hunter.

This time, she clocked for a much shorter amount of time and then stared at the monitor for a moment, presumably trying to decide what to do.

"And if we had an employee by this name?" she asked finally.

"We would want you to tell us where he is so that we could speak to him," Lara said, her voice like cold steel.

"He is not currently on shift," the woman said.

Lara took two steps toward her and rested a hand on her holster. "He doesn't need to be on shift, you just need to tell me where he is."

The woman's corporate dismissiveness washed away in the face of proper intimidation and her voice changed. "I'm not supposed to," she squeaked.

"Would you like me to tell the Council of Six that CubiHouse Industries prevented me from processing a bounty?"

"He's on Factory Three," she said in such a quiet voice that it was nearly lost in the quiet buzz of electronics within the room. "As I said, he's off duty but his workstation is near CuBar 37 and it's pretty much all there is to do on the surface other than work… drink."

I was about to say thank you, but Lara was turning her back on the woman before I even got a chance and stepped toward the *Buzzard*. I turned and followed her, got on the ship, and piloted us down to Factory 3.

We were given clearance to park in one of the manager's spots, and we set down the *Buzzard* on the small planet that did nothing but produce tiny, collapsible houses for use on planets around the universe. They could be stacked to make apartment buildings, set into larger structures, or situated on their own. Lightweight but constructed of sturdy materials, weather resistant and complete with their own air and water filtration systems, CubiHouses were found on nearly every planet.

Factory 3 built the version of the home designed for humans, but other factory planets built ones to suit the needs of many of the differing species throughout the universe. As long as they were willing to spend the money to buy them, the company would produce them.

A girl I had met in a bar once took me back to her CubiHouse and I had thought it was nice and clean and understood why they were so popular. Now, seeing one of the planets on which they were produced, it was hard to believe.

The light of the nearby star was nearly blotted out by the belching smoke, covering the world in a blanket of dark brown light, cut through by only the occasional streetlight. Tenement houses lined the streets, broken up by a bar every few blocks.

As we made our way out onto the streets, we watched the miserable people head either to or from their jobs, bodies slumped like vultures, faces sunken and dark. The air tasted like burning rust. Everyone moved as though they were walking on a high-gravity planet. I had thought that Bussel was an industrial planet, but it was nothing compared to this place. At home, there was life outside industry but here, there was nothing but work, homes and bars.

"At least if they are drinking, they don't have to think about what kind of life they are living," I said, gesturing to the flickering neon lights above the dark doors to a bar.

"Have them spend their meager wages on booze and housing more like," Lara said over her shoulder, the respirator in her mask working hard to filter the particles in the air.

"This is what our Consortium of species has become," Ned said miserably. "This should all be automated. None of these souls should have to be doing this. They could be working some job they enjoy, doing something that fills them with pride; not laboring their lives away until they drop dead."

"Not a bad point," Lara allowed, and I realized that she had let Ned into the system in her helmet. They must have done it while I nodded off at some point, but it was a surprising step. I knew she wasn't going to stay with us and still didn't entirely trust Ned, but to let him into the systems she was wearing said something.

"One step forward and two steps back," he said and fell silent.

The streets were quiet save the occasional person lurching from one place to another or little clusters of people outside the bars, talking quietly. Everyone was pale, with red eyes. Without day and night cycles or the proper light of a star and with the burning air, the people all had a uniform look about them; a look made all the more homogenous by gray work uniforms.

The bar numbers were ascending as we passed each one and the fact that every one was nothing more than 'CuBar' followed by a number only added to the drudgery of the place. Once we arrived at 37, we stopped, and Lara turned to look me over.

She reached out and pulled the collar of my jacket up, tapped a fist against the stolen chest plate she encouraged me to wear now that I was playing the part of a bounty hunter, shifted the taser to be more noticeable, and handed me a set of keys to the handcuffs hanging from my belt loop.

"You look the part, Spears," she stated.

"Who knows, maybe in another life this would've been me," I said, resting my hand on the grip of my stomper.

"It might've been," she agreed. "But since it isn't, I just want you to stand there and look intimidating. I expect the people of this planet are tough and will look out for their own. They're not going to want us poking around, asking questions."

"I expect that's probably true," I agreed.

"Assess the situation and make tactical decisions," Ned advised both of us. "We've come this far and don't need to jeopardize ourselves now."

Lara and I nodded at each other, and I followed her into the bar, stopping in the doorway and leaning my shoulder against the frame, my hand still resting on my weapon. The place looked as though it had been mass produced as well, the whole place having the appearance of having been stamped out of a press and then screwed together in an afternoon. An afternoon a long time ago… in a hurricane. Everything was chipped and worn, the standing room in front of the bar so weathered that it sank several centimeters down.

Kilara Vex stepped up to the bar and waved the bartender over. He was a big, tired looking man with a shaved head and messy beard. Surveying the room, I noticed that nearly everybody had this look. Some had beards or five o'clock shadows, others had shaved heads or unkempt hair but they were all muscular with sunken features. And all of their eyes were on the bounty hunter at the bar.

She laid her badge on the countertop, flashing it to him before putting it away and replacing it with the holoprojector. Soon, the image of Bud was staring right at the face of the bartender. I watched all of the people around the bar shift nervously. They obviously knew him.

"Don't know them," he said in a gruff dismissive tone and turned his back on Lara.

"Try that again," she said, and her voice sounded like the barrel of a weapon pressed against his head. Because, even though she hadn't pulled it out, she might as well have.

The bartender turned back, placing his hands on the bar and looming over her. "Don't know them," he said again.

"Goes by the name Marco Markov, though he is actually Bud from Pleasant Planet," she said and at that, a ripple of whispers began making their way through the bar. People began shifting in their seats and a few on the far side of the room stood up and began cracking their necks and knuckles threateningly.

The mention of his name had changed the mood in the room immediately and I knew a fight was brewing when I saw it.

30

"Don't make me say again that I don't know 'em," the bartender said, his voice deepening and face darkening under the dim lights of the bar.

"Tell me where he is or I will bring the full wrath of the Conclave down on this place," she said, her hand beginning to slide toward her weapons.

"The conclave ain't nothing but a bunch of folks looking out for themselves. Best thing you could muster would be some scrappy handful of hunters what couldn't do shite against the lot of us," he said and several of the bar patrons began to move in around Lara. "CubiHouse protects their own and there ain't nothing you can do about it."

The gruff man shot a look across the room and out of the back of the throng popped Bud, crashing through tables and throwing over stools on his way out the back door. At the same moment, several of the patrons jumped toward Lara and she spun on them, a clean roundhouse sending her heavy boot slamming into the face of one, his jaw cracking before spraying the man next to him in spittle and blood.

"Go after him!" she ordered me. "I'll handle them."

I broke into a sprint, sending my fist into the side of one of the thugs surrounding Lara before I jumped over a table and followed Bud out the back door. As I entered the rear kitchen that didn't look like it had been used to prepare food since it was constructed, I saw a foot disappearing out of the door on the far side.

I continued after him, hoping to gain on him with each long stride. My boots slammed across the kitchen and as I turned the corner, crates full of empty beer bottles came crashing down around me. Glass shattered and sprayed the floor with the sticky, slick liquid. I threw my arms up to send the remaining tumbling crates out of my way and jumped over the glass as best I could, crunching down and feeling shards press into the sole of my boot.

Bounding up the stairs, the door to the outside slammed in my face but I threw a shoulder out and knocked it open, seeing Bud continue up another street that looked exactly like the previous one. Like the rest of the people we had seen here, he was fit and still hadn't broken a sweat running away.

He repeatedly checked over his shoulder to see that I was pursuing him but in my heavy layers in the disgusting air of this environment, my lungs burned with each breath.

I had the thought to try and pull out my stomper and attempt to slow his pace, but I knew I wasn't a good enough shot to take out one body part on the run. The weapon wasn't reliable enough even if I was a crack shot and opening fire in a work zone unfriendly to us seemed as unwise as it was dangerous.

Instead, I just pushed myself to run harder, forcing my legs to pump, sending me tearing forward down the darkened road. We were nearing two smokestacks that pierced the sky, spewing dark smoke to mix with the putrid air. Flakes of ash snowed down, coating everything in a light gray sheen cut only by our footprints.

Bud disappeared around the side of a crumbling building and when I followed, I saw that he was leading me toward the assembly line. A conveyor belt rattled slowly forward, bisecting the road. Massive pieces of wall were being lifted from one belt onto the other by operators controlling mechanical arms and once they were down, more people scurried onto pathways along the belts, running out with parts which they bolted into place.

The belt stretched on into the distance until it terminated at a further bank of mechanical arms, picking up the partially constructed homes and moving them to the next stage of assembly. Bud leapt up onto the conveyor belt, shaking the system and causing one of the workers to fall over. The man screamed a curse before turning to see me in pursuit and shouted something inaudible but undoubtedly derogatory at me.

At his voice, the other workers looked up from what they were doing, and it wasn't long before I felt bolts and screws and nuts clattering against my jacket and pants. Hard metal struck the side of my head, nearly knocking me off of the conveyor belt. Running along the moving track that shifted and bounced under my weight was difficult enough without being pelted by metal objects.

"Help me!" Bud shouted, getting the attention of his coworkers. One reached out an arm to try and trip me up, but I leapt over his reach, landing on the moving rubber beyond, having to catch myself from tumbling forward.

When he shouted again, several men with industrial size welders made contact with the metal in front of me, creating a wall of sparks. I threw up my arms to shield my face and pushed through, smelling burning hair and feeling the hot sear of a thousand tiny flames.

"Stop now!" I called after him when I had cleared the falling sparks, but the man wasn't stopping and was creating more distance between us with each stride. He knew where he was going and the workers were all trying to help him. This was giving him a distinct advantage in his escape.

He cut across the conveyor belt to the other side, leaping off and continuing between two buildings. When I left to do the same, a woman pulled free the sink she was attaching and threw it at me. I leapt out of the way just in time but as the heavy-metal slammed against the conveyor belt, it sent a wave through the floor that tossed me forward slamming me into the side of a CubiHouse.

I threw up a hand to brace my impact, but it was too little too late, and my entire right side cracked against the metal. But I couldn't stop. I pushed myself off, my shoulder searing.

One of the workers jumped me as I cleared the side of the wall, swinging at me with a length of pipe. I threw my head back just in time to avoid the metal that rang out as it struck the side of the house. Adrenaline surging through me, I snapped up and grabbed the pipe, yanking it clear from the man's grip and seeing his face register with surprise and fear before bringing it down on him.

Metal crunched cartilage and I was back in pursuit before he even hit the ground.

Bud was halfway up the next street by the time I leapt down onto solid ground. In anger, I chucked the pipe up the street at him, and it whistled through the air before clattering on the ground a few meters away from him and doing nothing except giving him a reason to look over his shoulder and see that I was still following him.

He pushed open the door to one of the massive buildings on the side of the street. A few paces and I was at the door, throwing it open and hoping that he wasn't waiting inside to cold cock me.

I was relieved to find that he wasn't but when I saw the room full of people with mallets, hammering strips of metal into various shapes for different purposes, I stopped running. The man I was following pushed through yelling and pointing at me. Heads turned and hammers were brandished, and I knew that heading out onto the floor would be the last thing I would do in this world.

A few times in my life I had seen scrappers band together against some common enemy and knew the camaraderie and brotherhood that existed in the labor force. They didn't have to know me or what I was there for, all they had to know was that I was trying to hurt one of their own. Those hammers would drop on me one at a time until the pulp of my body lay in the middle of the floor.

Looking around the room, I saw a catwalk that cut up and over the space. I turned and rushed up the steps, clattering to the raised surface and rushing across it over the heads of all the workers who were now gawking up at me.

"Just stop!" I called after him in desperation.

I knew he wouldn't and if we kept this up much longer, he would lose me.

He pushed his way out of the door on the far side of the room and I slammed into the railing where the catwalk terminated, hooking a right angle down into stairs. Rather than waste time, I threw myself over the side of the staircase, leaping down just as a hammer whizzed by. If I had run forward, it would have hit me in the jaw and sent me crashing down. As it was, the hammer hit the wall beyond and fell to the ground as I landed.

Following Bud out, I saw before us a massive, elevated track where giant claws gripped completed CubiHouses and carried them away for shipment. Homes in an endless stream dangled away and I watched as Bud ran up a gangplank astride boxes before hurling himself into the doorway of one, pulling himself in.

I clattered up the plank behind him, accelerating alongside the moving homes and jumping without a second thought. My chest slammed into the floor, feet dangling as the ground dropped further and further away. My fingers clutched at the smooth floor before I threw my arms back against the door frame to pull myself up and in, causing the square to swing.

The space was small with a kitchen on the right side and the living space that converted into a bedroom on the left. Across from me was a rear door through which I could see the front door of the next CubiHouse. On and on they went like the funhouse in that old traveling carnival that Lutch took me to when I was a boy.

I saw Bud disappear out one and into the next, sending the homes swinging into one another. Up on my feet, I cleared the space and leapt through the door of one and into the next, landing as if on the bow of a ship rocking in heavy waves. The one I had vacated swung back and crashed into the one I occupied, sending me falling forward. But I caught myself and kept moving, seeing the man I was chasing getting further and further away.

Being uneasy as I ran through the CubiHouse caused a memory to flash in my mind.

Lutch and I were on a scrap site where a new colony ship had miscalculated the gravitational pull of a nearby planet and, when trying to slingshot around it, was pulled down to the surface, killing most of the inhabitants. The bid had been huge, and we were only given access to scrap on one small grid, but it seemed like a wealth of material at the time.

That was the first time I had seen a CubiHouse. Several of the homes had been stacked and lashed together with industrial chains but had come apart when the ship crashed to the planet and the boxes were scattered in pieces.

"Up there," Lutch had said, pointing to one that was half smashed on top of a pile of rubble. "Go see what you can find."

I was so excited. It was the first time he had sent me to assess scrap on my own. It didn't matter that it was perched precariously on top of shifting metal or that I didn't have a clear sense of what I was even looking for. What mattered was that he trusted me to do it.

Scrambling up the side, my grip was true, and I popped from pipe to broken platform to hanging piece of flooring until I had reached the top. After pressing my body between the half-opened door, I found myself inside a broken CubiHouse. Everything was dented, cracked, or otherwise damaged, and it was strange to see the life of a person compressed into a tiny, destroyed space like this. Clothes were strewn about, packages of food were shredded and scattered, and picture frames were shattered on the floor with the eyes of deceased starfaring travelers staring into nothing.

I made my way through the space, lifting this and poking through that but finding nothing of value. When I stepped into the middle of the floor, putting my full weight on it like the incautious child that I was, it collapsed. The latch which held it into place had cracked on impact and I fell through to the rubble below, landing on my back and knocking the air from my lungs.

My head was ringing and, for a moment, all I heard was my gasping. But a sound cut through the numb silence: laughter. Hearty, uproarious laughter echoing through the ruins as Lutch appeared in my vision.

"I figured the emergency exit might have broken in the landing," he gasped through his levity. "But I never thought you would fall for it so perfectly."

He offered his hand and pulled me to my feet, though I almost collapsed back down to my knees. He kept me upright, grinning down at me.

"What did we learn?" he asked in the tone of parents the universe over.

"Not to trust you," I wheezed in answer.

That caused him to laugh again. "Aye, you certainly shouldn't trust me but that wasn't the lesson you should learn."

I sighed theatrically. "What was the lesson I should learn?"

"Know your surroundings," he advised, his giant finger in my face. "Always be aware of where you are. We spend our lives in the junk, and everything is a danger." He paused for dramatic effect. "But it doesn't matter where you are or what you're doing, you should always take inventory of your surroundings. You never know when that might save your life."

Those words rang in my head as I jumped between another two CubiHouses. Bud had cleared the space between us and I was now in danger of losing him.

"Ned," I grunted, throwing myself through another house.

"Hank," he said back in a calculating voice and I knew he was analyzing everything. There was something in the way he spoke that let me know he was learning and taking it all in. He was doing everything I hadn't been doing all those years ago with Lutch.

"Track Bud and when he reaches the middle of the next Cubi-House, drop the bottom emergency hatch door," I commanded through the puffing breaths.

"Copy," he said, and no sooner had he answered than Bud took one more running step and the floor dropped out beneath him.

He cried out and slammed against the side of the vacant house, throwing his hands down to keep himself from falling through but sliding and having to grip the moving box with his fingertips.

I kept surging forward, moving from house to house until I caught up with him dangling over the ground now far below.

"Help me," he groaned, the tips of his fingers white with exertion.

I leaned down and made a show of pulling the handcuffs off of my belt, clamping one around his wrist before reaching down with both hands.

"Don't try anything," I threatened, trying to sound as imposing and threatening as I could and feeling like I did a pretty admirable job of it.

"I won't, I won't," he promised because he was pleading for his life, but I trusted him about as far as I could throw them.

As soon as I had hauled him up, he staggered to his knees and threw an ineffectual punch that I dodged easily and paid back in kind. My hard scrapper's hand connected with his jaw, rattling his teeth and sending him staggering back.

Springing forward, I spun him and clamped the cuffs closed on the other wrist.

31

"Let's get him out of here," Lara said when Ned guided her to our position.

"Agreed," I said, pushing him up the street in the direction of the *Buzzard*. It had taken some time for us to reach another platform for us to disembark and it certainly had been a harrowing experience for Bud to make the jump with his hands clasped behind his back. Since then, he had not said much but I watched him make eye contact with all the people that we passed, pleading for help with his eyes.

"Guess you had no problems handling his friends at the bar?" I asked.

Lara turned and I knew the face she was making even from underneath the mask.

"They would've needed twice as many," she said.

"Just you wait," Bud threatened and was rewarded with a quick gut punch.

She looked back at me. "Good work catching him."

"Thanks," I said. "He almost got away. Almost."

"It was actually I who caught him," Ned grumbled quietly in our ears.

At the same time, Bud commented, "you didn't do anything to catch me, I fell through a hole in the floor."

At the dueling comments, I could see Lara covering her amusement in her body language: a hand moving toward her face. She maintained her serious bounty hunter's affect, but I knew her well enough to know when she found something entertaining.

The moment of levity was short lived.

From an alley between two housing complexes, a group of five people emerged, ready for a fight. There was a particular gait and posture people assumed when they wanted to fight and it was known the universe over as, I assumed, it had been throughout all of human history; the squared shoulders, wide steps, balled fists and hard face.

"Your friends learned the hard way not to interfere with bounty hunter business," Lara said, resting one hand on the hilt of her blade and the other on her sidearm.

"Let 'im go and you can be on your way," one in the front said. He was the perfect picture of a leader of a group of thugs: tall, bald with a dented head and missing just enough teeth to be noticeable from a distance.

"You really don't want to do this," Lara said, letting her words hang in the air. But the group of toughs were continuing toward us.

I pulled out my stomper. "Come any closer and I'll drop him here now."

They called my bluff. "No, you won't. You don't wanna drag no corpse outta here and he's not worth it to you dead."

I pointed the stomper at the lead man.

"You won't shoot me, neither," he growled and took another step toward us, now just an arm's length apart.

"You want the two on the right?" Lara asked me in a stage whisper.

I looked the two over. A wiry man with wild eyes and a beefy woman whose face revealed her disinterest in the fight. "Yeah, I can take those two."

"You think you can take us just like that?" the leader said but Lara answered with a fist.

Before he could even react, she had set her feet and struck out with a hard fist to the stomach, causing him to keel over. When he did, she grabbed a fistful of hair, holding him in place just long enough for her to hit his nose like a sledgehammer. When his head shot back, blood sprayed into the air and one of his accomplices immediately broke, running back into the alleyway.

Weapon in one hand and the scruff of Bud's collar in the other, I wasn't in a particularly good position to start a hand-to-hand brawl. Lowering the stomper, I fired once into the ground, the loud boom of my weapon snapping through the air like a thunder strike. The woman who hadn't wanted to be in this fight in the first place shook her head and grabbed the thin man beside her, pushing him at me before turning and running as well.

The man held up his hands but careened into Bud. I let go, allowing the two of them to topple into one another. Bud, unable to catch himself, fell back and crashed to the hard asphalt as the wild-eyed man was able to stabilize himself and rushed me.

I attempted to swing the butt of the stomper at him, but he batted it out of the way and crashed into me, sending me and him toppling to the ground beside his friend. When I hit the ground, the weapon discharged again, the bullet shattering the window of a nearby building and eliciting a scream from someone within.

The man landed on top of me and gathered his wits enough to throw a punch. When the fist connected with my left eye, white flashed and my vision blurred. When he raised his hand to punch again, I deflected it with my left forearm before bringing the side of the stomper up against his temple. Metal cracked against bone, and his head snapped, eyes rolling back a moment before blinking back into ferocious focus.

He wailed on me with both hands, swinging wildly. A few blows made it through my upheld arms protecting my face. Since he was straddling me, I brought a leg up and slammed it into his backside sending him splaying over me, hands crashing to the ground behind me and I was up and on my feet.

Despite his injuries, he was up in a moment as well, but his once-mad eyes were now dazed. He assumed the position of a boxer. Or, rather, somebody who had watched boxing a few times and thought they understood it.

I set my legs, holstered my weapon and waited for him to come.

He did. Taking a step to clear the distance between us, he threw a right hook, and I moved out of the way with ease before throwing a hard right jab directly into his nose. It was the knockout blow I'd been looking for and he crumpled to the ground.

I turned to see Lara simply watching me with her hands on her hips.

"You know, that wasn't too bad," she judged.

"Thanks," I said. "Didn't get a chance to see what you did but I assume you made short work of them."

"I did," she bragged and then gestured behind me.

I followed her finger to see Bud wriggling away like a fish on the dock.

"That's just pathetic," I said, walking over to pull him to his feet.

The main thug sputtered something from the street.

"Don't get up," Lara warned but he just rolled to point his face away from us, sputtering blood onto the street.

"Let's get out of here," I said, not wanting to go through this again. We had been lucky that several of the employees didn't want to fight but we wouldn't get lucky again.

"And fast," Lara affirmed, and we took off toward the *Buzzard*, pushing Bud though he threw his shoulders around and dragged his feet like a child angry about having to leave the party early.

He continued to put on a show of lollygagging the entire rest of the way through the factory city, but we met with no more resistance and soon we were back on the *Buzzard* and lifting off the planet.

"Where to?" I asked Lara. "Where do you turn him in?"

"The Conclave," she answered without hesitation. "They will process him there and take him to his next destination. Sometimes the client wants direct delivery but with the Consortium themselves, they prefer batch deliveries."

She looked into the little window opening of the broken bathroom we were using as a cell for Bud. "I hear Conclave processing is far worse than the government," she said with a nasty smile. "And I'll be sure to let them know that you had your friends turn up against a hunter as well."

All the smug and cocky bravado he had shown before was now gone and all that remained was fear.

"I have information," he said, his voice pleading but sincere.

"Really?" I asked, admittedly intrigued, and then felt an elbow in my ribs.

"They all say this," Lara whispered before speaking at a volume loud enough for him to hear as well. "I get this offer every time. You're all the same. Once you get caught, you think you can weasel your way out but it's never true."

"It is this time, I swear," he said, and I looked into his eyes through the little opening in the door. I had always prided myself on being able to read people, and I felt like this man was telling the truth.

I reached out and pulled Lara's elbow, then guided her toward the cockpit and out of earshot of Bud, who shifted in the room to try and follow us with his gaze.

"We should hear him out," I insisted.

"Hank," she said pityingly. "I mean it when I say that they always try this. Literally every time I pick up a bounty, they try to offer me some bigger fish. When I was young, I would chase those leads and end up getting nowhere at best and losing the bounty at worst."

"You're right, I have no experience with this, but if there's a way we can double our profit, we should do it," I said, thinking about all of the improvements I wanted to make on the *Buzzard*. "There's no harm in letting him tell us."

"He's the mission," Ned said in my earpiece, obviously not risking speaking through the ship. "And we have only so much fuel.

Our reserves are not such that we can chase our tail around the universe."

"Let me try?" I asked though it really sounded more like begging.

Lara let out a little snort but nodded. "Sure, have at it."

I expected her to follow me back to Bud but instead, she turned her back on me and headed toward the cockpit. Making my way back to the bathroom, I looked through the little sliding opening whose existence I had always questioned.

"Prove to me that what you're saying is true," I said in a low and serious tone.

"I'm a Peacer," he admitted without hesitation. "Even just admitting this puts me at risk for execution so you should know what I'm about to tell you is true."

He had a point. Peacer rebels were nearly as high on the Consortium's wanted list as people harboring AI. They were certainly not at the same level and didn't have Inquisitors hunting them, but they were high-value targets. His admission did put him in a dangerous position and, if I had the foresight to record it, would have meant as much as he had said. Such as it was, it was little more than something I could try to leverage.

"Okay, so, you're a Peacer, and…?"

"And I have information on someone the Consortium really wants," he said in a whisper as though his people might be able to hear him.

I leaned in, fixing him with a serious gaze. "Who?"

"Thorpe, the bomb-maker," he said in such a whisper that I could barely hear it. "She's one of the top five most wanted people in the universe. I can give you her location if you'll just let me go.

No one ever has to know that you caught me, and you can bring in a much bigger, more valuable target."

"You'll tell me where the bomb-maker is and we just let you go?" I asked incredulously.

"Yeah," he said, nodding his head vigorously. "Just leave me here and you can go get Thorpe."

I laughed. "You must think I'm some kind of idiot?"

"No, no, I'm serious."

"Oh, I believe you're serious about knowing the location of Thorpe, but you must think I don't have two brain cells to knock together if you believe I'm gonna leave you here with some information you feed me."

Her curiosity must've gotten the better of her because I saw Lara out of the corner of my eye, standing and listening to the conversation unfolding.

"You tell us where she is and take us to her and I'll consider your deal," I offered.

The look on his face changed. "If she sees me, I'm dead."

"I thought the Peacers were, you know, all about peace," I said, my tone a bit more patronizing than perhaps I meant.

His face screwed up in irritation. "We are about universal peace but understand what it takes to achieve."

"A bit of killing is what you mean?" I asked with an eyebrow raised.

"We'll do whatever it takes."

I shrugged and pointed in the direction of the cockpit. "She just wants to take you right in and I'm fine with that. I could use the money. So, either you can tell us where he is and take us to him or you can get 'processed,' whatever that means; though I'm sure it's… invasive…"

"I can't, they will kill me," he said and while I believed him, I didn't sympathize with his predicament. I wanted him to tell me where the bigger fish was.

"Okay," I said dismissively and turned to walk toward Lara who was standing just far enough away for Bud not to see her.

"Wait," he called after me and I smiled.

"Yes?" I asked, sure to cover my satisfaction.

"She's on Utopia," Bud said, disappointment in himself clear in every word. "She's there, and I can take you to her. I mostly just have a career, but I was trusted to go there once before, and I can do it again."

"If you're some hot shot rebel, why were you back on the factory planet?" Lara asked, taking a few steps forward. "Were you back there trying to gain more support for your people?"

Bud snorted a laugh. "You think being a Peacer is a full-time job for all of us? You think they pay the bills?"

"I guess I assumed they did," Lara said.

"Yeah, me too," I agreed.

"Well, they don't."

"You learn something new every day," I said.

Lara smiled. "You really do."

"Shall we go to Utopia?" I asked, and she bobbed her head.

"It's your fuel we're burning," she said, and the two of us walked to settle ourselves in the cockpit.

Ned shut the door behind us before his voice came through the speaker. "I think this is an unwise decision."

"Why is that?" I asked.

"Marco Markov, aka Bud, was the mission, and we have him," Ned asserted. "We have guaranteed funds in hand. Lara picked him because he could achieve what we needed, and we have him now. Running off on some secondary objective when we have already accomplished the first is unnecessary and foolhardy."

Lara reached out and brought the bounty board back up on the screen, then twisted the dial to scroll all the way up to the top of the board. She tapped her finger on where Thorpe's name was.

"Look," she said to Ned. "She might not be as high value a target as Bud thinks, but she is still worth a good amount of money and worth our time… if Hank's instincts prove to be correct."

"And you believe they will?" Ned asked, sounding utterly unconvinced.

She looked at me and back to the console of the ship. "He's usually right about these kinds of things," she admitted.

"You said yourself that claims like this never prove to be true," Ned reminded her. "It was less than five minutes ago that you said it."

She rolled her eyes. "Yes, I know, but I also rather enjoy saying 'I told you so.' So, it's win/win for me."

"Fine," Ned groaned. "Let's go find this phantom bomb-maker."

32

"Utopia had been the planet most similar to Earth when it was first discovered by early colonists. As a result, people had flooded there faster than anyplace else and development happened rapidly. Those early settlers had told themselves that they were not going to do to Utopia what they had done to Earth. They were not going to milk the planet for all that it had until it was a husk of its former self.

"But, as they say, the road to hell is paved with good intentions," Ned continued as we hurtled through the gyre. "This amazing new planet was clear-cut and decimated within a century. Humans have become so efficient at converting resources into what they needed that the planet's population grew exponentially.

"It was the first instance of true, unfettered growth on a planet. There were no alien species to contend with, no harsh conditions, radiation, or natural disasters. Nothing standing in the way of the colonists. They felt like Europeans discovering North America except without the previous inhabitants pushing back against their presence.

"Utopia has become one of the most populous planets in the system and now has to trade for a vast majority of its goods. All of the advantages it once held have dried up, and in many ways, it appears to be neo-Earth," Ned concluded. "Would you like to know more?"

"I think we're good," Lara said. "I don't remember asking for this information in the first place. I've been to this planet a ton of times."

"I thought it was interesting," I admitted. "I think I've been to more populated planets in the last few days than I had in my whole life up to this point. Most of the places I've been to are nothing but destitute scrap sites."

"That's a bummer," Lara said, and it took me aback for a moment.

We had been so caught up in catching the bounty that it hadn't occurred to me how hard a turn she had taken. When we had first met up, she had been so hard and cold but now she seemed to be having fun. Ned, too, seemed lighter since she had come aboard.

It was sad to know that she was going to have to leave us. Her presence seemed to make all of us better off. I wondered if that was part of the reason I had listened to Bud in the first place. Just to extend our time together. Then it dawned on me that it might be the reason Lara agreed to it. If perhaps, despite herself, she was happy for the company and didn't want to see this come to a close so soon.

"I had always kind of assumed that the life of a scrapper was a bit more glamorous than I think it actually was," Lara said.

"Glamorous is about as far from the word I would use as possible," I said with a laugh. "I mean, look at this place."

Lara let her eyes drift around the cockpit, stopping to look at the dangling wires, rusted-out holes where there used to be bolts, and uneven plating held together with duct tape and cable ties.

"I suppose it all seemed so much more grand when I was a child," she said.

"Can't argue with that," I agreed. "The first time I stepped foot on the Buzzard, I was in hog heaven. I don't have to tell you that it was the opposite of everything that we had known. Our lives have been so small, feeling so pointless, and even just being on a starship for the first time was…"

"Freedom," Lara completed the thought. "At least that's what it was for me."

"Exactly," I agreed. "Knowing that you were in a vehicle that can take you anywhere, that can take you… away."

Lara nodded slowly, thoughtfully.

"When did you first leave Bussel?" I asked.

She looked at me, but the lightness was gone and I realized that talking about her past was not something that ever seemed to go over well. Whatever she had been through after Lutch had taken me in was not something that she seemed keen to discuss further.

"It was a few years after you left," she said, sounding like she was forcing the words from her mouth. "And it was several years after that before I had my own ship. You should see it. It's new, state-of-the-art, with all of the tech and weapons you could want. It's the opposite of… this. I've never loved piloting but being behind the controls of Retiarius is different."

"I'd like to see it," I said, allowing her the change of subject she seemed to so desperately want.

"After we stop at the Conclave I'll need a ride back to my ship, and you can check it out," she said.

"Sounds great."

"Maybe I'll even let you take her for a spin," she said.

"Really?"

"Not a chance in hell," she said with a laugh.

Ned piped up. "May I take her for a spin?"

"You neither," she said, putting her feet up on the console and leaning back in her chair. "I wouldn't trust either of you with my baby."

"I can be very gentle," Ned said in an almost seductive tone.

"Don't do that again," I admonished, only half jokingly.

"Agreed," Lara said, smirking. "It's weird how quickly I adjusted to talking to you. We have to be careful not to get too complacent about it. Just because we're all shooting the breeze doesn't mean it's any more safe for you in this world."

"I never forget that," Ned said in a serious tone.

"Good. Don't," Lara said seriously just before we washed out and into orbit around Utopia.

From space, the planet did look somewhat similar to the images I had seen of earth but with less green. The blue in the cloud cover was reminiscent though.

I opened the automatic door and called down the hallway to where Bud was locked away. "Where are we landing?"

"Gibson City," he shouted back, and the door slammed closed again.

"Gibson City is named for one of the planet's early inhabitants, and, though he was killed by those he lead after being discovered embezzling, the planet still bears his name," Ned said in the flat affect of a tour guide, just before our comm array lit up.

Once again, Lara answered the hail and user credentials to get us a landing spot in the city center, and we dropped down. The towering skyscrapers lit up at night as we passed through the clouds. Rain plunked down and streaked our window as I guided us to our spot. We had determined that a planet of this development might have more active AI sensors than others, and it was best for Ned to lay low.

He would still be in our ears, but he wouldn't be engaging with any systems or attempting to hack anything unless he absolutely had to. There would be Consortium Prefect presence on the planet in addition to an inquisition hub. We all knew that we had to be very careful as long as we were on Utopia.

After setting the buzzard down, we were greeted by no fanfare as we had been before. Here, I just parked the ship in the huge concrete lot beside several other ships, and Lara used her Hunter badge to pay a reduced fee for the spot.

When I pulled Bud from the bathroom, then walked down the stairs and toward the rear of the cargo hold, he looked up at me pitifully. "Do you have a jacket I could borrow? And maybe we could loosen these cuffs?"

I laughed. "Remember when you tried to punch me after I dragged your ass up and out of that hole in the CubiHouse? Well, you can think about that when you are getting rained on."

"Asshole," he muttered under his breath but obviously loud enough to be heard.

"Just take us to Thorpe so we can be done with you," Lara said, now masked and in full Hunter persona.

"Where did we park?" Bud asked as I pushed him down the ramp and out into the rain. It was really coming down, the wind sweeping sheets of hard drops to the earth and making it hard to see in the dark of night.

Streetlights provided limited light, and it didn't take long for us to be soaked through. Bud squinted up at a street sign. "There's a place you could've parked a bit closer, but this'll do," he informed us. "Just start heading this way," he said, nodding in a direction up the street.

He turned to look over his shoulder at me. "Think you could at least walk on the awnings?"

"Only because I want to," I told him, shoving him forward across the street and under the curved plastic awnings. The neighborhood seemed dead in the night. There were no open businesses except one corner liquor store in the distance, and half the buildings seemed empty, the storefronts shuttered.

A cab landed nearby, and a couple stumbled out, then rushed hurriedly from the apartment building, before disappearing inside.

"All CubiHouses inside there," Bud noted with a surprising sense of pride.

"I have to ask," I began. "Why would you leave a place like Pleasant Planet for a factory world?"

"Let me ask you something?" he said irritably. "Does this planet seem like a real utopia to you?" When I didn't answer, he continued. "No. So maybe it's safe to assume that a planet full of nothing but plants isn't that 'pleasant' just because it says so in the name."

"Seemed like a nice place to me," I observed, remembering the light and warmth fondly as the cold rainwater squished in my boots.

"Seemed like a nice place to anybody who just visited," Bud snapped back. "Guessing where you're from ain't so great either."

"Where I'm from is a pit stop on the way to a pit stop," I told him.

"Turn left here," he said, and we ran from one awning to a ripped and dipping one across the street.

Squinting up into the rain, I saw the buildings becoming even more ruinous. Where the buildings behind us had seemed half populated, these seemed completely vacated or crumbling into disrepair. Husks of vehicles that were melting with age lay parked along the side of the road and every now and again I could make out the flickering light of a garbage can fire somewhere within one of the buildings.

"Charming neighborhood," I noted, and Lara threw a look back to silence me.

We continued forward without talking and without the benefit of any cover as, here, there was nothing left to provide any protection. We walked for what felt like an age, sloshing forward miserably until finally Bud stopped us.

"Building's right there," he said, pointing to the withered remains of a brick factory. "Now, let me go."

"We'll let you go when we have Thorpe in custody," Lara said in such a way that left no room for a counteroffer.

"Fine," he sputtered, and we moved toward the building cautiously. Large gaps covered the walls, but the building was mostly intact. Looking inside, we could see nothing but darkness. The door facing the street was blocked off by a mound of rubble. We hurried around the side and saw an open doorway.

When we reached it, Lara threw up a hand and knelt.

Coming up beside her, I saw a thin wire half a meter off the ground that stretched across just inside the door frame.

"Trip wire," she said, and I nodded, before getting down and reaching into my toolbelt while she took over keeping an eye on Bud. I pulled out a penlight, clicked it on, and poked my head through the doorway to examine the explosive. It was not what I expected. Given that the woman held the moniker "bomb-maker," I had anticipated some kind of sophisticated system.

Rather, it was little more than what amounted to fishing cord strung across to a grenade safety pin slid most of the way out. Though rudimentary in design, it would certainly do the trick if a person wasn't paying attention. I reached out and placed a hand on the grenade, then slid my thumb into the ring at the end of the pin. With my left hand, I pulled out nippers and snipped the line.

Using the nippers to grip the screw, I loosened the ring clamp that held the grenade in place and slid it out, then popped it in my belt for future use. I looked up at Lara and gave her the thumbs-up.

"We have to be careful," she said as though seeing a booby-trap within the first few steps hadn't made me already feel the same way.

"Just leave me out here," Bud pleaded. "I'm going to get us killed. I don't want to die like this."

"He's going to be more of a liability," I agreed.

Lara turned and moved like a flash of lightning to start doing something with her finger, before plunging a nail into his neck.

Within a moment, he slumped to the ground, whatever sedative she had used on him taking effect immediately. She laid him down, leaning him up against the doorframe, and turned back to the building, then lifted her own flashlight that was built into the side of her sidearm.

Inside looked like an unremarkable abandoned building. There was nothing to indicate that anybody lived here, and we began making our way from room to room, looking for signs of anything. We found a pile of clothes and an old cot, but they looked like they had been abandoned long before Thorpe got here.

Furniture was stacked in what appeared to be an old break room, and we pushed our way through. I was able to see dueling staircases leading up and down a few rooms away. Lara saw the same thing and headed that direction. Before she walked to the doorway, I put a hand on her shoulder and stopped her movement. She turned to look at me, and I held up a finger telling her to stay here.

I grabbed a short piece of piping off the floor and threw it. It went skittering through the doorway like a rat. When it did, something snapped, and a heavy repurposed door came swinging down on a hinge above the frame. The front was overlaid with protruding chair legs fashioned into long spikes.

"Thanks," Lara whispered.

"No problem," I said, moving forward and pushing the swinging door back up, allowing her to squeeze by me before dropping again. "Safe to assume she knows we're here now."

"She's probably got cameras all over the neighborhood," Lara hypothesized, and I figured she might be right, and the bomb-maker would know we were here.

"Up or down?" I asked, pointing to the staircases.

"You go up, I go down?"

I cocked my head at her. "Are you kidding me? You're the one who made me watch the entire Phantom Mansion series, and splitting up is always what gets everyone killed."

"Those are movies," she said flatly.

"Even still," I answered, and she shook her masked head, water cascading off her.

"Fine," she said, and began to move toward the stairs leading down.

As I followed her, I couldn't help but pull my stomper out and point it as we moved, pressing the pen light up against the bottom of the grip. I knew that it wouldn't do anything against another trap, but it made me feel more secure having it at the ready.

When we reached the bottom of the stairs, we entered a room full of parts and pieces stacked on shelves and desks. Another cot was set off to the side, but this one had blankets folded neatly on top and a dog-eared book just beside it. There was a strong metal door at the far side of the room, but it seemed too easy, and Lara looked back at me.

"See anything?"

When she asked, I appraised the room once more, looking around for anything that might be a trap. There was a small rug between us and the door, and I crept over to it.

"Be careful," Lara demanded in a whisper.

I knelt beside it and lifted up a corner to see that there was a panel just underneath it. Turning back, I pointed down to it and made the hand gesture of an explosion. The two of us walked around it and reached the far side of the room, and when we did, my brows knit together.

I leaned in, pressed my ear against the door, and heard the thrumming beat of a drum and then the wailing twang of guitar.

"She's listening to music," I said.

"It's a trap," Lara warned and raised her weapon as I reached for the door release. I pressed it and swung the door open, revealing the bomb-maker's lair on the other side.

33

Music flooded our ears and light blinded us from inside the room as we both entered with our weapons raised. Blinking quickly, we assessed the situation and stared in confusion as the redheaded woman in heavy leather gloves, boots and an apron danced with her back to us. She was holding a soldering iron in one hand and pliers in the other. The project she had been working on was sending a stream of dark smoke streaking into the air from her workbench and a cracked and flickering screen in the corner of the room was showing the music video to the loud tunes.

Lara and I kept our weapons trained on her as she continued to dance around, raising her hands above her head and spinning. When she turned to face us, she screamed, and the metal face protector fell down.

"Don't move!" she demanded, dropping the pliers and pulling a detonator out of her pocket.

"*You* don't move!" Lara screamed.

"Good one!" mocked Thorpe in a childlike manner.

She was younger than I was expecting, looking hardly older than mid-twenties and I would never have thought we were going to find an explosives expert dancing around. The whole situation was bizarre and, more than anything, deafening with the screaming music blaring.

I moved around her with my weapon raised to turn the little screen off, plunging us into a ringing silence.

On the workbench just behind her, the smoking object twitched. From my new vantage point near her side, I could see that it looked like a robotic arm; specifically, a forearm from about the elbow down through the hand. It was crude, fashioned of the kind of scrap I wouldn't even bother hauling from a site, but it was functional. I could see the fingers twitching and tapping.

The room was barren except for the bench covered in tools, the television she had been watching and a bank of monitors showing views from around the building above. This confirmed Lara's suspicions, and I was grateful the bomb-maker had been too distracted by her fun to have noticed our approach. Quickly, I checked and saw Bud still slumped beside the door where we left him sedated after he led us here .

"What are you doing here?" Thorpe demanded, flipping her face covering back up and then brandishing the detonator like a gun.

Neither Lara nor I lowered our weapons. We both kept them pointed directly at her.

"I am hunter Kilara Vex, here to collect a bounty on you," Lara stated, her voice carrying the weight of absolute authority. "Come with us peaceably and no one has to get hurt here."

"No one has to get hurt," Thorpe parroted sarcastically. "You two broke into my home and are trying to take me in."

"We did and we are," Lara stated.

"But that doesn't mean you have to respond with violence," I put in and I noticed the slight twitch from Lara. She didn't want me involved but I didn't care and I wanted to prevent this from devolving into gunplay or whatever explosions Thorpe held at her fingertips. "I know that the Peacers are looking for universal peace and there is no need to kill us to achieve it," I said. Not the best case I had ever made but not bad given that I was pretty sure all three of us would be blasted apart if she pressed the button.

"You know nothing of the Peacers," Thorpe said, her words spitting from her mouth.

Before Lara could simply demand the woman give herself up again, I spoke. "So, tell us."

"Put your weapons down," she demanded, her eyes flicking back and forth between us.

"Not a chance," Lara stated.

I didn't know what her plan was here, but I didn't want to find out the hard way so I lowered my stomper and holstered it at my belt line. "There," I said, showing my palms as I raised my hands. "We've come all this way and I would like to know more about the Peacers."

I didn't know if she would fall for it and didn't know if Lara would remember our old con, but I had to try anyway.

When we were kids, Lara had an aptitude for stealth. She could move as silently as an owl and disappear without a trace. It was why she hadn't been caught when Lutch found me that fateful evening. It also meant that she could snag a bag of chips off a rack without being noticed so long as someone kept the shop clerk distracted.

That job fell to me. It taught me to both run my mouth and ask the kinds of questions which encouraged others to speak. It turned out that most people wanted to talk about themselves or about whatever was irritating them at the moment if given the space to do so.

"I've been feeling lost in the universe, and I think that you guys might have something to offer me if I just had more information about your cause," I added, laying it on a bit thick.

But it seemed to work. Thorpe's face unclenched ever so slightly, and she stopped looking at Lara, focusing on me instead.

"I used to feel that way too," she said sympathetically. "My Sector paid higher taxes than any other in the Universe and my whole family had to work just to survive."

"That's exactly what it was like for me!" I exclaimed. "I was orphaned before I even got to know my parents and had to start working before I was old enough to appreciate how young I was. I didn't even have a childhood."

"Exactly," Thorpe said, taking a step toward me and nodding. When she did, Lara moved almost imperceptibly closer toward the bomb-maker. Or, at this moment, arm-maker. "The Consortium takes advantage of all its citizens and gives us nothing in return. The Sectors should decide what's best for themselves, and one governing body should never decide what's best for other species."

She continued to make her point, but Ned couldn't hold his tongue and his passionate whisper filled my ear. "That's why the Sectors send representatives! People of all species can have a voice in the government that serves them and works in their best interests.

A unified universe is stronger than a divided one! Working together is what defeated the Enemy AI and the only way to ensure that we can face whatever comes next."

"And Parliament does nothing," Thorpe continued. "The Triumvirate holds all the power and the three of them always just work in their best interest and never for that of the people. Everything is upside down and we need to tear it down and start over again with all the Sectors working for themselves."

"The Sectors divided would never be able to withstand any kind of unified foe," Ned screamed as quietly as he could so his voice couldn't be heard out in the room. "If a strong enough foe were to gather strength, they could isolate the Sectors and defeat them one by one. Then we would be a universe united… by subjugation."

As the conversation unfolded, Lara moved again, seeing exactly what I was doing and taking advantage. Behind Thorpe, I saw Bud begin to stir.

We needed to get her into custody before our other bounty escaped.

"Are the Peacers looking for more new members?" I enthused, trying to sound as much like a naïve and pliable potential recruit as I could.

"We are," she said and dropped her hand ever so slightly as she took another step toward me. "We need all the help we can get to prepare for what's comi—"

At that moment, Lara sprang forward, blade slicing with a blur through the air and bisecting Thorpe's wrist. She screamed as her hand streaked blood down to the ground, the detonator rolling away.

We had her.

I moved to grab the detonator off the ground at the same time as Lara reached out to subdue our target. But as she did, the arm on the table propelled itself up. The back side where an elbow would be unfurled more fingers and projected itself at Thorpe's back, exploding through her chest and showering us in blood.

Thorpe sputtered and fell to the ground, metal fingers dripping crimson protruding from her chest.

I was in shock, staring at the sight before me when my eye was drawn to movement on the screens over her shoulder. Bud was getting up.

"It's an AI," Lara accused, reaching out for the arm and yanking it free from the fresh corpse.

"I'm attempting to communicate," Ned informed me.

I opened my mouth to warn them of the other bounty's awakening but before I could, the world erupted around us. The ground shook, the walls cracked, and the sound of the explosion blew out our ears. Both of us were thrown around the room and debris slammed us before dirt filled the room like a cloud.

A low hum rang in my head and I coughed into the darkness, seeing nothing but the beam from my penlight beside me on the ground. I reached out with a shaking hand, lifted it, and pointed the light into the brown fog.

"Lara," I croaked before an explosive cough erupted from my lungs.

"Hank," she said from somewhere in the haze and I saw the faint outline of her light nearby. Both beams wobbled as we moved toward one another. Soon, the dusty outline of my old friend came into view. She was coated in a heavy layer of dust but was still gripping the robotic arm in one hand and her handgun in the other. A chunk of the ceiling was stuck in her hair and a stream of crimson streaked down her neck from some unseen injury.

"A consummate professional to the very end," I said, pointing to the arm before sputtering a cough.

"You know me," she wheezed. "We have to find Thorpe."

"Hopefully the body wasn't crushed," I said in a grim half-joke. Lutch had often used humor as a way to cope with tough times and, toward the end of his life, was trying to make light of everything. As it was the behavior I saw modeled, I had adopted a similar affect.

Lara coughed but didn't answer, the two of us sweeping our beams over the ground until we saw the body of the bomb-maker. An arm came into view, and then a torso but much of her lower half had vanished under a large slab of following concrete.

"Does this mean you'll only get half the bounty?" I asked.

Uncharacteristically for when she was on a job, Lara chortled a laugh. "You haven't changed much, Hank."

Chuckling and helping her to free the body, lifting it up and onto my shoulder, I smirked. "I guess neither of us have."

"How many dead bodies did you guys play with as kids?" Ned asked and the comment caused the two of us to laugh again. "It is also possible that you are both concussed. It is advisable to obtain a MediScanner for the *Buzzard* when finances permit."

"We might be," Lara admitted through her ventilator before coughing again. Whatever systems she had in there were straining against the sheer amount of dust.

"I would also advise you to check on Bud," Ned reminded us And we both turned in the direction of the stairs, moving as quickly as we could. "I expect that he was the one who triggered the implosion, but I would still like to collect double bounties if possible."

"You would make a hell of a hunter, Ned," Lara said as we moved around the plate under the rug which had miraculously not been set off during the explosion. If it had, we would likely have been entombed in the other room.

"Thank you, Lara," Ned answered graciously. "I believe you would have made an excellent soldier of the Consortium as well."

"I can't imagine anything I would enjoy less," she retorted without even having to think about it.

"Sadly, I am coming to understand why that is," Ned admitted.

We were carefully pulling ourselves up the crumbling staircase, bricks falling under feet and chunks of wall coming out as we braced ourselves. The body slung over my shoulder, only complicated things, the weight of it shifting with each step. It was not unlike carrying a dripping bag of scrap back to the *Buzzard*.

"Seeing what the Consortium has become has given me a lot to think about," Ned continued. "I had hoped that we were building a better, more just version of the universe. But I see now that our nature has prevented this reality."

I thought about what he said and where we were. "Seems like Utopia itself is a pretty good representation of what you mean."

"That is an astute observation," Ned agreed. "This planet fittingly named Utopia is emblematic of promise-versus-reality."

"The two of you get surprisingly deep," Lara observed, climbing over a block of wall blocking the path out of the building.

"We are both men of the world," I self-deprecated and Lara scoffed.

I moved around beside her, lifting the spiked door again and allowing her through. She stepped in beside me and took over propping up the heavy wood so that I could move through with the body before lowering it slowly behind me. The dust was mostly settled up here, and the light of morning was beginning to shine onto the planet, bathing the ruins in an incongruous golden yellow light.

After traversing the rooms toward the front of the factory, we discovered more destruction but not a body.

"If he's smart, he'll lay low," Lara suggested.

"Nothing about him suggested an abundance of intelligence," Ned asserted.

I nodded. "I have to agree."

"He managed to escape from us," Lara noted. "Can't be that dumb and it isn't just dumb luck either. He got us here, annoyed us into separating from him and probably thought he killed us by setting off the implosion."

"When you put it like that…" Ned began.

"Right," I agreed. "Best not to think about it that way."

"I always think about that," Lara said, her voice dark and heavy with emotion. "One mistake can cost you everything."

Her tone had shifted so radically that neither of us answered at first.

After a long moment and when we had finally reached the street, pulling off our masks to breathe in the natural air, she spoke again. "Let's get her to the Conclave and get paid."

34

THE CONCLAVE WAS like nothing I had ever seen before. The bounty hunter city was built on a small planet in the middle of nowhere, protected by more starships and patrols than I had ever witnessed, anywhere. When we pulled into orbit, Lara had to submit her credentials quickly or we would have been blown out of the sky. Then, she had to answer several questions as to why she was aboard my ship, who I was and what we were doing before we were given access to land in her spot.

As we descended toward the planet, huge anti-spacecraft guns followed our movement until we set down. The entire place had a feeling of security and mistrust unrivaled by even the Scrapper's Guild headquarters. It also had a grandeur I had not expected. All of the buildings were constructed of what looked like marble and towered over the cobbled streets. Statues of famous bounty hunters lined the roads, plaques at their bases explaining their exploits.

I read what I could as we walked past them and gawked at the shops beyond. Armorers, weaponsmiths, cage designers, ship outfitters and every other kind of hunter accoutrement could be found right here.

The other hunters who strode by took no note of us, but I pulled my jacket closed, zipping it up to hide the armor which I should have left on the *Buzzard*. The fact that I was carrying what was obviously a body bundled up in a piece of old tarp didn't seem of any interest to anybody either. And it wasn't long before I passed another person who was pushing a cage with a naked man cowering inside.

The world of the bounty hunter was very different from that of my own but certainly held its own appeal. The Junkyard, base of operations for scrappers, had a look to match its name. It was dirty and gritty, just like the people who inhabited it. But here, the hunters could walk around their magnificent city (where all of the buildings looked like ancient temples) with their shoulders held high.

It was not only a difference in design and self-ascribed value, but it was also a fundamental difference in money. The bounty hunters made a lot of it, and while certain conglomerated scrapper groups did well for themselves, scrappers, by and large, did not. As a result, we lived in squalor, and the hunters in grandeur.

"This way," Lara said, pointing up the Via Falco, a road with fewer statues and shops, mostly adorned with brick buildings with heavy metal doors under holographic signs. It was one of the few places where I saw any modern technology. Here, there was an obvious, or even aggressive, reverence for the past.

Approaching a door which said Falconer Zenobia in red hologram, Lara pounded a fist against the door. She glanced up and down the street a moment before knocking again.

"Come on, old woman!" she called and after a moment, the door swung open.

Old woman was apt. It was hard to believe that the little old lady who greeted us was a dispatcher of hunters. That was, until she spoke. The lady with bundled white hair atop her dark-complexioned face and sharp emerald eyes spoke with a tongue like a whip.

"Such a loud noise from such a skinny waif," she said, and it was hard to believe anybody spoke to Kilara Vex in such a way.

"I may be skinny, but I could still kick your ass," Lara snapped back, a smile growing on her lips.

"I'll be long buried before you could hold a candle to me, young lady," the old woman fired back. She was short and hunched but still wore heavy plate armor and a gun slung at her side. If she wasn't a foil in one of the Interstella movies, it was a real missed opportunity. Her wizened eyes fell on me. "Who's your handsome friend?"

One of her eyebrows went up before winking at me.

"I bet you were a real slayer in your day," I said, winking back.

"Who's to say I'm not still?" asked Zenobia with a sassy smile.

"No one wants to think about that," Lara put in, starting to step toward Zenobia who moved out of the way, allowing us inside.

"Jealous," the old woman said loudly as she passed, and I watched her eyes move over me when I stepped into the small room. It was little more than a computer station across a table from a few chairs carved out of stone. A display screen was mounted into the wall beside the table and flanked with sconces holding little candles or busts of people of various species.

Mounted on the wall behind Zenobia were weapons of various designs. Some melee, some projectiles, but all of them deadly.

After setting the body down and settling myself on one of the stone slab chairs, I pointed to the armaments on the wall. "Those are from vanquished foes?"

Zenobia looked at them before settling into her chair and shaking her head at me. "Those are the weapons of the hunters who I've sent out and who came back to me in the same state as that." She pointed to the body of Thorpe.

I saw Lara's eyes flash up to a heavy particle weapon coated in far less dust than the others and bite her lip.

"I'm hoping not to have to mount Vex's blade up there anytime soon," she said and smiled at Lara who seemed lost in thought. "What do you bring me?"

Lara cleared her throat. "Bounty number," and she rattled off the identification code.

"I thought you were after Marco Markov?" Zenobia asked.

"I added the third bounty to my list just before reaching Utopia," Lara told the woman.

Zenobia punched the keyboard buttons with a heavy hand before picking some glasses up off the table and sliding them on to perch at the tip of her nose. "Ah, yes," she said. "I see that now."

She opened a drawer in her desk, sliding out a hand scanner and biodata reader. Shuffling over to the body and sliding the tarp down. She took a sample before setting the reader down and scanning the bomb-maker's face. Moving back across the room slowly, she plugged both into her computer and sat back at her desk, letting out a long exhalation as though she had just run a marathon.

"Have to confirm," she explained to me as though I didn't understand what was happening. "You are a new hunter? A disciple? I don't see anyone here under Vex's name."

"No," I answered with a smile. "I'm Hank Spears, a scrapper."

"A scrapper?" she exclaimed in surprise. "Not many scrappers who can help take down one of the Consortium's most wanted. You might be in the wrong field, young man."

I waved her away. "That's very kind but I think I was getting in Lar—er, Kilara's way most of the time."

"He's being modest," Lara added quickly. "He was surprisingly helpful."

Zenobia raised an eyebrow. "I've never known Vex to talk like this."

"We are old friends," I said and when I did, Zenobia's face registered recognition and she turned back to her computer for a moment.

"That's how I know your name!" she exclaimed. "You ran afoul of one of the bosses of the Twelve Cartels…"

"It's all a misunderstanding," I justified, and Zenobia gave me a look that made it clear she knew I was full of shit.

"I see," was all she offered and looked at Lara. "You could bring him in too."

Lara smirked. "I thought about it."

"I'm sitting right here," I protested.

"We know this," Zenobia said. "And my suggestion of you becoming a hunter is retracted."

"I can't become one now?"

She admonished me with a look. "No one can apply for a license whilst they are under a bounty."

"I see," I said. "And it's fine; I don't think I am anything more than a scrapper anyway."

I wasn't sure I believed the words anymore and was happy that Ned was busy examining the programming of the arm and not in my ear or Lara's mask. Both of which we had left on the ship.

"You're far more than just a scrapper," Lara said and put her hand on top of mine for just a moment before patting it like a coach saying "good game."

"Vex has been so tight lipped about her history," Zenobia said, grinning at me. "I think there are a lot of questions that I would like to ask you."

Just then, the machines plugged into her computer chimed and flashed a green light.

"Saved by the bell," Lara said, though her voice betrayed her nervousness.

"You are quite a lot wealthier," she said to Lara. "This was a big one for you and you are moving closer to a new rank."

Lara tried to keep from smiling but I could tell she was pleased.

"It was pretty easy, honestly," she admitted, sounding ashamed.

"We almost got blown up," I reminded her.

"Yes, but that was our own fault and we ended up catching Thorpe unawares," she said dismissively. "A bounty who is singing and dancing when you walk in the room is not particularly difficult to takedown. And we almost got blown up because I didn't administer enough sedatives."

"I think that's a pretty self-effacing way of seeing what happened," I said.

"It is the hunter's way," Zenobia put in. "It is how we learn from our mistakes."

"We can also learn from our successes," I said. "We don't have to diminish ourselves to learn. We can grow by seeing things for what they were, not only from nitpicking."

The two women looked at me with flat expressions until they both burst out into laughter.

"A scrapper would say that." Zenobia cackled.

I had no reply for them.

"When you face death at every turn and each job you go on risks ending with your weapon on my wall, you have to take things a bit more seriously," Zenobia explained, more patronizing than I thought was entirely necessary. "I know there are risks to your job but the scrap doesn't fight back. It doesn't shoot you or claw for life.

"The people we hunt all see us as the adversary. They believe that we are the thing that stands between them and freedom. Or them and life. And often, they are correct. They will do anything to survive or escape. So, we must study every mistake we make and learn from it. We must come to understand all that we have done and try to do better each and every time. Otherwise…" She hooked a bony finger at the weapon which had drawn Lara's attention earlier.

There were counterpoints I considered, but I also knew there was truth to what they were saying, and I wasn't going to presume to tell them their business, so I let it drop.

"What is next for you, child?" Zenobia asked Lara.

"I'm going to help Hank sort his ship out and he will give me a ride back to my own," she said before adding, "he needs to have his registration signaler removed."

"Costly endeavor," she noted with a hint of something I couldn't quite distinguish in her words.

"But then I will get right back to work," Lara justified as though she was explaining herself to a disapproving teacher.

Zenobia smiled. "You know he would be proud," she said softly, and Lara's face tightened.

"I know," she replied so quietly that the words nearly disappeared into the air. "But I still have a long way to go."

"Not as far as you think," Zenobia said, and I felt like I was the third wheel in a conversation I wasn't meant to be hearing.

Lara stood and patted me on the shoulder. "Buy me a drink?"

"Sure thing, so long as you're paying," I said with a laugh.

"It was nice meeting you, Hank Spears," Zenobia said with a coy smile. "And if you change your mind and ever wish to become hunter Spears, you come back after clearing up the situation with Resh."

"It was nice meeting you. And I have to admit that Hunter Spears has a nice ring to it," I said, and I meant it.

Watching the way Lara interacted with the universe, the way that doors opened for her and, of course, how much money she made, it was hard not to see the appeal of what she did.

The life of a scrapper was one of toil for little gain. It was relentless, exhausting work for little money. Honest, difficult work done by hard working people. But there was never going to be the kind of money in it that I would need if I wanted to help Ned track down this weapon.

And, of course, I had burned my bridge with the Guild anyway. By breaking into an official scrap site, I had made it so that I would never be able to work as a licensed scrapper again. I didn't know if I would be able to get out from under the thumb of Resh, but I would try and if I did, coming back to see Zenobia might not be the worst idea.

I might get myself killed on the first job I ran as a hunter, but unless I could find a way to parlay my scrapper work into some kind of real money-maker, I had to consider all my options.

This might all be moot anyway, I considered, thinking about the fact that, even without a registration signaler in the *Buzzard*, I was in pretty bad shape. I might not be on the run from every entity in the universe, but I still had very few prospects.

Maybe Edgar can help me out?

I didn't like the idea of having to go back to him for help or the fact that he might have to make sacrifices for me, but I was running out of options.

When we left the building, Lara guided us up the Via Falco to where it intersected with the Via Vinarea. The streets were aptly named, making it clear what you were going to find on them based on just the designation alone. But rather than being a street with a series of different bars and Taverns, there was one massive, multi floored bar full of bounty hunters, sitting around and jawing.

Every hunter had their own unique look and style and there were even a few species sitting at the tables out on the street in front of the building that I didn't recognize. The more time I spent away from Bussel and the surrounding planets, the more I was coming to realize how truly vast this universe was. I had met several species, more than most probably, but I hadn't even begun to scratch the surface apparently.

"Should I be in here?" I asked nervously. "Couldn't somebody just hit me with a brick and bring me to Resh right now?"

"No bounties in the Conclave. I brought you here so no one can claim you. Another bounty hunter rule," Lara explained as we stepped through the door to the expansive bar.

Though this building used electric lights, they were disguised to appear old-timey. A brazier set in the center of the room had a flame in its center which produced no heat because the fire appeared to be shaped, blown glass with flickering bulbs within. Metal tables were filled with patrons, and I realized just how many hunters there were. I had never known any, had only heard rumors of them, but now I understood that they were far more in numbers than I had known.

There were bounty boards framed like art, changing by the moment and displaying available bounty jobs. I saw the prices being offered for some, the staggering fees a person could be paid for bringing in pirates, crime lords and even politicians—if a hunter could get to them.

On the walls, massive mosaics of intricate tiles showed images of hunters collecting bounties throughout the universe and behind the long stone bar was an image of a man with a club held high in one hand and a dead lion in the other.

"Orion, ancient god of the hunt," Lara informed me, following my gaze. I could swear I learned something different about him but just had to trust that the people here knew what they were talking about. "There is a certain devotion to the ways of old here."

"I picked up on that," I said. We sat at the bar, and it didn't take long before a Kyrog in a large tunic lumbered over.

"Two belts," Lara ordered, and the man nodded before turning away to mix our drinks. I watched the bartender work for a moment, noting that nearly every bartender I had seen recently had been of his species.

"I feel like all I have done since leaving Bussel is go from bar to bar," I noted, and Lara simply nodded.

"That's the life of a hunter, too," she asserted. "No matter where you go in the universe, bars are a natural meeting place and tend to be where the information can be found. Drinks loosen lips so there are few places better to root people out."

"That makes a certain sense," I said, and the bartender returned with our drinks. It was some jet-black liquid on ice. "I hope it tastes better than it looks."

The corners of Lara's lips pulled down in a showy expression of worry. "It's an... acquired taste…"

"All the best things are," I said, raising my glass and taking a sip. "Oh, why?" I rasped at the taste of the alcoholic concoction.

"I hate it too!" Lara burst, laughing until she turned red. "I just wanted to see you try it."

"Ugh," I sputtered. "Just like that milk."

"That's right!" she said, pointing at me and laughing even harder as she remembered when she tricked me into drinking spoiled milk a moment after trying it herself.

Wiping a tear away, her laughing slowed and we stared at one another for a long moment.

"It really has been so great to see you," I told her, and I had never been more honest than I was at that moment. "We were up a creek when you found us, and since then, our fates have changed. I don't feel like I'm about to die anymore."

"Now you feel like you have a few months to live?" she asked with a smile before sipping her drink and wincing at the taste.

"Something like that," I admitted. Turning to the bartender, I gave a quick wave to get his attention. "Got any Bussel Brews?"

He nodded and then checked with Lara with a glance. She

nodded. "Tab it, too," she told him before turning to me. "I can't even remember the last time I had a Bussel Brew."

"You remember the first time we had them?"

"I do!" she exclaimed, tapping the bar with a nail. "We broke into that place, oh, what was it called?"

"Fat Gus's," I reminded her.

"Right!" she said, a genuine smile breaking out on her face. "And he had nothing worth stealing but there was a fridge full of beer. We were so young, but it felt like finding gold."

The bartender returned and set the two amber bottles in front of us.

"It even looked like striking gold," I said, remembering the way the fridge full of beers looked when we swung the door open in the dark and it glowed like a treasure chest in a movie.

"You remember what else happened that night?" she asked, raising an eyebrow, obviously trying to get a rise out of me.

"It was the first time we kissed," I said, rolling my eyes.

"First and only," she said as though I had offended her by not trying it again.

But I shook my head and took a sip of the beer that tasted like home. "No."

She slapped me on the shoulder. "That moment in the orphanage play does not count."

"Did our lips touch?" I asked and now it was her turn to roll her eyes.

"Got shut down, you know," I said quietly after a moment.

She cocked her head. "Our orphanage?"

"Yeah," I told her.

"That's too bad," she said, taking a swig. "They really tried their best with us."

"They did," I agreed. "Not that you and I made it easy on them."

"That we did not," Lara said and held her bottle up. I tapped mine against it and we fell silent again.

There was so much history between us and we had met so far from home that it felt like there was so much and so little to be said all at once.

"I know you don't want to talk about it but…" I began but Lara started talking at the same time.

"So I have been thinking about your situation," she started and we both chuckled and stopped speaking. "You go."

"No," I said. "I think yours is far more important."

"I've been thinking about your situation," she began again. "And I want to pay for your registration signaler to be removed out of my cut of the Thorpe bounty; the other half of which I want you to have so that you can start turning your life around."

I shook my head no. "I can't let you do that," I announced.

"You don't have a choice," she stated unequivocally. "What I choose to do with my money is my own business and if I want to give it to you, I will."

"I know better than to argue with you."

"Good," she said. "I think what you're doing is noble and worth doing. I would never admit this in front of him, but I think that Ned is telling the truth and trustworthy. The work you guys could do might change the universe. And this universe needs changing. You and I both know that."

"That we do," I agreed.

"I want you to be able to, at the very least, have a fair shot at accomplishing something. And the only way you're going to be able to do that is with some money. And we both know you're not going to be able to make any money doing little freelance scrapping jobs. Not while you have… everyone and their mother after you."

"Right," I snorted, thinking about all of the groups who were after me.

"And that's one more thing I'm going to do for you," she said with a clever little smile. "I'll go talk to Resh on your behalf. I know what's coming for you and if I can take at least one of those away, I will."

"You can't," I said, feeling immense guilt for all of the things she wanted to do for me and my inability to pay her back.

"Stop trying to tell me what I can and can't do," she said and this time, she sounded like Kilara. "I told you already that I want you to do some good in this universe so let me help you do it. Friends don't abandon friends."

I finally decided to ask the question again that I had known I wanted to ask since she began to move in on Thorpe while I distracted her. "Why don't we stick together?"

She broke eye contact, looking at her beer as though it was going to have the answers. "It's too dangerous. The enemies you've made, I don't want. I want to help you, need to help you, but I can't come with you."

"As much as it pains me to say it, I completely understand," I admitted. "I wish that you could join us more than anything, but I understand why you can't. And, honestly, it's the answer I wanted to hear. Because, as much as I might want Kilara Vex by my side, I don't want to put Lara Shen at any risk."

She smiled sincerely at me. "You've become quite a good man, Hank," she asserted. "When all is said and done."

"Thanks," I said in a questioning tone.

"And I really think you might just be able to do great things."

35

We spent the night at the Conclave. With bounty money, I rented a hotel room not far from Lara's apartment. I showered and, at her recommendation, shaved. On the Via Taberna, we shopped and got supplies for the *Buzzard*.

Lara introduced me to a mechanic who knew how to remove registration signalers. Despite the fact that I wanted to make any and all repairs myself, she also convinced me to allow him to work on the ship itself. He repaired and upgraded the shield generators, patched a few of the most egregious holes and installed the MediScanner Ned had requested.

For a fee that was akin to highway robbery, he also restocked my fridge and pantry, replaced my bedding and replaced the lightbulbs that had burned out.

When I went to pay the man with my half of the bounty, he waved me away.

"It's all been taken care of," he said, nodding in the direction of Lara who, herself, had also purchased a few upgrades.

"It's not just your ship that we need to outfit," she had told me and reached around the side of my body, sliding her hand around my waist and pulling out my stomper. "Does this thing even shoot straight?"

"It shoots," I said with a shrug. "I don't know about straight."

She set it down on the table of the weaponsmith beside her blade, giving me a chance to get a good look at it for the first time. It was blue and seemed to glow with some kind of internal light. I couldn't tell what material the thing was even constructed of, and I thought that I knew most elements found around the universe.

"My version of the *Buzzard*," she told me as she handed it to the one-eyed weaponsmith in a tank top.

The weaponsmith took both weapons and told us to come back in an hour.

"Your heirloom is nicer than mine," I said with a laugh.

"Worth more, too," she said in a tone that made it clear she wasn't joking.

Guiding me toward an armorer, she had me step into his stall and pick out some new clothes.

"Workman's coveralls aren't going to keep you safe from a bullet or a beam," she said gravely. "You can keep the boots and the jacket and, of course, this," she said, knocking on the chest plate I had stolen from the hunter I had killed. "But you need to have it altered and painted in case we run into one of his friends around here. No one can collect your bounty on-planet, but that wouldn't stop somebody from following us out of here and blasting our asses back to the stone age when we leave orbit."

"I want to keep this too," I said, handing the armorer my tool belt. "I've never gone anywhere without it, and I don't want to start now. But I also think it needs another holster, as well as a few other additions."

"Now you are thinking," Lara asserted. "With our powers combined, we might just keep you alive long enough to actually accomplish something."

"I'm only alive now because of you and anything I accomplish after this will be because of the foundation you're setting up for me right now."

"I know," she said and smiled before pointing at some of the tears in her stealth suit. "I'm going to have some of these holes repaired and I don't think we need to watch each other change," she said and gestured in the direction of another armorer who was going to help her.

We both spent some time getting our outfits upgraded before grabbing our weapons and heading back to the ship. Once we had boarded and were alone again, Ned finally spoke.

"I've analyzed the arm," he informed us, and we shared a look.

"I kinda forgot about the arm," I admitted.

"Not me, I totally remembered," Lara lied.

Ned didn't say anything for a beat. "Anyway," he said finally as though he was speaking to two children. "The arm is an artificial intelligence from the Old War that has been wiped and reprogrammed so many times that its core programming is no longer accessible even if it's still somewhere in there."

"What does that mean?" I asked.

"It means that the arm could be programmed by us to suit our needs the same way Thorpe had programmed it as a kill switch."

"The Peacers are using AI?" I asked, astonished.

"No, I don't believe that Thorpe let anyone know she was using the technology and there was no code to indicate that anyone other than her had been involved recently," Ned explained. "But I believe that you are missing the point."

"So, what's the point, then?" Lara asked.

"The point is that we have found something which we could program to serve as a companion for someone who needs it," he explained, and Lara spread her hands in confusion.

"We could bring it to Libby!" I exclaimed excitedly.

"You can't see but I'm tapping my finger to my nose," Ned joked.

"What's a Libby?" Lara asked.

I smirked. "Mind if we make a pit stop on the way back to your ship?"

When we arrived at Suniuo Station, Ned told Libby it was us and she allowed us to dock, turning on the lights and allowing us into the command room without the bells and whistles she used to scare people off.

"A week ago, I thought AI was extinct," Lara groused. "Now I know three. If the Inquisition ever gets a hold of me, I'm in as deep as you guys."

"The Inquisition has no reason to suspect anything of you," I assured her though I wasn't entirely sure I believed what I said. She had spent a fair amount of time with us and we both knew that there was a realistic risk that she might see John Gregory's face again and that he had seen hers.

"You guys are back!" Libby exclaimed excitedly. "You brought the girl back too! Is she staying with me? You best not be here just to ask me for another favor and expect me to give it!"

"We *do* come bearing gifts," Ned informed her.

"But it's not me!" Lara put in. "Just to make that crystal clear."

"Aww, but I want one," Libby said.

Lara stutter-stepped and looked up at me. "That was creepy."

"You think that comment was creepy? You should have seen this whole place before," I noted. "But Libby's good people."

"I'll have to take your word for it," she said, and I set my bag down as we stepped into the command room. Lara gawked up at the face on the massive screen whose eyes were watching what I was doing as I pulled the arm out and set it down on the floor.

Between the fingers at the front and the bonus manipulators at the back, it moved around like a four-legged creature, cowering and staying close to the bag.

"It's so cute!" Libby exclaimed.

"I'm happy you think so," I said.

Ned didn't miss a beat. "I hope this makes us even and shows that we are men of our word."

Lara's eyes darted from the screen with an AI face, her childhood friend who she reconnected with as a bounty and an artificial arm nuzzling my leg like a dog. "This is the weirdest moment of my life."

"What should I name it?" Libby asked, ignoring Lara but I looked up at her and couldn't help but laugh.

"Can you imagine telling you and me as seven-year-olds about this?" I asked with a laugh, and she just shook her head.

"I wouldn't believe it if I wasn't seeing it for myself," she said and then dropped her voice to a whisper. "We also should have cleaned it before bringing it here," she noted. Dry flecks of Thorpe's blood flaked onto the hard station floor.

"It's better this way," Libby answered excitedly. "I have a whole creepy motif happening up in here, so it totally works."

"Oh, good," Lara said apprehensively.

"Libby," Ned put in. "Now that we are square and you can see that we are to be trusted, perhaps we could work out a deal where we use this station as a base of operations?"

"Bring me more presents like this and you have a deal," she said before cooing at the arm. "Come here, Army, come here… I'm still workshopping the name."

"I don't like Army," Ned said without missing a beat. "Feels… disrespectful."

"Oh, shoot, okay," Libby said. "How about King Arm-thur?"

Lara and I shook our heads. "Okay, I'll think about it for a while," she said. "But, you know, sure. If you guys want to come visit safe harbor or whatever, that would be totally fine."

"I might start coming up with a way to get this station off official records as well, then," Ned said. "The last thing we need is more people poking around here."

"Add it to the list," I joked. "Though, thanks to Lara, that list has actually shrunk some."

"It's true," Ned agreed. "Thank you both."

I let a little smirk cross my face. "I didn't think you were capable of gratitude."

"I am when I have something to be grateful for," he quipped back.

"I see how it is," I retorted.

"But, really, Hank," he began in a sincere tone I rarely heard from Ned. "Be better and I'll be grateful."

At that, both Lara and Libby burst out loud laughing, and I just shook my head, unable to help a little smile.

Things finally felt like they were trending in a positive direction. I had been resupplied, the *Buzzard* had been repaired, I was going to be able to put Resh in the rear view and we now had a place where we could be safe and hide out while we figured out what to do next. I had been on the run since the moment that I had met Ned, but now it seemed as though we might finally be able to turn things around and investigate this threat.

The arm shifted away from me and began walking toward the screen displaying the face of Libby while Lara and I watched.

I turned to my old friend, thinking about all that she had done for me and how far we had come since she pulled a gun on me the first time she discovered Ned.

"Thank you," I said, looking her right in the eyes.

She turned to face me and smiled.

"That's what friends do," she said. "They are there for each other."

"I know," I said, "but you didn't have to do any of this. When you realized that it was me, you could have just turned me in or left me alone. But you chose to come with me, chose to take a risk on me and helped me at every turn. It was a remarkable thing that you did and now, I'll never be able to repay you."

"Certainly not on a scrapper's salary," she said with a laugh.

"You know what I meant."

She nodded and reached out, putting a hand on my shoulder. "I know what you meant, and you don't ever have to repay me. I've lived a life where I try to do right and don't know if I'm succeeding but I feel like by helping you, I'm doing something good because you are doing something good."

"Could all be a lie," I suggested, and she smiled.

"It could."

"It isn't." Ned interjected. We both grimaced. "Did I spoil a nice moment? I've been told I do that."

"I can totally see that," Libby added.

Lara squeezed my shoulder and I reached across my chest to put my hand on top of hers.

"Okay, let's get you back to your ship."

36

"That's when William fired and dropped the only shatter bomb we had left," Ned said, continuing to regale us with stories of the war as we rode the gyre back to Port Tortue. Lara and I were both on the edge of our seats and leaned in to hear what happened next. "I had done all of the calculations and knew the bomb would miss by a small margin. It would damage the exterior of the base but wouldn't be enough to disable the shields and win the fight."

"Oh, no," Lara said before covering her mouth as though she had been caught saying something she shouldn't. Or maybe she just didn't want to appear as invested as she obviously was.

"But my calculations had failed to take one thing into account," Ned said, pausing for dramatic effect. "The air conditions... wind. Without being able to know every detailed contour of the planet, every previous weather condition and all the other factors that had ever gone into creating the wind in that moment, I couldn't accurately calculate it. But somehow, William had known exactly how much it was going to help carry the bomb.

"He was smart like that, instinctive. He could see things that others couldn't. And apparently, he could calculate things that even a computer wasn't able to. It was an innate sense. Certain people are born heroes and William West was the very definition of that.

"The bomb dropped directly into the vent, rolling the entire length of the shaft and down into the power grid. I tell you both, the explosion that followed was a top ten easy, maybe even top five. A moment later, the shield lost power and our boys were able to jump from their trenches and begin the forward assault.

"Cult leadership sent their best at us but there was nothing that they could do without their shields and soon, we had overwhelmed them, taken back the factory and freed the city. It was one of the first great victories and a turning point in the war."

"Man, if the museum on Bussel told stories like this, maybe it wouldn't be so boring that the kids sneak out back to smoke," I said.

Lara laughed. "That's right! Myles got in so much trouble for taking half the class out back."

"But not us," I said, remembering the moment.

"Why not you?" Ned asked, sounding bored by the change of subject.

"Because the two of us used the opportunity while the chaperones were distracted to sneak into the gift shop and snag a few things. Hank, as always, distracted the clerk and I pinched a few toys for us. We got so much use out of those toy soldiers, I can't even tell you."

In a dull, mocking droll, Ned said, "Oh, please go on."

"She stuck a bag of toy soldiers under her dress and snuck it all the way back to the orphanage and we played with them for years. That boy, Myles, stepped on one of them and broke his gun; Lara broke his nose."

She put her feet up on the console. "I did."

"Also," I said, turning to her. "It was great that you picked up on exactly what I was doing with Thorpe."

"I knew that move the second I saw it," she said excitedly. "It was like we picked up exactly where we had left off. I mean, obviously you look quite a bit older and... I don't think dumpy is the right word but..."

I cut in. "It's the Scrapper outfit!"

She chuckled. "I know, I know."

"I used the MediScanner on you when you were checking it out and determined that you're well within a healthy weight range for a man your age," Ned added.

I ran my hands down my face, feeling my smooth chin for the first time since I was old enough to grow a beard. "I don't like either of you," I said without any intonation.

"Nah, he's lying," Lara said with a broad smile on her face.

"I know this," Ned said as though he hadn't picked up on the sarcasm. "Arriving at Port Tortue."

We strapped back in and prepared to wash out at the space station. When we did, something seemed different. The normal traffic that had surrounded the port was nowhere to be seen and bits of scrap and pieces of junk floated in the area like around the wreckage of a ship.

A knot formed in the pit of my stomach, and I only had one thought. "Get us in there, I have to check on Edgar."

"Are you sure you want to do that?" Ned asked.

Lara added, "Whatever did this might be on the station."

"It could be a trap," Ned continued.

"It's almost certainly a trap," Lara added before a realization dawned on her. "My ship! Ned, take us in and we will have a look around."

"Shall I start hacking the systems to discover what happened?" Ned asked as he took control of the *Buzzard* from me and began to guide us into port.

"Not yet," I said. "We will have a look around and let you know what we find. I don't want you to get caught intruding on a system and drawing Inquisition attention unless you absolutely have to."

"Understood," Ned said. "But I will begin poking around while keeping myself veiled just in case you change your mind."

"Fine," I said, staring out the window at all the debris.

A pirate ship spun slowly in place. When it turned into the lights from the *Buzzard*, we discovered that it was only half a ship, torn in two by missiles.

We pushed through toward a closed docking bay door. As we approached, the heavy metal began to separate, allowing us in.

"What the hell happened here?" Lara said, less as a question than an exclamation.

"Illegal industries run the risk of being shut down by the Consortium," Ned said. "Throughout history, piracy has been cracked down on by many, but specifically, by politicians looking to advance their careers by saying they defeated pirates. Famously, Gnaeus Pompeius Magnus waged a war on the Cilician pirates in the year—"

"Not now, Ned," Lara barked, and he stopped speaking immediately.

He set the *Buzzard* down and we disembarked quickly, our newly refurbished weapons at the ready.

When the door to the port opened, we were met by an eerie silence. It was like entering Libby's station for the first time but this time, it was real. The blood stains that streaked the walls were fresh. When we knocked on the closed doors we passed, they were locked tight. The occupants were either dead or too terrified to open up. Either way, we weren't getting any information from them.

After stepping over a dead mechanic, still clutching a red wound in his belly, I broke into a sprint down the hallway, desperate to get to the center. Lara was right by my side, and I registered that she was speaking but not the words she was saying. I was so focused on checking on Edgar that I was aware of almost nothing else.

When we reached the walkway that faced the pillar of businesses at the center of Port Tortue, I stopped, my heart thundering as I stared at licking flames and ruptured metal. The place had been torn apart. A few of the floating platforms lay crashed along the catwalk but I rushed around and over them, tearing for the nearest bridge.

Recognizing some of the businesses I was passing, I realized that Ned had put the ship on the same level as Edgar's bar. It was a small kindness, but I appreciated it. Looking back and forth, I saw that there were no people to be seen anywhere. An occasional body littered the path but, for the most part, it seemed that the occupants had fled.

This place had been so full of life, so packed with people milling about and having a good time and now it was destitute, a lifeless shell of what had existed before. I couldn't believe that the government would do something like this but also figured that it was the only entity in the universe with enough manpower to achieve something like this.

When I rushed around the corner, closing in on the El Tropico 2, my foot skidded on a pool of blood and I slipped, sliding down the hallway and coating half of my body, staining my jacket. I coughed and got to my feet, taking careful steps toward the bar, not knowing what to expect but fearing the worst.

Smoke billowed down the hall when I approached the bar and I saw embers sparking from the scorched tables and bar. Bright red and yellow glowed from inside blackened wood and the false wood's melted plastics drooped and dipped, frozen in time as the melt solidified.

Black air singed my throat when I hurried to the bar and looked over. Edgar wasn't there. Perhaps he had made it out alive, was hiding in the back, or had used the same tunnel to escape that he had sent me through.

A hint of gray caught my eye, and I turned to see the hand protruding from around the side of the counter behind the bar. After leaping over the bar in a quick move, my feet landed heavy on the ground, and I braced myself so as not to slip on the blood still coating the bottom of my boots.

I ran to the end of the counter to see Edgar, his lifeless eyes staring up at the ceiling.

The sound that surged out from within me seemed to shake the very walls of the station. My guttural scream of misery, anguish and guilt roared from my very soul. Seeing the cauterized skin on his chest under the burned ring of his Hawaiian shirt through my tears, I suspected what had happened.

But when my eyes focused enough on his face to truly see him, I knew with absolute certainty. In the skin of his forehead was burned the mark of the Inquisition.

This wasn't just the Consortium cracking down on pirates.

This was for me.

This was all for me and Ned.

I screamed another time, standing and pressing the trigger of my stomper toward the wall, riddling it with bullets just to feel something.

"Hank Spears and Lara Shen," a voice thundered from behind us, and I turned with the heavy handgun leveled right at his helmeted face. The Inquisitorial armor protected him from head to toe, the red plates shimmering in the low light and the black robes flowing in the air of the fire response systems. "You stand accused of conspiring with the enemy, of working with the inorganic, of colluding against the Consortium and disrupting universal peace."

I didn't let him continue. Though I knew it wouldn't do anything to damage him, I unloaded the rest of my magazine into him, bullets crunching against the reinforced armor. The man did not flinch.

"Turn yourselves in and no further harm will come to anyone," he threatened.

Lara looked at me then back at him, slowly beginning to unsheathe her blade.

"No further harm?" I roared. "You killed all these people. Destroyed the lives of everyone here. You murdered…" I looked back at the body of my uncle, the lifeless remains of my family.

But before I could speak, the Inquisitor took another step toward me, hand on the hilt of his own weapon. "It is a small price to pay. A small price for protecting the universe from the greatest threat it has ever known. A small price to cut the infection before it can spread.

"I would burn entire planets to protect the people of the Consortium. There is no cost too great. No line in the proverbial sand."

He took another step toward me and Lara moved to the side by another stride. She was good and I knew that if we had any chance to defeat this man, it would be together.

"The threat is not the AI," I said through gritted teeth. "The threat is you."

"If you believe that, then you are truly lost. You have been corrupted by the purest of evils and you will be cleansed before the universe can be cleansed."

"Cleansed like all these people?" I demanded, sliding out the magazine and replacing it with a steady hand. I was overwhelmed with anger, fear and grief but I remained in control of myself.

Lutch had instilled in me a calm determination. The harder and more challenging things got, the calmer and more resolute I had taught myself to be. After falling through the floor of the Cubi-House that first time, I never did again. I learned. I learned because my father taught me.

So, now, in the face of a threat the likes of which I had never seen, my hand didn't shake.

"Yes," John Gregory said through the thick red helmet with grim, frowning features. "That is precisely what I mean."

He moved toward me once more, each footfall like a thunderclap, and Lara swung even further to his flank. Slowly, our plan was working.

Then the station shook as a distant explosion tore through the port.

"That will be your starship, Miss Shen," he said, and I realized that it wasn't us who were setting the trap.

Lara's rage immediately overtook her, and her blue blade sliced the air from her side as she rushed toward the man.

His sword met Lara's, the molten glow sparking against the oceanic sapphire of hers. She swung wildly, attacking without her usual grace and form. The Inquisitor's movements were smooth and calculating, his parries fluid and easy as though he was her instructor trying to exemplify how to properly fight.

In her anger, she continued her relentless onslaught, and he kept batting her away with ease.

I raised my stomper but there was no shot to take in the confusion of combat and no way I could enter the fray without only making things worse for Lara. If I survived this, I would need to train and learn to fight so that I would never find myself in this situation again. Until then, I kept the barrel of the weapon trained at the Inquisitor, waiting for an opening.

One came when Lara overextended herself, slicing down through the air with a wild move that John Gregory easily sidestepped before swinging a massive, gloved hand to strike the side of her face, sending her hurtling into one of the tables. Mugs and glasses shattered and crashed to the ground beside one of the most adept fighters I had ever seen—now totally outmatched.

Looking for the gaps in his armor, I began firing the stomper again, watching the bullets tink harmlessly off him. He turned and began stalking toward me and I realized that I had no plan other than to get him away from Lara.

At his approach, I turned and took a few steps away from him, looking over his shoulder to see Lara lying limp on the ground. His weapon glowed, heat crackling the air around it.

That gave me an idea and, knowing that I had to do something, I turned toward the bar and grabbed a bottle of Starfarer's Finest, an incongruously named alcohol that tasted like paint thinner. The moment that John Gregory got close enough to swing his blade and remove my head from my shoulders, I whipped the bottle at him, the flammable liquid exploding against his sword and spraying liquid fire around the bar.

Having known what was about to happen, I turned my body away from the flames, took one massive step down the bar, and then grabbed hold of the counter and threw myself over in the direction of Lara.

The Inquisitor let out a furious grunt, the fire dousing him but not slowing him.

As patches of flame licked at his body before sizzling out, he looked like a vision of evil, turning toward us. I knelt and picked up Lara from under her shoulder, her head limp but small mutters escaping from inside her mask as she came to after the hammering blow.

"We have to get out of here," I told her, beginning to walk out of the bar, waiting for her feet to catch up. "We have to get to the *Buzzard* before his acolyte does."

The words seemed to rouse her some and I felt her legs begin to pump, the two of us running for our lives from a man who seemed to want nothing more than to watch us suffer. Any pretense of interrogating us was long gone and now he just wanted us dead.

So, we ran.

Lara could not keep up her usual pace and her blade looked as though it was going to fall limply from her hands at any moment, but she kept pushing, kept running.

But the man was close behind. With long strides, he seemed to be keeping pace with us without even having to jog. Every time I checked over my shoulder, he was bridging the gap between us, getting closer and closer by the moment. Smoke trailed from his billowing robes, giving him the appearance of some monstrous ethereal presence. He was the Inquisition made flesh.

Soon, we had neared the docking bay hallways, knowing we were closing in on the *Buzzard*. I hoped, more than anything, that we reached it before the woman who the Inquisitor had called Imogen. If she got there first, we were done for.

This would be where our story ended.

I would have come this far, survived this long just to see it end at the tip of a blade.

But soon, we saw the door to the docking bay, both of our bodies pushing to reach it, but before we did, the pale young woman with red hair and huge eyes with red irises stepped from a hallway, blocking our path.

In her leather glove clad hands, she gripped a long, ornate spear whose hooked point was alight with a low flame. When she twirled it in front of her, the air was left with red streaks floating between us.

Inquisitor Gregory stopped behind us and Lara and I looked back and forth like trapped rats on a sinking ship. The man lumbered toward us as his acolyte continued to slice the air with her flaming weapon.

"I'll take him, you take her," Lara suggested. "Maybe one of us will get out of this alive."

"No, we both will," I said. "We'll take her together and then get to the *Buzzard*."

She didn't wait for me to say anything else and the two of us moved in on Imogen at once. I raised my weapon, squeezing off a few shots into her chest plate and causing her to react just long enough for Lara to strike out with her blade. The internal power of the weapon crashed against the woman's Inquisitorial armor, blue sparks streaking the air.

Imogen swung the spear, the shaft striking Lara's shoulder, but I took the opportunity to leap forward and grab the weapon just below the flaming point. Imogen's eyes registered shock just before Lara's foot struck her side. She was thrown back and lost her grip on the spear, which I yanked free.

I turned with the weapon in my hand and threw it straight for the chest of the Inquisitor lumbering toward us, hoping that the flaming tip could penetrate his armor.

All hope was dashed when he batted it away, sending the spear clattering to the ground beside him and he continued to walk forward. He was in no hurry to reach us and, as seemed to be his nature, was savoring this moment, enjoying the fear he inflicted on us.

I bent down and picked up the stomper which I had dropped to grab the spear while the two women continued to battle behind me. When I glanced back at them, it seemed that Lara was the more skilled combatant, but it was hard to be sure. I raised my handgun and, knowing that it was pointless, began taking slow, single shots, one after the other.

Crack.

A bullet sparked against his helmet.

Crack.

Another tore through his robe.

Crack.

His chest erupted in a torrent of bullet fire, sending him staggering back.

Turning, I saw a turret blazing with relentless shots. Shells fell like smoking metal rain and I took the opportunity to turn my back on the Inquisitor. I bull rushed toward Imogen but when she saw me, she fell back, clearing a path for us down the hall.

The barrels of the turret turned a deep crimson, the storm of bullets not letting up.

"Get out of there!" Ned ordered.

He had come through for us. He had been watching through the earpiece and hacked the Port's security system just in time.

If the Inquisitor had any doubt that we were working with an AI, there would be no question left now. But, as we ran toward the *Buzzard*, none of that mattered. What mattered was that we were going to survive. We were going to live to see another day.

The door to the docking bay opened and I took one last look back, seeing the turret run out of ammunition just before Imogen hurried over to aid her Master. As I turned back to the ship, I could have sworn she stole a glance at us, but I didn't know for sure.

Ned had the *Buzzard* activated and facing toward the bay doors, retracting the ramp as soon as our feet were on it.

The two of us dragged ourselves to the cockpit just in time for the door to the station to seal as the large bay doors to space opened. In the rear-facing camera, the tip of the Inquisitor's blade began to sear through the metal, but it was too late.

Ned took us out, and we entered space only long enough to activate the already charged Tidal Drive and wash us into a gyre.

We had escaped. Such as we were.

While the gyre rolled around us, I thought about Edgar. About his child and his mate. All of the people who had lost their lives or livelihood because of us. Or because of those who wished to harm us.

My mind was a soup, and when I looked at Lara, I knew hers was as well.

"What do we do now?" I asked.

37

Lara didn't answer.

Ned didn't even say anything.

The sound of the *Buzzard* working was all that could be heard in space.

In the silence, I wondered if Edgar's family was killed as well. I had more questions than I could even begin to contemplate, so I put one to words just to fill the cab with something.

"Was it more Inquisitors or the Consortium military or Prefects who destroyed the Port?" I asked. "And how did they track us? And why do all that?"

I had more but I didn't put voice to them.

"Do you actually want to know?" Ned asked in answer. "I was able to access the Port's security systems and have a clear picture of what happened at the port."

"I want to know," I said and turned to Lara who was still just staring at the gyre, looking as though she might scream or bury her knife in my chest at any moment. I couldn't tell for sure but knew better than to push for any answers at the moment.

"It was all three with the aid of the Consortium Navy," Ned explained. "At first, they surrounded the port and said that it was being seized under Inquisition authority. All of the pirates who tried to flee were pursued and eradicated. Then, the port itself was boarded and swept.

"A handful of Inquisitors backed by Prefects and Marines began tearing their way through the port, destroying businesses and terrifying citizens. They weren't shy about killing or harassing, more than happy to wreak absolute havoc on anyone they came across," Ned said, his voice breaking.

"They destroyed whatever they wanted, making an example of everyone they came across. Even tourists who had committed no crime and done nothing except be at the wrong place at the wrong time, suffered at their hands. It was a disgrace of the highest magnitude."

He stopped speaking for a long moment and I waited, unable to say anything in response.

"When we met, I had believed in the Consortium with absolute dedication, with the unwavering faith in the system I was brought up to trust. It was a faith that I thought was well founded and something that I was proud to be a part of.

"Witnessing what I just did, I don't know what I believe anymore. From the moment we met John Gregory, I knew that the Inquisition was a zealous arm of the government, but I had hoped that it was just a vocal minority cut off from actual authority. Now I realize that this thing that I helped to create, that I lost friends to defend and that I believed in more than anything else in this universe, has been perverted. It has been corrupted and destroyed."

"I'm sorry, Ned, that must be a hard pill to swallow," I said, and I meant it. Though it wasn't quite the same as losing a family member, Ned had lost everything he had believed in. It was a tragedy in its own right, and I was sure he felt as lost as I did.

"Thank you, but it pales in comparison to what you are going through," he said. "Edgar was obviously a good man and wanted to be there for you no matter what you had done or what you were running from. He died because of my very existence, and I will do my utmost to help you right this wrong. In whatever way you see fit."

I almost couldn't bring myself to ask the next question, but I had to. "Did you see it?"

"I did," Ned said, his voice so quiet that I instinctively reached out to turn up the volume on the speaker before realizing it was just the sound of his grief. "Inquisitor Gregory knew exactly where he was going and what he was doing.

"After he had killed your uncle and the others had cleared out the port, he sent them all away to wait for you. As we predicted, it was a trap."

"And it would have worked if not for you," I said. "Thank you, Ned."

"It had to be done and I'm just sorry that I couldn't help you guys sooner or actually kill the bastard. I wish I could have done more," he said miserably.

"You did everything that you could, and we got out of there alive," I reminded him. "That's a lot."

"You couldn't have stopped her from destroying my ship?" Lara asked in the tone of an accusation, her voice cold and detached.

"I was still trying to mask my presence, I'm sorry Lara," Ned said.

"Mask your presence?" she hissed. "The Inquisition knew we had been there, knew who we were, what difference did it make that you were hiding yourself?"

"I didn't have all that information at the time and did the best I could as I gathered more intel," he snapped back, sounding testy now.

"Gregory was already on us when my…" she began again but stopped speaking, folding her arms and curling inward.

I had seen this before. This miserable reaction when she was truly wounded. I had been respectful of the fact that she didn't want to talk about her past, but I also had to ask, "Why does that ship mean so much to you?"

She turned on me with eyes raw with tears. "What does the *Buzzard* mean to you?"

"A lot," I admitted. "Lutch left it to me."

"You understand then," she said, letting the words hang. "It was his. I was going to carry on his legacy and…" She trailed off, pulled out the blade he had also passed down to her, and stared at it.

"I'm sorry, Lara," I said. "For all of this. From the second we met up, your life has become worse."

She looked up from the weapon, a single tear rolling down her cheek.

"I feel the same way about both of you," Ned said, his words cutting the air. "I had no idea that my very existence was going to change both of your lives for the worse."

"Edgar is dead," I croaked. "Your ship is gone and a connection to the past, severed. Ned, your entire belief system has been destroyed."

"We know!" Lara shouted.

"But it isn't our fault," I continued over her. "We are blaming each other and ourselves but we didn't make this world. We are all victims of it. And we can't just sit here and snipe at one another until we all feel too shitty to go on."

"You're right," Ned said, his tone not quite matching his words.

I turned to Lara who was back to gazing at her blade.

"You don't have to keep helping, Lara, you've done so much," I offered. "I'll take you anywhere you like and I'll repay you when I can. For all of it."

"You still don't get it!" She jumped up from her chair, pointing the tip of her blade at me. It wasn't meant as a threatening gesture but had that effect all the same. I leaned back in my chair, holding my hands up defensively.

"Get what?" I asked.

"I'm not going to leave you now, I'm not going to just disappear when you need me," she screamed, another tear rolling down her cheek.

"Okay," I said quietly.

"Hank," Ned put in. "For a man who seems to understand people pretty well, you have one big blind spot."

"No," Lara said. "You don't have to."

"You're right," Ned answered. "*You* should."

Lara glared down at me. "You left me."

"What?" I asked.

"You left me that night," she said again. "When you met Lutch, you just dropped me. You know I was happy for you and never expected you to bring me with you, but I didn't think you would just go with him and never talk to me again."

"I visited," I protested meekly and before she could even speak again, I continued, "No I didn't. Not enough... I was so happy to have found someone, to be out of there that I guess I just forgot about you and everything you had done for me."

"You did!" she screamed, letting the years of pain I had caused her out in her words. "Your life had changed, but mine didn't. I needed you more than ever, and you weren't there. Even when you visited, you weren't there. You would send little absent messages, not respond for days or weeks, and eventually, not at all.

"You were the person I was closest to in the whole world, and you abandoned me like it was nothing. After losing my parents, I didn't think I could have my heart broken again, but I did. It took me years to recover, years to become a new person and escape the version of me that you had left behind, and then you came crashing back into my life.

"I knew things wouldn't be the same the second that I saw you, but I never thought they would become like this."

She trailed off and I said the thing that I needed to have said a long, long time ago. "I'm sorry."

She nodded but didn't answer.

"Only now do I understand how sorry I am. I thought it was just that I showed up and messed up your life as it is, but I didn't realize I had also messed up your life as it was."

She wiped the tears from her face, letting it grow hard once again. "I've blamed you for so long," she said. "But you also made me the person that I am now. If you hadn't left me, I would never have needed to forge my own path. I would never have snuck on that ship and... and changed my own fate."

"Don't give me credit for that," I said and meant it. "Whoever you became after me was not because of me but because of yourself."

"Oh, I'm not giving you credit," she said with a wobbly smile. "I'm just saying that your actions set me on a path. And, maybe now, they will again."

"You really want to stick with us?" I asked.

"I would get out if I were you," Ned joked.

Lara chuckled and shook her head, her hair falling in front of her face. "I shouldn't but, as I said, I'm not going to abandon a friend like some other jerk I know."

"It takes a real talent to be that nice and that mean all in the same sentence," I observed, and she did a little curtsy.

"Are we going to be okay?" I asked after a beat.

"We are," she answered. "But man, oh, man do you owe me."

"I don't want to think about how much that is," I grimaced.

"The ship was nice when I got it, but I also put all of my earnings into it, so, you know…"

"Are you sure you don't want to stab him just a little," Ned asked with a laugh. "I mean, he really blew up, quite literally, your whole life."

"Not helping," I said as Lara eyed her weapon again.

"Like he said," she began. "It's not on him. Not really. And it's not on you."

"I guess that means we all have to go prove that the Enemy AI weapon is real," Ned said excitedly.

I nodded. "Sure."

"But first," Lara said, and I looked puzzled at her.

"What?" Ned asked irritably.

"We have to go see Resh and try to get the bounty off your head," she said. "If I'm stuck on this ship for the foreseeable future, I don't want to run the risk of being blasted out of the sky by a far better equipped bounty hunter."

"Fine," I said. "Let's go see one of the most dangerous men in the universe."

38

It felt odd going back to Bussel. Even though it was home, somehow, it felt distant to me now.

"When were you last here?" I asked Lara who seemed to be lost in her own moment while we guided the ship down to the planet's surface.

"I haven't been back since I left," she said. "When I left, I thought I left this place behind."

"But you have a relationship with Resh?"

"A *working* relationship," she clarified. "And it's all predicated on my work. I have picked up many bounties for him, securing a strong position in case I ever wanted to come back here. But I haven't had any reason to visit him or chat in person or anything like that."

"I see," I said, realizing once again that I didn't actually understand the life of a bounty hunter in any practical sense. "You seem to have had a really clear plan for yourself."

"I did," she nodded. "I never wanted to be caught off-guard."

"I really ruined that," I noted, my guilt still at the forefront of my mind. And, as I was beginning to realize that this would happen often now, I thought of Edgar.

I believed what I had told Ned and Lara: that I wasn't the one at fault. It was Inquisitor Gregory who killed my uncle. But I also lead the Inquisition right to his door.

At that moment, though there was little that could be done about it, I wanted revenge. Not only on Gregory himself, but also the system that allowed it.

This time it wasn't just about finding the weapon and protecting the people of this universe from the threat waiting for it, but also about changing a broken system.

Our relationship with the machine had swung too far one way and we had only ended up hurting ourselves as a result. I would help Ned and hopefully, change the universe for the better as a result.

But first, I had to get out from under the thumb of a crime lord.

We dropped down toward the planet's surface and after a moment, Resh's estate came into view. As soon as Kilara Vex had asked for an audience, we were quick to get an invitation, but I had worried what was going to happen when the *Buzzard* came in for a landing. That was, until Ned reminded me that with the registration signaler removed, no one would know what ship we were operating until we had landed. And it was a safe assumption that the hired thugs protecting Resh's compound wouldn't have an encyclopedic knowledge of all of the starships in the universe.

This was confirmed when we landed and four big bruisers were waiting to greet us and escort us straight to Resh. Lara and I were fully masked and in our full bounty hunter regalia as we stepped from the ship and out onto the landing platform which abutted the estate itself built into the side of Mount Bussel: the mountain which overlooked the city of Bussel—unsurprisingly, the namesake of the planet of Bussel.

Beside the platform was an expansive garden, the green of the plants and grass dulled by the yellow orange sky. There were people tending to the flowers and trimming the hedges, but no one was walking or appreciating the grounds.

"Kilara Vex, welcome," a Kyrog guard in a fine suit said. Though his words were friendly, his demeanor was all business.

Stepping through a flower arch into the garden, more thugs fell in around us and I worried that the moment I pulled down my mask, they would simply beat me to a pulp.

Guess I'll find out, I thought, with more armed goons stationed around the garden following us with their eyes. The Kyrog guided us into a small hedge maze, taking us this way and that before we reached the center where a staircase flanked by two marble statues led down into the mountain.

At the bottom of the stairs, the Kyrog ran a card over a reader and the door slid open.

Stepping into the estate there was not the subterranean layer of tight metal walls and security systems that I had been expecting. Rather, we were asked to take our shoes off so as not to damage the carpet but we were allowed to keep our weapons because, apparently, they would be useless here.

"The room is fitted with a specially adapted inertial damping field from a starship to slow and stop anything above a certain minimum mass traveling above a certain velocity ," the lead thug informed us. "Bullets hit the floor before they make it even a meter."

The comment seemed to be less a threat and more posturing. Just a way of letting us know that we were powerless in this place. As if being surrounded by a dozen armed guards didn't give one that sense already.

"What about particle weapons?" I asked.

The Kyrog fixed me with all his eyes and then grinned mischievously. "You wouldn't even wanna find out what happens if you fired one of them in here."

"No, see, that answer actually just makes me want to find out even more," I told him with a half-smile, but he hardly reacted to my words.

Once our boots were off, we followed the man from the little anteroom out into a beautiful open space of white carpets, elegant seating at ornate tables set with fine cutlery and a huge window that lined the entire far wall, looking out over the city.

"Everything the light touches is Resh's domain," Ned whispered in our ears before chuckling at his own comment, though I wasn't sure why. Resh did all but own this planet and much of the sector.

My feet sank into the thick carpeting, and I wanted to wiggle my toes but knew better than to do so. We continued past a grand piano and paintings of what I assumed were Resh's family members. There were more guards around the room and one standing by a security panel, watching everything that was going on in the mansion.

The entire home was beautiful and opulent and far too fine for a place like Bussel.

When we reached the far side of the room, all the men but the

Kyrog stopped. A massive gray hand knocked lightly on the door, announcing our presence and it beeped before swinging open.

We followed the bruiser in, and he stepped to the side, allowing us to approach Resh's desk, which was positioned in front of more massive windows so that the sinking sun bathed the room in a blinding orange glow. The backlit man stood from his chair and walked over to us.

I had only met Resh once before when he had been making the rounds in the city and came by the shop to threaten Lutch. Seeing him now, I still felt as intimidated as I had at the time, though he was markedly older.

His face was tanned and leathered, his once jet-black hair streaked with white. His shoulders were wide and squared at ninety degrees with his neck and his nose bent at an unnatural angle at two places. His ears were cauliflowered, and the suit he wore looked as though it had to be sewn onto him, it was so tight over his muscles. Though he was undoubtedly twice my age, he looked as though he could still throw a punch that would flatten even the most seasoned boxer in one hit.

"Kilara Vex, as I live and breathe," he said with a light affect, as though they were old friends. He didn't have to make a show of acting threatening, everything about the man and his environment did that for him.

"Resh," she said, extending a hand. "It's good to finally meet you in person."

"Likewise," he said, shaking her hand before holding it out for me. "Who's your friend?" he asked, addressing her and not even looking my way.

"He's who I'm here to talk about," Lara informed him.

"Okay," Resh said after shaking my hand and walking back around to sit at his desk. "Please, sit, have a drink."

He spread his arms in front of the desk in a welcoming gesture and pulled the bottle out from under his desk, pinching three glasses together with his fingers and setting them down before pouring short sips of the booze that was undoubtedly worth more than my life.

To my surprise, Lara pulled off her mask and clipped it to her belt.

"Whoa," Resh said in exaggerated surprise. "Never figured the deadly Kilara Vex to be a beautiful broad."

"Thank you," Lara said, the words carrying the sound of pure disgust. "But I am not here to talk about me, I'm here to talk about Hank Spears."

Though it was hard to see his face with the darkness enveloping his face, I could sense his brows furrowing. His head turned, and from within the black of shadow, two eyes glared at me.

Pulling down the mouth covering and removing my goggles, I revealed myself to the man who had made my business unsustainable, whose operations had destroyed the life of my father and who had sent bounty hunters to kill me.

"What do you think you are doing, bringing him here?" he asked Lara venomously. "This man is a poison. He's got the Consortium running themselves ragged looking for him and you drop this bag of shit on my doorstep?"

"This bag of shit is an old friend," she said. "So I have come to parlay."

"Parlay?" he spit. "I should have one of my boys come in here and pull his head off, do all of us a favor."

Lara reached across his desk, sliding the two drinks he had poured for us across the wood and plucking hers up to have a sip. I could see the white of his teeth as he grimaced.

"Hank's being hunted, sure, but we got his signaler removed so he can move freely without being hunted. We knew better than to bring that heat to your doorstep. But you also can't sit there and tell me that you don't have a few folks with rap sheets hanging around. Let's be honest, here: you, yourself, are on that same list that he's on."

When she finished speaking, she shot back the rest of the drink and set the glass down with a thud on his desk.

"You do live up to your reputation," he said with a chuckle. "Though I don't know where you're smuggling that pair of balls in an outfit that tight."

He peered over the desk to appraise her in the admittedly skintight stealth suit. But this act didn't faze Lara. I knew she had a temper, but she was too smart to let it flare at a moment like this. She stayed calm and collected, her poker face a perfect mask.

"I'm not here to talk about me," she said. "I'm here to pay off his bounty and walk out of here."

"Much as I would enjoy watching you leave, I don't think the deal you offer is something I want to take," he said. "This man was in my employ. His father was in my employ. He not only owes me money but also brought a heat down on me that caused me a great deal of stress. I don't really like being stressed. So, here's my offer: you leave him with me, and I'll pay you his bounty, then get to watch that sweet little ass sashay out of this room."

I turned to look at her and saw contemplation on her face. She could get out from under this. She could leave me behind here and now, take my ship, and start over. It would also repay me in kind for abandoning her. There would be a certain poetic justice to it, and I wondered if all those thoughts were going through her mind too.

"Take the deal," I said.

"Oh, he speaks!" Resh laughed. "But he's right. Take the deal."

She turned to look at me with a mixture of confusion and heartbreak plastered on her face.

"And for you," I said to Resh. "I have another deal. Let me work for you. I'm one hell of a scrapper. Let me do what I'm best at but do it directly for you. No Guild, no middleman, just send me to get supplies and bring them back for you. It'll be profitable for you and it's the only thing I'm any good at."

Resh seemed to consider my deal and for the first time since stepping foot on the estate, Lara spoke as herself and not Kilara Vex. "A scrapper?" she exclaimed. "After everything, you are going to go back to just hauling junk?"

"It's all I know," I told her. "Everything else, it's something I am not. Like I am doing an impression of someone else."

"But everything Edgar said," Ned said, his voice carrying the same disappointed astonishment as Lara's.

"I need the money, and this is the only way I know how to get it," I said with a certain finality and Lara's face twisted into disgust with me. But I smiled at her.

Turning back to Resh, I stood, and Lara followed suit. "Do we have a deal?" I asked, taking down the drink in one quick swig and extending my hand across the ornamental desk.

"This has been so pathetic that I'm inclined to agree to it," he said, adding condescension to cover the fact that he knew a good deal when he saw it. The fact that I was a wanted man was likely no different from half the people in his employ and something he could work around.

It would have been easier to kill me but now that I was here and offering my services in an untraceable ship, the deal was worth taking.

"I heard you say you need the money, so I'll offer you a good deal: five percent on everything you haul in," he suggested, proffering a crocodile smile.

"Fifteen," I said optimistically, thinking he might offer ten at best.

"Seven," he said, sounding impatient, and I nodded, knowing he wouldn't offer anything else.

"I can't believe you," Ned sounded as deflated as I had ever heard him.

Resh smirked at me as though I was the most pathetic thing he had ever seen in his life. And, in that moment, perhaps I was.

Out of the corner of my eye, Lara was watching, taut as a bow string.

The crime lord stood and reached across the desk, taking my hand in his hard, calloused mitt.

I clamped and did the one thing no one in their right mind would do.

His head blotted out the light of the sun and I could see the anger in his eyes when I pulled his arm, dragging his body across the desk with one hand while the other reached for the taser Lara had affixed to my belt, pulling it free and slamming it against the man's vascular neck.

At the same moment, Lara spun and crossed the room in a lightning quick pounce, jumping up and plunging her blade into the neck of the Kyrog before he could even pull out the gun from inside his jacket.

Resh fell limp against the desk while his henchman slumped to the floor, blood spurting from his neck.

Lara looked over at me and I put the taser back before hurrying around and beginning to heave the man onto my shoulder.

"Good thing they didn't make me take my gloves off with my shoes," I noted, knowing I could not have tased him if we had been shaking barehanded.

"Hank," she sputtered, staring at me in disbelief. "I bought it. Right up until the last moment, I believed you."

"Me too," Ned admitted.

"I'm tired of letting the universe dictate the terms," I said, crouching down and getting under Resh so that I could lift him onto my shoulder. "Here, now, is when we turn it around."

"What are you going to do with him?" Lara asked before adding, "if we can get out of here alive."

"When we get out of here, I'm bringing him in and taking Zenobia up on her offer," I explained quickly, carrying the unconscious Resh to the door and pulling my stomper out with my right hand. "And after that, I can pay you back or we can stick together. Whatever you want."

Blood dripped from the tip of her blade, seeping into the white carpet. "You're stuck with me now," she said.

"I wouldn't have it any other way," I said, and we began to hear shouting from the other side of the door.

"But how the hell are we going to get out of here?" she asked, seriously questioning if I had any semblance of a plan.

"Together," I told her. "Ned, can you get into the system?"

"Already in," he said.

"I knew I could count on you," I said with a smile, Resh's belt pressing hard into the flesh of my shoulder. He was all muscle and it showed in his weight. "And is it true about the dampening field?"

"It is," he said. "There is a man on the far side of the room with manual controls so he can turn it on and off for the benefit of his allies."

"That's exactly what I was hoping you would say," I told him, having noticed the operator on the way in. "Think you can override and give us the advantage?"

"Sure, but every time he flicks that switch, the system will fight back," he said. "There will be some inconsistencies."

I turned to Lara. "Does that outfit Resh loved so much work?" I asked and she wasted no time in pulling off her belt and handing it to me before pulling on her mask and tucking her hair within it. Once she had affixed the neck to seal herself in, the stealth suit shimmered, and she disappeared. There was a slight blur like a gas leak when she moved, but otherwise she was hidden.

Even her blade was synchronized to the system and its internal light faded to invisibility after she wiped the blood off on the padding of a fancy chair. She moved to stand by the door, compressions in the carpet being the only giveaway as to her presence.

"You make straight for the system operator, and I'll distract the others while Ned gives me clean shots and keeps those thugs from ending this before it even begins," I said, my heart racing.

I worried that my plan was insane, that this would never work but I didn't let that fear show and, for the first time in my life, I was truly taking my own fate in my hands. I wasn't just trying to survive, running to the next thing or away from some danger. I was taking action and fighting back.

"Everyone ready?" I asked.

"Ready," Lara answered as more and more shouts emanated from the other side of the door.

"Yes, sir," Ned answered seriously.

"Open it," I said to Lara, and she swung the door open, wavy air the only indication that she had darted from the door until blood sprayed up from the throat of one of the men.

"He's got the boss!" one shouted and the operator turned to change the magnetization.

The thugs were in a semicircle around the room, every one of them positioned near some piece of cover. I ran from the doorway and toward the piano, planning to use it in case Ned couldn't make it work.

"Now," the operator called, and the room filled with the sound of discharging weapons.

I kept low but pressed forward, waiting for the impact of bullets around me but they never came. Confused shouting followed as the goons and the operator blamed one another.

"Off," Ned said, and I ran from behind the piano, raised my stomper, and put three slugs in the chest of a man standing just beside a statue of a naked woman.

Another cascade of blood as Lara traversed the room toward the operator and I kept running, moving into position behind an island bar and grunting at the weight on my shoulder.

"Now!" the operator shouted and once again, all the thugs fired their weapons at once, their bullets slamming to the ground in front of them as Ned overrode the system.

"Go," Ned said, and I ran again, popping off a few shots in the direction of another but hitting nothing but art as the people I was shooting at had figured out that something was amiss.

One was even smart enough to return fire, the glass beside me cracking and spitting shards down on me.

"He is hacking the system," the operator yelled. "It must be—" but his words were cut off with the top of his head when Lara swung the blade through him.

"Off," Ned said, and I popped up from behind the bar, winging another guard in the shoulder with a bullet from my stomper.

"On," he shouted, and I watched as they returned fire flaccidly.

"Off." I squeezed off more shots, and Lara moved around from behind them. Only one of the thugs got wise to what was happening and tried shooting at the rapid blur making its way toward him. But it was too late.

Lara plunged her blade into his chest, the specks of blood on her suit and dripping down her blade the only thing that was beginning to give away her position.

"Off," Ned said, and I emptied the rest of my magazine into the remaining thug.

The room was now empty of enemies, and I hurried toward the bloody blade by the door to the stairs. I was straining under the weight of the unconscious man and the bullet wound in my shoulder that had almost totally healed, now screamed out in pain.

"Good work," I told Lara.

"We're not done yet," she said, using a keycard she had swiped from a body as it fell before her to open the door. "I counted ten more guards on the roof."

"Right," I said, letting the magazine slide from the weapon onto the soft carpet before awkwardly trying to jam another one in the bottom of the stomper. Invisible hands reloaded the weapon quickly and I stepped into my boots, taking a deep breath before hurrying up the stairs to engage in a second firefight.

"Wrong," Ned said as we reached the top and saw bodies torn to shreds, smoking anti-spacecraft weapons and the *Buzzard* hovering right in front of us, waiting to take us away.

"Impressive, Ned," I said, and he spun the *Buzzard* so that we could clatter up the ramp. I dropped Resh on the ground, rubbing my shoulder. Lara pulled the mask off and shook her hair free.

"You, too, Hank," he said. "That was a hell of a plan. Almost worthy of William West."

Lara looked at me excitedly with her mouth open.

"I don't think I was ready for that," I said like I was accepting an award I didn't believe I would win.

"We don't have to make a big deal out of this," Ned said.

Lara and I smiled at one another.

"We absolutely have to make a big deal out of this," she said, walking over and patting me on the back.

We dragged Resh to the converted bathroom that I decided was going to become a holding cell and then moved up to sit in the cockpit.

Ned had us ready to lift off and we strapped ourselves in, preparing for the journey.

"Ready to become Hunter Spears?" Lara asked.

I took one last look down at Bussel, unsure of when I would return but sure that my life as a scrapper was being left behind on the planet's surface.

"I'm ready."

39

Resh had come to by the time we got to the Conclave and was screaming threats at us the entire way from the *Buzzard* to Zenobia's. Accustomed to the sight, hardly any one batted an eye at two hunters pushing a target through the street but many did take note when they realized who it was. I heard his name whispered as well as that of Kilara Vex.

People pointed at me and asked each other who I was that I could be keeping such company and dragging in one of the heads of the twelve families. Others began to appear from inside buildings or were pointing from the windows above the streets. I had never received any attention like this, but Lara seemed to be reveling in it.

"You and your friends are dead!" Resh screamed at the top of his lungs at me, drawing even more attention.

A hunter in elaborate golden armor stopped and stared as we passed.

Lara squealed with delight at the attention. I had never seen her more excited. Well, not since meeting her again, anyway. When we were kids, she would get excited about little things all the time and it was nice to see her acting that way again. Even if it was over the fact that we were bringing a man to undoubtedly be executed by his government.

The existence of the cartels was another example of what the Consortium had become since Ned's time. The crime lords greased the right palms and stayed in operation by paying off Sectoral Governors, but they were also wanted by the government. At any point, some zealous Prefect Officer could decide they wanted to go after these criminals but instead, they were allowed to operate while their activities were condemned in Parliament by the very people who allowed them to continue.

Bringing in this bounty was going to be a big deal for a short period of time though it wouldn't be our names that made the news. Instead, some member of the government would say that their crackdown on crime had been a success and people in the capital would tell themselves that they were a little bit more safe until the next celebrity did something interesting and a new criminal stepped in to take Resh's place.

The one thing that would change was my fate.

"I want the bounty on me lifted and I wish to turn in my first bounty," I announced to Zenobia as we stepped into her office.

The old woman gawked at the sight before her.

Getting up from behind her desk, she walked around and looked at the three of us before pulling out her glasses, placing them on her nose and repeating the process.

"Let me stand on ceremony," she said as though it was a great inconvenience. "Who so nominates this man?"

"I, Hunter Kilara Vex, so nominate this man to enter at rank one by the name of Hunter Spears."

Zenobia nodded and grinned at me.

She looked as though she was about to speak but Resh butted in. "You are seriously going to do all this in front of me? Just let me go and I might let you live, old hag."

I could hear the sharp inhalation from Lara just before Zenobia moved faster than I had ever seen a human being move. With unnatural speed, she stuck him in the side with something and he collapsed to the ground, spittle pouring from his mouth.

"Where were we?" she asked herself, but I simply stared at her in awe. "Oh, yes, the weapon," she said before looking me over and turning to ask Lara a question. "Does he have a weapon of ceremony?"

"I have this," I answered, pointing to my stomper.

But Lara spoke over me. "He does not."

"You will see to that?"

"I will," Lara answered.

"Then he will remain rank one and under your eye until this is remedied, understood?" Zenobia asked, setting her eyes pointedly at Lara.

"I understand."

"And you have earned a new rank as well I believe," Zenobia said and stepped close to Lara, putting a hand on her cheek. "You have come such a long way, my dear."

"Thank you," Lara said, her voice nearly breaking.

Resh twitched on the ground.

"You know what I am going to tell you," the old woman said, looking for a moment at that one weapon on the wall that seemed to mean something to Lara and that I took to be her mentor's non-ceremonial weapon.

"I know," she said. "I do it all for him."

"No," Zenobia scolded. "Do it all for yourself but know he would be proud."

"Yes," Lara corrected herself, dropping her head like a child being admonished.

"And you," Zenobia turned to me. "I hereby declare you rank one Hunter Spears under the watch and to the tutelage of Kilara Vex until such a time you are deemed worthy."

I looked back and forth between the two women. "Should I bow? I feel like I should bow."

"You don't have to," Lara said.

"I'm not opposed to it," Zenobia smiled. "But you do have a lot to learn."

Stepping back around her desk, she got her tools for identifying s bounty and got to work on Resh while Lara and I sat and waited. Even though she had lost her ship, my old friend seemed genuinely happy at the moment, and I was grateful for that.

I had come back into her life and caused so much chaos that I was grateful to turn it around for her. And, of course, for myself.

Without Resh's bounty on me and with a steady stream of income, the three of us could begin an actual investigation into the super weapon. The Consortium and the Inquisition would continue to hunt us but it would be far more difficult without a registration signaler giving them a heads up. Additionally, with the money from turning Resh in, I could change the look of the *Buzzard* some and make it even more difficult for them to find us.

Things might just turn around and we would finally be able to start doing some proper good in the universe.

"Confirmed," Zenobia told us before pressing an intercom button on her desk. "Consortium pickup."

It wasn't long before two women in pseudo-Prefect attire arrived and put Resh on something that looked like a gurney. Strapping him down, binding his hands, feet and neck, they rolled him away for 'processing,' whatever that entailed.

When they pulled him through the door, I felt a certain satisfaction in seeing him carted away. Though Lutch had his own demons, and would have found ways to feed them, Resh had facilitated the path he stumbled down and helped speed along his decline. And while it wasn't some great vengeance, I did know it was a small good.

"Your new account, Hunter Spears, has been credited with half the bounty," Zenobia informed me, turning her computer monitor to show me the new balance.

It was more money than I had ever seen in my life. Not a set-up-your-retirement-fund amount, but enough to start this new life off right.

I hadn't said much since entering the office, but I did have questions.

"What do the ranks mean?" was the first thing that came to mind.

Zenobia steepled her fingers, seeming to think about the answer for a moment. "Access," she said finally.

"You're going to have to give me a bit more to go on," I said.

That clever smile split her face again. "With every rank, you gain priority access to available bounties, more doors open to you and different shops are revealed."

"Scrappers do things differently, you bid on jobs, setting the cost against what you will earn," I explained.

"While that is different, there are inherent similarities: only those established scrappers could afford the higher profit jobs and here it is the same, except that the hunter's rank is the barrier for entry," Zenobia explained. "You will find that there are a great many differences between the likes of a scrapper and that of a hunter. But I believe that your past will help to shape your future. What you have seen and done will make you more capable in this new role.

"You also have the help of someone who, themselves, learned from the best," she said, pointing at Lara who was sitting back and smiling.

"What, me?" she asked when she noticed that the two of us were staring at her.

"Yes," Zenobia said. "You will help guide Spears."

"I will," she said absently, and Zenobia returned to her computer for a moment.

"As expected, you have achieved rank three, Vex," she said, and the pride was unmistakable in her voice. Like a proud parent, she looked at Lara and grinned.

She looked giddy for a moment before her face fell. "This almost makes up for…" trailing off, she sounded like it was impossible to say the words. "The *Retiarius* was destroyed."

Zenobia registered no reaction other than bobbing her head up and down one time.

"She was a fine ship," the old woman said. "But she was just a ship."

"No," Lara said, her joy turning quickly to sadness.

"Yes!" Zenobia said, knocking her knuckles lightly on the table. And though the sound was quiet, it carried inherent weight. "I know what that ship meant to you, what it meant to him. But it is just a thing. Others can be built or bought but what you have forged here is much stronger. You have lost an heirloom, but you have gained an ally and helped strengthen the Conclave. These are more important than things."

Lara turned to look at me, considering the words of her mentor.

"And we have the *Buzzard*," I reminded her.

She rolled her eyes but smiled. "Right," she uttered. "We have… that…"

"Hunter Spears," Zenobia announced, drawing our attention. "Congratulations."

"Thank you," I said, trying to embrace the moment and not feel like an imposter. I had earned this.

"Take him to the Hephaestus," Zenobia said, and they both ignored my puzzled look. "For both of you."

Lara stood and I did as well, the meeting seemingly coming to an end.

"Thank you for everything," I said to the woman.

"Don't thank me yet," she said with a slight air of menace. "The road you now walk is not an easy one. You have seen the great rewards, but it comes with a great cost. The life of a hunter is not like that of a scrapper and while your roots might be sturdy, you will have to grow stronger with every day."

"I understand," I said, treating her the way I treated Lutch when he was first teaching me the ropes. And, in many ways, this moment was similar. I was beginning something new and would have to learn a whole new skill set.

"Come," Lara said, nodding appreciatively at Zenobia before leaving the building and turning, walking us quickly in a direction we had not gone before.

The gawkers were all gone, and the streets were back to normal but things were different.

"No turning back now," she said, looking over her shoulder but not slowing her pace.

"Good," I replied and meant it.

A few streets later, we approached another massive building fronted with stairs leading up to a door just beyond a series of columns. Before the building was a marble statue of a hunter wearing a duster jacket, with a rifle slung across his back, hammering a sword laying across an anvil. The weapon was a hologram, glowing red as though it had just been pulled from the forge.

Lara led me up the stairs, not pausing for even a moment to stop and look. She was eager to get done whatever awaited her. I kept a quick pace behind, following her into the tall structure where a huge room awaited us. Within, armor and weapons were placed on racks and dummies all around. They were mounted on the wall and even hung from chains affixed to the ceiling.

We traversed the space with me gawking at armaments the whole way to the back of the room where an Iskini awaited us behind a thick podium. The scaled species were uncommon, their entire population having been secluded on a single planet in a far sector until recently and I had only seen a few in my entire life.

Its wings fluttered as we approached, and a sound came from

somewhere in its large ovular head. The insectoid eyes reflected us in hundreds of adjoining cubes. A translation device sitting on the podium spoke in words we understood.

"What brings you to the Hephaestus?" droned the electronic words.

Lara presented her personal hunter's emblem. "I have been granted rank three," she said and the Iskini reached out with one of the mandibles that protruded from its chest, picking up the emblem between pincers and examining it. With another, it checked the truth of her words on a computer within the podium behind which it stood.

"You have earned a new rank," it confirmed, turning and picking up a hammer before pulling a metal bit and setting it in the forge built into the wall at the back of the room. It didn't take long for the tiny scrap to heat up and the Iskini reached into the fire as though it was nothing, plucking up the hot bit and dropping it on the emblem before hammering it into place.

I could feel Lara's excitement beside me and when she was handed back her badge with nothing more than a third little scrap of metal adorning the side of the circle, she looked as though she might cry. But she maintained her composure.

"Thank you," she said in a monotone to cover her excitement.

"And you?" the speaker on the table asked as the large eyes turned to face me.

"I am Hunter Spears," I said, hearing myself say it for the first time. "I need an emblem."

"One now," it said. "Two after your first catch."

I nodded my understanding and watched in wonder as the Iskini forged the symbol for me, using its bare pincers to shape the emblem before hammering it together and dropping it in a bucket built sitting beside the creature's curved legs. The water bubbled and steamed and, a moment later, the badge was set before me.

I picked it up and stared down at the symbol of the bounty hunter in my hand.

I was not just a scrapper anymore.

Now, I was something else, something more. With this, I could earn the money I needed to help Ned, to help the universe.

I thought about what Edgar told me that my father had said, and I smiled. Now, I could make him proud. I would explore and do good. It wouldn't be easy, but it would be worth it.

With the emblem in my hand, I turned toward the universe as a new man.

EPILOGUE

With the bounty money from Resh, I was finally able to procure enough fuel to take the multi day gyre trip to the last coordinates Ned had from his investigation into the Code name: Extinction.

After spending a week at the Conclave, making adjustments to the *Buzzard* as well as further outfitting ourselves, we set off to discover if there was anything worth investigating two hundred years after the discovery of this clue.

We hurtled through the tube, and I was sitting at the workbench that now had a few functioning supplies. It wasn't the old tools comprised almost entirely of rust but new, state-of-the-art devices that made what I was doing even easier.

Lara stepped from the room beside mine that she had made her own, spending a good amount of money to get fixed up the way she liked. More than anything, the fact that she had outfitted her own room on the *Buzzard* was indicative of the fact that it was no longer just that she didn't want to abandon her friend but also that she wanted to be a part of what we were doing. Of course, she still wanted to catch bounties and further both of our careers, but we were also going to help Ned investigate the ancient threat.

After making her way down the hall, she stepped up behind me and watched as I affixed another leg to the small machine I was working on.

"It looks like a spider," She observed.

I shot her a judging glance. "That's obviously what I based the design on."

She groaned theatrically. "How many more days before we arrive?"

"Actually," Ned answered. "Only a few more minutes."

"Good," Lara cheered. "Feels like I've been stuck on this boat with you two for a month."

"Back atcha," I said with a wink before returning to the small robot I was building.

She moaned again. "We might also need to find some more crew members so that I have someone to talk to that isn't a military intelligence or a person who I knew when I was still in diapers."

"Says the girl who was working alone until I came along," I mocked.

"Well, if I'm stuck with some people, I would rather have more," she justified.

Ned piped up. "It would be unwise to let more people know about my existence. Every person who learns about me is put in even greater peril."

His words landed on me like a ton of bricks. During our time off, I had Ned investigate Edgar's mate and child. He had discovered that they had not been at the port when the attack had happened. Of course, I was grateful for that but couldn't shake the guilt of the loss that we shared. I wanted, more than anything, to find them and tell them how sorry I was and to get to know them.

But I couldn't. All I would do by going to see them would be to put them at greater risk, so the best thing I could do for them was to let them grieve without me.

"The most prudent course of action is to remain a foursome until such a time as it is necessary to bring another into the fold," Ned continued.

Lara looked up to the speaker in the corner of the room. "You count Libby as a member of the team but not our new arm friend?"

"Seems pretty rude," I put in.

"The arm's programming is so rudimentary that it is more akin to a cat," Ned stated flatly. "Would you count a cat as a member of the crew?"

"Ooh, we should get a cat!" Lara exclaimed excitedly and I hoped she was just making a joke to irritate Ned.

"I believe you missed my point," Ned assessed, before adding, "intentionally."

"You know what," Lara said in mock astonishment. "I think I might have."

"Thankfully, we are arriving now," Ned said in an obvious show of changing the subject.

I finished what I was doing and joined Lara in the cockpit just before we washed out into space to find… nothing.

When we entered space, there was nothing interesting or noteworthy. Nothing at all.

"This is anticlimactic," I said.

"You would have preferred a military space station still fighting a war that ended two centuries ago?" Lara asked pointedly.

"I suppose I wouldn't," I admitted. "But after all this, I was hoping for something."

"Activating scanners," Ned said but I could hear the disappointment in his voice. This had been the culmination of everything we had worked for and to get here and find nothing would leave us at square one. Or maybe a negative square since we would not only have no clues to go on but we were still being hunted by the Inquisition and Consortium.

"Do you think we need to get him some kind of consolation cake or something when nothing turns up on the scanner?" I asked, joking to make up for the disappointment we were all feeling.

"I think we are going to need to do more than that," she said. "But I'm itching to get some more bounties under our belts."

"You're just excited about your new rank," I said with false dismissiveness, staring out the window while Ned continued to scan.

"I am," she admitted. "And I know you are too."

"I think it'll be satisfying to earn more in a day than I earned most years as a scrapper," I said, trying to play it off.

"Yeah, yeah," she waved a hand, seeing right through me. "I know you're excited to help bring in some bad guys."

When I opened my mouth to speak, Ned cut me off.

"Nothing on the scanners," he said, sounding as morose as I had ever heard him. Admittedly, I understood how he felt.

We were doing all of this, putting ourselves through so much, because we wanted to find this weapon and help the universe. If the trail ended here, everything was going to be a lot more difficult and complicated.

"Run them again?" I suggested. "We could shift position and rescan?"

"No," Ned said. "There's no point in that. This was the location, and there's no drift in space. If something was here, it would still be here."

"I guess we just turn back," Lara suggested.

"I suppose so," Ned said mournfully. "Hank, you drive."

"Sure," I said, reaching out and grabbing the controls. I stole a glance at Lara, who looked as worried as I felt.

As the *Buzzard* turned, a single star caught my eye. It waved unnaturally for just a moment, wobbling the way the world had when Lara was wearing her stealth suit.

"Could any systems on a ship still be operational all these years later?" I asked, knowing the answer.

"Certainly," Ned said. "If it was using solar power, that star could be keeping it working this long."

"That's what I thought," I said with a laugh and fired the forward-facing missile battery right toward the faint shimmer.

The micromissiles streaked through space before exploding against a ship's shields.

"Hank," Ned said in absolute astonishment.

"This is why it takes a person and a computer working together," I reminded him. "Because we can each do things the other can't."

"Sure, but…"

"You really hitched your wagon to the right star," I said in exaggerated self-satisfaction.

"Ugh, are you going to be like this all the time now?" Lara griped.

"It's safe to assume that he will," Ned put in, whatever moment he had now gone.

I felt him take over the controls and guide us forward, setting off another missile burst, the explosions against the shield allowing us to see through to the ship itself.

I marveled for a moment. "Is the shield on that thing *also* a cloak?"

"It is," Ned answered, maneuvering us into position so that we could board once the shields were down. "It seems like a lot of technologies have been lost since the war."

After another round of sustained fire, the old shields failed, and we were able to glide into position beside it. Ned activated the docking tunnel for ship-to-ship contact and grumbled about the fact that it almost didn't work.

"I can't remember the last time it was used," I said, before adding under my breath, "if ever."

It took a while for the docking tunnel to align with that of the other ship, and as we got close, I got a good look at it. Wide with gun emplacements along the top and bottom, the medium-sized sloop was the kind of vessel that the cult military would fly into a battle and be used to shoot down the smaller starfighters.

Ned continued to explain more about it and its uses as we put on our atmosphere suits, getting ready to board the craft whose oxygen had undoubtedly run out years before.

The *Buzzard*'s tunnel was able to seal against the receiving slot on the cult ship, and soon we had closed the door behind us and were crossing the narrow passageway.

Lara made the comment that I had been waiting for. "Told you we were gonna need new space suits."

"You did," I said and made sure to tell her what she needed to hear so that she didn't have to hound me about it. "And I said that I didn't know if we would need them, and you were correct."

"Got that right," she said just after Ned depressurized the tunnel. "And don't you forget it."

"I should have the door open for you in just a moment," Ned informed us, and before he had even finished speaking, the door on the far side of the tunnel began to open. Carrying the particle weapon that I had taken from where I found Ned, we entered the sloop.

The design of the interior was very different from anything I had seen before.

"What is that?" I asked when I saw a short pillar of tubes and wiring.

"That is an interface console," Ned explained. "Where the augmented humans could plug directly into the ship and activate different parts of it. The cult wanted man and machine to be one in all things, believing that it was the only path to true perfection."

"That's… intense…" Lara said, looking at one of the consoles while we moved down the dark passageway to an open space with doorways leading in many directions. More consoles were placed in a ring at the center of the room and books and papers littered the ground. I knelt and picked one up, opening it to discover that the faded pages were written in a language I didn't recognize.

"It was a code," Ned told me, as always, looking through my camera earpiece. "They were changing it all the time and using it to communicate. Our best analysts, both human and artificial, were always trying to crack their codes, but it was one of the places where the fusion of man and machine seemed to have us beat."

We heard a sound, and I jammed the book in my bag, then placed a second hand on my weapon and continued forward. I had a good sense of the direction of the command center of the ship, so Lara and I walked that way without hesitation.

"Where's the crew?" I asked.

"Cult craft could operate with as many or few crew members as they needed since automated systems could fluidly take over when an operator moved on. Think of it as the way you and I pilot the *Buzzard*," he explained, and I realized that there was a lot more I needed to know about the Old War if I was going to be investigating this threat with Ned.

Toward the aft of the ship was the command center. Here, there were no windows, and I didn't have to be told why. If the people and systems operating it worked in perfect harmony with the scanners, radars and cameras, there was no need for use of the naked eye out of a window. Instead, they could fortify this room better than any other room on the ship and keep it safe from enemy fire.

At first, the space appeared to be totally unoccupied. Nothing more than a few chairs sat around a holographic display table. But in the corner was another chair that had been blocked from my view as I walked in, but that Lara was making her way directly toward. I moved in beside her, and the two of us stared at the body in the chair.

Though I wasn't sure body was the right word.

This person had obviously begun their life as a human, but part of their face, pieces of their arms, and their entire bottom half had all been replaced with mechanized parts. It was the kind of thing that was the stuff of Inquisitor Gregory's nightmares, and even I couldn't believe what I was looking at.

The metal half of his face stared into space, while the organic half was partially melted away, undoubtedly beginning to decompose before the lack of oxygen halted the process when the air ran out.

"Get me closer," Ned said, and though I didn't want to, I stepped toward the cyborg.

"I can't believe things like this existed," Lara said, and Ned was quick to answer.

"It was common, pervasive even," Ned explained. "This was the norm throughout much of the universe and only became problematic when the cult began wanting to force it on others. Honestly, it's hard to believe how alien it is to you."

"A lot can change in two hundred years," I noted.

"Truer words…" Ned said before going silent, and after a moment, I jumped back, pointing my weapon directly at the body.

Its mechanical eye flickered on and turned a low red.

"Calm down, it's just me," Ned said, his tone making it clear that he thought I was a wimp for reacting the way I did. "I had to power it up in order to intrude on his system."

"You're in the brain of a two-hundred-year-old half-man half-machine at the moment?" Lara asked.

"I am," Ned answered as though it were nothing.

Then we waited a long moment.

"They were headed home!" Ned said, excitement hanging on his every word.

"Where was home?"

"Not a where, a what," he exclaimed. "It was the name of a space station: Home. But now we do know *where* it is."

Amazon won't always tell you about the next release. To stay updated on this series, be sure to sign up for our spam-free email list at jnchaney.com.

Hank will return in HUNTER'S RISE, available on Amazon.

CONNECT WITH J.N. CHANEY

Don't miss out on these exclusive perks:

- Instant access to free short stories from series like *The Messenger*, *Starcaster*, and more.
- Receive email updates for new releases and other news.
- Get notified when we run special deals on books and audiobooks.

So, what are you waiting for? Enter your email address at the link below to stay in the loop.

https://www.jnchaney.com/star-scrapper-subscribe

CONNECT WITH MATTHEW A. GOODWIN

Check out his website
thutoworld.com

Connect on Facebook
https://www.facebook.com/ThutoWorld/

Follow him on Amazon
https://www.amazon.com/stores/Matthew-A.-Goodwin/author/B07TXWJBWX

ABOUT THE AUTHORS

J. N. Chaney is a USA Today Bestselling author and has a Master's of Fine Arts in Creative Writing. He fancies himself quite the Super Mario Bros. fan. When he isn't writing or gaming, you can find him online at **jnchaney.com**.

He migrates often, but was last seen in Las Vegas, NV. Any sightings should be reported, as they are rare.

Matthew A. Goodwin has been writing adventures about spaceships and dragons since he was a child. After creating his first fantasy world at twelve years old, he continued to write in his spare time. He spent his days as a zookeeper, but when his son was born, he decided to pursue his lifelong dream of becoming an author.

Having always loved sweeping space operas and gritty cyberpunk stories that explored man's relationship to technology, he penned the international bestselling series, A Cyberpunk Saga. His passion also inspired him to create and cofound Cyberpunk Day ™. For more information and FREE content, visit **thutoworld.com**.

Printed in Great Britain
by Amazon